The Desolate Garden

The Desolate Garden

Heirs and Descendants Book 1

Daniel Kemp

Other Work By This Author

Percy Crow
The Secret
Once I Was a Soldier
A Shudder From Heaven
Why?
Reasons
And for children or those still young at heart:
Teddy And Tilly's Travels

Contents

Chapter One

Poison Ivy

The first time I saw her was three days after I was told that my father had died.

All the national newspapers had carried the story in their first editions; most describing him as a private banker, others as simply a financier. All had speculated as to why. The majority of the more respectful had suggested pressure, and stress in the current financial world. However, the most popular tabloids had repeated the accusation for which he had successfully sued them, that his money had come from unscrupulous and tyrannical rulers of various African countries. Only this time they glossed over some previously mentioned names, and added the word 'alleged.' They had not known that he had been murdered.

* * *

"Tell me a joke," she said. She was seated at the table nearest the bar in the Dukes Hotel, in London's St James's.

"What?" I replied, in complete surprise.

"I've had a really shitty day, and I need cheering up. Come and join me," she suggested, enticing me in from the lobby.

She was about thirty but, in the dim seductive light of the world-renowned Martini bar, I could have been wrong by ten years either way. She had long curly dark hair, penetrating large eyes of an indeterminable colour, and a very attractive face. As to her figure, I had no way of knowing for sure but, from what I could see, she was quite petite. A colourful shawl draped from a glimpse of bare shoulder, and the cut of the red dress she wore was modest and high. What stood out was her perfume. The clear, smoke free atmosphere carried an array of sweet aromas, mingling with the gin and lemons and the fresh damp air of the outside night, but hers was the sweetest. It reminded me of raspberries ripening on autumn canes, mixed with jojoba oil and honey. I smelled of whiskey and tobacco; not the catch of the night, I supposed.

"What makes you think I'm here on my own and not with my wife?" I replied flattered and interested, but guarded, unforthcoming to her obvious appeal.

"Well, you're not wearing a wedding ring for a start. Want me to go on?" My new friend said playfully.

I nodded my acquiescence, adding, "Why not…I've got nothing better to do with my time," trying to seem disinterested, which I definitely was not.

"Your shirt could do with an iron and the suit has seen better days, your hair needs a trim and, quite honestly, you look out of place. Not a local…by many a mile. Up from the country for a day or perhaps two, no more than that I'd say. You've been dragged here reluctantly and want to get back to the farm as soon as you can. Anyway, I only asked for a joke, not a page by page description of your inactive life."

"Perhaps my lady friend is equally unattractive," I responded to her accurate assumption and correct observation.

"That's an old-fashioned expression but at least it establishes that you're not gay, plus you're not pretty enough anyway. I'm Judith by the way. What did those lady friends of yours call you, when you were younger and playing the field?"

"Am I that ancient? Thank goodness I left my bath-chair back in my room. I would have felt embarrassed had I have brought it."

* * *

This was the second invitation I'd had in three days to have a conversation with someone I had never met. All of a sudden my hitherto selected social circle of friends was widening; and one of those acquaintances was not welcome.

Joseph, my butler, had answered the front door to the knock I had heard, and was now standing in front of me announcing the arrival.

"There is a police officer wishing to see you, Sir. Shall I show him through?"

"Lord Paterson? I'm Detective Chief Superintendent Fletcher of the Special Branch. I've got some news for you about your father...may I come in?"

It had been the previous Sunday, around about three in the afternoon, and I had just driven home from my local pub after spending all morning blasting crows out of the sky. I reeked of alcohol, sweat, and cordite. The twelve-bore 'Purdy' shotgun lay dismantled on the gunroom table, and the rest of my gear was scattered around the floor. He glanced at the gun.

"Been busy, Sir?" He asked, in an official police tone.

"Yes. One of my tenants keep sheep, and they're lambing. The crows pick out the lambs' eyes almost the minute they're born, nasty creatures, so I lend a hand killing as many we can. My license is in the estate office, if you want to see it? Incidentally I'm not a Lord, only a lowly Honourable." I replied, without looking at him.

"I never knew that about crows. As for the license, that won't be necessary." He paused. "I'm afraid that your father was found shot in the head by the housekeeper at his home in Eton Square, London, at ten past one this morning; so, as I understand it, you are now a Lord," he stated, in the standard perfunctory, manner that the police inform relatives of the unfortunate. "Can you think of anyone who may have wanted to kill him?" He enquired, without a change of tone to his voice or any pretence of remorse.

The shame of it was that I could not. However, that did not imply that he had no enemies; only that I had been unable to discover them, and I *should* have.

"Absolutely none. He was the last person I would have thought of to have had enemies. It might have been money they were after…he had plenty of that," I declared, not trying to hide my indifference.

"He was alone in the ground floor sitting room. There were signs of a forced entry Sir, and the housekeeper says that he was alone that night. He had no company." His monosyllabic style of speaking was beginning to annoy me.

"Was there anything missing?" I asked, knowing exactly what the housekeeper meant by *company*.

"No, Sir, nothing that the housekeeper or his valet knows of. I was hoping you might be able to provide some information, throw some light on it. Has he been in touch with you lately?" He asked, fingering the bespoke carved stock. "Very lovely gun. Expensive, I expect," he added.

"Yes to the gun, and no regarding him being in touch," I curtly replied. I had never had much time for the police and he was not changing my opinion.

"Has he written at all, or perhaps telephoned you in the past with any worries he had…any problems he was having with anyone?"

"Can't help you there. A private man my father, not one to wear his heart on his sleeve."

"You wouldn't have any of his old letters to you, would you?"

"No, sorry. I don't keep things like that." I took a sip from the glass of whisky I had poured in readiness for the gun cleaning ritual that I always enjoyed doing myself. I had not offered him anything, nor was likely to, even though he looked the drinking type, grey inanimate eyes, a bulbous red nose under which was a nicotine-stained moustache and, even further down, a fat rounded beer belly. I was not in a social or generous mood, and had no wish to adjudicate on the innate evils of modern society as seen through the eyes of the law.

"It's just that we could not find the exchange number for the home here in Harrogate on any telephone records of his. Clearly he didn't like the phone or is it you that's got an aversion to telephones?" He asked, smiling, as if attempting to ingratiate himself. But I was not in any sort of a jovial conversational mood, either.

"Look... he and I didn't get on. We haven't spoken to each other since he left before my mother died. I haven't spoken to him or seen him in almost two years and, quite frankly, I don't give a toss that he's dead. If that's all, Detective Chief Superintendent, I've got lot more important things to do than discuss the personal relationship the two of us had or *didn't* have."

My abruptness and directness had shocked him, or perhaps it was my inhospitality and his need of a drink that hastened his departure, I was not sure which. However, before he left what he considered to be an unfinished conversation, he summoned me to London the following Wednesday to meet with a Government Official. He did not name him, nor his office, but declared. "You will be met at the station, and we will expect your full cooperation in all of this, your Lordship. It is, as you will appreciate, a matter of great importance. I look forward to your collaboration at our next meeting." Irascibly, he stressed the *'next'*, as I closed the door behind him.

I had no qualms over the forthcoming journey to London, other than my complete distaste of that city and all who traversed its capricious streets. What did worry me though, was the question of who had shot my father? I could think of a reason why it had happened; but had no idea who could have done it!

"The name's Harry, and I think I must be the joke after how you've described me. Harry Paterson, how do you do Judith?" I shook her proffered hand, adding as I did so, "You certainly don't look out of place, and you are far too beautiful to be on your own." I had decided that diffidence was no longer necessary. A shield and a sword would be better if all conquering I would go.

The waiter had arrived and was hovering with his drinks menu, and the obligatory bowl of nuts. No everyday peanuts for the ritzy clientele of this bar oh no, here they were offered salted macadamias and olives, with crunchy pretzels in various shapes. I would have preferred the roast spuds at 'The Spyglass and Kettle' a pub back home. But for the prices they charged here they had to appear more chic than wholesome, I supposed. I ordered another gin martini for my new companion and asked for my 40-year-old Isle of Jura single malt. I had checked before I had booked that they stocked it otherwise I would not have been at this particular hotel. However, with hindsight, given the cost that they charged per glass, a more frugal man would have brought it with him. 'Mean, I may be, but never to be seen,' was an old maxim that my father had many occasions quoted in my presence; I wished I had never heard and remembered it!

"Call me Judy, and I'll call you, H. Never had a drink with a Harry before, or at least, anyone by that name that I can remember. What's your joke?"

She was an easy conversationalist but not, as I first suspected, an easy woman. It would not have been the first time I had been approached by an escort in a hotel bar and I'd used a few bars, that is. I won't admit to anything else, or deny that I hadn't been tempted, but I had never succumbed. I had never needed to pay for what came easily to me.

"Let me see." I played for time, searching my memory for amusing lines I could repeat to a woman who, in this light, was an extremely desirable and sexy young lady who I fancied as much as the Scotch before me. I was out of practise, and having been drinking before I had arrived back in my hotel, was faltering badly at the first hurdle. I was more accustomed to ribald horsey female types, swigging beer and telling stories of successful matings of stallions and mares of one kind or another, usually as inebriated as I.

"Ever heard the ones that end 'that's how the fight started'? No? Then, if you're sitting comfortably, I'll begin." I started the little anodyne tales of animosity between partners or family that I had heard somewhere in the past.

"One year I decided to buy my mother-in-law a cemetery plot as a Christmas gift. The next year I bought her nothing. When she asked me why, I replied, 'Well, you still haven't used the gift I bought you last year!' That's when the fight started." There were several like this, and I found myself joining in her laughter as I recalled as many as I could.

She refused a third martini, opting for a mineral water instead, explaining "I'll need a clear head in the morning."

"I hope tomorrow won't be as bad as you say today was," I said, still waiting for her to expand on why her day had been as shitty as she had said.

"I'm not expecting any difference for a considerable time, I'm only too sorry to say. Do you want to know why that might be Harry?"

"Thought you'd never tell." I was on my fourth Jura and set for a night of bliss, as my undoubtable charms had obviously seduced her, or so I thought!

"It was because I was ordered to meet you, and you haven't disappointed me. You're exactly as your file reads. I can summarise it in one word: *chauvinistic.* Thought you'd scored, didn't you? Shame…you couldn't be further from the truth. I've got to hold your hand all the way through the debrief. I'm your liaison officer, and I'm stuck with you. How did your reunion with our lord and master go? Was Trimble wearing that sarcastic smile of his? I find it so irritating, how about you?"

"Who are you?" I was completely thrown by this reference to Peter Trimble, my previous drinking partner, who I had left half an hour ago at Box 850. I had then arrived here for my final night, before I could return home and find the refuge it gave me.

"I'm in the same business as you, Lord Harry, except I'm across the river at Five. Did you and 'C' come up with any idea as to who bumped off Daddy? What's the time of your train tomorrow? I'm to travel back with you, and can't let you out of my sight. Lucky me, eh?"

"I've forgotten," I lied. Trimble had said he was to appoint someone to run me through everything; only he never said it would be a woman!

"Don't be such an asshole Harry, and take your thumb out of your mouth. It's not very edifying for us serfs to see the nobility sulk. You'd better let them know back at your palace, so they can make up a room for me. Tell them to make it as far away from you as possible. No sleepwalking; it's not allowed."

"I'm on the 12:43. First class of course. Doubt your expenses will cover that." Slowly, I was recovering from the shock.

"No expense to be spared in your case H, orders from above. While we're on the subject, can you claim for bedding all the virgins in the Kingdom of the Patersons? Do you still have that role to fulfil, or are there none left for the new Earl to indulge? Heard of your investiture and gone running off to the hills, have they?"

"Got me on that one I'll have to check in Burkes peerage. If it *is* one of the privileges of office, can I add your name?"

"Most certainly not, H. I'm past that painful stage of life but I'm glad you recognised that purity in me. See you at King's Cross. I'll be wearing a white rose and carrying a newspaper under the Station Clock. Look out for me, won't you? I'd hate to miss you in the crowd."

She left to catch a taxi, quietly mouthing the words and the tune to the song 'Poison Ivy.' "You can look, but you better not touch," she murmured, looking pleased with herself.

Chapter Two

Dark Blue Lilacs

The name of Paterson, with all of its lineage, had been affiliated with banking since John of Gaunt, in 1342, persuaded the *Compagnia dei Bardi* of Italy to lend his father, King Edward the Third, 400,000 gold florins to continue the Hundred Years' War against France. Our ancestral line went indirectly to that King and his daughter, Elizabeth of Lancaster Duchess of Exeter, and more particularly her husband; John Holland and an unnamed mistress.

Our first direct genetic line to banking was to be found in 1407 in Genoa, where most of the royal houses of Europe deposited their money, at the *Banco Di San Giorgio*.

When England broke away from the Catholic Church in 1534 the then English King, Henry VIII, severed all links to that bank and ordered our lineal relative, Lord Phillip Paterson Earl of Harrogate, to return home and establish the *Bank of Saint George* in England. At its conception it operated in the same manner as its originator, handling the money of the Royals and other wealthy individuals. By the 1850s and the start of the Crimean War, it had evolved into what it still was on the death of my father, Elliot: the covert financial funding of all things the British Government wanted surreptitiously hidden from public scrutiny.

The Patersons, throughout the centuries, had been prodigious at bearing a male offspring to take up the chalice the bank presented.

Only on one occasion had they faltered at the production of honest, upright, dependable bloodstock from which to draw on for the Bank's wellbeing. That juncture happened late in the nineteenth century, when the then Earl of Harrogate was only able to originate one son amongst his flock of eight children; and he, unfortunately, was convicted of manslaughter, killing a fellow card player whilst defending himself. The fact that the other man carried a single-shot revolver, and the heir apparent was unarmed, saved him from the charge of murder, because the horrendous injuries inflicted far outweighed the defence of one's own life. He was sentenced to a lenient prison term of three years, the only period in its history that a female Paterson ran the Bank's affairs.

You would never, through the years, find this bank listed in any directory, nor was it regulated by the Financial Services Agency nor governed by the Bank Ombudsman of its day. It was not even situated in the prestigious City of London; it had no need to be. With Victoria's accession to the throne, and a permanent royal residence established, Queen Anne's Gate, a relatively quiet street running parallel to Birdcage Walk and within easy walking distance of the Palace, the Houses of Parliament and Eton Square was where, if you were in the know, you would find that office. It was hidden behind a highly glossed black painted door, free from adornment of any badge or crest or name, with just a simple brass plaque stating 'Private.'

For a hundred years or more what lay beyond that door was never altered nor changed. A card system index introduced in the late 1800s was its only modernisation to its recording of secret British interference in the affairs of other nations.

In the Bank's developing years, deposits and the payments of profits were conducted in cash. Bags, or in some cases, chests, were deposited with my ancestral custodians and carried from palace to palace. Once, on a visit to Leeds Castle for some sort of pageant, there was an attempt to steal the monarchs treasury chest. In that attack by raiding Danes, The Honourable Jeremiah Paterson gave his life fighting alongside Henry, his King, and 'Keeper of the Royal Purse' was added to the name Paterson, alongside all its other titles.

In time, promissory notes, then cheques, took away most of the need of cash, but this bank still dealt in a commodity little mentioned in today's society; that of trust, on which all good partnerships are built. The vaults at 'Annie's', as the offices at Queen Anne's Gate became known, were full of banknotes and share certificates. Files on investors, past and present, were overflowing and the urgency of more space was prominent in the incumbent Patersons mind, so he exchanged the cash which littered his floors into bank Bearer Bonds. These bonds were extremely convenient in the transference of cash. They took up little room, as they were printed on a single sheet of paper, and covered any amount from a thousand to a million pounds or more. They could be used as currency, the same as cash or cheques, and were payable on demand from any commercial issuing bank. They carried a small amount of annual interest, as effectively the buyer of the bond was lending that commercial bank his money. One other facet of these sheets of paper was their anonymity. There was no name on them; simply a number which denoted the date of issue and the promise to pay the bearer the sum of money the bond was worth! In less scrupulous hands than the Patersons, it could have been an indiscriminate and easily abused system of handling money.

What appeared to be the start of a slide into oblivion for the Patersons began with the election of a Socialist ruling party in 1945, and its stance on pro-decolonisation of the Empire. To Lord Maudlin Paterson it seemed that the part that the Patersons had played in the building of that Empire was about to be betrayed. It was the final straw in the haystack that was enveloping him. Poor Winston the war boss, the leader of all free men, had been shown the door by a grabbing, ungrateful public, and an American named Marshall was throwing money at Britain's defeated enemies with none coming to the victors. Instead we, the only bastions of democracy left in Europe at the start, were subsidising that loan by being forced to repay huge interest on that debt for holding out until they deemed it time to step in and reap the glory. The bank, however, had prospered well. The war had proved profitable, through Maudlin's astute structuring of the assets he held on behalf of his clients, in stocks of American financial institutions, petroleum companies and currencies; but he baulked at becoming the Orwellian image of an American 51st state.

He made a monumental decision and contacted his old Etonian and Trinity college friend, the then head of the Joint Intelligence Committee, without the knowledge of the Foreign Secretary or the Cabinet Office, to whom his bank was responsible. He offered the resources of 'Annie's' directly to the SIS, the Secret Intelligence Services, behind the government's back. Chief, or 'C' as he is always known, accepted this patriotic proposal and adopted the Bank of Saint George under his secretive umbrella, thereby removing it from the clutches of the all-embracing arms of a nationalising programme for the supposed public good.

With the bank beyond the grasp of Attlee and his penny-pinching auditors, he could work his magic to his heart's content, safe in the knowledge that his largesse would hide his illusion. In 1956, at the conclusion of the crisis over the Suez Canal, the secret side relinquished its sole interest in the Paterson bank. It preferred to share it with the new Prime Minister, Harold Macmillan, as he, with the SIS, sought ways to retain influence in the disappearing British Commonwealth whilst Maudlin sought more ways to secrete the names of the 'others' he now cared for. On his retirement, my Grandfather Lord Phillip Paterson managed the bank's affairs, but never delved too deep into the double entry bookkeeping accounts as Maudlin kept tight reins on his son. In 1981, my father, Elliot, took over the running of the bank.

Thanks to the birth of another brother, about the only thing I was grateful to my father for, I was destined towards a diplomatic career or in one of the services, it was always the youngest male who had the bank to look forward to; the rest of us Patersons were left with choices. My dynasty had seen conflict from the heights of Agincourt and the fields of Waterloo, to the slopes of Gallipoli, and on to the mud of the Somme and the sands of North Africa. They had served their country in those wars and in all the battles in between. Some of them were spared. Others were not.

After my own dalliance, I had a commission in the Blues and Royals and saw operational duty in Bosnia and Afghanistan, I was disillusioned. After nine years and a few months I came to the conclusion that the Army was not the life that I wanted. I was not that brave. For those that had charged the French archers, or the machine-guns and tanks, I had the uppermost respect; but for my part I had seen enough wanton death caused by political ineptitude, and news reporters wanting to be *newsmakers*, to realise that wars had changed. In my formative years of understanding of just who was who, depicted in the dull soulless portraits hanging in the Great Hall and corridors of the family home, I believed that the Patersons had invented the word *patriotism*… only I didn't want to wear the cross of Saint George so conspicuously.

As far as the diplomatic world was concerned, I had more self-respect than to simply regurgitate the policies of politicians, and had scant regard for in their sanctimonious crusade for personal power and fame. I wanted the ability to shape and control what was happening, not just to react to the situations made by others. I moved sideways into 'the office' and the dim and shadowy world of The Defence Intelligence Staff, gathering information in the ongoing war against the undermining of this great country of ours.

* * *

I entered this prominent world of ours on the 29th of July 1970, and was given over straight away to my wet-nurse. I survived that experience and moved on, to various nannies, tutors and instructions, in all things needed for an Earl's first born to assimilate and learn from. I attended the Methodist Ashville Preparatory School, just beyond our estate, when deemed necessary. When I reached the age of 13 I was sent away to Eton College, carrying on the long tradition of Patersons as 'King's Scholars' boarders. My feet found the same indentations made by previous family members to the doors of Cambridge and Trinity College. While there, I spent most of my time making up for my lost childhood years by sharing beds with as many women scholars as I could.

I displayed no prejudice to them being over-me or under me-graduates, as long as they furthered their education with my body. I was as attentive at my tutorials and lectures as my wandering mind and aching body allowed me to be, as it searched for other suitable experimental, or previously experienced, participants. At my Finals I received three 'one ones' in Engineering, Mathematics and Chemistry, and two 'one twos' in Physics and Economics, but had there been examinations for sexual prowess and endurance, I could have plastered the four walls of the dining room at Harrogate Hall with *'double first'* certificates. And they were enormous walls!

Chauvinistic; not an incorrect word to describe me, I admit. I've never been completely sure whether I had a choice as to my relationship to women, or whether it had been passed down through the male chromosomes of John Holland, but I had never experienced a wish to form any lasting deep commitment to, or from, any woman that I met. My imagination could not stretch to the wearisome life of couples arguing or compromising over each others' obligations within their partnership. I was too selfish to share my life and risk criticism, and neither would I have recognised the saintly sacrifice many make in times of illness or approaching death. In this respect it could be levelled at me, the charge of being a hypocrite, because that is precisely what my father did. He left my mother when she was diagnosed with terminal cancer citing his own inability to cope, but my defence would rely on the fact that I would never have married in the first place.

The stance I took over his departure owed more to my own weakness, I suspect, than his own. I'm not proud of my psyche, and neither am I ashamed. I am what I am; and it is only me that has to live with that.

As far as my father was concerned, it was a different matter. He did not have only himself to answer to. On the surface, he seemingly had everything: a beautiful wife, five children who, for the most part, were happy and contented with their lives, and a lifestyle many could only imagine. He had the estate here in Harrogate where he could play the 'gentleman farmer' role with his Holsteins and Herefords whilst enjoying his hunting and his stables of polo ponies and those of his thoroughbred race horses. They had added seventeen trophies, in his time, to the bulging cabinets where the accumulated silverware was kept, showing the Patersons equine significance over the ages.

There was the Eton Square mansion with its eleven bedrooms, of which he only ever used the one, and only four others were occupied, the housekeeper with one maid, a cook and his valet-cum-secretary George. He had been in the Paterson employ for forty years; from boy to man, fourteen to fifty-four.

Abroad was the house in Portofino, Italy, where his yacht a sixty foot two-masted schooner, was moored. Occasionally, scholastic calendars, scholarly agendas, and 'Annie's' permitting, we holidayed there as a family, until he found his own world and withdrew himself into it again. He was a complex and introverted man with many interests that kept him away from his family in Yorkshire. Horse racing, as I have said, and also the polo and sailing for which the schooner Britannia was on show; having been either sailed by him, or delivered to Cowes for the biannual 'Fastnet' race, coming runner-up three times in the challenge cup. What was more important to him than any of these things were his 'women-friends'.

He had started keeping a mistress a year after marrying my mother, Alice, who was aware of all of them. He had six in total, throughout their 39 years of marriage. He had a penchant for professional partners: a famous classical singer the daughter of a titled family who dabbled in interior design, a barrister who has since taken silk, a college professor (who, innocently, I introduced him to) and a film executive. His final extramarital consort was a first violinist, whom he was still seeing up until his death, even though it was her father who caused that defended lawsuit with his allegations of financial corruption.

The thing they all had in common, my mother told me days before her short, but uncompromising, illness claimed her life, was that they all made him happy. A strange thing for her to say, but nevertheless, that was what she said.

"He needed the distraction that they gave him," she had said. "I couldn't give him all that he required, other than legitimate children, and for that blessing I always loved him. He loved me back, but in a different way. Love doesn't die Harry, it kills without sorrow," she concluded.

I had never had the opportunity to truly know her spending most of my later life away from home. But I had always loved and admired her, and, on her sharing of that information, respected her even more.

In my early years, when I had time with her, it was her reasoning that endeared her to me so much. She never did adopt the 'I know best because I'm an adult' line. Instead, she sat and spoke to me, not *at* me. She was gentle in her words and explanations, and a patient listener to mine. There was always a smile and a reassurance from her, and I felt a sense of belonging when with her. Something I never felt from my father, to whom I was never close.

He had left her to die when he heard that she had just a small amount of life left in her, informing my sisters, Rose and Elizabeth, that he could not handle the situation of dealing directly with death; they would have to. I was overseas at the time, June 2008, as was my middle brother Maurice, but I managed to return for those final days. My youngest brother Edward, who lived in a rented flat in Cadogan Gardens, would not be released from his London duties, he informed us. He added, as an afterthought, "I will not allow him to see your mother during her decline." Sage words from such a learned man!

He was a user of women, in my opinion, rather than an admirer of them. I'm both, I suppose, having already admitted to my disconnection and unwillingness to any commitment. However, my addiction to women is not solely driven by sexual appeal. I hope I am not so one-dimensional and one day, I may change.

It was my brother Edward who first raised concerns about my father when he approached me at Alice's funeral.

"There's something amiss with Dad you know. I can't put my finger on it, but something's not right. Do you think you could have a word?" He stupidly asked.

"Don't be as foolish as you look Teddy. Mum's dead. Learn to wipe your own backside there's a good chap."

I then walked away from him, and from all things to do with London.

Chapter Three

Red-Veined Snake Head Fritillary

I've never been one to reminisce, to rediscover memories locked away in parts of the mind only psychologists know about, but in those last few days that I had with my mother, I found myself swept away in her nostalgia. I had not thought of my father as being a handsome man but there, in the photographs of their wedding, stood a person I could not recognise as him. As to her beauty, the wedding memorabilia only testified more strongly in confirmation of what I already knew. As to the man beside her, it was a stranger that I stared at. He looked taller than I remembered with jet-black hair combed back from his forehead, sharp clean features in a strong commanding face far more mature than the 26 years of age that he was then. There was a dashing, debonair look about him, a nonchalant character whom I could believe had swept my mother off her feet, as she had told me. He was not the person I had always remembered him as.

"He was impetuous then, Harry, romantic and audacious a lot like you are today, I suspect. He was dangerous around women. Are you the same?" I didn't answer that question of hers, but understood entirely what she meant.

To me, he had always been an eccentric old man with no hidden charms or fascination. I searched those photographs and more, to find some of us together, but could find none. No snaps of us two kicking a ball or hitting one, riding ponies and whirling mallets in unfinished chukkas or leaning over the side of the boat and landing fish. In fact, none of us being father and son. Perhaps there were no secret memories, none there to find, even had I have looked closer. No shared happiness, no laughter, no hugs and certainly none of affection. Perhaps he had entered my life as he had left it; a disillusioned, self-obsessed man.

As I have said, to me he had never changed. He was portly in build and slow in movement, more deliberate than made so by his slightly excessive weight. He had thick white hair parted at the side, dull blue eyes shaded by broken red veined cheeks and nose, and his constant spectacles, wearing his reading variety permanently around his neck. At all times he was smartly dressed, his pocket watch suspended from his buttonhole by a double gold chain and carried in the breast pocket of his suit jacket. Always grey light or dark; pinstriped or checked, but always a shade of grey, for his daily London attire.

"I never wear black, too sombre…looks like you're in mourning," he explained. "Blue is for those continentals, the Italians and Southern French, goes with their colouring. And never, *never* wear brown that's for those shirt-lifters. Lots around in my day, especially up at Cambridge. Mind you Harry, the breeding ground was Eton. Never could spot them there…I wasn't their type. Now there seems to be more Queens than Kings everywhere, even here!" We were in Boodles, his London club, too many year ago to recall, but I can remember vividly what he was doing, he was renowned for it. Expounding on life in general and demonstrating his practised skill at cognac consumption, there was no one in the family better at both.

In the winter months, he would say, that his hat matched the colour of his overcoat, as would his gloves and scarf, but not the colour of the green rubber boots that he wore on his walk to 'Annie's'.

"Look after your feet son, and they will carry you through life without complaint." This was, perhaps, the only sensible advice he ever gave me.

He was not particularly tall, maybe it was my mother who made him appear so in that nuptial snapshot but strode in a military fashion, straight-backed with swinging arms, pacing out his steps with his silver-topped walking stick. He had served in the Coldstream Guards before his inevitable transfer to the bank at the age of 39. Longevity lay before him in this role and maybe it was this that had burred away at his impulsiveness, dulled the sharpness and taken away the spirit that shone from those photos. However, his self-assurance and assertiveness stayed with him for all to see. It was only with me that he let that curtain rise, and then only briefly, months before his death.

Most banking Patersons lived well into their eighties. Five had reached the three-figure mark, and the normal age of their youngest to take outright charge of the bank was in their late forties. Elliot had been the youngest, but he had been the exception, as his father Phillip was quick to point out.

"I had enough interference from your grandfather. He kept his nose in the trough almost until he was dead, and that was not until he was ninety-three! I'm not going to make the same mistake. I'm going before you're forty; you can have the worry, boy." When I was told this story, I wondered what could have been meant by the word *worry*.

In 2003 Elliot began the transfer of all the Saint George files onto computer discs, and that was when his trouble-free complacency began to be interrupted irretrievably.

Eight months before the shot was fired from the Slovak semiautomatic pistol found beside my father's body, he had spoken to me on the telephone. At a younger age I would have replaced the receiver on hearing his voice, but I recognised his courage in taking that step. When I left him on the threshold of Eton Square almost eighteen months previously, having used most of the expletives in current usage and some, I'm sure, I conjured up on the spot as he stood there open mouthed and traumatised, I had left him with no doubts into the advisability of contact between the two of us.

"Harry, I am sorry that I have to disturb you, but I have no option. There is something terribly amiss in some notes I've found of

Maudlin's, and I don't know what to do about it." There was an element of fear in his voice; I had heard fear at the end of telephones too often in my life not to recognise it.

"Thought of confiding in Edward? Why trouble me with it?" There was not much compassion in my response to his call for help.

"He's too young Harry, too young for most things. It's big and if I'm correct, it's still going on. It's certainly over my head, and I'm way out of my depth. I think Maudlin was a spy working for the Russians, and I'm not sure how I can save the family name."

"Where are you speaking from?" I asked.

"I'm at my club, why?"

"Have you told anyone else, anyone at all?"

"No," he replied, in a questioning tone.

"Good. Don't call me from home, or from the bank. Tomorrow…no do it tonight, there must be somewhere open in your godforsaken part of the world for it, it's only seven thirty buy a mobile phone, a pay as you go one, no contracts understand? Then buy a twenty-pound top-up card, and charge the phone overnight. I'll call you at 'Annie's' in the morning, no, that won't do. Stop at that call box you pass in Hobart Place and ring me here with the number. Remember to write it down before you leave."

"You're being forgetful, Harry. If it's a number, I'll remember it," disdainfully he replied.

"Have you enough cash? I don't want you using a card."

"I expect so."

"That's not what I asked, was it? How much have you got on you?" I asked, curtly, with no respect.

"Couple of hundred, I suppose. Haven't looked."

"Well, now would be a good time, don't you think?"

There was a pause whilst I heard the sound of the rustling of paper.

"I've got one hundred and sixty in notes. Will that be enough?" he asked, innocent of the world beyond his own.

"Yes, that will be fine. Dad…don't tell anyone about this, not even George. When you get the phone, look through the security options and put a password in it, so no one can access it without your say so. If George sees it and asks about it, tell him it's for another of your liaisons…he'll understand that or, better still, say that your young violinist is causing you trouble again. Tell him that her father has found out that you haven't broken it off yet and you need a different number to keep the sordid arrangement going. After all, George might be able to relate to that, you being almost three times her age." I stressed the *'her,'* hoping he would notice. The knife that had only grazed my mother was buried deep in my heart.

"I understand," was his only reply as a momentary silence split our conversation. "I'll do as you say," he added, eventually.

"Good, and I will do the same tomorrow. No more land lines, or personal mobiles, never that okay?"

"All a bit melodramatic, the need for all these precautions, Harry. It's only a suspicion, after all."

"Maybe, probably. Let's hope so…but better to be cautious Dad, just in case there *is* something in what you say. We don't want the good name dragged around needlessly, do we? Keep all this between the two of us for now, and remember the old war motto: *Keep Mum, She's Not So Dumb.*" He was one for platitudes, my father. I enjoyed the usage in return, for once, knowing he wouldn't miss the ridicule in my voice. I had his acquiescence, but not only that; I also had the same feeling of fear and trepidation as he did.

"Make that call here early in the morning. We will have to arrange times to call and other ways to contact each other. By the way, don't ring again tonight, I'm out," I had added trying to sound as impassive and as unconcerned as I could.

"I hope I'm wrong about Maudlin, Harry…I honestly do."

I said goodnight, but I didn't think he was. I had found some old photographs of Maudlin whilst rummaging through the family photographic chronicles, and one in particular had caught my eye. I needed answers and, I needed help in finding them.

Chapter Four

Hibiscus From Malaysia

She was there as she had threatened to be, waiting at the gates for the East Coast Line and beckoning me enthusiastically.

"Over here, Harry Paterson!" I heard her call, above the commotion of King's Cross station.

The rose and the newspaper were missing, but that was not what had caught my attention. It was her hair; I had been wrong as to its colouring. It was a patinated copper, the colour of the flames of a fierce bonfire, a beautiful combination of red, brown and orange, and extraordinarily striking.

The first thing that caught my eye was that hair, as it flowed in time with her waved greetings and brushed against her impractical pink linen coat. Then her skinny legs, which ended in the cream leather high-heeled shoes. She would have been better suited in boots, and warm ones at that. The late March weather in London had been touching the lower 70s on the Fahrenheit scale, whereas in Harrogate it had barely risen above freezing, and I had no intentions of telling her! The absence of a suitcase caused me to wonder if the outfit she wore was her only clothing, and I remarked on it.

"Have you got a spare pair of everything you need in that document case?" I asked, when I was beside her.

"Oh now, don't you worry about my welfare, H. I'm more than capable of looking after myself in that regard. *Censeo et Conslio* family motto, or *Resolve and Purpose* Harry, if you're a bit short on your Latin. Have no fears about me."

She was jumping around like a demented child who had never been on a train adventure before. I did have a singular fear of being arrested for the transportation of a live skeleton on British Rail, for which I'm sure, there must be some law against in the lost journals of the Empire.

The fact that my father held the position he did had meant that a Government enquiry had been inevitable. However, my position within the SIS had complicated matters, and had led to the appointment of Judith Meadows as my personal inquisitor, the would-be discoverer of the truth as to who may have committed the crime. I had called Peter Trimble that morning and was told all I apparently needed to know about her, which was not a lot!

"She is good at what she does, Harry, very thorough." That, along with her surname, is all the information I got.

As I had approached my would-be interrogator, my annoyance was slightly tempered by the realisation that not all was lost. I had been right about her face.

She was indeed very attractive, with large hazelnut shaped green eyes, my favourite colour. I decided on the age of 32, short without the heels, which somehow accentuated her slightness. She reminded me of a pink mannequin displayed in the windows of fashion shops, one of those minus zero size females who are advised to eat air for sustainability.

Since my university days and my indiscriminate fascination in women, I had graduated in selection and had settled on a preference for voluptuous, sensuous types. The sultrier the better, and the more full-figured the more magnetic. Judith had none of these desirabilities, and her vivaciousness only underlined my distaste and my hostility.

"Did you stay for more to drink last night, or did my departure spoil your evening?" She asked, as she linked her arm through mine and pulled herself close to me.

"I'd rather we didn't play happy families, Judith. Or should I address you as Miss Meadows, or Ma'am, as you're the senior officer here?" I detached her arm and quickened my walk so that I was a few steps ahead.

"Don't be petulant, Harry. There's no seniority here, only friends. Actually, I'm a Mrs, even though I don't wear a ring. Please, slow down, I can't walk that fast in these heels!"

"Why aren't you at home caring for him, instead of frequenting bars and accompanying chauvinists layabouts to their country lair? By claiming to be married are you trying to avoid any virginal duties you may have with the new Earl on his estate? I thought you knew all about them, but I'll be glad to fill in the missing details."

She stopped, tugging at my sleeve as she did so. "My husband died, Harry; five weeks after we married. He was a Major in the Ordinance Disposal Regiment, on active service in Afghanistan. He was blown up into little pieces. I would be obliged if you weren't to mention him again."

There was a deep determination in those green eyes perhaps tinged with sadness, I'm not sure, but certainly spirit and a great deal of tenacity. She was, as I was beginning to understand, a stubborn, intransigent woman; self-contained and belligerent at times.

"You brought him up, not me," I answered, in my defence.

"No, you used the word *'Miss'* in a disparaging way. I'm acutely aware of your enmity towards me and the resentment you must feel over others examining your father's death. I'm here to help you, not trick you," she replied, truculently causing a brighter colour than her hair to wash over her face, blemishing an otherwise pure complexion.

'Help' not 'trick' me... strange words to use, I thought. Could she know what I was already hiding, or was this the subtle way of the practised interrogator?

'Tell us what we know you're concealing, and we'll give you a candy bar.'

Suddenly I viewed Mrs Meadows in a different light. Perhaps her zero size did not match the zero evaluation I had given her. I made no reply to either her offer or threat.

"I've sent two of our sitters up to your place by road. I've phoned ahead and forewarned them of their coming and their requirements. They won't need accommodation, we found them berths in a local hotel. I thought about using your stables for them when I found out that you don't keep those racehorses of yours anymore, but decided they deserved better, the poor souls. They have all their equipment in a van, but I sent my car up with them. Can't bear to be parted from it for too long and, who knows? We might want a drive up to the moors, you and I." Judith had regained the composure I had displaced, returning to her bullish best as we took our seats. I contemplated her words whilst exchanging tiresome banalities for the remains of our journey.

After Alice's death, my father had taken permanent residence in London, having no need or want of Harrogate. He had sold the estate's racing stock at Newmarket and the polo ponies had also gone long before this; his age, other pursuits, and the lack of interest in the sport shown by my brothers and I being a contribution in his decision. These changes had led to the letting go of our stable manager and most of the hands, now we had only the six horses in the stables for riding out or the occasional point-to-point race. I hadn't hunted in years, nor had I thought of it much since the changing of the laws, but her comment made me think of the chase of the fox, as long as the scent wasn't wrong and it was not me that was being chased. There was to be the full response to such a situation, recording machines both audio and visual and the electronic data readings of pitch in speech. It was not quite a polygraph; more refined, it showed the slightest agitation, because most in my trade could lie with conviction. That is, if they knew what was a lie, or the truth, if it stared them in the face. Why, then, the need of a drive and away from the recording of Lord Harry Paterson, Earl of Harrogate, I wondered? Was that where the trickery made its entrance?

That evening, after dinner, we began the first episode of what was to be a challenging time for both of us. I was changing that first opinion of mine; albeit slowly. Her car, a Porsche Panamera, one of those four-door saloon types that are shaped like a coupé, had been loaded with matching luggage, and her obvious wealth could not have come from Civil Service pay alone.

She had dressed for dinner, something I had not expected nor done since dining with my mother. I was waiting without a tie but luckily I had a jacket, otherwise her rebuke may have been more severe.

"Harry, we have to have rules. Rules are what I live by, and I love a good routine. After breakfast, through lunch and one hour before dinner, we work. We go back in time and recollect all that we are trying to forget; or hide. We play by the SIS house rules that we both understand. At dinner we adopt the rules of the upper classes, of which you are most notable, and as are my own family. I am Lord Davenport's daughter, he is the Queen's private secretary, amongst many other things. Heard of him?"

I had...by accident one could say. His father, Judith's grandfather, was one of those I was investigating in the mysterious photos I had found, now cut short by that gunshot of Sunday last.

"No," I lied, but we were not in the library where the machines now lived, we were in the lounge beside the huge log-burning fire. She had discarded the pink travelling coat and now looked considerably warmer. Her hair was pinned to her head and woven into a circle at the back. The long crimson dress covered every inch of flesh except for her neck wrists and ankles, and although I have already spoken of her slight figure, I could not deny her femininity.

Joseph, my father's butler had stayed at the Hall when he had left, and had been in the room through all her detailing of the code to be adopted throughout her stay. He had just finished pouring our drinks, so no doubt the rest of the household would soon know of my guest's high principles, I thought.

My sisters had, like Elliot, long departed, and now I was the only Paterson left here in the hereditary home, but I was not alone. With Joseph I had inherited two footmen, my own valet, two cooks and three kitchen maids. There was a housekeeper with four maids to care for the thirty bedrooms and all the grand rooms that were constantly in use, a chauffeur who had met us from the train, and three gardeners. Oh yes, and three stable-boys, and one stable-girl. All, apart from the gardeners and the stable-hands, were housed on the estate which covered some 220,000 hectares and contained four tenanted farms, as well as our own. A colossal undertaking which I took over from my father on retiring from the Army and, then, my partial retirement from the SIS. I say partial because they never really let you go! They don't know how to trust anybody on the outside.

"I'm going to bend those rules of mine at little tonight H. After all, that's what rules are for, don't you think...to be broken a bit?" Her head was tilted to one side as if to accentuate her question.

She waited for an answer, but all I could think of was making love with a skeleton. My imagination tried hard to stretch that far but I was unfortunately, ahead of myself again.

"Well, I do anyway. Let's get some background filled in. Start with your childhood, and your relationship to your late father." Her requests were more demands than mere inquires; they carried a note of compliance rather than the choice of disregard.

I painted that failed closeness in flowing, complimentary terms of harmony and kinship; it was easy for me to do. It was how I had dreamt it should have been since I was sent away to boarding school, something I had emotionally built on every day of my life that I spent there in nigh solitude, bereft of love and affinity from anyone. I was a good liar. I'd had plenty of time to conjure up an idyllic adolescence, and I told my imaginary story well.

I had been fifteen years of age when great-grandfather Maudlin had died and thirty-one when his son Phillip had passed away. Both had been instrumental in my life, even more so than my own father. They had filled my head with tales of the adventures of their siblings or their forbears, and my head had swollen in pride. Grandfather Phillip's eldest brother had seen action in the Korean War and the Malaysian Conflict in the middle sixties, and I heard of his exploits first hand. Phillip and Gerard would sit in this very spot with me, on one or the other's knee, listening to those deeds in avid attention. Then Phillip, not to be outdone by his elder, would praise his own efforts in 'Annie's' involvement in the protection of British interest in the Far East. Both would refer to Maudlin in an almost religious manner, never in my memory addressing him as 'father' or simply 'Dad.' Only the words 'he' or 'him' and, less occasionally, *The Old Man* were used whenever reference was needed to my great-grandfather.

"They even named a military operation after *'him'*, you know. *Operation Claret* they called it, an intelligence lead incursion against the Indonesian forces. I was with the misinformation section, SIS by any other name, but that was what they called us then. We were spreading falsified rumours amongst the Chinese, stirring them up against the President principally. Anyway, it worked, and an opportunity arose to assassinate him; his name was Sukarno if I remember correctly. I led that operation, Harry. I saved the day, and saved Malaya becoming a communist extension of Indonesia," Gerard told me.

"It was *'he'* who provided the funds from 'Annie's', then covered over the Government's connection and any trail leading back to the Foreign Office. It allowed BP to continue out there, and protected our rights to the rubber," Phillip informed me.

So the bank became pivotal to me and my interest deepened, leading to my knowledge about Saint George, and broadened my interest into lies and as Gerard had put it; *misinformation.*

"You're fortunate, Harry, that you don't have the responsibility of the intricate nature of the bank. It's an elaborate affair, and only *'he'* knows the full complexity," one of them had added, but I forget exactly who.

We were together, *'he'* and I, on the first of August; three days after my ninth birthday and six and a bit years before his death. I recall the day well, because I was to make my debut in the Halls cricket match against the estate tenants. The house was fully staffed in those days and, with the stable hands, there were more than enough adults to fill the eleven needed. However, the day had coincided with the unexpected arrival of my grandmother's sister and her entourage, compelling most of the staff's withdrawal. I was to go in last and had received batting advice from Maudlin. Fortunately, my uncles Charles and Robert were making a good show of things, and with my grandfather standing as one of the umpires, I considered my position in the proceedings as being well protected. *He* used his shooting stick in my coaching as a bat and displayed the forward defensive stroke as practised by Jack Hobbs, a contemporary of his and an England and Surrey batsman.

"Play a straight bat to everything young Harry, and play yourself in. Always give yourself time in any position in life before striking out. Cricket mirrors our lives in many ways, and that metaphor will stand you in good stead in both. I always found it best to keep something in reserve... to lure the bowlers in to believing you've nothing in your armoury then spring the trap, and dispatch them all over the place!" He swivelled his stick around imitating imaginary cricket strokes with agility and aplomb. "That's how I have survived for so long in this complicated world. Never let anyone know all there is to know about yourself my boy. And I'll tell you another thing, if you have a secret; bury it deep so even you don't know where to find it!"

His conversations always captivated and meant a great deal to me as he usually spoke with such clarity and logic. With this one, in particular, I can recall his words clearly; they contained neither. I never understood what he meant by not being able to find your own secret, until now. Needless to say, none of these accurate recollections were related to Judith. The story that I told contained snippets of truth, mixed frugally with lashings of fiction. The exaggeration of dreamt happiness was not fabrication to me; it had become my reality. My lies had become my truth.

I never, for example, mentioned the fact that her own grandfather had been a pallbearer at Maudlin's funeral. I hid the knowledge that I had discovered from the photograph, hoping she would bring that up, and not me.

Chapter Five

Friday Crocus

We ate breakfast from the arranged dishes set out in the dining room and, whilst I ate heartily of scrambled eggs and sausages, I marvelled at her small appetite; one piece of dry toast, a small bowl of cereal with imitation milk and an equally small bowl of pears. I felt obliged to eat more than I would have normally, as if to distance myself from her, and spare cooks concern.

"I'll see Mrs Franks, the housekeeper, mid-morning and order dinner. That way, everyone knows who will be required and for how long. I prefer seven-thirty for dinner. I'll tell cook not to prepare so much tonight. Perhaps you would like to share my plate? It would save on the washing-up for the kitchen staff."

"I was about to compliment you, Harry, but your sarcasm is not welcome. I'm too polite to comment on your own pig like consumption. Are you jealous H, or is it that you're insecure in your own body?" With that now charismatic cant of not only her head, but rebuke, she chided me.

"I'm perfectly content, thank you. I was worried about you and your obvious anorexia and how it is to affect my kitchen. I don't want cook going to all her efforts to feed you, when lettuce and a few radishes would suffice. Would that do you for tonight's dinner?"

"If your questionable humour would take a break for a while, and if you are asking what I would like to eat at dinner, then pork would be lovely with loads of crackling and all the trimmings. Then, if I am unable finish it all, I can at least imagine you there wallowing in the gravy. But, have no fear Harry. I will be hungry by *eight*, ravenous like a horse!" I had not missed the emphasis on the eight. It was the beginning of the bantering between us; however, Judith normally got her own way.

I sought out Mrs Franks and ordered tea, coffee for Judith, a light lunch of vegetable soup for her and beef and pickle sandwiches for me at eleven, and dinner, as instructed, at the revised time. I then joined my uninvited guest in the library to face my inquisition.

"Before we start, and before I switch on all this equipment I would like to say something off the record Harry, by way of introduction, as it were. I believe your father was murdered and not killed by accident whilst disturbing a burglar, or anything like that. I know that this is what the enquiry is meant to find out and I shouldn't decide its outcome before we have looked at everything and every possibility; however, I wanted to take this chance to tell you where I'm coming from, and where my questions are leading. I suspect that you believe the same as I do. This is our way of eliciting from you all the names that are hidden from us and temporarily out of your mind, bringing them back into the spotlight, so to speak. Then, of course, your thoughts on how he was murdered and by whom, okay?"

In my experience there is nothing 'off the record' when dealing with the *Service*. Even how you wipe your nose can be important; if you change from using a paper tissue to a cotton handkerchief it can have repercussions, and probably investigations into your bank account! I nodded my commitment to the cause, and lit my first cigarette of the day.

"Do you mind if I join you in that habit, H? I resisted last night when you smoked I'd given up for Lent but I just can't do it, not with you indulging. I'm afraid I've come with none. Didn't know you smoked. Anyway I've got none myself, hate to be a ponce and all that, but I'm going to have to be." She could be as incessant in speech as she was in gestures, her hands forever brushing away imaginary specks or stroking her hair or brushing against her lips, all seemingly involuntary. She hadn't read my file very well. I'd been a smoker since university, and that would have been there in the notes, if only for the life-covering insurance that comes free in the security business.

"Feel free. I'll add it to the bill for board and lodgings unless you think of a way to repay my hospitalities... just joking. Throwing it up in the air, seeing where it lands," I gave her the most artificial, contrived smile I could manage.

She mimicked it and returned it with interest. In a more effective way, cute and quick, she replied, "That reminds me... you must show me your bedpost before I can eventually leave this place and get away from you, I would *love* to count the notches. I seriously doubt there are any, especially if the repayment of hospitalities is what you rely on for seduction. You must save thousands on the heating bill; ever thought of turning it on?"

"Now who's being sarcastic? I've had to replace all four bedposts twice, I'd run out of room for any more notches." My reply fell on unimpressed ears, as she showed her disinterest with a simulated yawn and the feigning of sleep, angling her head to her touching slender hands.

"As to the heating, well normally, there's someone close by to keep me warm."

"Hmm, as shallow as I thought. Let's get down to work shall we? I want to start with you, Harry. Run me through your file. Start at Cambridge. Were you approached, or did your family connections lead you to us? Were we something you stumbled upon or was that your goal from the beginning?"

I told of my military career in the Guards, citing the boredom and inability to react to situations spontaneously as the factors leading to my retirement, and how great uncle Gerard's experiences had influenced my choice of offering myself to the SIS.

"So you came to us, then. Tell me what you expected, and then lead me into how you first got involved. Last night's summary of your upbringing was good; most concise I thank you for it. This time I want you to be more expansive, more detailed, right up until the time you were approached in Moscow three years ago." She had done some homework, if not all.

"I left the brigade in 2003, in the June of that year. When I left Cambridge I went straight to Sandhurst, in Surrey, having decided upon that at Uni. It wasn't a vocational calling or anything like that…my first love lay in the science of Chemistry. I just felt the need to do my bit, if that doesn't sound too silly. I did the full forty-four-week course, and was presented with the Sword of Honour on its conclusion."

She interrupted me. "What's the significance of the sword Harry? What's it for?"

"Best Officer Cadet on the course," I answered.

"What rank were you on leaving?"

"Captain, but I was promoted after Bosnia, before my first tour in Afghanistan. Too many Captains and not enough Majors, I suppose."

"Really, go on, please. Why us?" She was making notes in shorthand, and I hoped that the reference to being a Major did not bring back painful memories of a lost husband. I had honestly forgotten and should not have added the silly joke at the end, but I chose to leave it, and not apologise.

"I got an invitation to see Trimble at the Joint Intelligence Committee rooms in Derby Gate, in the Old Scotland Yard building, that September."

She interrupted again. "Develop it more, H. What did you do from June until September who invited you to meet 'C,' or was he 'C' then? No, it was Fleming as Chief. Peter has sat in the chair from December 2007."

"I mooched around. All right…I'm sorry." I saw her raise her pen in protest, ready to admonish me for my brevity. At that moment she reminded me of the piano teacher who taught my two sisters to play. They were three years apart, Maurice coming between them, so I had ample opportunity to see her at work. She was also a tiny woman, at least, that's how she appeared to be to me then with equally graceful, slender long fingers that she would raise and wave in time with the metronome, balanced on a sideboard, in the music room, before bringing them down when she required the lesson to begin.

"I spent time here. Elizabeth was still at home. Rose had married the year before and I had missed the celebrations, so I visited them in London and stayed a few days, they had a house in Rutland Gate. Came back here, did a bit of riding, worked around the place…that sort of thing."

"Too brief, again. Remain celibate throughout all this time did we?" She asked, with a hint of annoyance in her voice.

"I wouldn't have thought so, no," I replied.

"Nor would I. I want everything, Harry, even the dirty bits. I promise I won't blush. If it helps, and if you kept them, refer to diaries. Did you keep them?" She asked, astutely.

"Yes, I did, they're in my private office. Please, Miss, can I leave the room and fetch them?" I raised my own arm and childishly asked to be excused.

"Do be a good boy and hurry back, I'm on fire with anticipation. Oh, and could I have a coffee and perhaps a couple of chocolate digestives? No, wait…make it one, or I might shatter that illusion you have of me being reputable and selective," she asked, with a very seductive smile.

We went through those written records of the missing months in fine detail, taking hours over its deliverance and scrutiny eating lunch as we did so. When names appeared she made separate notes in a black and red hard-backed book, stopping me for the spellings and addresses. I went on to describe how it was that Trimble had invited me to London and the interview that took place between the Ministry of Defence and the Houses of Parliament after he had travelled up to Harrogate with my father and two others: an Antony Willis from the Foreign Office, and Donald Howell, a Cabinet Office official. Judith showed great interest in these names, nodding her head vigorously and confining them to that *'soon-to-become holy'* book of hers.

They had come for a shooting weekend as the boxed guns unlocked from home lockers, or retrieved from Asprey's, the Royal Jeweller's private gun cabinets, bore evidence to. The opening of the season had been delayed that year from the twelfth, because of the extreme severity of the preceding wet winter which had depleted the stock of grouse and woodcocks, so a later start had been decided upon. It was a Thursday, the day of their arrival, Elliot always shut up shop at lunch time on Thursdays; that's if he went to 'Annie's' at all that day, as it was earlier than his normal time of arrival.

It was the following day, before the first drive, that Peter spoke to me. "I hear you're at a bit of a loose end nowadays, old boy." He handed me a piece of paper.

'Come to this place, on this date and time that I've written down for you, and I'll see if I can find somewhere you can hang your hat.'

"That was his approach, and how I came to offer myself up."

"Did you speak to Peter or the others in that party much over that weekend, Harry?" Judith enquired.

"Not much, no. We exchanged shooting stories and all that sort of thing. I think one of them mentioned the Army, but it wasn't Peter…must have been Donald. I seem to remember he had served in Second Para in the Falklands, now I think about it."

"Was the topic of the UN's role in Bosnia ever brought up at all?"

"No."

"So, they spent their free time more with Elliot than you, would you say?"

"Yes, I'd say that was true," I replied.

"Did Antony Willis mention that he was in the same year intake as you at Eton, Harry? Or wasn't it necessary? Did you recognise him and chat into the wee hours, reminiscing?" She asked, patronisingly.

"No, he never said anything, and I certainly never recognised him. A few years had passed by, however…he probably never made a connection."

"Hmm." Her lips tightened as she moved the pencil around in her fingers in a rolling motion.

She had made copious notes throughout our day and had changed the tapes twice in both machines, smoked far more of my cigarettes than I had, and had complained when I opened a window, requiring

Joseph to arrange the fetching of a cardigan and shawl from her room. Now she sat curled up in a winged red leather reading chair, arms crossed, with her hands inside the sleeves of her thick woollen red and orange cardigan. Her feet were tucked under herself with those pages spread across her uplifted knees, her head tilted slightly, enabling her to read. Occasionally she removed her right hand to turn from one sheet to another, but there were no words uttered, as she remained silent throughout her revision.

I poured myself a Scotch and asked if she would join me. Without averting her eyes or lifting her head, she replied, "Yes, that's very kind. I'll take some water with mine... could you put it here for me?"

The pointed finger again, only this time it was not raised; instead, it indicated the oblong table that separated us. I considered a protest in the intended adulteration of my single malt, but considered it useless. I simply rang for the water and changed the Jura for a Bells.

John, one of the footmen, appeared, and as he cleared away the lunch trays onto the trolley, she addressed him, still engrossed in her manuscript.

"Joseph, please pass on my compliments to the kitchen. The bowls of crocuses on the lunch trays were a delight, as was the soup. That's what I was going to remark upon at breakfast, Harry, before our conversation became diverted. Your front lawn looks wonderful, there must be a million crocuses out there!"

"Thank you," I replied. "And thank you, *John*," I added.

"Oh, I'm sorry," she said to John's back as he left, and she added water to her whisky. Her attention now returned to the room. "I was miles away, intrigued by your recollections."

"No matter. I'm sure he's pleased by the promotion."

She gave a tiny smile; but whether it was to my riposte, or to her findings, I had no way of telling.

Chapter Six

Home-Made Plum Wine

Saturday morning broke with all the conventionality of an English spring weekend morning; it was thundering with rain. I had risen early as I had neglected the farm business for three days now. My travelling to and from London, and my day and a half there, plus the day in the library meant that there was work to catch up on. I was in the estate office, and had briefly been able to consign Judith to the back of my mind. I had managed about two hours of work, when I caught sight of a figure at the open door.

"I'm sorry, did I disturb you? I've been here for a couple of minutes just standing and watching. Nothing else to do in this monsoon. I was hoping to saddle up one of your horses and trot off for a canter, build up an appetite before breakfast, but no can do, worse luck. Were you busy?" In the professional matters we had touched upon she had been direct and to the point, but not so her standard discourse, which encompassed many things before she got to the point.

My perception of her so far had been mixed, which the relationship to the figure in the photograph had only helped to complicate. With Maudlin knowing her family, I wondered how much she knew of the Patersons. Her appeal to me was twofold. Firstly, I found her challenging in an intellectual sense. The way she had introduced herself to me at Dukes was clever, something I would have been proud of myself. Her approach had completely disarmed me, and taken me by surprise. She was quick-witted, sharp and seemed intuitive and shrewd in her deliberations. Her second appeal lay entirely with her physicality; again, it was the challenge that attracted me. In physical law opposites attract, and my positive sexual chromosomes were being drawn inexorable towards everything that was once negative to me.

"Yes, I was." I was going to leave my answer at that, but I was regretting some of the ridicule I had aimed at her. I continued in my reply, "The milk count is down, and we're waiting on the vets' report. It's a worry. We've had problems with an influx of badgers this winter, and it could be TB in the herd. There's conjecture as to if badgers do spread the disease, but if there weren't so many liberal tree-huggers about in this neck-of-the-woods, then I'd trap them all. The badgers I mean no; come to think of it…I'd shoot the huggers as well!"

She pulled up a chair beside me and stared at the chart on the computer screen.

"My, you *are* radical. Hope that doesn't reflect your own political views. I marked you down as being more of a liberal than an intolerable right-wing fascist. Don't worry, it's only rhetorical, no need to divulge your leanings. I'm not here to find any sleepers hidden in any of the panelling."

I wondered about that throwaway remark all through breakfast, and barely said a word apart from polite answers to Judith's sincere questions regarding the estate and its management. Mixed with the memories of Elliot's first declaration of suspicion of Maudlin, my emotions were ragged and my thoughts confused. The eight months I'd had to examine those files, the ones that had caused the anxiety in father's life, were unfinished and inconclusive. The photographs I'd retrieved from my mother's memorabilia had unearthed some surprises, but nothing overtly connected to the unaccountable missing monies. In total there was £300 million that could not be found amongst the ledgers from 1935 to 1970; in today's money, that equates to roughly £2 billion.

I was following her along the corridor from the dining room to the library, it was as if she was in a hurry to continue from where we had left off the previous evening; or was it, I speculated from her tactical remark, only minutes ago?

"Do you think you could have some sort of portable heater brought in this morning, Harry? It was freezing enough in there yesterday. This wind and rain chills my bones."

I considered the obvious reply, "They're on show, that's why," but my change of nature prohibited me. I liked me being understanding and humane, so I decided to continue to like myself.

"Of course I can, I don't suppose it will harm the books for a day or two. My apologies...I don't feel the cold as much as you must." I just could not help it, but it was not as blatant as before.

She had the same cardigan on, but had replaced the black leggings she wore under her skirt on Friday for thick beige corduroy riding trousers.

"We'll be here longer than a day or two, H. A week at least...maybe more."

"I had better send out for more cigarettes then," I offered, courteously. She stopped and turned to face me, smiling like the proverbial Cheshire Cat.

"In that case, could you order Rothmans for me I find your Dunhill too strong and too big. I seem to be wasting more than I'm enjoying." She most certainly was not a diffident girl!

"Nothing too much for Madam, nothing at all!" I was quickly becoming annoyed at liking myself.

We entered, and as she was about to load the recording equipment with new tapes, I touched her hand. She did not recoil; instead, she looked dispassionately and detached from me, as if to emphasis her Wednesday evening warning of *no touching*. Or, was it simply shock?

"Before we begin this morning's session, I'd like to ask you something off the record, and I'd like an answer to it, Judith; again, just between the two of us."

I had let go of her hand, but she had not sought to distance herself from me. We remained close and we were looking directly into each others' eyes.

"Yesterday in your preamble, before these machines were on, you stated that your mission was to find out who murdered my father, and how. You never mentioned *why*. I don't believe you make any oversights. I believe there is a purpose behind all that you say, and all you don't."

"I believe the same could be said of you, Harry. Neither of us are fools. Your father was a very important chap, perhaps more than you realise. I have no reason to ask why. I know why…it was to cover up something he had found out. But here's the thing H, did he know what he had found, and did he tell you? Want me to turn them on now, or do you want to cry on my shoulder and confess all the sins of your family in private?"

They were whirring, and Judith was into her stirrups. I was confused again. Was I being suspected in some way in a cover up, or the actual murder? Sometimes, honesty can be too much. Her acerbic little diatribe had found a mark. How did that anodyne remark of 'out of sight, out of mind' come into existence? Certainly not from our trade. Keep both eyes fixed on that round object, catching rather than dropping it otherwise you could end up dead!

"We grow plums in those huge poly-tunnels of ours, over where the racing stables were once. We sell the wine made from them all over the world. Our biggest market is in Japan, would you believe? Top restaurants in your own town of London stock it. It's becoming very fashionable, I'm told. They even had a bottle at Dukes, if you noticed. Before its full fermentation it's quite acidic. Remind me to offer you some of that immature, sour, variety before you depart."

"I'll take it then that you don't want to shed your tears all over me, Harry?"

"Haven't got anything to cry about, Judith. Unless you're going to tell me that your leaving today then I'd cry a bucket but, knowing that you're not, I won't bother. Incidentally, have you heard anything from the police about the CCTV at Eton Square? Have they got any pictures?"

"Yes, they have, from the outside cameras. The hood was black, the trousers black, the shoes were black, the face might have been black, but whoever it was never smiled for the photographic session. Went in through the front door, though. You can see them drilling out the lock. You can buy little, almost silent ones nowadays at any DIY store. Slow speed varieties, the same sort used in some departments of ours. No deadlock. I understand from George, the valet chap, that Elliot had a habit of entertaining late at night, and one particular lady visitor had a key. There were no cameras on inside the house. This, apparently, was Elliot's last job on retiring to his bedroom."

Without further comment or hesitation, and without waiting for any reply of mine, she threw the first ball. "I'm going back to last night, I got how you came to us. I'm clear on that. What I want to know now is how your skills suited our purpose, what use did we put you to, and what was it that you expected."

"Trimble said he wanted me for my degrees, but mostly I think it was for my name. Together they suited his purpose admirably, as he put it. I was to be seconded under the Defence Intelligence Staff banner, and apply for a position in a private English company who would be favoured in a forthcoming takeover of certain petrochemical assets owned at present by BP in Antwerp. "With your qualifications they'll snap you up. You will be in there at the start, and you will open doors for them. You'll be making history, my boy!" That's how he sold it to me."

"Were you expected to make that history for him directly, or through a handler?" her eyes narrowed as she asked.

"He told me, "Only ever to report to me Harry. No dirty hands on you before you step through my door...I should say not! We don't want you corrupted and shown the other side of life too soon. Only pure unadulterated chemicals for you to work with. Refreshing bubbles bubbling away above your Bunsen burner. We'll strip them clean, the two of us together, with you carrying the cross of Saint George and me sweeping up behind."

"Were those the exact words he used, Harry? It's seven years ago, now."

"Perhaps not verbatim, but the essentials and the references are his, plus the terminology. He was so excited about it all. I might as well have not been there. He reminded me of a dog with a toy almost jumping through rings. I'm sure that, had there been burning ones and I'd asked him, he would have jumped without questioning it."

"He never showed any exuberance or jauntiness towards you when here, on that shooting weekend. No high spirits whilst banging away at all those grouse?" She asked.

"No. If anything, I'd say he looked downcast and gloomy. He never said much at meals or on the drive…he was a bit subdued, as though he had a heavy load on his mind."

"You said that he spent time alone with Elliot. Did your father reflect Peter's mood, do you think?"

"I honestly don't remember. He was never a 'hail fellow well met' sort of person…a serious man, my dad. And I suppose it's true that familiarity does breed contempt. You stop looking for signs, after a while."

"Hmm. I'm surprised, Harry. You have struck me as a very deliberate and observant man. Why wouldn't you notice if your father was either nonplussed or excited, I wonder?"

"Possibly because he always seemed that way to me, back then." I had added the 'back then' quickly, as my lie about the close happy family ties in my previous recount had to be maintained.

"Hmm, yes…possibly, I suppose." She opened the red and black book for the first time, and scribbled something quickly.

I had lied about Elliot's reaction. On the Sunday, the day they all departed, he did something completely out of character. 'Give me your hand, Harry. Congratulate me. I've been able to help my country,' he said, before patting me heartily on the back. In my silent reflection I almost missed her next question.

"Did Willis and Howell meet your father separately or were they always together at their meetings?"

"Always together. I never saw father on his own with either of those two."

"Are you sure?"

"Yes, certain."

"Hmm...I see."

This idiosyncratic 'Hmm' seemed always to proceed the need of additions to the black and red book of hers; sometimes hastily, as though she didn't want to stop the flow, other times more deliberately, as though she needed time to think about my reply. This was one of the latter. She sat with her chin resting on her clenched hands, staring at the pages. Her lips pouted in a frown, in deep thought, until at last she gave a tiny sigh and said, to no one in particular, "Could be." Then she immediately carried on.

"When you were accepted into this BP buy-out company, how was Peter's reaction? The same euphoria, or a different reaction altogether?"

"Different, yes, as though he expected it. He seemed a touch pensive, I remember him saying, "all well done then Harry. Get yourself settled, and I'll be calling on you when I have the need." Very perfunctory, it surprised me."

"What was your role inside the petrochemical company? I've got the name on file, also your position, but I want you to tell it and, like before, expand on it. Tell me what you worked on, and what were its uses."

"I first worked on Polymers and man-made fibres; that category breaks down into many products, all used either by consumers or in industry. Polyethylene is what your milk comes in all the takeaway cartons for coffee, soups, etc. Polyvinyl chloride, PVC, makes pipes, amongst many other things. Polypropylene goes into appliances and packaging, then there's polystyrene and polyester, nylon and acrylics. All these products are made from spin-offs of the oil industry: liquefied petroleum gas, natural gas, or crude oil."

"Let me try to summarise all that if I can. Where there's oil these polymers can be made, is that right?"

"At present, yes, but you need the expertise. That's where the science of chemical engineering comes to the fore, and folk like me. Biofuel is the future."

"Go on, Harry. I'm all yours."

"After a year or so they moved me into the speciality chemical field, which is a high-value, rapidly growing market where the products have diverse applications in the industrial world. There's electronic chemicals, commercial gases, adhesives and sealants, coatings for high-grade projects, and the materials needed for the decontamination of anything from used oil to nuclear waste. The biggest growth of all is in synthetic organic polymers, and that was really my personal forte. They're made from waste products ideal for the developing world, where there is no oil, or very little."

"You might have to excuse my ignorance in something that you are obviously so expert in, but could you reverse this process, and create fuel from polymers?" Judith innocently asked.

"You have it. That's the end game; fuel from waste products or existing bio-diverse products farmed for fuel, like used cooking oil or seaweed, for example, not the agricultural produce that was first suggested. There are investigations into other methods too, but I have no wish to appear too esoteric. Many compounds are found in polymers, carbon being the most important. It's a common factor, so most have the consistency to ignite. Benzene used to be added to petrol as an aromatic compound polymer. It made it smell better but it can still be used for other purposes. It's still used as an additive but also, in the right formula, a substitute. Phenol is used in anything from cosmetics to antiseptics, from aspirin to herbicides. Ethanol is pure alcohol. There are other elements that, if combined with phenol and ethanol, give you a petrochemical base constituent. From that, the replication of fuel could be, in theory, constructed. It's a long way off replacing non-restorable assets, but it's on the right tracks.

There's another thing though that's more relevant and more of today's world. In the Northern Hemisphere, Russia and Canada in particular, there are billions of barrels of oil locked up in the rock strata and under deep sand, but the cost of extracting this wealth of oil and gas has been prohibitive. Now, though, with the technology that we have developed in this country, and the cost of conventionally drilled oil, it's proving more cost-effective. There's a theory going around that the Russians have cut back in production to hike the price up, so that their vast reserves locked away can be extracted. Their only trouble is that they don't know how to do it, and don't want to pay for the knowledge nor the expertise needed. They want to steal it!"

"That's interesting, very interesting. All that within your remit, Harry?"

"Well, not just that now, no. I got shifted over into the biotechnology side, which is vast. I focus on metabolic pathways of pathogens, manipulating these using biochemistry. It truly is fascinating. Take protozoa, as an example. It's a single-cell organism living in algae that feeds on organic matter and lives in the soil, so after drilling or extracting the oil..." I was not allowed to finish, as an obviously bored Judith raised her hand and waved for me to stop.

"As you say, a fascinating subject, no doubt, but I really have heard enough, thank you. Managed all this as well as us and the estate here, did you?"

"Oh yeah, easily. Part-time for them and you, plenty of time for other things. I found a niche for myself." I would be a liar to deny that it was not my aim to be boring. I liked being in control for a while.

"Hmm. I can see that." She rubbed the back of her fingers as if suffering the first symptoms of arthritis. "I want now to move on to your first venture into the field for us, and to how Trimble kept his reins on you."

"He would simply phone. I was living in a company owned apartment, about 25 kilometres from Antwerp, in a place called Mortsel. He called me there three days before my first operation."

"Before you go any further, was there any; *'living in'* company to soothe away your aches and pains in Mortsel, H?"

"No, no one permanent. There were a few transient relationships I pursued at the time but nobody stayed to do my washing and ironing, no."

"You're so romantic, Harry. I do so miss that age of romanticism, don't you? I'll need their names, give them to me at lunch, will you? Carry on. What did he say?"

"He said he had sent me something in the post. I was to open it, and take the contents to a Lutheran Church in Grönwohld near Hamburg, in Northern Germany, and to leave it there at the far end of the chancel on the lectern side of the church. I was to do this by nine-thirty on the following Sunday, one hour before the first gathering of the day."

"What was in the parcel?" that narrowing of her eyes again.

"It was a small lithographic print of a robed figure giving communion to a bearded, kneeling man. I was to place it upside down on the shelf that holds the song books in front of the first pew."

"What were you to do then?"

"Well, there was something I had to do before that. I was to knock on a house…number 17 Steinern and ask for a Dietmar Kohl. If I was asked who I was, I was to give my full name, Lord Harry Paterson, adding that I was an old friend."

"You obeyed that directive, Harry?'

"Yes, I did," I declared.

"Hmm…strange. After that, you went straight to the church and left the sketch…then what?"

"I didn't find it quite as easy as you put it. I was trying to hold myself together a bit; I was thinking of Richard Burton in *The Spy Who Came In From The Cold.* Peter had said to wait until the congregation had left and then, to see if anything was left."

"Like what?"

"He didn't say, only that whatever it was it would be underneath the pew where I had left the print on view."

"Tell me that there was something there, Harry, please?" she demanded, excitedly.

"No, there was nothing there that time." I paused just long enough to let the disappointment fill her face, then added, "But I found this; the second time I looked."

Chapter Seven

Pink Carnations

We were to have a rescheduled start after lunch. Judith had requested the change, stating her need to research something, leaving the subject unclear as she carried the photograph away with her. I was left alone beside the roaring fire that I had instructed Joseph to light, but suddenly I felt cold.

I remembered how I was shaking on that short walk from my car to that house in the quaint hamlet with the unpronounceable German name. The knock was unanswered, which I was thankful for, as I felt no words would leave my mouth as it was so dry. I was trying to hold my breath in the silent church in case I made a noise as I laid the sketch on the pews, and, again, as I tiptoed across the stone floor in my exit. Then the wait, and the return. It was as if everyone that Sunday was watching me. Trimble had said that if there was no reply, then to go back the following Sunday. I searched and searched, down on my hands and knees, but found zilch. I really didn't want to come back and face the same torment, but had no choice.

The next Sunday I think I was shaking more as the rain bouncing off my coat would testify. I suppose it was the mood that I was in that made that rain feel, and sound, like gunfire zipping through the air, targeting only me. There was no one else foolish enough to be out in such weather, which made me feel more conspicuous and vulnerable. I didn't know what to expect, a policeman or a gun; I was that paranoid. My mind was going over and over, thinking I had been set up. The first time they'd had a good look, and this time they know who to shoot. Anyway, I was a good boy-scout, and I got over it, and went in. I found it straight away the photograph, I mean. It was held up under the seat by sticky tape. Then my curiosity took over. I stayed for the service; I don't know why, it was not as though I would recognise anyone. It was just a show of bravado on my part I guess, plus I wanted to see who sat in that pew and had caused me all this mental anguish. The thought of punching him crossed my mind but it was left empty, just like the emptiness my anger had to endure.

I had never experienced nerves before as I did that day, even in Bosnia trying to keep a thankless peace. The other time I had seen action well, *seen* is not the right word, *heard of* would be more appropriate was in Afghanistan. There I had listened to others on field telephones, hearing their response to fear and danger, whilst I liaised with OIC's, Officers In Charge. I never once, on either tour of duty, saw a bullet fired. I never had the opportunity to test myself in tense situations or under hostile fire. In truth, I felt a fraud amongst brave, disciplined, men, and that is what led me to retire. I had been nervous before, however, and one specific time now came back to me. I was trying to forget that first drop-off by thinking of other things, when the phone call from my father came flooding back.

* * *

He had texted me his number and we spoke in depth of his findings. We communicated on Mondays or, if unable to do so, Thursday afternoons. My father was a systematic man, for whom the term 'habitual' was invented. 'Annie's' was only open on Tuesdays, Wednesdays and Thursday mornings. The weekends from Friday to Sunday were, when my mother still graced this life, spent here amongst his material belongings, or in London with his lovers when the need for more covertness was unnecessary. Thursday afternoons and Monday were his. Mondays he would spend travelling and lunching at far flung restaurants he had read reviews of. He would then tour the surrounds on foot, weather permitting, visiting galleries or antique shops. He was selective in the areas he chose, of course, but generally he spent that day just amusing himself and, presumably, the other party to his life.

"Mondays are quiet in London, Harry. Good day to get out and about a bit. Go to Notting Hill...the good parts, mind you or the Borough and the City. The air is a bit cleaner on a Monday."

Thursdays were his indulgent days: massage at the Dorchester, wet shave and hair trim at Truefitts and Hill, call in at Lobbs to see how the shoes were going, pick up a good new wine at Berry Bros, lunch at the Connaught, and even see a matinée, if one was showing that caught his eye, or hers.

The copies of the journals he sent me, the ones that had been unearthed in a previously unknown safe hidden in the concrete floor, did not make good reading. Against some numbered bonds that were lodged, amounting to £7.5 million, were the initials MA. Three bonds in all were removed from the bank; the first in June 1936, then November of the same year, and finally May 1937.

The next time those MA initials appeared was in August 1946, and for varying values. More were removed at sporadic intervals, until they ceased on the 14th of April 1970. The largest amount went missing in September 1956: four Bonds totalling £66 million. From 1946 to 1956 the scale of withdrawals, compared to the total sum, was meagre: about £20 million, or two million a year. Then, in '56, two other initials were joined to MA...RD, and £186.5 million went missing in the following years and were never returned, nor were the recipients names recorded.

As far as Elliot's suspicions over a Soviet Union connection, they seemed to be borne out by a scribble in the margin of that 1936 ledger. *2397 Baskov. District 19. Leningrad.*

* * *

"No news from London, I'm afraid. Been on to both us and the Branch. No one's been into the men in blue and put their hands up and said 'It's a fair cop, governor,' I'm sorry to say."

My family oriented analysis had been stopped dead in its tracks by Judith's all-singing, all-dancing return.

"You can remove your rear end from my chair, as well. At least it will be warmed up when I get mine in there. By the by, Harry, did you know that both my great grandfather and grandfather knew your great one, Maudlin Paterson?"

I feigned disinterest and ignorance as I vacated the toasting spit, and resumed my allotted position.

"Yes...now, there's a coincidence, don't you think?" She waited for an answer, as I waited for her continuance. As nothing was forthcoming, I broke the stilted silence first.

"I suppose so. Small world, eh?"

"Getting smaller by the day, Harry. Want to know how they all knew each other? Well, I'm going to tell you, even if you don't want to hear it. Edwin that's the great one on my side of the trilogy, was a year older than your Maudlin, and a year apart at Eton and Cambridge, where I doubt they knew of each other. They went their separate ways after schooling, with my Edwin ending up in the Foreign Office straight from the age of 26. That was in 1917. Over the years he worked his way up the ladder, aided by his title, as is the way of things, ending up quite big. He was also aided by the outbreak of the disagreement between us, the good side, and that bad lot lead by Herr Hitler and his gang of testosterone driven murdering thugs. Lord Edwin Davenport was His Majesty's Ambassador in Vienna, that hotbed of Machiavellian spies.

For three years before his appointment, and for the entire time that he was there, and that was until 1945, he regularly received requests from Lord Maudlin to forward on letters addressed to an Andrea Isadora Mafalda Cortez in Leningrad in the USSR. Your own M got himself a nickname; Pinky, he was called thereafter, in the corridors of the FO. Don't look so worried, H. He was never considered a spy. Not many I've heard of thought he sent the Kremlin our Crown

Jewels through the diplomatic bag," she laughed in an insulting way. "My grandfather followed precisely Edwin's steps early in his passage of life, signing on for the FO at the same age of 26 in 1947, and regularly confirmed, to the continuing interest of his father, that Pinky was still active.

At this time, Edwin headed up section X1, the anti-Soviet section of the then SIS but, can you believe this, not one of them, or any of the minions working the wires under them, bothered to ask Pinky what he was up to! By around 1956, three years after Stalin's death, communications were relaxed between East and West, and Maudlin no longer had the need of diplomatic channels. Whether he persevered in his correspondence I can only speculate on and, I guess, so could those in 'The Office' at that time." She leaned closer to the fire and rubbed her hands together, as if to say, 'I've got you; haven't I.'

"Would you like to comment on what I've just said, Harry, or did you know about all these carrying-ons of GG Maudlin and didn't want to play with the rest of us?" She adopted the seductive, accusing, smile that I was becoming used to.

So, no one knew what went on after 1956, but it must have been substantial; otherwise why had Judith mentioned all of this, and why had so much money vanished after that date?

"Nothing I can say, other than I admire your knowledge. As I said, I knew very little of Maudlin and no one in my family has ever spoken of it. Perhaps it's innocent. Maybe he played chess by post with an old friend."

"Yes, that could well be it," she said, sitting back in her chair and almost laughing. "I admire your optimism, Harry, in all your shades of life, but I doubt that you're that naive," she declared after some seconds, never altering the stare from those green eyes at me. Then, without delay, she continued. "Okay. Let's get back to business, and I'll stop all my show boating about our connections. Tell me of your second trip into the field, and Trimble's instructions. Did he phone as before, or use a different method? Take me for the walk, H and, please; do it slowly."

"He wrote this time. It was January 2006 and I was still bedding down in Mortsel and before you ask, I was not in a permanent relationship, nor was anyone there when I opened the letter, nor did I leave it around for someone to read. I opened it in my office at work, and shredded it. There were no other women that I was involved with, that I have not given you the names of already. On the back of the photograph was a date and a place, where I was to go and meet the face on the front." I was a little tense and it did not go unnoticed.

"All right, Harry. I sense aggression somewhere there, where has that come from? Don't be ashamed of your past. Without a history we won't know how to avoid making the same mistakes in our future. I'm referring to your promiscuous behaviour…nothing else, no hidden innuendoes I assure you."

"I've never thought of you as the insinuating type, Judith. I'll just carry on and ignore the connotations about my personal life. I was going on a delegation to Canada to present the companies credentials to the regulating bodies in Vancouver, and to start the bidding to open several plants there. I assumed that she was working for ADM international, an American competitor of ours, who, along with two other companies from Japan, were also present. In the photograph she was about 29 years of age, five foot seven in height, long black hair, good figure.

All in all, a foxy glamorous-looking girl, and as you would well expect…I was looking forward to making her acquaintance. Her name was Katherine Friedal, and I was to introduce myself as me. He gave me no cover name, and I was surprised by that. I thought by now that, having run the gauntlet once, so to speak, I warranted cover this time. I texted him on the number that he had given me as a contact, and the message I got back only confirmed what he had already written. "Introduce yourself as Lord Paterson. That will be the name on the delegates list, it cannot be avoided." I complained about it when I got back."

Judith was alternating between both her books, but had not interrupted her writing, nor looked likely to. I watched her delicate fingers as her left hand drove that pen across the pages making many underlines or crossing-throughs, sometimes circling motions in a heavy hand as if to emphasis something already written. I carried on with my recollections.

"Industrial espionage was, and still is, rife in my line. An attractive women in the same business was especially dangerous, as she would understand any technical jargon that might be blurted out in the heat of the moment."

She gave me one of the inquisitive stares that usually followed her idiosyncratic, 'Hmm' one where her lips pouted, eyes widened, and she tilted her head to one side.

"That's novel pillow talk, Harry… chemical formulae? I'm all aghast at what you get up to in bed with your conquests!"

The compulsion to respond to her irony with a 'come and see' was strong, yet there was another impulse that restrained me more forcefully. A feeling of wanting to be liked by this women. Not in a sexual way, not really well, that's what I told myself, but more in a respected, companionable way. It led me to lie: "Gorgeous, she was, but there was no way on this earth that I was going to get hooked up in any arrangement with her, and that you can take as gospel and verse!" I had my fingers crossed as I told it, and wished strangely that it was true.

"We met on that first evening, there was a reception held in a municipal building of some description. I'm not sure what it was called now, or the Department we were dealing with. I just tagged along with the others. Anyway, I helped myself to a drink and approached her. She was surrounded by other admiring men and obviously enjoying all the compliments they must have been showering her with. Me, being the irrepressible confident soul that I am, I figuratively dived into the ruck, and went searching for the ball.

"Hello… Katherine, isn't it? The manager sent me over to ask you to leave; your absolute beauty, charm and radiance is making every other woman in the room look so terribly ugly. I'm Lord Harry Paterson, and if you would like to take my arm I'd be delighted to escort you anywhere else you'd like to go."

"You cad you, fancy pulling rank like that! That's some line, I've just got to say. Did she faint? I know I would have from embarrassment! Did you get away with it?" I had Judith's visual attention this time, as she almost fell out of her fireside chair.

"It's not original. I'd heard it somewhere and it was, honestly, the first time I'd used it."

"Well, you're not using it on me, Harry Paterson. How did it work on Kathy...a quick KO, or did you die from a slow death?"

"She took my arm, of course. Who wouldn't have, apart from you?"

"Cut to the quick, H. Don't feed me the images from the bedroom mirror, I'm hot enough already from the heat of this fire. What did she say?"

"I suppose you mean apart from the obvious...that I was fantastic, an Adonis, things like that."

"Shame omnipotence can't turn back time. Even the gods must suffer from slowing metabolism. The seams are showing on the costume, Harry, you're only just about holding it together!"

I didn't feel the need to reply, so I carried on. "She said: *He will meet you in Moscow on the sixth of September, it is all arranged.*" She also slipped something into my jacket pocket as I brushed against her, through the crowd at the bar, to get two more glasses of champagne. I have it here."

I laid the stiff blue envelope on the table and pushed it towards Judith, who opened it. Inside was a Visa card, the numbers corresponding with an account at the Impexbank of Russia. The account was in my name and had been opened one month before this Canadian meeting, but not by me. There was 250,000 roubles in it, about £5,000. More than enough for the two nights that someone had reserved for me at the National Hotel, opposite the Kremlin. Attached to the Hotel confirmation form was a leaflet promoting the Michel Jarre concert to be held on the evening of the sixth, celebrating the 850th anniversary of the founding of Moscow. There was a seating plan, centred on the performance stage. I was in row D1, seat number 101 an aisle seat, which I was thankful for, as I could stretch out my invalided knee."

Judith was busy penning into her book, when she asked, "Did she work in the same business as you suspected?"

"No, she said she worked for CNN and was there covering the negotiations for her news channel. The release of the reserves of trapped oil would be big news, apparently, not just for the economy, but for the tree-huggers that I love so much."

Still not looking at me, she asked, "So, you had no worries about discussing your work when you bedded her, then?"

"I'm getting a mite peeved at your questions into my private sexual affairs, Judith, and I can't see the relevance, but I'll answer it; of *course* I did!" My chivalrous intentions were goaded too far, and was not capable of continuing in this role of gallantry.

"Thought so…you do run to form, H, don't you? Where did you meet Trimble when you made your complaint, and what was his reaction?"

"We met in the back of a London cab. I'd taken the cab from the rank outside the Terminal at Heathrow, ostensibly to Eton Square, asking the driver to pick someone up on the way. Trimble, collar turned up, and wearing a tartan cap was in the Grenadier Pub, down a cul-de-sac off Belgrave Square. I had asked the driver to turn in. We waited a few minutes, glad handing outside the front but watching for followers, and when none appeared I paid the driver off. We walked through the front door of the pub into a courtyard at the rear, then out into Knightsbridge, catching another cab to Crockfords, in Curzon Street. As to my complaint, all he said was that I was in no danger, and to stop worrying."

"Did that soothe your troubled mind?"

"That was all I got, so it had to…I had no other option."

"Did he mention the photo at all?" she asked.

"Said he had a copy on file. He never mentioned the name though, of the file, that is."

"Did she give you anything else, Harry like a card, or the means of getting in touch?"

"Yes, got it right here close to my heart." I patted my breast pocket, then added, "Do you want it? Are you a bit jealous, Judith?"

"Hmm…no, Harry, but I'll take a copy of the details that is, if you can part with it for a few seconds without passing out on me. Did you ever phone old Kathy, Harry, out of office hours, as it were?"

"Now who's being insecure, Judith? I didn't. I just knew that someday the two of us would meet, and I didn't want her memory to jeopardise our mutual regard for one another."

"Did you and Peter have a profitable evening, gaming at Crockfords, or did you come close to losing the Estate?"

"I don't gamble Judith. I like sure things; only certainties."

Abruptly the conversation finished as Judith's mind was transfixed elsewhere.

* * *

"Right, now that's out of the way, it's time for me to change. I'm out tonight, old thing, something prearranged I just can't get out off. No, you can take that silly look off your face, it is official business. I'll be back in the wee small hours and I promise not to disturb you if you trust me with a key, or is it a swipe card you use to get into this fortress? Will you miss me?"

"I'll count the seconds that we are apart. Can I help you change? Help with your buttons, or, perhaps choosing the dress? Something silky and sultry, I would think?" I had returned to my old self and felt much better for it.

"No, you can't, and I think tweed and something woollen would be more suitable this evening. I feel a chill in my bones."

"If you do feel like disturbing me, please do. Other than that I'll hold my breath and wait for you at breakfast. Do hurry back."

Chapter Eight

Where Life Begins

Peter Trimble teamed up with the Directorate of Military Intelligence, Section Six, from the sanity of the outside world in 1978. He was almost 29, and immediately became a sub on the 'Garden File', directly under the supervision of the then 'C' Dicky Blythe-Smith. That file had been opened in 1961 by one of his predecessors, Maurice Cavendish, when irrefutable information was mysteriously intercepted at GCHQ.

A cryptanalysis of previously used pages, of an intended 'one time pad' encrypted message, pointed at a certain Harold Adriano Russell Philby as being, beyond doubt, the 'third man' in the Burgess Maclean scandal. Stanley, the name used, by the Soviets in these messages, had been nicknamed 'Kim' after the young Indian of Rudyard Kipling's novel, having had been born in the Punjab and spent time in the Indian Civil Service. This was a major breakthrough for the SIS, *as one time pad* messaging, that is encrypting words and letters into numbers to which an additive key from a *'one time pad'* was added, was unbreakable.

The code had been corrupted by the reuse of entire pages of previously used material, allowing for its decryption. At the time, it was taken to have been an oversight at the Soviet manufactures of their secret communication equipment, or simply a lucky break as can happen in life. No one considered it to have been deliberate, other than Cavendish. Philby had been supplying information to the Russians since before the Second World War but had been cleared of spying charges; even being vindicated by Prime Minister Macmillan in the House of Commons in 1955. He was an acute embarrassment to all in the upper echelons of English society, especially the Intelligence community. Cavendish, either in collusion with the Government or on his own, decided not to use that undeniable evidence and arrest and prosecute Philby; instead he allowed him to escape to the Soviet Union, where he was beyond the reach of journalists and the full exposure of his treason.

By this action the cryptanalysis was not apparent to the Russians, and project *Venona;* the name given to this decryption continued into the eighties. More oversights and lucky breaks came the way of SIS. Had Cavendish been clairvoyant, or just plain lucky?

Set against Stanley's banishment away from the Secret Services, were the unanswered questions over the full and exact damage he had done. The only avenue into that investigation left open to Maurice was the time honoured one of leg work; that of going back and over everything Stanley had done, or everywhere he had been stationed.

Two separate and seemingly unconnected items were thrown up by 'subs' working out of 'the office.' The first was when the department was situated at 54 The Broadway SW1 in 1963. A bank account, under the name of Stanley Russell, was held at a branch of the Martin's Bank of 63 Long Acre WC2. It was opened on the 14th July 1936 with a deposit of £2.5 million plus change, then another of exactly £2 million in November of the same year, and finally one of £3 million, again with change, in May the following year. There had been no withdrawals. The writing on the application form filled in by Stanley was identical, conclusively, to that of Philby's.

Lord Edwin Davenport, as British ambassador, had a great deal more to do at the outbreak of war than just the forwarding on of a fellow hereditary peers' letters. He delegated Philby to that task, who was attached to the Embassy in Vienna throughout the early war years, supplying valuable information to the Allies. Edwin had noted down all the details of the three letters. However, it being such a small inconsequential event, it went unnoticed and unrecorded on Stanley's file until Peter Trimble, ferreting around as all good 'subs' are meant to do, unearthed it early in his career, in the Westminster Bridge Road building that then hosted the SIS. This was the second item. Taken apart, as well might they have been done, owing to the fifteen-year gap in their discovery, there was no connection; but put together as Dicky Blythe-Smith did, it added up to one thing, and one thing only. Lord Maudlin Paterson was sending money to a person in Leningrad, and Stanley had intervened in the delivery.

The next thing that Dicky had to decide upon was how to approach the problem of an errant, supposed ex-custodian of a private bank, in which the SIS had a distinct interest. After due deliberation he abandoned protocol, adopting a radical approach rather than the more conservative prudence that the situation may have demanded. He sent the young, inexperienced, Trimble to parley with the aged Lord at Harrogate Hall.

"I'm sorry to trouble you, my Lord, but I have come to speak to you about some letters you wrote to a Señora Cortez in Leningrad starting in 1936 and then going on for many years," Peter stoically declared.

"Yes, young man... and what interest are they of yours?"

"Well, Sir, we believe that Kim Philby that abomination of a man took some money from those letters for himself."

"What money? Was there money in them? What makes you think it was mine?" indignantly he asked. Come on, speak up, man!" he contemptuously demanded of young Peter.

"Well, nothing really, other than we've found a bank account of his with £7.5 million in. We just wondered if it could be yours, Sir?"

"Are you accusing me of being a spy, or a fraudster, or both? Make sure that Blythe-Smith is in his office on Monday when I shall walk the ledgers over the bridge to him. Tell him that he should not have sent a boy to do what he could not face himself, and also; to have his apology ready and for good measure, his resignation. I will be speaking to the PM this evening about this."

The Director of MI6, as the Secret Intelligence Service is popularly referred to, has only once resigned. If it was a more regular occurrence it would cause an unnecessary furore amongst the servile citizens it is supposed to serve, and this edict was applied to Dicky, who sent a letter of abject apology to Lord Maudlin and attached his report to the *Garden* File. There it stayed until Peter Trimble assumed the role of 'C' in 2007, and the haunting memory of that ancient meeting was remembered.

Where the complexity of my father was introspective and self-absorbed, Maudlin's was the opposite; he was an extrovert, gregarious, and in his young days, an utterly carefree man. In some ways, Judith reminded me of his methodical way of thinking and his painstaking attention to detail. He had selected Vienna as his chosen route for his correspondence, with care and deliberation. His inbred suspicion of all things foreign narrowed his options it must be said. However, it was still an inspired choice. The fact that Stanley had intervened was beyond his comprehension or his control. It had been through his foresight that GCHQ had been endowed with the unique facilities that enabled that institution to decipher the code that had lead the SIS to his door! It was in 1946 when he had contacted Meredith Paine, the then 'C,' and proposed the expansive program of improvements to GCHQ capabilities, prompted by his own experiences of gathering information; but he had no fears of any investigation. The secrets were, as he advised me, buried deep.

The air route for mail was complicated in the late thirties. Through Germany was the direct route; however, the tensions between that country, Britain and the USSR made that choice unreliable. The route via Scandinavia was unusable, due to the unrest, prior to the 'Winter War' between Finland and its unhappy neighbour the USSR. A route through North Africa and the Middle East was feasible, but long in time and therefore capricious. Notwithstanding all these obstructions, the overriding consideration to Maudlin was his inability to write in the Cyrillic alphabet and his well-founded mistrust of some Soviet postal worker being able to read English. So, he settled on Austria as his safest bet; and until that interview, had never known where his money had gone.

He had no replies from Andrea to muse over for ten long years and had often worried about her welfare, until in September 1946 he received a rerouted letter from her, informing him of her poverty and asking for help.

He was a learned and erudite man my great-grandfather, gaining his knowledge from wide and expansive fields; not relying solely on his academic lessons for his insight on life. He had been aggrieved that he was the last son and in line for the Standard of Saint George, as he had sought a more adventurous life for himself than that.

At the onslaught of the 'War to end all Wars' he had enlisted, against his father's will, in the Royal Horse Artillery and immediately was given the rank of Captain. He saw action on the Western Front, the Sinai Peninsula and in Persia and ended the war as a Colonel. He was commended on four occasions, and wore his awarded Distinguished Service Order and Bar, along with his other campaign medals, with great pride. By 1922 he had retired from the Army, much to the relief of his father and Alfred, the third-youngest brother of the quartet of Paterson sons but not, to their horror, from hostile activities. He volunteered for the Irish War! There, in Ireland, the seed was planted that grew and led to his acquaintance with MA; or, more correctly, Andrea Isadora Mafalda Cortez, who unbeknown to him then, was one year old.

Maudlin's responsibility lay in the gathering of information of the Irish Republican Armies' intentions and tactics, and in this role he recruited an assembly of men known as the 'Cairo' gang. For three years Maudlin's handling of those seven Protestants, as they went about their trade, was impeccable and faultless... until one day when he made a mistake. He vowed there and then, standing on the street where their bodies lay, never to divulge confidential, intimate secrets to anyone, even if they are, supposedly, on your side!

"Never trust your friends with confidential information Harry, they will ultimately let you down. Keep it to yourself. Never allow yourself to think that a friend is as reliable as you are in keeping a secret, because they won't be. Just remember that you can only ever rely on yourself, and no one else." Another snippet of knowledge my great-grandfather gave me, and I was trying to live up to him in keeping the faith.

Chapter Nine

Snowdrops

"If it's all the same to you, Harry, I'd like to get out today. I'm a bit of a botanical freak, and I love spring, with its promise of new life. Today looks like it will be lovely. How about the moors? If the crocuses are so wonderful here, I bet the snowdrops, up at that height, are truly marvellous."

We were at breakfast on the Sunday and I hadn't heard her return from her night's excursion, but I had broken away from tradition. There seemed little point in having a selection of dishes from which to choose, carried upstairs from the kitchen and presented in the dining room, as she had eaten the same dishes on the mornings of her stay. One slice of dry toast, brown, of which she had left half, a bowl of one shredded wheat with skimmed milk, and then some tinned fruit in their juices. She had decaffeinated coffee, whilst I had tea. As far as my own breakfast was concerned, I was perfectly happy with my normal routine of raiding the refrigerator for delights, and having my tea either in my office, or the estates.

I found the formality of the first meal of the day wearisome and over indulgent, especially with my own consumption of the last few days. In homes such as mine, it is not unusual to have breakfast served; however as my guest ate so little, I had decided to dispense with that ritual, and had brought Judith's favourites from downstairs to the table. I had also prepared a plate of cold beef, left over from the previous night's dinner, for myself. Cook, with her pleasant habit of cooking too many, always kept the crispiest roasted potatoes left untouched for my snacking, and I had a few of these on my plate as well.

Judith was surprised and complimentary with the care I had taken over the arrangement of her preferences, but still felt obliged to criticise the contents of my own.

"You'll die young from high cholesterol poisoning if that's what you pig out on in the mornings. No wonder you're overweight. You could lose a few pounds, especially around your waist. I haven't seen you eat anything healthy since I've been here," she declared, in a gentle voice solicitously adding. "How are the cows? Have you heard from the vet with his report, yet? That reminds me... your hair could definitely do with a cut. You'd look silly with a pigtail. If you want, I could do it for you? I used to cut an old boyfriend's hair once, made a good job of it too, even if I say so myself. I'm no Nicky Clarke, but neither do I need a basin to put over your head. I'll tidy it up for you."

There was no mocking in her speech, no hint of inane criticism or witty indulgence. I thought I detected a sense of fond warm-heartedness that could be easily be taken as affection. All of a sudden, my breakfast table had taken on a different perspective. Had I married this women in my sleeping hours, whilst I had been drugged and stupefied? I quickly glanced at my left hand to see if the ring of captivity had been slipped on, or if the ink from the register had stained my fingers. Where did this concern come from if not from a marital partner?

"Yes, it would be nice to get away," was the trite statement I was able to make. I felt as though I was suffocating in the intoxicating air! "By the way, did you have a pleasant night and a peaceful drive?"

"Don't want to discuss it, Harry. Boring as being at a nun's convention discussing the virtues of contraception. Do you think we could have an hour's ride together straight after this? Nothing too strenuous with all that floating around inside you of course. I'll be kind!"

Again, where I would have made some clever remark about *'a ride together,'* I didn't. I was lost and incapable it seemed, of regaining my sanity.

"Why not?" I replied, thinking it was better than 'you wash, I'll dry' which any moment soon would be my suggestion. I should have said that the report from the vet had indeed shown some infection in the herd, and that I must lend a hand in the inoculations, but I didn't. I made things worse.

"The only thing is, I really must be at St Michael's, our local church, by ten-thirty. As the new Earl it's my duty to attend on the first Sunday of each month. This one is special, anyway. It is to commemorate my father, and I'll be expected to say a few words. Would you like to come?" I insanely asked, still caught, unexplainably, in her dazzling headlights.

Overnight I had become the doting, dutiful husband of a malnourished refugee rescued from the Third World. *Better stay clear of the hot roasted spuds at the Spy Glass after church*, I thought, as I struggled to free myself from this malaise.

"There was something I was meaning to ask you, Harry. I hope you don't mind…it's a bit personal."

In the trancelike state that I was in, I doubted that I could have kept any private matter from her, and I was not mistaken.

"Ask away, Judith, do."

"Well, you smell in the mornings. There's a whiff of chlorine in the air when you're around. You don't use it as a deodorant, do you?"

"Funnily, no. I swim every morning, spend a good hour or so in the pool. I have done since I was a child."

"You've been holding out on me, H! Have you got a pool here?" She was on her fruit course and almost dropped both fork and spoon, holding on to them at the cost of her half eaten toast, which fell, plate as well, noisily to the wooden floor.

I was helpless, caught with my trousers down at my ankles. I had been trying to keep the pool strictly to myself, but I was caught in her hypnotic presence and was unable to escape.

"Hadn't I mentioned it?" Bedazzled I replied. "No, I hadn't had I, must have slipped my mind. I promise I'll show you after breakfast and sort you out a costume to wear. There are steam rooms there, a sauna and heated relaxing loungers. Help yourself."

Another time I would have substituted *'a couple of handkerchiefs'* for the word costume, but that seemed an age away. I attended church alone; whilst Judith enjoyed my secret. However, by the time of my return I had regained my senses.

It was a six mile drive to the part of the North York Moors National Park nearest my favourite pub, and I hung on for grim life for every inch of that journey, as she hurled her car into every blind corner with seemingly reckless disregard for everything. When we had ridden out, earlier, she had shown no signs of this kamikaze trait, being comfortable and judicious, canny and perceptive. We had done the schooling jumps then ventured out across the estate. I had not removed some of the gallops from the racing stable days, and along these she had shown good riding skills in her posture and balance, beating me easily in a pretend race. I was heavy now, in my fortieth year, having given up on almost all sport, since a complicated knee injury I had sustained whilst playing rugby for the Army had curtailed my participation.

I played the occasional round of golf, if the arthritis in my knee allowed at a nearby course, or took some part in the annual estate cricket match in which to vent my anger. Other than that, and the occasional ride with my swim each day, there was nothing in which I could exert myself. I had always been heavily built; it was in the family genes. In my youth this had been to no disadvantage, having never been bullied nor ostracised at schools.

Apparently I was everyone's 'best pal' if house-mates were threatened with any the *'Seniors'* pranks, and at Eton there were many. One such was the variation of the 'Wall Game' where there was no ball and goals were often scored, unlike in the real thing. Every Ascension Day, after the conventional event, 'Oppidans', the Seniors, would suspend first year King's Scholars, called *'fags'* over the curved wall and drop them, spread-eagled, into the mud below. A goal was scored each time a 'fag' rolled over in that mud before being able to extradite himself from the all-clinging morass!

Nobody dared to argue the point with me when I refused, none too politely nor gently, to a particularly noxious Seniors offer to partake in this tradition. I hit him once and promptly knocked him out, then calmly turned from the rowdy crowd and walked away. Overnight I became my dormitory 'fellows' champion and, on more than one occasion, was offered up to resolve a matter which they had with other Seniors. I, for my part, had no inclination to refuse!

I was, however, no warrior more a *worrier*, as she drove to the Moors that Sunday afternoon. When I had the time to think I wondered if her husband's death had made her suicidal and when at last we stopped, that was exactly what I asked her.

"Now, you look here, Lord Harry bloody Paterson. Don't question things that are nothing to do with you. My private life is precisely that; private. If ever I decide to speak about it, it will be my decision, not yours. Got that? As far as my driving ability is concerned then you are perfectly safe with me. I love to drive fast. I hold an advanced driving certificate, which I gained after completing the Metropolitan Police Advance and Defensive driving course at Hendon. The top academy for such things in the world. I am also the holder of the women's lap speed record in Formula Three cars, and on 500cc motorcycles, at both the Brand's Hatch and Silverstone circuits. So button up, Harry, and don't pontificate on things you know nothing about." My views on self-preservation clearly did not harmonise with her own.

We both sat in an uncomfortable silence for a while, me determined not to apologise and Judith, in her state of disgruntlement, staring straight ahead. I broke the stalemate with a deep sigh and, at the same time, offered my cigarettes.

"At least it was invigorating. Would one of these help?"

"I've got my own, thank you. Joseph left 200 in my room yesterday. You know, if you didn't keep tripping up over your ego, you wouldn't be such a pain."

The silence had returned, only this time it was Judith that spoke first, having discarded the melancholy mood I had caused.

"You're holding something back, Harry, and I don't mean about hidden facilities at that house of yours. Why would Peter Trimble want you in the first place? Why not use an experienced field agent? I don't think it was only for your expertise in the chemical industry. I believe it was for your name, your title and it all stemmed from that tie-up between the bank account, and Maudlin's denial of having anything to do with it. Now, from where I'm sitting, only you can provide that link, and I believe you know what that is. You've painted a rosy portrait of your family bond, yet conveniently forgotten your father's reaction after that shooting weekend when obviously the backing of the bid for the takeover, of those BP assets in Antwerp, were discussed. He would have been over the moon, surely, with the chance to help his country and all that. I bet he partied into the morning!

You're trying to lock me out because of some egocentric reason, and that's not going to help in discovering who murdered your father if that... *is* what you want to find out! I'm going to be completely upfront with you, and tell you some things about me that just might, hopefully, help in opening you up. I have a master's degree in Psychology, Sociology and Psychotherapy, and I also lecture on experimental Psychoanalysis when I get the time. I was headhunted whilst at Oxford to join Joint Intelligence, and have been there since 2002 when I was 27, so now if you're quick you'll know I'm 36... anyway a divergence. Back to the point. I've had one file to concentrate on since that day, and it's directly handled by Peter. It's cross-referenced with a file coded *Garden* of which, with my classification, I've been privy to only smidgins. I've been fed crumbs for nine years just to keep me drooling. Then I get this break; unkind on your Dad, but wicked for me. Someone wants to wipe away a memory or take revenge. And I'm backing the first of those options!"

She was on a private crusade, as if to fight evil dragons. The intensity of that glare in her green wide eyes and the tightening of her upper lip that said, *come on, I'm ready for you,* was there for all to see, but it was only I that witnessed it; and I was happy that it was not me she had in her sights.

"I need you to work with me Harry, seriously. I need to find the rhythm that's running through those two files: *Garden, and Cockpit Steps,* my one, about all of you in the Paterson clan."

"I wouldn't know who wanted revenge on my father Judith. I really can't think of anyone. To my knowledge he has never done anything that would warrant someone to hold a grudge and kill him."

"I didn't expect you to. We've got to lift the lid on what Maudlin did together, and find out what he bought with his money before the war and if I'm right, what he kept paying for after it. That's what I need your knowledge for!"

"I don't know how I can help you."

"Yes you do, Harry. You can make me deliriously happy by telling me that your father found the missing link and told you, and then H, you can confirm my suspicions, and tell how you went digging and came up with zero. Now, I know that I'm right and you're playing for time, hoping I go away and you can carry on being the Inspector Clouseau in your own private 'Pinky' pantomime, but you're not going to get anywhere doing that. You haven't had the access to what I've had, and you're not likely to. I've got what you want dates, names, and coincidences. You've got the ability to make those opaquely unconnected occurrences glue together, and make the whole thing stand up."

I wish I could say that I sat and thought for a while, but I didn't. I discarded the valued memories of patriotic Patersons and seemingly betrayed them. I was free now from Morpheus, the mythological god of dreams, and in full conscious control of my thoughts. It was the renascence of my conscience, and a relief to share.

"I know about the money. It was from the bank," I revealed, blatantly.

Turning in her seat towards me and leaning forward, she eagerly asked "Was there more, lots more, Harry? And did it start in the late fifties?"

There was a strength and ferocity to that question, a belief in the knowledge of my reaction and answer. To what coloured door did I have the key to, and what was on the other side if we open it, I wondered?

"Look, Harry, over there. Snowdrops, can you see? I told you that if we looked, we would find them. Spring…it's a new beginning," she said, sitting back buoyant and perky; now in the driving seat.

Chapter Ten

Hops and Juniper Berries

My mind was muddled. What had made me give up that knowledge so easily? Was it her charm, or a weakness in me? I hadn't seen any droplet of spellbinding liquid added to my tea at breakfast that would have magically changed me into a blubbering traitor, but here I was, passing on the family's hidden secrets without resistance. I had previously considered myself strong and reliable but what was I now, I wondered?

I suggested the Spyglass and Kettle as a divergence, a time to gather my thoughts, and Judith agreed. This time the drive was sedate and beyond reproach, but we had missed my favourite roasted treats. I had never taken a women before to my debauched tavern. Now it seemed appropriate to share it, as we were about to share more relevant revelations in the forthcoming days. There were conspicuous head-turnings and restrained greetings from the raucous locals, and pure indifference and slight annoyance from the less frequent patrons, who did not know me. I had always felt at ease here amongst friends who treated me as no different from themselves. I was not the son of a Lord, just Harry, a bit of a scoundrel who had a few amusing stories to relate. Overall, good company.

There is a part of the pub, near one of the log fires, that had been christened 'The Worrier's Corner.' It was normally occupied by elderly pairings, discussing the woes of humankind today compared to their time, and their standards. Nothing was ever overheard emanating from that corner that was not better done, tasted, used or made in their days compared to today. Perhaps they were right in their collective refusal to participate in the righteous grind of progression, which can often seem onerous and exacting in the increasing anarchic society the elderly find themselves in.

"Always wore a shirt and tie to the pub on a Sunday... not like today, when anything will do. There's no respect nowadays, you know," one of their number had once rebuked me, when I'd arrived from the middle of ploughing and had been rightly told to leave my boots outside.

As I approached the bar, Judith had noticed that the *'Worries'* were leaving, the call of a nap after lunch being more pressing than another pint of John Smiths and continued arbitration, so, unaware of the native connotation given to the spot, she sat in one the vacated settees.

"Sorry to hear about your father, Harry. We were all shocked. How are you? I take it that the funeral will be here and not in London?" An unnecessary question, I thought from Jim, the landlord, before I realised that my father's absence from Harrogate for the preceding years had not gone unnoticed.

"Of course, Jim," I replied. "He had too much work down there to get home; it wasn't your beer," I light-heartedly joked.

"Has a date been fixed yet? We would all like to come and pay our respects. I've been asked a thousand times if I've heard anything," he asked, whilst getting my order.

"No, it's been a complicated matter, but when I'm able to make the arrangements I'll get Joseph to pop in and tell you. Does he still come in on a Monday night for his cribbage match, or has he beaten everyone here so many times that he now goes elsewhere to find his opponents? He tells me that he's a master of the game," I commented, still managing a smile.

"Well, he's been playing it long enough... should have learnt something by now. It was him who told me, last Monday. I'd missed it in the papers. Don't have much time for them, comic books the majority of them. As for the news on the telly, I give that a miss as well. All doom and gloom. Except for that one in the morning on BBC, Simon someone, he cracks a joke or two when he can, and if he can't; at least he smiles. Always finds something cheerful to say. It would be a better world if there was more like him." Jim was an effervescent character who, according to stories, had been an actor in younger days, prompting one of our number to question whether he had swallowed the scripts on more than one occasion! Without pausing in his pouring, he changed topics.

"Did you get a chance to see the game in Dublin? We were poor, weren't we? It's good to see you, and in such good form. I'll tell your lot to leave you in peace, if you'd like?" he solemnly offered.

I thanked him for his consideration, then waved and mouthed a *'No'* to the beckoning gestures from the far end of the bar before carrying Judith's gin and slimline, along with my usual, to our fireside chairs in readiness for the first delve into the truth.

She had her back to me with her mobile phone to her ear, looking intently at the flames as I put the glasses down. "Yes, I see. He's here now. Of course I will. Later today, if that will do? And you'll collect... fine."

As she closed her phone she turned from the fire, but the severity of the flames still remained. Where the happiness had been, an intense morbid gloom had replaced it, blending the hearth to her face as well as to her hair. I saw her cheeks indent as she clenched her jaws together, another characteristic of hers when troubled.

"That was Trimble, I've got some bad news I'm afraid." She leant across the dividing beer stained table and touched my hand.

"Your brother Edward has been found dead in his apartment this morning. He was murdered, H. No question. We're to resettle you out of harm's way until this is cleared up. Peter has his cleaners in at the bank, searching for needles in haystacks, but it's imperative that we finish the puzzle in double quick time. Who knows... you may be next on the list."

There was no need of concerns over breathalysers on our retreat to the Hall, as the drinks had been left untouched. I watched the fading view of the pub as it passed into the distance from the wing mirror of the Porsche saloon, and the immediate chance of discovery as to the origination of my troubles passed, too. I packed some bags, whilst Judith packed hers, left notes for the estate manager, and gave reasons of arrangements to be made in London as my excuse for the unplanned return. To the unflappable Joseph, I gave a more detailed reason.

"Edward has been murdered, Joseph. It seems as though he and father had ventured into an investment arrangement with another company in a buyout of a failing corporation. One of the directors of that enterprise lost a great deal of money before Dad's involvement, and according to the police, is suspected of committing these heinous crimes. They are searching for him now, so I'm leaving you to reassure the staff. When I'm able to confirm the date of the interments I will; however, from what I can gather, they may need more time with the bodies. You know what petty officials are like and all the boxes they love to tick."

Joseph disliked officialdom, believing that as head of this house, there was no paid employee in any *service*, of any description, that was above him. We had shared a dram or two, on leave in my Army days, when many degrees of authority had been discussed; and I had learnt, from hard experiences, that it was best to stay on the better side of Joseph rather than deal with his petulance.

"I'll tell you one thing, Sir. They're all the same, these politicians, no matter what colour they wear. Incapable of telling the truth and never did a day's work in their lives most Liberals, and all the Labour ones. Read about the lives of real people in books, but never experienced it. Then they spout on about how we have to live ours. Take this socialist lot, bringing us all down to the lowest denominator. No grammar streaming, yet they send their own children to private schools. Denounce private medical care, but where do they go for their health needs? Some dirty filthy NHS hospital where you have to be able to understand Swahili? I don't think so! Why is it that those who have come from nothing, perpetuate this class division, always referring to the working classes as though they are no different? They like to associate themselves with the ordinary man, until it comes to peerages or jobs in Europe, earning astronomical money for themselves and their own. They're in it for the power and prestige it gives them; nothing else. Give me a man who creates opportunity any day, rather than one who wants to regulate us all and leave himself exempt."

I remember that evening clearly. I'd chanced upon Joseph in the Spy Glass, and listened to him harangue the Socialist Government of the day, quoting shed loads of cases in education and health to substantiate his argument. His conviction was overwhelming. I held no such vehement views being, as I suspect like the majority of us, indifferent or rooted in tradition. I sought refuge in prudence that night, and have stuck with that philosophy ever since.

"I'm ready, Harry. Are you?" Judith was in the Great Hall, as her bags were departing through the door. There was an apprehensiveness in her question, and an anxious expression on her face.

"Impetuosity can get you killed," I remarked.

"Not while I'm around with this," she replied, lifting aside her pink coat and exposing the gun in her shoulder holster.

"Have you one, Harry?" she asked; needlessly.

* * *

Edward had been tortured to death. He'd been tied up and gagged, then cut with varying degrees of ferocity until his throat had been sliced open. There were dozens of disparate lacerations, reported by the on-scene pathologist, all seemingly done to cause increasing levels of pain. A long term friend had been the unfortunate one to find his mutilated body, when he had let himself in to the apartment that Sunday afternoon, after Edward's non-appearance at a gathering the previous evening. He had called the police, who in turn had called Trimble, who was left with the hapless task of forwarding on the pitiful news.

Our drive to Judith's house on the edge of Clapham Common was one full of contemplation; of the past and the immediate future. I was to stay at her home while the bank was closed, and Trimble's men went through the contents in search of the answers. "In 1946, they started again for a steady ten years. Nothing substantial compared to the whole, nothing over three million per year then, in 1956, £66 million in paper bonds disappeared the same day, 16 September; the first time the initials RD appeared. From that date until 1970, the rest of the £306.5 million walked out. Maudlin covered the missing bonds in two ways my father told me. One by shrewd investments, writing most of his windfalls against the missing bonds, but also by false arithmetic, by simply carrying forward the wrong balances in his ledgers. If you didn't look hard, you wouldn't find them, father had said," I told her, as she fed me questions, intent on the road ahead.

"That fits," she announced clinically, eyes fixed straight ahead.

"What fits what?" I asked, surveying the road for clues.

"We lost track of someone connected to an eventual big fish in '56," she confessed to me.

"Like to tell me who?" I enquired.

"No, not yet, H… I'm still mulling things over in my mind. But don't worry. I will reveal all in my own good time, I promise. Don't want you slipping away now, do I? I'm going to get a coffee at the next stop; I think it's going to be a long night. Do you want one, Harry? I've not got your brand of whisky at home!"

Chapter Eleven
Yellow Forsythia

When Paulo Sergeyovitch Korovin married Tanya Malonovna Kuznet-soka, originally from Lithuania, it was not because love had brought them together. It was more a case of obligation on Korovin's part, and the aspirations and connivance of Tanya. Paulo's mother could speak little Russian, and when she fell ill, and Tanya nursed her, it was through Paulo's interpretation that her symptoms and require-ments were conveyed.

Tanya and her five siblings were poor even by Northern Russian standards. Her mother suffered from chronic bronchitis and was only able to work few hours in the machine factory, a two mile walk from their communal apartment block. Her father, who had lost a leg in the October revolution of 1917, received scant recompense for his sacrifice other than the pride he was constantly reminded he should have. The illness suffered by Paulo's mother, on the other side of the partitioning wall, came as manna from heaven to the Kuznetsoka's, as the family were willing to pay for their daughter's time, and handsomely at that. For two and a half years this arrangement went on, until death took Andrea away, and Paulo repaid Tanya and kept his promise.

Tovarisch, to give Paulo his full Russian name or far more com-monly referred to as simply Comrade Sergeyovitch, was, at the time of his mother's death in 1955, twenty-three years of age, and had served in the KGB for three years since leaving Leningrad University, where he had written his final thesis on international law. He had joined the Communist Party when he was sixteen and at the time of the wedding, working in the fifth Directorate dealing in counter intelligence, widening his thoughts on his own expectations of life.

On their arrival in Leningrad in May 1935, Andrea Isadora Mafalda Cortez was 26, and her son Romario three. They were part of the Basque refuge's evacuated from Spain at the start of the Civil War to the Republican supporters; Russia. Andrea had sewn money given to her by her lover and the father of her son, Lord Maudlin Paterson, into both her own and the child's clothing, hoping that their temporary communist hosts would not search them too thoroughly.

"I managed to get it in roubles, and it should see you through for a year or two. I will send more for the boy and yourself as soon as I can; you may need it."

Maudlin told her this, after he had said that his homeland of England was out of the question for them to relocate to, owing to the position he held. He never quite explained what that was, but knew it would be sufficient for the practical and realistic Andrea. It was to be the last of his escapades, as his own father was, by now, showing the first signs of dementia and by 1939 his future lay at 'Annie's' door. He sought one last dash, before representing his country through the Bank of St George in a much more restrained way.

Ireland had ended badly for him. On the slaughter of the *'Cairo Gang'* his cover had been blown, and his patriotism and respect for others smashed, so he had looked for more adventures elsewhere in a solo role, unconnected with the echelon of rank. Spain was the obvious choice, with the tensions between the ruling Republicans and the Nationalists, led by General Franco, rising by the day. He offered himself to the British Foreign Office and was sent to San Sebastian, on the northern coast, to monitor the arrivals of the volunteers to Franco's fascist army. He simply noted their names, and feigned friendship.

He was forty-three, with a family of four children at home in Yorkshire, but that did not stop his philandering eye selecting the beautiful, dark-skinned, Andrea as his next mistress. She had fallen pregnant early in their relationship, much to Maudlin's initial annoyance; however, Andrea's appeal was deeper than one just based on sex. Maudlin had found love for the umpteenth time in his lecherous life. That version of his love had lasted an abnormal amount of years compared to other moments of *amore* he had endured previously, but one year later it was beginning to wane.

She had told him, in one of their heart-to-heart conversations, of relatives who had settled in the City of St Petersburg in the time of the Tsar and of its golden steeples and marbled halls; so it had seemed to him to be a perfect place in which to park-up his mothering lover. He was as good as his word when he received her one letter home allowed by the Soviets, addressed to him at the Embassy in Madrid.

The bonds were dispatched with no enclosed letter of remorse or sympathy. He was unmoved emotionally, by her and his son's distress, confident in the solid belief that they were far enough away to cause no such pain in his own life, and money would solve their predicament. Daft, he was not at least in a monetary way, never expecting them to be cashed to their face value in some High Street bank but he believed, sincerely, that the black-market would cash them for her and give in return sufficient roubles for their wants. However, he was unaware of Kim 'Stanley' Philby's intervention. In any case, by November the following year, that so-called love for Andrea had been replaced by a new, more opportune one, named Veronica, who lived around the corner in Hans Place SW1.

The earth moved from beneath Maudlin's feet when, in July of 1946 a letter, redirected from the Madrid Legation Ministry, arrived at his Eton Square home, and he was forced into a whole new direction. He did not recognise the writing, but knew instantly who it was from.

Part of Maudlin's benevolence had been invested by Andrea in the absorption of the English language, taught to her son by an émigré who had fled the British Isles, seeking the neutrality of the USSR at the start of the war in which to hide his cowardice; only to find himself conscripted into the Red Army in 1941, where his conscientious objections counted for nothing.

"Listen well to these lessons, my boy. You will never regret it. The language will stay with you all your life, if you listen well." Andrea had told her son, as she ruefully remembered her own inability to concentrate at Maudlin's feet. His proficiency in Spanish was, unfortunately, their preferred means of parlance.

Maudlin's illegitimate son had penned that letter of 1946, in which he detailed his and his mother's plight. He told of how they had been unable to locate the relatives and were still at the Baskov address and how he had been educated at school number 193 in that district. How the leather-jacketed 'Chekists' had issued them new papers, identity cards, and new names. Andrea, he told, had expected money, but none had come. *She does not blame you, father. She never has. It is the system that she holds responsible.*

She had spoken to her son of how time must have moved on in Maudlin's life, and how she accepted that, ascribing no accountability to Maudlin in any way. He quoted his mother's words again, when he wrote: '*You were a kind man, and I knew what I was doing in our affair. I was aware of your marriage. You were as honest to me as I was to myself.*'

He went on to say how they felt betrayed by the Soviets; and imprisoned by them.

We cannot leave this country as they told us we could. They say it is Franco's fault, not theirs, but not all countries have been overrun by fascists, surely? We are housed like animals, and treated much the same. You cannot trust anyone, as everyone is frightened by the authorities. Mother has made friends in the Postal Sorting Office, where she works, so that is how we have been able to send this letter. If I have been successful in reaching you, then I will acknowledge any reply you make. Please, if there is anything you can do for us in the way of money, we will love you forever. The political officer in the Sorting Office is the one who taught me my English, and is a particularly good friend. Address any letters to Tovarisch Sereyovitch Korovin. He will be less suspicious, and not jealous. He signed the letter Paulo.

Rather than ignoring the cry for help that lay on his desk he picked up the challenge, and began to pull his ex-lover and his child free from their misery. He sent Bonds in smaller denominations than before, and again in roubles.

He cautioned Paulo to be vigilant in their exchange, and begun to school him in the arts of deception.

"If you're asked where they came from, tell them that you got the money from an uncle abroad; say Spain, it will suit your cover story better than England. If you can use banks over there, then enlist the help of others, and pay them well for their silence. If you have to rely on the black market then use the same man, if it is at all possible. It will cut down the chances of you being discovered. Do not spend the money in large quantities, or waste it. Use it to buy influence and favour, and note well who they are, the people who take your bribes. You may be able to use that information. Use the system that you're in to further yourself within it. Buy your status, but be careful. Get a sound education through your own endeavours on which you can build your foundation. There is nothing I, or anyone else, can do regarding repatriation. There's an iron curtain being pulled across the whole of Europe, and Stalin has the cords. You must wait until it is reopened."

"That bastard Stalin! A curse on Russia!" Paulo would repeat over and over, whenever he was alone with his mother.

Those, and more, were the words of wisdom and advice that Maudlin passed on to his son, and Paulo began to admire his father through those dispatches. The frequent references to secrecy particularly impressed him and stirred his already fertile imagination. Not being one to sit on his hands and let life unfold before him, he decided to change his lot. On joining the KGB, he was immediately noticed for his excellent English and his devotion to the Communist cause. In 1956 he was selected to become third Naval Attaché and assistant translator at the Soviet Union Embassy in London. In readiness for the State visit of First Secretary of the Communist Party; Nikita Khrushchev, and his Foreign Secretary, Bulganin.

By now, Paulo had relayed the sad news of Andrea's passing, and of his own marriage. He had explained the full reasons of this, and detailed the commitments he had made to Tanya. After carefully reading his letter, Maudlin developed a deeper affinity towards his son. Why this was, is a matter of conjecture. Judith, with her understanding of the human psyche, could well have diagnosed some sort of regressive personality disorder dating back to his abandonment of Andrea and his son. A feeling of guilt, compared to Paulo's acceptance of his responsibilities and reaction to those. Maybe it could have been a repressed feeling of inadequacy. However, Judith wasn't there to pass judgement, and even had she been, it would have had no bearing on the outcome. Whatever it was, he denied it no longer. Maudlin congratulated his son on his well thought-out plan, and offered his help.

* * *

Judith had parked the car about thirty yards from her home in Brownswood Road in the leafy London suburb of Clapham, just off the Common, opposite a huge, yellow flowing forsythia, swarming in bees. My nemeses; as my reaction told.

"Oh, don't be such a girl, Harry! They're only bees."

"To you, maybe, but I'm allergic to them. You could have found a better place!"

"That's who went missing, Harry. A girl. The person we lost track of…and never found."

Chapter Twelve

Water Lilies

In April 1956, Lionel Crabb a frogman, once of the Special Boat Services or SBS, and a highly decorated hero of the Second World War went missing underneath the warship that brought President Khrushchev to Portsmouth harbour. He was working for MI6, in attempting to ascertain why the ship caused no echo passing over the underwater sonic beacons in the Solent, and the diplomats had their knickers twisting around their necks. We denied all knowledge of underwater swimmers lurking around the ship, until the Soviets declared that they had him; and wouldn't let him go. We said he was out testing new equipment; they said he was a spy. It was in the only time in history that the *'Chief'* resigned. The newspapers were awash with bellicosity. *Give him back, or else!* They screamed. *Get stuffed!* The Soviets replied, and they sailed off, into the night.

Tanya seized her opportunity. 'You must take the first chance that comes your way don't wait for the door to be opened for you! You are to be the companion of the Ambassador's wife. It is their way of showing how they care for us peasants. There will be receptions and planned visits…you will know when it is right. Memorise the address. If he is not there, tell them to call him. Make them understand that it is urgent.'

I wonder if it was my father who made this incident happen? Paulo contemplated, when he recalled the instructions he had given his wife.

When Paulo received his posting orders to London, he pleaded his case for taking his new wife with him to the bureaucrats. He begged for compassion and leniency in recognition of her sudden blindness, offering to have his meagre salary docked for her air passage in way of recompense. No one bothered to examine Tanya, nor did they refuse Paulo's request.

"Comrade Doctor, do you remember me? Yes, you treated my mother. Well, I came across this new, shining, stethoscope whilst on official business at the Leningrad Medical Laboratory, and having noticed that yours was old and worn out, I thought of you. Please accept this one. Oh, I nearly forgot...here's a new blood pressure recording apparatus as well. Yes, I know they are extremely difficult to come by. What? You've been waiting almost a year? You should have told me! I've been fortunate since becoming a KGB officer in making many friends. If you're short of anything in the future, do contact me. Oh, I almost forgot something else in my excitement. While I'm here, could you do me a small favour? My wife of two months has an eye infection, and I do not want to leave her here, alone, while I am in London with First Secretary Khrushchev. Yes, him. I work for him you know. Write me a note to say she must go with me, please? Address it to his secretary and I'll pass your name upwards, perhaps reaching his exulted ears."

Since the news of his new assignment, he and Tanya had thought hard and long about how she could accompany Paulo to England, what temporary affliction would persuade the officials to show compassion. Paulo remembered a warning he had been given when he acquired the poison laid down to deter the rats that infested the block each winter.

"Wear gloves when you put it down, and hide it from any children. Whatever you do, don't touch your eyes afterwards without washing your hands it can make you blind," the chemist, whom he had bribed, told him. They practised for the remaining weeks left to them in Russia; testing quantities and effects, how much weeping was enough for sympathy and not too much for inquisitive attention or worse, examination, until they reached a comfortable enough compromise.

The day after Lionel Crabb's disappearance, the wife of the Russian Ambassador was told that all things were to appear normal, and she must keep her prearranged visit to the decadent Harrods Store in Knightsbridge. Appearances were to be kept up, no matter what the circumstances, and how harsh she would find the experience. Mrs Ambassador had never considered the task of escorting Mrs Khrushchev to one of her favourite stores as being burdensome. The opportunity presented many advantages that could be exploited; the one of free gifts came readily to mind.

Tanya saw things differently through her weepy eyes. It was not commonplace gifts she sought, but the gift of promised freedom. It was all she had dreamed of; and now was the day that all could come true. *My great Paulo has arranged this for me...I must take my chance,* she thought, and she prepared herself for the challenge.

There were three cars that set off that day from Kensington Gardens, whilst the rest of the Embassy staff busied themselves on more pressing agendas, such as what to do with Crabbs floating under battleships. The first heavy Zil, specially imported from Russia, carried the armed guards who were to protect the wife of the First Secretary. The second automobile would carry the lady herself, along with Mrs Ambassador, Madam Katrina, who would have preferred her usual British car with its obvious luxury to the practicality of this Russian beast. In the third was Tanya, and the other companions to the more important ladies who travelled before them.

London Police had surrounded the building, but democracy ruled that day and had not closed the department store, instead limiting the number of shoppers to a manageable size. Had it have been Khrushchev himself, it would have been a different matter. Luck still held for Tanya.

She had to use the toilet, she told Comrade Madam Katrina. "Yes, I can manage, my eyes are not so bad today, thank you," she replied to Mrs Ambassador's concerned question, and was allowed to go alone. The self-sacrificing Katrina preferred the comfort of an escort at her side, and the closeness to the attention of the Western Press with its flashing cameras, that the entourage brought.

"I will come straight back, yes. I promise I will not stop at the jewellery counter and ask for that huge diamond ring you admired so much." Tanya joked, as she dabbed the tears away.

She kept her word in regards to the diamond, but not her word on the rendezvous. The calm Tanya took her chance, and left by the side door. She jumped into a cab, thrusting her note of the memorised address into the drivers hand, then went the short distance to 16 Eton Square and the welcoming arms of her father-in-law, Lord Maudlin Paterson, now Earl of Harrogate.

"All is done, Comrade Petronikov," Paulo reported to the Head of Station at the Russian Embassy in London. "She has been placed as we arranged."

Tanya gave Maudlin the letters sewn into her coat lapel, and he began to read. The first part of the first letter was all about how they were to contact each other and where Maudlin was to deposit the bulk of the money, as well as arrangements for his 'everyday expenses incurred', as Paulo put it.

I have found inducement, and the fear of my position, powerful weapons in the forced concurrence of others. I have been subtle and selective in its use, and will continue in this way. However, as I climb higher in this corrupt organisation, I will need more elaborate means to effect that coercion. I will need something from you soon, to cement my position and that of Tanya's. Add one to the Cardinal number each day, until twenty-one, then start again and wait patiently for my contact. It may be years before I am able to help in changing the world.

The second part of the first letter was the surprising part, and the one Maudlin had not been prepared for.

Tanya carries my child, your grandchild inside her. It was a moment of indiscretion on both our parts, but not one I am regretful of. You are a great man, as I have come to recognise over our time through our correspondence. You have proved your devotion to me and made ample recompense for the years my mother and I spent in isolation, none of which can be attributed as your responsibility. Your responsibility can, now, be demonstrated in full. Treat my child as your own, I do not expect knighthoods bestowed upon him or her I understand your personal position but I do expect what I know you can give: respect.

The second letter, he filed away in a ledger at 'Annie's'.

In October of the same year, Maudlin was in Boodles where he was joined by a leading Civil Servant from the War Department. After the exchange of pleasantries and several glasses of a splendid Chateau Margaux, he learnt the unpleasant news that our special friends, the Americans, would not support the action being taken in the Suez by the British, the French, and the Israelis.

"They're going to pull the plug, old boy, and back Nasser. They think the Reds will get involved if we don't all pull back!"

The following day at the bank, Maudlin used that second letter, adding his numbers to the first, and under Tanya's pseudonym 'Mother', wrote her first message to Paulo. He addressed it to the Mail Box Number in the premises that dealt in such commodities in the Earl's Court Road, next door to the station, two stops on the district line from Notting Hill and a stone's throw from the Russian Consulate. In March of 1957, when the remains of the Army of Occupation left Egypt, the Russians consolidated their Mediterranean anchorage in Alexandria, thus freeing their Baltic fleet.

"It is not a great secret, Comrade Korovin. Lubyanka thinks it was inevitable, and the Kremlin agree; however, it means we can bring forward our preparations. Congratulations, Paulo! Your agent has done well."

Over the next few years, the information that Maudlin supplied using Tanya's code name was low-grade material, such as the launch of a Skylark rocket from Australia, freedom from British Sovereignty for Singapore, or the stationing of USA Thor missiles in Norfolk. However, all of this, plus what he did at home, established Paulo's rise in the hierarchy of the KGB.

"She is long-term, my *Mother*. Maybe it will take thirty years to ingratiate herself significantly within their structure. Be patient, my friends. It will be worth it in the long run... Just you wait and see, Comrades!" He announced to his increasing list of devotees and disciples, now-well practised in the black art of deception and lies. So they did, and they are still waiting to this day for something of consequence to come from 'Mother.'

From *Garden,* Paulo's chosen code name in this operation, came enough to fill that opened file. It kept Dicky Blythe-Smith's hands as 'C' busy and happy. It was never started by the mistake made at the KGB headquarters, the Lubyanka, by an incompetent communications operative. It started with the unearthing of a then current British subject, in cohorts with the USSR.

Chapter Thirteen

Red, White and Blue Petunias

"I'd better go fetch the dog. He's with Phyllis, my neighbour. She looks after him when I'm away, which, thank God, isn't often nowadays. I think he suffers from a recognition defect and forgets who I am if I leave him too long."

Judith's house was one of the myriad of Victorian terraced homes gracing this fashionable side of London. They were elegant in a modest way; two-storied, bay-fronted dwellings built of yellow brick, with alabaster pillars and scrolled motifs added to enhance their outward appearance. There was a short front garden of no more than three paces along red and black tiling, then an enclosed porch with glazed ceramic glistening tiles reflecting the overhead light, which had either been left on when she had left, or was on a timer. An imposing stained-glass twin-paned door with two deadbolt locks was opened by Judith, and I followed her in.

"On reflection, I'll leave the dog until the morning, you've had enough shocks for one day as it is. Welcome to my home," she announced, ushering me past, kicking the mail and the assorted leaflets lying on the floor to one side. We were in a surprisingly wide hallway, with a side table under an ornate mirror, doors and arches leading off into the house, and no expected staircase.

"I had it all altered before I moved in. Daddy's money paid for it, of course, but it is all my design. Makes the entrance look bigger than it really is without stairs, don't you think?" She pronounced. "Go through the first arch on the left, Harry. You'll find a bow-fronted high, yew cabinet that hides the drinks. None of your brew, I'm afraid, but there *is* whiskey in there; help yourself. I'll have that gin and tonic I missed out on now if you'd like to do the honours. I'm going to run my stuff upstairs; make yourself at home."

I heard footfalls on iron treads, which I figured were spiral steps somewhere to the rear of the house. I considered giving an offer to help, but I could not resist the temptation of a good nose around and the thought of a drink in solitude was impossible to pass up on.

I was in an illusionistic room with geometrically angled white painted lines on a black background, diminishing in width towards the front window, giving the perception of depth and space. The furniture was of an art deco mode: bright red and yellow leather armchairs with sharp-edged hexagonal occasional tables between two groups of three. Everything seemed to have an allotted space. It was a cared for room in an intrinsic way, but not a room to live in and enjoy. I poured two drinks and sat in one of the chairs, as the Bang and Olufsen CD machine was remotely switched on and La Boheme filled the room. I was not alone for long.

"Feel like doing some work tonight, H? You're to see Peter tomorrow, and it would be good if I could say that we've made some progress." She emphasised the *'some'* and I took it as more of an order, than a request.

"Sure…if you tell me who was the girl your lot lost," I haughtily replied.

"The wife of a young attaché who went on, in later life, to become a member of their Politburo and, even later, a beacon towards capitalism and democracy. She's still around, I strongly believe. Anyway we counted her off the plane, but not back on it. Name of Tanya Korovin. Ever mentioned to you, Harry, that name at all?"

"Was she important to the Russians then, this Tanya? Did she give away our treasures?" I asked, still trying to keep my own agenda separate from Judith's. Where we both wanted to find the murderer, I still wanted to cover Maudlin's back. I was trying desperately hard not to disclose his involvement but was weakening by the moment ever since I was told of my brother's death.

"We can't be certain, as we never found anything about her. She must have assumed another identity, and then vanished. She obviously had to have help for that to happen, but from whom; we don't know. She may be, right now, copying the notes of the last security meeting of ours or of the Americans, and passing them on to Paulo we just can't tell. Tanya might be the biggest fish out there… or she may have genuinely been Korovin's wife, and he made her escape possible. Possibly she never applied for asylum here, because she was protecting her husband, and didn't want Paulo to be exposed back in the motherland… Who knows?"

That was what Maudlin was then, the Schindler of his day, a refuge for escaping refugees from the oppressive Soviet Union but *why*? Hedonistic reasons, or was it the same sense of patriotism that had driven the Patersons before him? Before that question could be answered though, the one about how he knew the Korovins had to be addressed.

"I have something I think you should see, Judith. It may be of some help in understanding how my family has come to be connected in some way to this." My resolve was still strong, however; even I could not refute that she had access to what I needed.

Apologetically, I gave her the code that my father had found in the concealed floor safe at 'Annie's', where he found the references to MA and RD appended to the ledgers of missing funds ascribed to them. From my satchel I placed those papers and books our shared table, on top of the yellow rug, shaped like a musical quaver, on which it stood. In the top left hand corner of the sheet of paper containing the 26 letters of the alphabet and the corresponding numbers, was a capitalised number seven, and in the right hand corner the name 'Tanya,' followed in brackets by the word; 'Mother.'

"It's a code, Harry! One of their one-time pad methods!" she exclaimed excitingly, almost overbalancing from the leather red and yellow chair as she reached forward to take hold of one. "You add a number to the seven each time you send or receive. Your father gave you this when he discovered the missing money, didn't he? Why have you been keeping this a secret? Been afraid of finding a red under the family bed, have you?" she asked, damningly.

"In a way, I suppose, yes. Scandals were popping up all over the place in those days, weren't they? Profumo, the Portland circle, George Blake, Blunt, the Queen's art curator… everyone seemed to have one in the closet. It was even more rife in America, more so perhaps because they had more things worth nicking than us. My father was worried that Maudlin may have been helping the Soviets not only with money, but other things as well."

She was examining the ledgers, and without looking up she asked, "Do you know what the initials stand for, Harry?"

"No, that's what puzzled Elliot and me. We thought that they referred to people… but whom, we didn't know. Hadn't a clue," I declared.

"Then let me enlighten you, and further your education in the ways of your lecherous forbears. MA was Maudlin's Spanish lover and RD his son, your… what is it? Step grandfather, born Romario Dominico Cortez, later to be known as Paulo. Now, here is a piece of the jigsaw, I must say. You've got Russian blood links in your lineage, Harry… and if what I'm assuming is right, it's got enormous arteries pumping red white and blue liquid diagonally through the veins. And not horizontally, as in the Soviet flag."

"I'm not following you, Judith. You're on a different page to me, old thing."

"Less of the old, if you don't mind but yes, I know I am. I've been one in front all the time, dear thing, and until now, you haven't been following me at all. I think it was Paulo Korovin you met in Moscow, and if that's right, then Trimble knows all about him and how he fits into the *Garden* file. Your little piece of paper here opens up a multitude of interwoven streams, leading eventually to the killer, Harry. Too late for brother Edward, but maybe in time to save you."

"If Peter knows all about Korovin and how I'm connected to him, then why use me to drag him out in Moscow?"

"Exactly, Harry. My thoughts entirely, and that's the road I've been trying to nudge you along all this time. Finally, you've opened up Pandora's box. Let us both hope that it's not empty."

"You knew about this, then? Maudlin's son being Paulo Korovin all along?" I asked.

She gave a little laugh as she refilled the glasses, and I hoped that we weren't in for the long night that I could foresee coming. As she regained her chair she kicked off her outdoor shoes, tucking those skinny legs of hers under her bum in the now familiar position of questioning repose.

"For all the years that I've worked exclusively on your family's *Cockpit Steps* file, I have never been able to piece together anything of note. Yes, I managed to uncover the fact that Maudlin had a lover in Spain in the thirties, that was difficult enough, because no one was left alive from those days. By sheer luck, and by trawling through endless documentation, I found an entry in the Embassy log that Maudlin applied for leave in May 1932. It stated 'family reasons' but I found an entry in his private bank account records from Coutts. He had drawn a cheque made payable to the 'Majestic Hotel,' Valencia, for the same corresponding dates. I checked with the hotel, and the amount he paid in those days could not have corresponded to one person's cost.

I figured that he wouldn't have gone all that way to conduct an affair; why should he have done? It was not as though his wife of 14 years was with him. She was at home in Harrogate caring for his three sons and one daughter. I checked. So, I became a bit inquisitive, and started on the hospitals in that city, thinking that I might get lucky and that he may have gone there for a birth. Sure enough, I turned up gold dust. In Santa Maria Hospital, on the fourteenth of that month, a baby boy was born, weighing seven pounds eight ounces. On the registration document, the mother was named as Andrea Isadora Mafalda Cortez, aged 22, and the father was a Martin Paterson, aged forty-four years, of no fixed abode.

As you and I know, it's best to change both names when trying to hide yourself away, but your Great Grandfather wasn't a true spy after all, and he did have a soft touch when it came to women. He wasn't that savvy, was he? The name given to the child was, as I've already stated, Romario Dominico; and, when the Spanish War started in 1936, we know that a great many of Republican supporters, and their families, had been evacuated to Russia. Now, for the first time Harry, I am able to connect the money that Peter Trimble had in 1978, which the then 'C' Dicky Blythe-Smith connected to Maudlin, to a distinct name, MA, his lover, and then in 1946 a year after the War in Europe had finished, RD, his son; it all fits."

She stubbed out a cigarette in the push down chrome ashtray in front of her, and then continued in her appraisal of what lay before her, not seeking, or needing, my comments.

"Now, Tanya we know about and her alleged marital status to To-varisch Sergeyovitch Korovin, to give him his full patronymic title, but known politely as our Paulo. On the entry visas he was said to have been born in May 1932, so unless Maudlin had someone else hidden away in the Soviet Union that he owed a favour to, Paulo and Romario are the same person. Are you keeping up with me, Harry? All ears and regrets for not telling me before, instead of hiding behind the past and your prestigious name?"

"I was reading from a different book, Judith. Surely if anyone can understand, then you can? Having a history and a title can be a weighty load to carry. It comes with responsibilities. I was hoping that what my father had found out did not lead down the path he suspected. Yes, I was concerned with our reputation... wouldn't you have been?"

"I don't have those worries, H. I'm only a woman, there will never be more than an Honourable to go before my name, albeit that I won't marry a hereditary peer."

"Are you proposing, Judith? If so, I would hate to disappoint someone as charming as yourself."

"Do be serious, Harry. At least that side of you I can stomach. In any case I've been there, done that, got the T shirt, found it didn't fit, don't want another one, but thanks for your offer."

"Good, that's out of the way, then. Take it that I'm sleeping in the spare room after all? There I was getting my hopes up for a cuddle, seeing as how I'm the one who's lost relatives and in grieving. Have you no sympathetic side, woman?"

"Not for you, Harry. More for my poor dog, actually. Anyway, we're a long way off bedtime. You need to hear one more story before it's jim-jams time. Hypnos only visits the righteous at this time of day, and you're as far from that as I am."

"Ah…that *does* sound interesting. Get down and dirty Judith, let's empathise with each other. You show first, then it's my go. Tell me about your sordid life. As you already know most of mine, it's only fair. That's where I can be of help to you. I'm very experienced. I'll point the way to your salvation."

Another laugh in mockery, and another drink; it was going to be a long drawn out night, after all.

"It's not me who needs saving, Harry. You forget, there's no one wiping out the Davenports. The dish of the day is Paterson. Let's waste no more time…take me to Moscow in September seven years ago, and don't skimp on it, H. Give me every button on his tunic, and how many hairs were on his head."

Chapter Fourteen

Topiary

"He was taller than me, about an inch or so, maybe six foot three. I put him round about sixty-eight years old, but I was out by four years on you, so I'm not great at estimating age. If this was Maudlin's son, then he would have to have been seventy-two. I could have been wrong, because he looked in good shape. He had a head of thick black hair I thought that it had been dyed, as it looked too perfect to have been natural but it certainly was not a wig.

He had what I would term a 'boxer's' face, a flat forehead with deep eye sockets under a pronounced eyebrow line. He wouldn't have made a successful pugilist as his prominent nose would have been a distinct weakness, and there was a line across the bridge suggesting that at one time it had been broken and snapped back straight. There was another scar on the left side of his chin about two inches long, his chin was the same as mine, squared and dimpled.

I could detect no more similarities between him and me. He had grey eyes, whereas mine are blue, thin lips where mine are thick. He did have something in common with you, though. He had a dog, a big hairy German Shepherd, which he had brought with him into the hotel. He made it sit obediently while he introduced himself, then he passed the dog to his chauffeur. I thought this a rather odd thing to do it was as if he was showing off the fact that he owned a dog!

Overall I'd say that he was an extremely confident man, someone who was accustomed to being in charge of situations, and had spent more time inside than out. His skin, although tanned, was not wrinkled by sunlight nor weathered by wind and rain or, I must add, by alcohol. There were no red veins on his face, no liver spots on the back of his hands. I would say an administrator, not an operative. That might have accounted for his bad neck which, from time to time, he rubbed vigorously.

An elegantly tailored man, with expensive taste in clothes. One who was accustomed to refinement, but I judged had come across them late in life. It was only a feeling...nothing I could put my finger on. There was a showiness about him, particularly with the silver-topped cane, for which I could not detect a reason. I find the same pretentiousness in those who have made money, rather than inherited it. It's as though they are aware that they might lose it one day, so they wear it big and loud for everyone to see and notice. With him it was the same. He wore a large, ostentatious diamond and emerald tie stickpin, with matching cuff links and a gaudy Rolex oyster. Oh, and a wedding ring. It all never quite gelled."

Judith interrupted me. "I'm now wondering who was the more insecure you, or him? I guess you were underdressed for the occasion, as usual...or is it just your latent snobbery bursting through?" She had not been able to resist the sarcasm, but I found it easy to pass over the chance of replying.

"He also had a two-headed eagle badge, with a mounted figure slaying a dragon, in his jacket buttonhole." I paused, waiting for any more sharp-tongued retort, but none was forthcoming. I carried on.

"There was a note in my room on my arrival stating that he would meet me at seven that night for dinner in the Princess room, and not to worry, as he would recognise me. I was punctual and he was five minutes late, but, as I said, I had noticed him standing in the hotel foyer as I had passed through. It was hard to miss him.

He had been with one other person, who I later found out to be his driver. His command of the English language was obvious and absorbing, although there was something obsequious about him. He continued to use the phrases 'my Lord' or 'your Lordship,' even though I had told him to call me Harry. Eventually it was me that felt inferior, as if the references had intended to be derogatory and not simply oily, or overused politely. He introduced himself as Sergey Andreovich Goganof and, in his words, 'a retired public servant.'

We spoke about England, music, Michel Jarre, and probably everything under the Moscow moon, but nothing of great significance. He mentioned the tensions in the previous USSR of Chechnya and the Ukraine, and implied that he had a hand in the settlement that had been negotiated. He was the type of person who could talk on any subject and feel comfortable without detailing too much of his knowledge. The only matters of a personal nature he gave away was that his time consuming passion was playing the saxophone. It had been Judo when he was younger, achieving a Sixth Dan Red and White belt, whatever that meant. Later, at the concert, I thought I knew why he had told me that snippet of information!

"This is my daughter, Katherine. I believe you have already met!" He said, somewhat antagonistically when we bumped into Katherine.

We had walked the short distance from the hotel into the square where she was waiting, but there was no sign of a Mr Friedal. The company she was with stood aside, somewhat reverentially, when we appeared. Boris, my nickname for the driver, had been behind us and still had the dog. He was excited when he saw Katherine…the dog, I mean. Whatever Boris was feeling was a mystery to me; a man of closed emotions, Mr Boris."

I was interrupted again in my disclosure by what I considered an unnecessary remark from Judith, coupled with an observation that carried a sense of apprehension.

"She had that effect on dogs, then no wonder you were attracted. Forgive me, I just couldn't resist it. On a more serious note, Harry, have you wondered why he would want to give us his daughter? They are the same man, I'm sure of it…the love of dogs and the Judo, they both fit. He's shown you them because he wants help, and he must want his daughter out as well."

"Out of what?" I asked.

"The game, Harry. He's had enough. It's as though he's asking to be brought home, collect the money stashed away somewhere by Maudlin, draw a card to pass jail, and land on Park Lane, if you pardon my Monopoly pun. You didn't happen to ask him about the broken nose and the scar on his chin, did you?"

"No, I didn't. Should I have done? And, while on the subject, any distinguishing marks elsewhere on his torso?"

"That's a shame...I never put modesty on your file. Only Korovin was in a car accident early in '81 whilst he was in Lebanon attending a Middle East Studies Group. He lost a girlfriend in it, but got out almost unscathed. Would have been nice to have tied him to that. You did say that he wore a wedding ring, this Sergey of yours?"

I confirmed this and continued describing the rest of the evening, the concert, the occasional recognition of others, either from Sergey or towards him or Katherine, her departure, and eventually his and mine. We had returned to the National and settled into the Nikki bar. He was the type of man who could speak of everything without ever giving a glimpse of himself. He was more interested in me, which again I found disquieting, and he questioned if it was I who had been sent for his interrogation. In fact, I asked Peter that when I returned to London.

'No, Harry, that was not the reason for your encounter,' he told me, but did not explain what was. He was built from the same bricks as Sergey, never quite answering a question in an expansive positive way.

Judith asked what were Goganof's last words on his departure, and I could recall them as if they were spoken to me an hour ago. At the time I put no importance on them, but now she had made a connection to the past, they held significant gravity: *I have always felt an affinity towards the English nobility, as though I belong in your House of Lords and not a mere commoner. We should meet again, and discuss our past in depth.*

"Is that what you told Peter, Harry, word for word?" An uneasy Judith asked me. When I replied in the affirmative, I did not hear any anxious voice with more questions, but I saw a concerned face looking into an illusionary space between the zig-zagging lines.

"Let me run something by you, Harry. It will probably sound silly but indulge me, for a second. Just suppose Peter did not know of Korovin and used your name and title to flush him out...why do you suppose he would do that?"

"To catch a Russian spy, put a feather in his cap, revenge for what Tanya had passed on to him all good reasons, are they not?"

"Hmm...plausible." Another drink and more silence, apart from Mirella Freni and a young Luciano Pavarotti as Mimi and Rodolfo in Puccini's masterpiece.

"I don't think your summary can be correct, H. That would mean that all my theories are incorrect. Tanya was, after all, working for the communists and supplied useful gems, and Comrade Korovin was not working for us. I'm sticking to my instincts. There must be another reason...but what it is, I'm not sure."

"Well, I can't think of one and I'm tired, Judith. It's not often that you lose a father and a brother within a week; I have a lot to think about apart from all this. I've texted my brother Maurice, the next in line for the bank, but have heard nothing back yet. He won't be eager to return from California permanently, and what he knows of banking can be written on the back of a postage stamp. I'm off to bed so that I'm all bushy-tailed for Trimble in the morning."

"Don't speculate on anything tomorrow, Harry. Keep to the point, plain and simple. I'm staying here for a while, to mull things over a bit. I've put your things in your room, second door on the right. You've got all your own facilities in there, so there's no need of us crossing paths in the night, is there?"

"Absolutely not, Judith. Got anything to munch on in the fridge, or is it empty and barren?"

"Ha ha. Good night," she replied. I left the untold story, and I left her there with her red and black book opened, beginning to write.

I had showered and shaved. It was a habit of mine to shave at night as, being fair-haired, my beard was not noticeable in the morning. I had parted company with Judith early, it was a little after ten, but I was truly tired, and nigh-on starving. I knew that if I had anything else to drink I would be ravenous and my stomach would start churning, an affliction the old get, and not even Pavarotti would muffle the sounds. Judith had thoughtfully, and as it turned out fortunately, laid out a dressing gown, I guessed one that had belonged to her late husband. I was beginning to think about why she would have kept it, and whether I should use it for the morning, when she was knocking on my door.

"Harry, I need you. Come down immediately, this is no time to sleep."

There on the table that I had left no more than fifteen minutes ago, was a hollowed-out rectangle plate on which sat an unedifying sandwich of stale-looking, curled edged, brown bread, with something white and green poking through.

"I had forgotten your creature comforts, H. Don't look so miserable…it won't harm you. It's goat's cheese and gherkins. That was all that was in the fridge, I'm afraid. Promise I'll buy some provisions tomorrow." Not even I was that hungry, but I was curious.

"Was there nothing else he said…did he mention Peter, for example?"

I was too tired to argue with her and insist on my need of sleep, hoping for pity, which I knew I would not find, and so I reluctantly retook my position in the, still-warm, chair.

"In a way, yes. He asked who initiated the first contact and who authorised that dead message I left in the church pew. He said it was old school, used by an old friend many moons ago and left to die. When I told him that it was 'C' he said that he had never heard of Trimble but laughed it off, saying sometime he would write his memoirs."

"Look, Harry. I know I'm right." She picked up from where she had left off previously as I, successfully, managed to ignore the culinary delight, but not the glass of Scotch that sat beside it. "In the sixties we decoded a message sent from Soviet intelligence proving beyond doubt that an agent that we believed was not Russian House, *was*. It was thought to have been a mistake on their part, someone slipped up on the coding but supposing it was deliberate, and Korovin made it happen?"

"That's a big assumption. Why should he, and how did he make it happen?" I asked.

"The *why* is the easiest to explain. He was overawed by his images of the free world, an English Lord as his father, and a wealthy one. I won't have it that Maudlin never let on to his lover that he was a peer. He might have used a false name on the birth certificate, but he would have flaunted his status in her seduction, would not have been able to hold himself back. Do you agree?"

"Yes, seems a reasonable deduction, Judith. Go on."

"I was going to add that it worked for you the first time with Katherine, seems a shame she gave you the heave-ho the second time around, but I will not be tempted."

I allowed her to believe that she had me there, as I hid behind our interpretation of the fifth amendment, and added - 'no comment' to the debate.

"Right. So there he is, in squalor and chaos, faced with a dying mother. Restrictions on communications are relaxed at the end of the war. Let's say Andrea is still a looker. There's no reason why not she's only 36 in 1946, and one of your lot would have had a discerning eye when it came to women. So, after a while in freezing cold Russia, she wants the warmth of a man. She goes out and gets herself a lover with influence over what can and can't be sent out of Mother Russia. That's when young Romario reaches out to Lord M.

Maudlin sends his thoroughbred stallion to the rescue, carrying more money, and this time it gets through, influential postman and all that. Not beyond the realms of possibility, is it?" It was my time for interrupting, as she raised her glass towards me, expecting a reply.

"That money he sent in 1936 never was received in Russia, then. What makes you say that?"

"The agent I was referring to in that decoded message was Kim Philby, of Cambridge notoriety. He got his grubby hands on it. Syphoned it away for a rainy day but never got it before we cottoned on to him. In the Treasury vaults by now, I should think, paying for more wasted lives and buying prestige for this country in some deprived worthless spot on the globe. Anyway, back to my rantings. Romario can't manage alone, so enlists Tanya's help in the caring thing for Mummy. Or, maybe she's his sweetheart? I don't think that, though otherwise, why let her go? No! The first one's right, I bet. Whatever. He tells her that, in return, he will help her escape to the benevolent Maudlin. How am I doing... still with me, H?" No recognition in my direction this time, and I had no chance of replying, as she continued in her appraisal.

"He tells his bosses that he's planted Tanya under our radar. With that, and the money that Maudlin keeps giving him, he buys his way up the tree. As to how he alters that code... I'm not sure, but he knew about the system. That's obvious. He gave Tanya and Maudlin a pad to work from, christened Tanya, *Mother*, in honour of his departed one, then plied his comrades with worthless information purportedly from her. If she was really working for them, then that means so was Maudlin, and I don't believe that there was any person more English in England.

Maudlin, having dabbed his finger in the elixir of espionage in Ireland, I would think that you've heard all that story, thinks he would like to taste the ambrosia again, so runs the now renamed Romario himself using Tanya as his cover. Eventually, Paulo drops the spy tag and resorts to what he knows best. That's lying on a different stage, one where every player seeks power and self-gratification, that of politics. That's what that badge represented; a member of the old Politburo. It was his way of telling us that was where he was from. I don't believe that any of those three were parts of a Russian doll... no way, do I. I'll tell you that story I was going to now, so sit back and listen, Harry, and see if you can make sense of it."

Chapter Fifteen

Garden Twine and Garden Stakes

"Preceding that intercepted code in 1961 by five months, George Blake, a Danish Jew who worked for the SOE from 1940, who you previously glossed over and Henry Houghton a Royal Navel Master-at-Arms and one-time worker at a secret underwater testing establishment, were exposed by the defecting head of the Polish Military Counter Intelligence, as Soviet agents passing our valuables on to the Reds.

Special Branch arrested about seven others the same day, including a very high flyer indeed. A man who went by the name of Gordon Lonsdale, but that was not his real name…it was Konon Trofimovich Molony, a Soviet military officer. What has all this got to do with our Paulo Korovin, you are about to ask? Well, I'm going to tell you."

Judith was a little drunk by now, having, like me, had nothing to eat since breakfast, but she was holding it together well, although she was slightly less lucid than normal. Whether that was purely due to the drink or her blatant excitement in being able to elucidate on her theory to a captive audience, I again would not pass comment as to the cause. It would paint her in a poor light, and that would not be fair. Mimi had died and Rodolfo had sung his last lament, but Judith was trilling on, resembling a curled-up canary perched in her chair.

"Our young Korovin was posted to Warsaw in 1960 as was Houghton except he was ours, of course, Houghton I mean. With Paulo the *our* is more maternal, not factual, you understand."

"Would you prefer to finish this in the morning, Judith? It may make more sense then," I suggested, in an avuncular manner.

"No, I deem it better that you hear it tonight smelly breath and all. Houghton was attached to our Embassy the *our* there I mean literally. Anyhow, he got himself noticed by the civil police. The first time was when he beat up his wife in a public car park outside a restaurant, but he was in the Embassy car, so pleaded diplomatic immunity and got away with it. The next time, he was caught dealing in coffee on the black market, to which he had no immunity. He was cautioned for the coffee, which I presume was confiscated, and used as a remedy for all the vodka those communists are supposed to put away. Anyhow, three days later he was caught again trading; this time in medical drugs, all apparently to pay for his excessive drinking habit. He didn't have a kind Daddy like me…I digress.

He was sent home to England, but not before the Polish Security Services had turned him with offers of his own vodka brewery. He had opened the floodgates at Portland, selling our underwater secret warfare things, that then went floating off up the Channel and down the Volga on their way to Moscow. Does the Volga flow through Moscow, Harry? No matter… what the… oops! Nearly said a naughty word! Better not drink anymore…I can get a touch lewd when I'm in my cups.

Blake was a different kettle of fish, all told. He was one of theirs *and* one of ours…worked us both. He worked for us up to when he got captured in North Korea during the war over there. Hated the Americans, despised their indiscriminate bombing of the civilian population. He was banged up for years with nothing to read, so read Karl Marx *numero uno* in Waterstone's in Pyongyang at the time, then turned Marxist and started to sell us out on his release.

Both these two, Houghton and Blake, were handled in London by Mr Gordon Lonsdale, aka Trofimovich, who traded not only in our secrets, but slot-machines in pubs and clubs the length and breath…I mean breadth, don't I? of London. Let me in my inebriated state tie it up for you, before I either make a fool of myself or fall asleep.

The head of the Counter Intel in Poland who came over to our side, and whose name I cannot begin to pronounce, got himself posted to their Consular here in town. He saw our twinkling lights and got carried away... I call him Leonard, okay? Leonard had a fetish that apparently his wife did not share, nor could completely indulge him in. He swung both ways, batted left and right-handed, couldn't make up his mind which sex he preferred. Liked it kinky, tied up with all leather and whips, mask and gags. You're drooling again, H... it's not me I'm talking about, it's dear old Leonard!"

"I can assure you that I was not, as you put it, *drooling*, Judith. I was following your every word avidly, with my full attention."

"Don't interrupt me, or I'll fall off my chair and make a spectacle of myself. I've stopped drinking and now I'm sober. See? I can touch my nose with my eyes closed... well, almost." She made a vain attempt, ending up with a red-enamelled finger nail stabbed into her cheekbone.

"Where was I? Ah, yes, bondage! Well, Leonard got trapped in the shit of a honeypot, and ask me who set him up for it." There was a pause in her oratory, and when I made no reply, she asked again.

"Go on, ask me!" Another pause, as I deliberately declined to indulge her, preferring to watch her unease as she wriggled in her discomfort. "Please, I need to pee... oh sod you, then! Wait here. *I shall return*, as General MacArthur said."

"Who was it, then?" I shouted after her fleeing figure.

"It was Maudlin, you oaf!"

I heard the sound of running water then the faint cry of surrender as Judith declared her intentions of retiring for the night; however, there was still time for a last command.

"You're due at the 'Box' at eleven. Don't speculate, Harry, be factual, and don't wake me if I'm not up."

"What about your dog?" I enquired, trying to punish her further.

"What dog? I've disowned him for the night."

"Your neighbour will not think much of you in the morning."

"F to the lot of you-let me sleep!"

I sat for a long while, running it through my mind, I had forgotten my own previous tiredness, stimulated by Judith's revelations and the not so far-fetched conclusions she had made. If it hadn't been Paulo Korovin who had told Maudlin of the Poles' predilection, then how did he know? It's not something you ask a complete stranger, is it? *Like to come to a stake party...I mean stake as in 'tied-up'?*

As far as the coded message was concerned, she had provided no cast-iron evidence, nor even any unsubstantiated. But it did have a degree of plausibility, a high one, so why not believe that Paulo was behind the message? If he had sold us Blake and the Portland Spy Circle, then why not Philby? All of a sudden, the credibility of Paulo working against the interests of his adopted homeland became more believable and probable. I needed to know more, and perhaps Peter Trimble in his office at Vauxhall could fill in some missing details.

Chapter Sixteen

Blood Red Poppies

The category of achievements made by Paulo Sergeyovitch Korovin to the erstwhile corridors of Soviet political power were wide and broad, and within their shadow he hid his light and prospered well. His entreaties to Maudlin regarding his son's future were always answered graciously and with sincerity. Concerning Paulo's pleas of learned guidance as to his own future, his father's advice was simple, yet complicated to achieve.

The life spent in espionage intrigue is a short life; nobody is able to keep the pretence for ever. Take the secure route of political influence, and that way you can change the world.

Paulo heeded that recommendation, as he did all Maudlin's opinions, and set his sights higher than the desk occupied by the Head of the KGB.

In order to accelerate his progress in that direction, he placed his fictitious agent *Mother* in America as a translator, one of only five assigned to a Strategic Studies Group, another figment of his imagination. He built this group up around known movers and shakers within the Richard M Nixon administration, and either plagiarised, partly or whole or added his own exaggerations to Communist operatives intelligence garnered across that whole Continent.

He played his game of charades expertly, attributing useful extracts to *Mother* and ones of little importance also. It was just enough to keep his seat as supervising officer of intelligence and counter-intelligence warm and snug. He answered to one man and only one; a man of great avarice and ambition, and whose love of power and money far outweighed his love of communism. He bought this man cheaply, then sold him at a great profit, propelling himself through needless years of wait.

Anatoly Petronikov, the same Head of Station in London when Tanya had made her escape, had slowly risen through the ranks in the fifteen years that it had taken Paulo to emerge from third attaché to Deputy Head of all things secret, to be, once again, Paulo's master. After Khrushchev was removed from power and the leadership split between Brezhnev, as First Secretary, and Kosygin, as Premier, Anatoly was elevated onto the ruling Politburo, where he tasted the real qualities of life. He had his Dacha in the Shvorovshiy Woods, on the banks of the Moskva River, and his motorised yacht on the Caspian Sea.

His illicit wealth came from many avenues, most recommended to him by Paulo, who, as previously advised by Maudlin, kept his racketeers close. Anatoly was known as a flamboyant figure, who took risks to please those above him. Because of this, they indulged him, and knew they had someone to blame if things went wrong. The devil makes work for idle hands and Anatoly's were no exception. His were caught in a comatose state, having delegated most of his work to his Deputy in order to fully enjoy his new privileges. He had a weakness for cocaine and loose women, both plentifully supplied by Paulo's contacts and these, ably utilised by Paulo, brought about his downfall.

One night during the winter of 1972, when Moscow vagrants were falling asleep under their ever-increasing blanket of snow, Anatoly did not have their misfortune in having to wait for the thaw of spring to be discovered. He was found dead alongside his equally dead lover, in the warmth of her apartment, where lines of cocaine abounded. An autopsy was performed and a pernicious substance found; on analysis, it was discovered that white, odourless, potassium chloride had been added to the mix. They had been murdered.

Paulo himself, led the fruitless investigation, personally interrogating many of the thousands of drug users and pedlars that were interviewed, but there were no admissions of guilt forthcoming. After some were executed for proven crimes and others sent to Gulags in forgotten region by Paulo, all was dropped and written off.

His discharge of the duties of Deputy Head of the KGB were exceptional and peerless. He had favours to be recalled, along with his established means of gathering information, plus his furtive mind. He plated up his appetiser for his now fellow Politburo companions.

Anatoly Petronikov was not one of theirs after all, he declared! His investigation had unearthed a bank account opened up in London four years previously, with cash deposits amounting to millions of pounds Stirling. All had been discovered when Petronikov's bank in Moscow had contacted the Moscow Centre over its transference. That divergence, along with his flamboyant lifestyle, condemned the unchallengeable Anatoly, and forced the purge that Paulo advised. They covered their houses, and sat back to watch Paulo at his licensed work.

Maudlin's involvement had paid dividends as the two had figured, so he took this opportunity presented by the situation to rid himself of many possible future embarrassments. Unfortunately it was only many, and not *all*, that were eliminated.

His penchant for the protection of all things English was not extended to other countries. He favoured neither east nor west, discovering rings of networks of spies from West Germany, France, America, and a paid circle of Russians smuggling atomic secrets to the Chinese!

He was awarded the 'Order of Lenin' and pronounced Honorary Secretary of what was once Leningrad but, by now, had returned to its pre-Stalin days of St Petersburg, setting the foundation on which he built his political career. His meteoric rise continued.

In 1979 he became the youngest ever member on the Supreme Soviet of the Soviet Union, and two years later he began a career abroad.

In March 1981, Paulo, this time trading under the name of Dmitry Posharsky, along with his *wife* and daughter aged eight, were sent to the Middle East under the false pretence of promotion of relationships between the Soviet Union and the Islamic States. His real intentions were not as honourable; he was there to foster links with anti-Israeli movements, and he did not have long to meet one.

Anacova was not his wife, but Katherine was their child, and luckily was in the Embassy, when the Hamas-instigated bomb exploded inside the cafe in Beirut. The suicide bomber, along with thirty-one others, was killed that day.

The embassy driver of their car swerved violently to avoid the flying debris and smashed, sideways, into an oncoming bus. He and Anacova were pronounced dead on arrival at the main Hospital in Lebanon's capital city, and Paulo was recorded with the slight injuries that Harry had noticed on their first encounter, along with a cracked bone in his neck. Two things remained indelibly engraved on Paulo's memory from that carnage. The first was the resolve never to risk his daughter's life again, and the second, a wonder at how a civilised nation could ever defeat one that held life so cheaply. He returned to Moscow a different man, and never had the chance to have his baptismal cross blessed in Jerusalem, as was his wish.

In the same year, something happened that was no accident, and almost tore Paulo's rapid travelling caravan to shreds. Ronnie Reagan was elected President of that other superpower, and his brand of rhetoric frightened the 'old ones' on the Central Council and in the Politburo. They feared for their lives and for all around them, as they believed that the USA would mount a first strike nuclear attack.

The escalation had started in space, with the so called 'Star Wars' programme being initiated, and was further heightened by the stationing of *Pershing 11* short-range nuclear missiles on the Soviet borders. Paulo's replacement at the counter intelligence desk was instructed to mount an intelligence-gathering operation on specific targets; those likely to be needed or warned for such an attack, and on the facilities that would need to be readied.

The operation was called 'Ryan.'

All hands were needed on deck, even old, semiretired, ones. *Mother* handler Paulo was recalled from Tripoli, his residence of work, where, by then, he had become quite an expert in Middle Eastern affairs.

The British Prime Minister, Margaret Thatcher, took part in a planned evacuation, as did most of the American Government, and the communications going between each of those nations went sky-high something all in the Politburo considered would proceed an attack. General Secretary Brezhnev and his second in command Andropov were acutely worried. That fear became worse when Reagan decided to test the Soviet Union's radar capabilities by flying bombers and fighters at their border, then breaking off at the last moment at intermittent intervals.

The American Naval activity increased dramatically, both in the Pacific and the North Sea, and reports landed on Andropov's head of seabed beacons being laid from Nova Scotia to Scotland and from Iceland to Norway. Paulo was approached to activate his *Mother,* and to get her observations from within that Studies Group. By now he was almost completely removed from NATO intelligence reports, so he could not enhance existing information and as the situation seemed mightily serious, he could not use his imagination.

He contacted Maudlin, who made enquires amongst his Tory friends at his West End club, and was delighted to inform Paulo that it was merely exercises. The increase in the radio traffic was down to Reagan's invasion of the island of Grenada. 'A country ruled by our Queen,' he added.

Paulo reported this to Andropov and his ratings went higher, as it coincided with reports that the newly appointed head of the American National Security had not taken part in the scamper for underground protection another prerequisite, as he would assume command if front liners were obliterated. The concerns of the Politburo were eased, but only somewhat.

Others within the Military urged a stop to the procrastinations, to pre-empt a first strike by launching their own! Things were getting tense. On the night of 24 September 1983, the tension increased as the

Soviet orbital missile launch detector, code named '*Oka*', reported the lift-off of a single Intercontinental Ballistic Missile from inside America. The Russian Lieutenant Colonel in charge at the ground installation dismissed this as no early warning radar had picked it up and in any case, he argued, 'they would send thousands... not one.' Within an hour three more ICBM's were detected, but again he rigorously stuck to his guns, and the '*old ones*' luckily for the rest of us, never drew their own.

All was not over. There was worse to come, and this was where Paulo saved the world as Maudlin had predicted. In November of 1983, two months on from when the Soviets found that their sputnik was malfunctioning, Reagan initiated Able Archer 83. The codename given to a NATO command operation spanning the whole of Western Europe. It simulated a conflict escalation, leading to a coordinated nuclear release. The name of the exercise, '*Able Archer,*' was used every year for such military operations; only this time, it differed from the past, in many ways.

The exercise incorporated a unique form of coded communications that the Communists had never heard, and this was yet another thing to worry about. There was more. All Western alerts were put on DE-FCON 1, a never before used state of nuclear release status. This level should not be confused by the movie or television version of DEFCON 5 which is, the lowest level of alert. The status rises to one, after which the world implodes, unless one party pulls back. When this information, garnered by the watchers, was related to Moscow Centre, more than one set of untrimmed eyebrows were raised in speculation.

The whole of this situation had been kept secret from the Press of the world. The Cuban lessons had been learnt well by the politicians. They resolved it would be *them* who made the decisions this time, unaided by the paparazzi with snapshots of floating missiles, or tank formations to worry the flappable public opinion.

To everyone, young and old, in the Politburo it seemed that war was merely hours away. Andropov was now in charge of all the Soviets, Brezhnev having died of a heart attack, and was listening to his advisors from his hospital bed, as some advised the pre-emptive strike option. Instead, he heeded the doves. Excluding the hawks to the back of his mind, but he took precautions.

He ordered the readiness of their own ICBMs, and *standby alert* of squadrons of planes in East Germany and Poland. The whole world was, at most, 36 hours from self-destruction; closer, many would later say, than it had ever been, including that crisis in the Caribbean. This time, it was the Russians who felt threatened. Paulo reasoned with himself that the KGB's reliance on observation alone, and not analysis, was not helping the situation at all. If anything, it was a hindrance. If the evacuation of heads of Governments, two years previously, were exercises, and the increase in communications could then be explained, then why could not all this activity have a simple explanation?

He knew little of Americans. Dossiers in Libya were confusing, but if they were friends of the English they couldn't be all that bad, he deduced. He took a gamble, a calculated one. Either he would save the world, or perish along with all his lies.

He coded a message from *Mother*: *It is a pre-planned simulation exercise only. It is a test of the defences. Do not under any circumstance react or open silos, or they will launch!*

Andropov pulled back from that precipitous brink on *Mother's* say-so alone, and fourteen hours later the NATO exercise ceased. Paulo had done more than save the world. He had shown the aggressors that mighty Russia had no need to worry or react to threats, as she knew her true strength and that would have been enough to see off the bullying Americans. One part of the Politburo heaved a huge sigh of relief, while another beat their chests in triumph. However, all parts congratulated Paulo and praised his *Mother*. He had been made for life.

* * *

Three days before Christmas 1983, Rudi Mercer was busy doing his budget forecast for the upcoming funding arguments and debate before his office closed for the holidays. He was, as Director of the Office of Collection Strategies and Analysis of the American CIA, privileged and entitled to the colour coordinated, latest technological telephone keypad that was now flashing orange, on top of his sandalwood, inlaid mahogany, desk. The silent call, he knew before he answered it, was from President Reagan's chief advisor, Pat Buchanan.

"I'm sorry to land this on you, Rudi, but it's from up top. I want you in London, England, as from yesterday. What would you do in the holidays, anyway? Watch a game? You can do that over there, they must have satellite. You'll find it best to keep working after that latest divorce of yours…they're getting to be a habit. Find someone who loves this work as much as you do, next time. There's a plane on standby with its engines running at Andrews…I'll speak to you when you're there. Oh, by the way, Secretary of State Shultz is going to hold your hand all the way. He'll brief you, it's very important Rudi."

Rudi considered the use of one of his holy trinity, the President, his priest, or his granddaughter, to whom he could air his displeasure. He never had a direct line to Ronnie, so abandoned all hope of reprieve there. He left a message on Father Leo's machine of regret at not being able to give the Mass reading at midnight two days hence, and spoke to his daughter, preferring her dulcet voice to the castigating words of a three-year-old, more used to unfulfilled promises, than a grandchild should be.

Superfluous was not a word on his lips as the cavalcade drove through the gates of the American Ambassador's English home in Regent's Park that day, and Rudi was whisked silently away from beneath his covering blanket to the second level basement below.

"Where did the Soviets get this study group from, Rudi? Do we have one, or is it something you invented to stop World War Three? Wherever this came from, it worked. Had they not taken notice of this, I'm telling you, Reagan was up for it! They were showing us everything; and we would have won!" The Director of the office of Transnational Issues of the CIA passed Rudi a translated copy of a report he had received a month earlier. It read:

It is a pre-planned simulation exercise only. It is a test of the defences. Do not under any circumstance react or open silos, or they will launch!

"I want you to find out where it originated. You're now in charge of the file named *Vagabond*; read it carefully, and use the information long-term. We want him high, so high he can't be reached. Do you follow me?"

Chapter Seventeen

Bleeding Hearts

My first night in Clapham was not a good night. Both Peter and Paulo's names kept coming back to me, as I failed in any attempt to find meaningful sleep. I tried to think of anything other than them, but nothing covered their names. Nor was I able to forget my starvation; so much so that I rose early at about six, intending on finding a cafe where I could at least end that discomfort.

To my surprise Judith was up already, dressed and full of the joys of spring, unlike myself. Apparently Phyllis, next door, was a light sleeper and would be awake at this time of day, so she was about to collect Hector and visit the Common for his morning exercise. As this would be an opportune time to meet her dog, so I was told, and take advantage of her local knowledge, I took her advice and tagged along.

Hector, turned out not to be the Goliath of a Greek beast his name had conjured up in my imagination, but a snappy, snarling, black and white mongrel with an unsocial disposition. He took a dislike to me, which was mutually shared. She had no first hand recommendations of nearby eateries, but promised to direct me towards the Underground Station on the South Side, where she said there was a profusion, from which to choose.

Hector was off his lead, skipping ahead of us and barking as he looked back at me. I had resisted the temptation of booting him over the crossbar at Twickenham and scoring the winning points against

France, but only just. Judith caught my undisguised animosity, and suggested a remedy.

"He'll come round to like you if you give him a sausage for breakfast. I think we'll come with you," she cordially invited him, and herself. The fresh air was beginning to clear my head, but now I felt my hangover returning.

"I was going to Eton Square this morning, then going on to Trimble, Judith. There's a great deal I must see to there. Maurice texted me last night, and it seems that his wife is dead set against him coming home for Annie's, the kid's schools and all that. So, I want to arrange to see whoever is in charge of it all now, and pass it on. Time for change, I think."

"I can make that happen, Harry. His name is Haig...David Haig, my boss," she said, as she threw the twig that Hector had returned.

"I thought Peter was your boss. Correct me if I'm wrong, but isn't he the head of Defence Intelligence, as well as everything else in our little world?"

"Yes, he is, but I report to the Cabinet Secretary. The Bank of Saint George and all your family are under his jurisdiction, as is the whole of the SIS. I did tell you that the Patersons were a special breed, didn't I?"

"You never told me that you were 'out of house' though, did you? Isn't that a bit sneaky?" Hector had abandoned the twig having, found a scent to follow.

"Well, you've exposed a little bit more of yourself, Harry, so it's only fair that I do likewise. Think of me as the rubber sole squad, all one of me. I go everywhere, but nobody hears or sees me. I have access to most things and everything, if Haig deems it so, not even Trimble can refuse...went over two years ago.

I am under Peter's wing and keep him informed of my findings, but not conclusions. Those I give to Haig. He's a relative of the First World War's General you know, Douglas Haig or Butcher Haig, as he was more commonly referred to. We are all on the same side, H, it's just that I bring different skills to the table. I'm very good at what I do, Harry. I read people's minds."

Well, she hadn't read mine at all. Where I wanted a slap-up full English, fried bread, the lot, I had to make do with it in a toasted roll! Greasy spoons didn't exist in fashionable SW4; only Italian chain coffee shops where tea came in a pot and not a mug, and an all-day breakfast was found, wrapped in cellophane, on the chiller shelf. Needless-to-say, Hector never got his sausage, but he did get a biscuit which Judith gave me to feed him with, and we became friends. Ah…

It was going to be a happy ending sort of Monday all round, or so I began to think. I managed to part from my escorts, neither appearing too sad at my departure, and took the tube to Victoria, walking the short journey from there to number 16. I had only been inside this house on one occasion and that was so long ago that I had forgotten when that was and for what reason. I knew the people there by name, but not personally, only ever meeting them all once a year.

Every Christmas the staff from London would spend the holiday in Yorkshire, at Harrogate Hall, where it was our tradition to wait on them. My mother would cook, or it would be more correct to say finish the cooking of the Christmas lunch, with cook's expert eye looking on, and we all ate together in the Great Hall. When we all lived together, I was in charge of my two brothers and sisters at the kitchen sink, where I delegated my authority ruthlessly. On Boxing Day we would do it all again, but this time as a buffet for all, as before, plus additional local guests. Again, I ran my siblings ragged. All this had stopped on my mother's death, and I wondered if I would still be recognised on the doorstep.

Mrs Hodges, the housekeeper, answered the door, and immediately burst into tears. Condolences were exchanged all around, as I met the rest of the household. George, on the surface, appeared as stalwart as I could remember; but underlining that intrepidness lay a degree of uncertainty, on which he was quick to elucidate.

"It's good to see you, Harry. We were all upset over the disagreement between you and your father, and speaking on behalf of everyone we missed the bonhomie that existed between the two homes. Your two sisters have visited, but we understood the position you took, and never at any time took sides. There's no coincidence here, is there? I mean...with both Elliot and Edward's murders...are they connected to the bank?" George had this distinction, apart from all the rest that worked for us, whereby he addressed every member of my family by their first name. It was something I had grown up with, as we had both entered the Paterson patronage more or less at the same time.

I was five months old when Maudlin, then seventy-eight, first announced George's entry into our tribe. My grandfather, Phillip, was then fifty and living here in London with my father who had a mathematical inclination, so I was told, and spent his weekdays in the capital. At this late stage in my life, I understood the real reason. Anyway, as a child I found George a welcome accomplice to my escapades, and the fourteen years of difference was to me, on the face of it, no hardship to either of us.

I spun him the same story that I had told Joseph, that of a vindictive investor still on the loose, adding that he was now believed by the police to have made his escape abroad. I hoped that this would quieten any nerves and misgivings that he and the others here held. He had never married, or even courted a lady that I could recall, but I had never had a reason or a wish to question his sexual leanings. I asked him as to his aunt's well-being, and was told that she was now in a residential home but going strong at the age of seventy-four, if a little forgetful.

I lingered for a while, reassuring everyone as to their future as far as I could, then took a cab across the river to the waiting Peter Trimble and the not-expected Judith Meadows. I had left one cloud of uncertainty, and walked into another. The Special Branch police officer I had first met just over a week ago made up our four-ball, and off we teed.

Judith led, uninvited, with her report of the days spent at Harrogate, but made no mention to the code I had given her, or the connection she had made to Korovin from it. When Peter ask me if there was anything I wished to add, I declined, agreeing that Judith's summary was accurate and detailed and she had covered everything. We all discussed my brother and his interconnection with Elliot and the bank, which we all agreed was the only thing in common, and therefore the motive behind the murders.

As none of us had any idea as to the culprit, the police were left in charge and we were discharged, with even more repetitions of "sorry for your loss" ringing in my ears. As I was about to leave I remembered a question I had wanted to ask, but had managed to forget amidst the chaos of my private life.

"Oh, by the way, I was meaning to ask if you knew…" I got that far in my enquiry before Judith spoke across me, as though I wasn't there.

"I suspect he's about to ask how long before we feel it's safe for his return home? The precious cows and not-so-precious badgers are waiting. Am I correct, Harry?"

"No, you're bloody not. I was going to ask when it would be convenient for me to arrange my father's and brother's funeral, actually, my dear." I replied, angry that I'd been trivialised.

"No wonder you've managed very little if you're at each others' throats like that every day. Do stop the childish quarrelling; perhaps then we'll get somewhere. To answer your question Harry, it probably won't be until we've caught whoever it is."

The inference that Trimble had made in his dismissive remark that neither of us were treating the killings seriously added to the fact that more time was needed in London in Judith's company, confused the already complicated feelings I had towards her. I felt exactly as Peter had described: childish, and not to be trusted, without her beside me, being my chaperone wherever I went. We were outside when I got my chance to rebuke her for her interference. I had felt my resentment building up inside as we had made our way out the 'Box' and into the early spring heat of the polluted air of Vauxhall Cross, but my chance never came, as Judith apologised.

"I'm sorry about that, Harry. I had to jump in…I wasn't sure what you were about to say. I didn't know if you were about to reveal all my deductions about Paulo. Thinking I had forgotten to mention it all. I really do think it's best for the time being to keep that to ourselves.

Don't want Peter getting overexcited at the moment, do we? There's nothing concrete to go on yet."

I felt like the proverbial putty in her hands as the wind spilled from my sails. I accepted her offer of a fish lunch at Scott's, as recompense for my loss of honour as she put it; but I could not resist alluding to my preference to trouts on plates, rather than in my face, as we attempted to cross the road, watching out for yellow taxi lights. Her green eyes gleamed in mild mockery, but there was no caustic retort aimed at me. However, she made a remark that caused me to think.

"Have you ever noticed, Harry, that it's not the questions people ask that are often discomforting? It's the ones they *don't* ask."

"Now you mention it, I suppose there was more they could have asked. It all seemed a bit perfunctory and half-hearted, as if they weren't interested much."

"That's because neither of them want to take responsibility and leave any blame sitting on their desk if it goes wrong, Westminster politics, Harry. They are almost all the same, the mandarins of power."

Later that day, still in her clinging company, I returned to Eton Square. There, I made the arrangements for the joint interment, at the mausoleum that adjoined the family chapel on the Estate, for the forthcoming Sunday. I hoped that the bodies would have been released by then, and all things would have returned to normal. I was being premature, I knew, but I needed a semblance of normality in my life, and a reassurance to all those close to me.

Judith was having a nose around. She had asked if I would mind, but it was said as more of an imposed instruction that I was obligated to agree to, rather than a polite enquiry. As I telephoned Joseph to tell him of the arrangements, she was examining the mounted photographs that were scattered around.

"Could this be Maudlin?" she asked, holding up a silver-framed photo of the man himself.

"Yes, that is he." It was George, who I had not heard enter the room, who answered her question. "He was about eighty in that still cuts an imposing figure, though. There are some others where he is younger around...I'll sort some out for you, if you would like? Of course, in the first floor office, there is the commissioned portrait of himself with Phillip, Elliot, and the young Harry, here. He was very proud of it. I'm sure Harry could show you. Will you and the young lady be staying for dinner, Harry? I'm sure Mrs Squires would love to impress you with her delights from the kitchen. She's been inconsolable this past week since Elliot's passing, and now what with Edward...well, I think it would do her good, if you could spare the time."

I accepted the invitation, not deferring or consulting Judith, nor with any thought to Hector's welfare, as I introduced my companion to him.

"This is Judith Meadows; she's helping out at the bank." I do not know why I lied, but it sped off my tongue before I had time to think. Perhaps it was the distraction of other concerns that led me to blur the truth.

Mrs Squires, like Maudlin, had always been spoken of reverently within our circle. However, I had Mrs Franks as my cook, and plenty of people to look after my needs. Inside my already overworked brain, I was wondering how I could keep everyone on in meaningful employment.

The Paterson's, and they are all I can speak of, always had servants, but they were never considered to be humble or lackeys. They were skilled men and women doing their own job in our homes, in which they also lived. They respected us as employers and we respected all of them as individual people, with their own needs and problems. As I saw it, it was my duty as a rich and privileged person to offer positions to good honest people who wanted to work for me, as would any person in business.

Nobody was referred to as a servant, only as staff, and they were looked after as part of our extended family. Now that my family was diminishing by the week, what could I do with this house and the staff who had their homes here?

Judith had found something on which to pass comment. "I hope you don't think I'm interfering, H, but don't you find that a bit familiar…him calling you Harry, and your father Elliot? It's as though he's a family friend, and not your father's valet and butler."

"He is a friend, Judith. A very long friend of my family and of this house and all who have lived here."

"Hmm…I see," she replied.

Chapter Eighteen

Prickly Gorse

"Elliot, I would like to introduced two colleagues of mine. This is Antony Willis from the Foreign and Commonwealth Office, and Donald Howell, the permanent undersecretary at the Home Office. Donald's boss couldn't make the journey as he's suffering at home with the 'flu, but Donald has his blessing and his nod, so can speak on behalf of that Department. Can your man take our guns from the car?" Peter Trimble made the introductions.

After my father's, self-congratulating slap on my back, he had recounted all of his meeting of that shooting weekend when I was recruited into becoming a spy. As time went on, he told of his successes in working with these three, and later the profits he made for the bank.

"We have a proposition we would welcome your comments on, and perhaps an opportunity for your involvement through St George," Antony Willis had said.

The proposal amounted to the establishment of a paper company in the Isle of Man, funded through the bank's money, which would then buy out BP's interest in those petrochemical plants in Antwerp at a favourable price subsidised by HM Government. A private individual who was working for BP had been approached and had agreed to front this company, lending credibility to the takeover, and the financial reports in the newspapers. The reason behind this, Peter told my father, was that the Americans and the Japanese, along with us, were working on the technology to replace gasoline as the principal fuel for cars, and an equivalent chemical answer to natural gas. The answer they were developing was renewable and cheap to produce, therefore highly profitable. There was, however, an added incentive for Elliot.

"The new-found wealth in Russia is trying to shut this down. They want to poach the secrets and then corner the market and kill the research." They had two interested parties, Elliot was told; the ones who owned their oil and gas, and the Mafia, who wanted to control those industries.

"We must do something to safeguard British interest in this sphere, Elliot. We must add extra weight." It was Trimble who had added the final plea.

That was enough for my father. All the right bells were ringing in his head; he had his chance to carry the banner of St George into the battle. "I was ahead of them, Harry, so I volunteered you. I knew that you would fit in, be your kind of fight," he had told me.

* * *

"I was chosen by Trimble, and that's how it came about."

"Did your father say if he needed to persuade them, or did they accept his offer of you straight away, Harry?" Judith asked.

"No apparently, they had someone else in mind but, according to my father, he swung the vote my way after extolling all my virtues."

We were back in the barracks of Clapham and recapping all the events that had directly involved me. Hector was asleep at my feet, having enjoyed Mrs Squires' plate of leftovers as much as we had enjoyed her cooking, and the refrigerator in Judith's pristine, uncluttered kitchen was full of goodies for my later pleasures.

"Incidentally, Judith... what happened to Messrs. Willis and Howell? Did they get ousted with the other Blair lot, or survive to stand and fall with Brown?"

"They both moved up the slippery pole, H. Being civil servants means they can't be shafted, only moved, so they've gone up in the world. Working out of Brussels now, the two of them. EU representatives on Trade policy, more mouths to feed in that junket. While I'm on the subject of dubious politicians and outright liars, let's not use the two 'B' names in here again, please. They don't sit well in my company."

I never pressed her on this, allowing her to decide if she ever wanted to explain. I thought that it may have been tied-in with the other unmentionable, her late husband, and I was not wrong. However, before I was made aware of that story, there was more of my own to narrate.

"You were fifteen going on sixteen when Maudlin died, Harry, weren't you? My father was there at the funeral, and told me of it. He said that it was a strange day, but never elaborated on the details. Tell me what you can remember, and if you can recall, who attended apart from family members?"

It was just over twenty-six years ago, on a freezing January morning in snow-covered Harrogate. It was a ridiculous day. I was nearing sixteen, carrying the usual teenage baggage along with several other suitcases called Lords, Ladies, Honourable's and privileges. I was too wrapped up in my own life, both at school and on the rugby pitch, to properly understand what was happening. Father had told me that great-grandfather had died some days before, and that his body had been laid out in an open casket in the chapel for the day and night leading up to the funeral. I thought that I would feel sick on seeing him on display there, and the thought of him lying there, overnight, was too nightmarish to think about. Elliot spoke to me, reassuring me that ghosts and wandering spirits were stories that mediums made up to profit from, and that I shouldn't be afraid as Maudlin loved and could never harm me. I wasn't sick, but I remember that I didn't sleep that night.

The coffin lay on pedestals, draped in black, with a single vase of white lilies beside it. If anything, I think I felt disgusted; he was grey and bloated, and it just was not him, to me. I remained unmoved emotionally, unable to react, whilst some around me cried and others bowed their heads. Phillip was speaking to me, but I never heard what he said. All I could do was look at his body and feel both sadness and indifference; an odd feeling, and difficult to explain.

I had known him briefly, but in the short time that I had with him, I remembered him in a childish, frightened, way. He was a big man to me, both in stature and presence, and had a loud voice which, when addressed to my young ears made me stop whatever I was doing and take notice.

With Phillip and father it was different. Obviously I obeyed them, as with my mother, but I could ignore their words of wisdom or censure them, poking my tongue out when they had turned their backs. Not so with *The Old Man* ,when *he* was at home. Towards him, that behaviour would never have seemed right why, I cannot say but that's what frightened me, if frightened is the right word to use, from an early age to when I knew him more intimately. The sadness I felt was not for my loss, nor, I'll be honest, for his death. It was for the others who were crying.

For me, death was not something I could comprehend; it was not the final chapter of life, but it was just another stage. I had him in my memory, and that was enough. The indifference was not, as you might think, because he would no longer be able scare me or intimidate me. It was not that kind of fear. I think it came from the fact that I never really knew him, and now he was not there to know. But what was the point of regret? Later in life I was told that I was the same with toys, or other possessions that were broken or lost. I never got upset about it but just carried on with life, accepted it for what it was, and never pined for something that had gone.

The day of the funeral was a farcical day, in my mind, because of what happened. One moment there were people passing the coffin, wiping their eyes the next, there was father in his red tunic, jodhpurs and spurs, taking the stirrup cup and leading the hunt! Elliot was Hunt Master, following all the other Patersons in that country sport, and the hunt had been arranged and so, I was told, Maudlin would have insisted on him taking part. How, I wondered, did they know that was what he would have wanted to happen, or was it them that wanted their own enjoyment? At the age I was, it was extremely confusing, but I never worried about it. I just put it down to grown-ups and how they knew everything!

I remembered plenty of mourners being unrecognisable to me, but on mention of the photograph of my mother's that I had found, showing Judith's father, her face brightened. It then dulled as I informed her that I had not brought it with me. She altered tack, and tried a different direction.

"Do you recall George there that day, Harry?"

"Of course I do. He was my mentor, or sort-of guardian. I don't really know how to describe our relationship...the age difference never seemed to bother him, and I was happy around him. He gave me confidence to try things, that on my own, I would never have attempted, silly things like climbing higher in a tree. Having him around felt like he would catch me if I fell."

"Did you notice, or rather can you remember, how he reacted at the funeral? Was he more upset than others, or not moved by it all?"

"He reacted the same as most of the other men there kept a stiff upper lip, I suppose. Although I was thinking of this today, and I do remember asking him about his future now that Maudlin had died. I'm not sure why I expected him to go, but I did. It wasn't that Maudlin favoured him above me, but I sensed something when 'The Old Man' saw us together."

"Did Maudlin see you two more often than, say, Phillip, or your father?"

"Yes, he did, but both of those were in London more often than in Harrogate."

"Hmm. What was it that George said when you asked if he was leaving the household?"

"He said that not only would he look after me and my brother Maurice who really he had little to do with, as he was only one or two then and Edward had not been born, but he would become my father's personal secretary, which I thought only women became."

"Did he say anything else, like why? Or, anything about himself? I guess you never knew where he came from, or why he was brought into family? After all, none of you were short of governesses or tutors, were you? And I doubt your father would have countenanced your tree climbing, had he known," she asked, in a motherly way.

"No, that's true. I never knew that part of his life, nor have I ever asked. He was just there one day, and that was that. I did, however, learn that he had an aunt living near Radlett, not far from the Borehamwood film studios in Hertfordshire. Funnily enough I asked him today how she was."

"So this aunt must have been spoken about often, then, for you to remember her, and ask after her wellbeing?"

"I wouldn't say that. It was well-known that George would visit her sometimes, taking food hampers from Fortnum's with him."

"Why hampers? Couldn't he have taken food parcels from your kitchen? Seems an expensive indulgence. Didn't you ever question 'this?"

"I suppose it was, but why is that so surprising? There was an account at Fortnum's, so why not use it? Everyone in our household was treated as family."

"All the Paterson staff run up bills there, then? Use the Harrods' account to buy their underwear, do they?" A look of astonishment had replaced the motherly concern. I sensed I was being accused of something; whether it was of being simple, or more serious than that, I wasn't sure.

"One more thing, Harry, while we are on the subject. You said that the money stopped disappearing in 1970, the year you were born. That would be the same year that George appeared...I have got that right, haven't I?" I looked away as I realised just how silly and stupid I had been, accepting things on face value. Now, I questioned Maudlin and Phillip's motives for those trips to the Home Counties which he referred to when taking George away from me, and driven off with Geoffrey the chauffeur. "Pure coincidence, do you think? Or, maybe, a repayment of a debt?" She poignantly added.

There was a long silence, in which we were both thinking of answers to that absorbing question; and again it was Judith who raised yet more, none of which were easy to rebut.

Chapter Nineteen

Gooseberry Bush

Paulo's letter, carried by the nineteen-year-old pregnant Tanya, caused Maudlin to take stock of himself. He was sixty-four years of age when she arrived at his door and still playing the field, happily oblivious to its consequences. Parenthood had been confined to the marital home, apart from his indiscretion with Andrea in Northern Spain. He had, always, taken precautions of one kind or another; including the recommendations of abortions on three occasions, none of which had moved him spiritually, nor led to a change of nature. He was not a religious person but sometimes, when he had nothing more pressing to consider, he sought the same insurance of eternal life that affects others concerned more in the material world.

Andrea was a churchgoing Catholic, and had Romario christened into the faith before his first birthday. The option of ending their child's life was not even discussed between the two. There was no alternative open to Maudlin other than to face up to his obligations, or so it seemed, and confront the conformity of his English life. Fortunately, another door was about to open.

A war was coming, and if Andrea could be persuaded to take his advice and follow her relatives to Russia then all reputations and consciences could be saved, and recriminations avoided. His son's continued existence, and the awareness of his own, had disturbed his world. The news of Andrea's death had resettled it, bringing regret, but also relief on the discovery of Paulo's ambitions. He had no wish to pursue his patrimony. He instead wished to further himself within his adopted society, and had asked for help in this pursuit.

Money would do the job, Maudlin reasoned. It always did even in the case of unwanted lives. That's what would propel his embarrassment up and away into the red skies above the Soviet Union, especially if espionage was his chosen path. *Remember the 'Cairo Gang,'* he told himself.

Maudlin's conversion to humanity was not instant, nor was it painless, and not only in a financial sense. It entailed his continuance at 'Annie's' until his death, never trusting his legitimate heir, Phillip, to all the knowledge of Paulo's significance. He rejected the country squire role that had been his intention to live in his latter years for the one of patron and subscriber to his Russian protégé, who had excited his imagination.

His first enthusiasm was driven by self-preservation. He had no wish of Paulo divulging his name and connection to any official of any colour, as he was aware of the possibility of pressure being put upon him to keep his secret hidden. His continued support, and recommendation as to GCHQ expansion, came after Tanya's appearance at Eton Square and the full recognition of both Paulo's potential and his own weakness and ineptitude in handling the situation during the war years. He should never have sent those bonds, he now realised.

He could not disclose Paulo to his associates in the SIS how could he? *Hi there, I've got a son in the red zone who wants to spy for us, any good to you?* What had happened the last time he had handed over the cognisance of undercover informants? That had brought on that cynical, yet deserved, comment about the mistrust of friendships, so he decided to run him himself. *He won't get anywhere... how can he? He'll probably get caught before he can even start. I'll make the effort. I suppose I owe him that much, at least,* the jaundiced 'Old Man' told himself.

He agreed to Tanya's defection, never really believing that it would happen, and was more shaken than surprised when she announced that she carried his grandchild. Not even the selfish minded Maudlin could now turn her away, although it did cross his mind.

He concealed the real reason for her arrival from the staff by shrouding it under a cover of secrecy, conveying the impression to his housekeeper that it was something the Government wanted to keep out of common knowledge, with all the intrigue and confusion over the Crabb incident going on. During her first night under his roof he considered having her driven somewhere far away and just abandoned, with no money, and left to fend for herself. He wisely reconsidered, realising that his plan would not work, even allowing for her lack of English, as she knew his address and would only return, bringing down Paulo's anger upon his house. He could do one thing and only one; to continue in the ways of the surreptitious plans of his Russian son.

Tanya stayed the one night in London, leaving early next morning for Holyhead, with Maudlin in the lead. She then, obediently, went onto Whitecliffe, north of Dublin, and the site of a Carmelite Convent where she was tutored in the rudiments of the English language in the six and a half months before she gave birth to a healthy baby son.

She had just turned twenty years of age when George was born. Often she was alone and overwhelmed, with only Maudlin to call on in times of agitation, and his appreciation of garbled Russian mixed with pidgin English was not the highest achievement in his life. Between the English Lord and the peasant girl from Lithuania, the name of George was settled on.

Tanya knew the depiction of her countries patron saint slaying the dragon that Maudlin drew. As for him, he calculated that the coincidence of that name with his bank, would be too obvious for anyone to recognise or question. He visited her every other weekend, staying nearby for at least two nights on each occasion until, eventually, her education had reached an acceptable, everyday, level. She could then be reintroduced into England; near, yet far enough away, from London and Harrogate so as not to cause any undue awkwardness.

Maudlin bought the house in the chestnut tree-lined Gower Avenue, Radlett, using 'Annie's' money, and set about making a history for

Tanya and his grandson. He knew about the creation of false identities, as it was something he had practised and had experienced, whilst in Ireland.

He visited cemeteries, gathering names of the deceased females of the same age as Tanya, then researched those names, matching places of birth and living relatives from electoral rolls, until they met his own requirements of anonymity and excuses for her broken tongue. From the cemetery at Brenchley Gardens, in the far-off suburb of New Cross, he got what he was looking for: a nineteen-year-old Estonian girl with the name of Loti Martins, rescued from the advancing German army in 1940, with British citizenship and no surviving parents. It was a more than suitable new identity for his daughter-in-law, Tanya Korovin.

As with everything within Maudlin's grasp, he fitted the story to the circumstances. He applied for a copy of the birth certificate at St. Catherine's House in the Aldwych, and then a passport with Tanya's photo attached from Clive House, with no problems encountered, Tanya adopted her new identity and moved into Radlett, unchallenged.

Nothing Maudlin did was ever random. Everything had a reason and a purpose and, most of all, these suited Maudlin first, and others second. There was an emigre, an escapee from the Bolshevik revolution with a story of a distant relationship to the Romanov Royal family name, whom Maudlin had been introduced to by a mutual friend from Boodles as a possible investor at the bank. He lived at nearby Elstree and had money invested in a new commercial television company. Maudlin had put him in touch with the executives of the enterprise, and advised his financial commitment to them.

"It's the coming thing, old boy. Auntie won't have it all their own way for long. There will be more channels on the box soon not just a BBC monopoly. There's money to be made in commercial television. Get in quick man and you'll make a mint!"

Feydor had done just that, and his newfound friend's prophecies had come true. He needed a housekeeper, owed Maudlin a big favour, preferred younger girls to older women, and missed the grandson he had been forced to leave back in Russia who had died in Kiev. He also had a soft, solicitous side, that counterbalanced the harsh aggressive Russian morality against single mothers from the Motherland with no evidence of pure unsullied backgrounds.

What better than a compassionate, presentable, fellow dissident to fill that vacant role, while sacrificing her own life and welfare for a lost brother's child? This is how Maudlin phrased his petition, adding as a stimulus, "She's as Jewish as yourself." Tanya was briefed, and left in no doubt as to the importance of living that story for George's lifetime. She paid homage at the local synagogue and became Auntie Loti to both Feydor and George, and remained so, until this day.

Chapter Twenty

Lucky Heather

'Lucky at cards, unlucky in love' is a metaphor that could be applied to both Maudlin and his son Paulo, although their form of gambling was not confined to the wager of money. Their principle speculation lay elsewhere; in the interference and risk to other's welfare and lives. Maudlin's lifelong search for his version of love had brought many conquests, but none had fulfilled his heart as much as the discovery of a fellow devotee to the enrichment of English wellbeing. As for the focus of this love, his son, his desires for emotional satisfaction were second to that of ambition and power.

Paulo was ambivalent towards love, as his upbringing had taught him that the reliance on women for his personal welfare was a mistake. He had thought Andrea had been weak in not pressing her claims on his father, of not somehow using his influence and money to secure a better life for herself, and him, in Russia. This reticence and humility had cost her life, it would not cost his, he vowed. Where she was meek, he would be assertive, and where she was effacing and subservient in her relationship with Maudlin, he would become conspicuous in his father's life and taste the riches that were rightfully his. Not however, through begging or simple paternal recognition.

There was no lasting resentment felt by Paulo in regard to his mother nor his father. He had, it's true, berated his mother on several topics, including her choice of Russia as their refuge, but his admiration of her acceptance of hardship without complaint had overcome his petulance and indignation. Where Maudlin was concerned, there was empathy and endorsement. His father had status and that could not be threatened for a mere love affair, no matter what the outcome. He would do the same if the roles had been reversed he reasoned, and when eventually the circumstances regarding Andrea's failing health proved too much, his prophecy came true.

His indifference to Tanya was palpable to everyone from the very beginning. There was no attraction either sexually or intellectually, no physical or spiritual magnetism... until one night.

There was nothing to distinguish her from most girls of the same age in Leningrad at that time in both their lives. She was sixteen, five years Paulo's junior, when he first used her in the nursing and everyday needs of his mother. She was shabby and uneducated, malnourished and grubby all things he could take care of, had he had a mind to, but he did not. Initially, he used her simply because she was available and his money had bought her parents. He was growing into the role of manipulating and affecting people surrounding himself, a life he excelled at. Then, when he was ingratiating himself within the corridors of the KGB, he found it more acceptable to be accompanied by a female companion than to be alone, and allow questions to be raised as to one's suitability and sexuality to be amongst the ranks of upstanding men.

Such things had happened during Stalin's last days, when excuses were being found to sort the hammers from the sickles, so as to dispose of those who stood out as different from the norm. Or, more correctly, the ones *perceived* by the most influential as standing out from the accepted and normal.

He began to groom Tanya; not only in corporeal ways, but aesthetically as well. Make-up and hairstyling were procured, and a new pair of spectacles stamped with the opposing 'C's' denoting the French fashion house of Chanel magically appeared. The black market was resourced to provide the clothing that not only Tanya would need, but also every other officer's mistress or wife would need, in order to wear to the upper echelons of the elite Communist Party Members' private meetings.

She did not pass unnoticed at these parties, and it was not only men who commended her appearance; women, too, applauded her elegant attire. Soon, Paulo came to hear of the compliments coming his and her way. He was, amongst many other things, a narcissistic man, wrapped up in his own self-importance and consumed by selfishness. As such, he considered Tanya to be his property; to be complimented, or not, by only him. The jealous rage he felt was not aimed at those who had admired Tanya they would help him on his travels, of course. No, it was aimed at Tanya...a much easier target to hit.

"Who is that woman you're with, Sergeyovitch? What a find! When you tire of her, pass her on to us, there's a good comrade!" She had a 'great those, great these, great everything,' apparently, but her looks went unnoticed by Paulo, until commented upon by his lecherous friends. That was when the, previously unnoticed, lust within himself began to grow. In later life, this Byzantium man would argue with himself that it was the death of his mother, only a few months before, that had confused his mind and driven him to that moment of madness. As to the truth of the situation...only he could answer, as only he knew what made him think of it.

They were walking through Nevskiy Park one autumn night, on the way to the communal apartment block that they still shared, after leaving Comrade Olgaovitch's party. They were dressed in the regulation grey topcoats, hiding his finery and her slender figure, clad in a revealing white blouse and a thigh-hugging short black skirt, teamed with knee-length boots made in West Germany. He suddenly pushed her on to the grass snapping, as he did so, a heel off those expensive boots, as Tanya fell awkwardly, catching her foot in the cobbles of the path.

"Why did you do that?" she cried indignantly, clutching her prized possessions!

It was then, no matter what he may say now, that the thought and intention of rape left his mind, as the act of consoling and commiserating her took over. He was honest, to a point, as he nervously admitted his desires for her. She, on the other hand, felt no self-consciousness in proposing the pact of sex for marriage and freedom made on those blades of grass, and not at the nursing bed as Paulo had told his father, thinking it wise not to show his frailties and weaknesses instead of the compassion and thoughtfulness contained in that message.

This was not the only deception he played on Maudlin. When he learnt that Tanya carried his child, it was not selfless concern for the wellbeing of that child that placed George in Maudlin's charge. Altruism was the contradiction to his real motive.

Paulo considered his own prosperity and success too important to be restricted by a wife and child. He calculated that now was the time that Maudlin could repay the debt he owed his mother and himself. And the repayment he would extract would be in the reversal of roles. It was time for his father to care for his son's offspring, whilst Paulo played the field.

He had, however, one handicap embedded in this decision: he believed in the teachings of God, and his mother had schooled him well in the ways of the Church and the scriptures of the Bible. His first step had been initiated by Andrea, with the baptism. He had then practiced the faith and had participated in the liturgy of the Eucharist, and he believed in the sacrament and of penitence. There was no reparation he could make to annul that marital union he had made in God's house; he must stay married to Tanya for ever.

* * *

Maudlin's luck had been made manifest in many ways, none more so than when a German high explosive shell killed all four horses drawing the gun carriage on which he rode, when in command of a field artillery squadron in 1917. He escaped with a shrapnel graze to his left leg, whilst the man beside him was decapitated.

Apart from this one wound, he was unscathed by the war, and carried no marks or scars of other campaigns he had involved himself in throughout his life. Health was not a primary concern to Maudlin, having never been beset by illness other than the childhood sicknesses that affected others of similar age. He had never broken a bone or twisted an ankle whilst he performed on the athletic track or playing fields at Eton and Cambridge, nor had he ever been thrown from a horse in all the disciplines he took part in. So, on the conception of the plan that Paulo had conceived, only then did it enter his head that one day he would die. How then could his estranged son continue in the furthering of English interests? He thought of the Civil Service perhaps the permanent secretary to the Foreign Office, he suggested to himself, then quickly dismissed that idea.

"Can't trust those buggers," he said aloud, while sitting alone in the library, drinking another glass of good claret from the cellars at Eton Square. "Couldn't make up their minds what to do with Franco, let alone Hitler in his early days. Appeasement…that's all they know. Paulo will be sold off to the first Russian bidder if one of their own needed to be swapped."

The Secret Service was out of the question. It was to them that he had turned before, telling about his informants in Ireland, and look where that led! Where was there for him to hide that secret? He set about on his course to reveal one mystery, by enmeshing it within another.

"Our children have a brother, my dear. No, there's no need to worry there's only the one. I've only made the one mistake and the boy's mother is dead, so I'm not involved anymore. I managed to smuggle him out of the great bear's cave with an aunt. They won't bother you or the family; I'll see to that."

Christina, like Alice in later days, was well aware of her husband's affairs and tolerated them as best she could amongst the myriad of things Maudlin's wealth could buy.

"I don't want anyone else knowing about this, Maudlin. I could not face the scandal," she bravely declared. "Have I your word?" she demanded.

The sixty-four young at heart Maudlin gave it, but never kept it. He hadn't given his boy scout's salute on making that affirmation, so didn't feel obligated. He told one other person in his legitimate family and, again, it was the abridged version. He saved the almost-complete truth for one other, who had to wait a further twenty-nine years to discover it!

To his reluctant heir apparent at the bank he gave a similar account, only this time he added, "When you pass away, Phillip, so does the secret. It ends at you." He ordered, and was obeyed.

He had to tell his youngest because he needed to prolong his interference with the bank's assets, plus he needed Phillip's help in establishing Tanya and George in Radlett. It was not possible for him to do it all alone, as much as he wished he could.

Fourteen years later, both to the rest of his family, and to the staff of both houses, he neither told the truth nor lied. He simply implied that George was related in some obscure way to the departed Christina, who had been dead for almost a year. He managed this in subtle ways, never directly connecting the two. He would hint at 'the wayward side of the Northfleet family,' or insinuate that one or two nieces were not quite of 'the right sort in male company.' At the Christmas gathering, the one just before George's arrival at Harrogate, his aspersions changed from intimations to outright accusations, albeit merely hearsay.

"It was once said, I'm not sure by whom, that Christina's niece, Josephine, had a promiscuous daughter, and I was led to believe he's her son. I made a promise to the Great Lady that if anything untoward happened I would step in, and I did."

He never elaborated on the circumstances that compelled his intervention, leaving that to any imagination that might exist among the gathered guests. "You all know how set she was on helping the wayward and downtrodden in life," he said, with a straight face. There was an undisguised look of incomprehension on the faces of those around the table that day, after the exposure of the otherwise-hidden charitable nature of Lady Christina, until Phillip added his considerable weight to the conspiracy, whilst attempting to swallow yet another whole bowl of trifle.

"She was always doing things, don't you remember? She chaired the Women's Institute and was a judge at the county show, and I know for a fact that she contributed to Shelter. I was with her when she visited St-Martins-in-the-Field in Trafalgar Square. She was made to pay at the door to get admitted!"

All were then happy and contented in the new, glorified, vision of their mother, or their mistress; handing out the coppers to the poor and wretched in her other life, away from the trappings of grandeur they all seemed to have always seen her in. The closest she had ever been to grim, they had always believed, was when dismounting in a wet stable yard. Had the circumstances that Maudlin had invented ever happened, then his wife, and head of the house, would have been the last person on Earth to have intervened. It might well have upset her lunch parties or afternoon tea gatherings, and that would *never* have done. Not in the society in which she ruled!

At the age of eighty-nine, Maudlin's luck began to run out. He had his first traumatic experience of old age, and suffered a minor stroke. He was advised by his doctors to moderate his drinking, abandon the consumption of red meat, and curtail his energetic lifestyle. As he attributed all of these things to his robustness and endurance, he chose only horse riding to give up. He did, however, decide to make arrangements for the continued furtherance of England's wellbeing.

Chapter Twenty-One

Ground Cover

In the letter that George opened from Probyn and Fellow of number nine Lincoln's Inn, Maudlin's solicitors, most of the truth was revealed, written on fine expensive cotton paper. One thing that remained unrevealed was Tanya's real relationship to him and that of the Patersons. However, one thing was extremely relevant to the murders of his complicated 'step' relative Elliot and his son Edward: the means of communicating with his father Paulo, and what to do with any communiqué.

After an admirably modest preamble by Maudlin, in which he described both his own and his Aunt Loti's role in extricating him from his entanglement inside Russia, George read on in increasing fascination. He had been a quiet, unpretentious, boy, not altering his approach to life on reaching young adulthood throughout the years he spent in Maudlin's company, either in Harrogate or London. He had not wished for much, as he had no need of possessions. All had been found for him by the Paterson family since his birth. They had provided a sound education, and comfortable homes first in the Home Counties, then mansions to live in. He had been given a steadily increasing income from which he had neither the need or desire to draw from in great quantity.

At twenty-eight he was a healthy, presentable, self-assured man, one who did not look beyond the day in front of him. He had no ambition to somehow 'better himself', as was the political philosophy of the then Thatcher government. He was content doing what he did within his vocation, as aide to all things appertaining to his philanthropic patron and all who bore the same name. None of this was to change, so the letter said… but how could this be so, with such monumental information laid before him? He came to the part where the lies began, overriding the interspersed truth.

You have come from rebellious and important stock. Your paternal grandfather stood beside Leon Trotsky, in a city then called Petrograd in October 1917, when he denounced the Tsar and the Royalist Government in a speech that lead to the uprising that changed Russia into the Communist Soviet Union of today. Your grandmother was a leading participant in the February revolution and had a seat, alongside her husband, on the first revolutionary council of the new Bolshevik Government of Soviet Russia.

I must have been tranquillised at birth, then, George thought, upon reaching the parts of the letter that interested him.

Your mother, Alexandra Rovasova Beroyich, died giving birth. She was twenty-six. You were born on the seventh September 1956 at 1745 Sredgnly Prospekt Leningrad, and you were named Sergey Gregorovitch. It was aunt Loti and I who changed it to George. Your father's name is Tovarisch Sergeyovitch Korovin also known as Paulo. He is a powerful and influential man, who wishes to bring his country closer to the West by political reforms. For this reason he has made many enemies but also, fortunately, like-minded supporters. It was they who aided your escape.

George thought that *escape* was a strange word to use; *unless I was in danger, which must mean that my father's life is equally threatened!* He rationalised, before reading on.

In the sealed envelope that accompanies this letter are the details of the code that you and he will use in all communications between yourselves. It is not as complex as it appears. There are examples of decoded material using the formula. Study these and practise with the numbers and letters; Paulo's life depends on your competence and accuracy with it. His means of contacting you are simple, while your means of contacting him are not. Again, it is imperative that you learn his methods well.

He will send an empty envelope, posted in West Germany, addressed to: Lord Paterson, 16 Eton Square, SW1. Marked on the flap will be a number between one and seven, and that number will correspond to the same numbered hotel in West Berlin that is enclosed with the code. You must be at the selected venue two weeks to the date on the postmark. You may never get that envelope, but if you do, don't expect to meet your father; that would be exceptional. In all probability, it will be a message to collect from the desk.

When you have deciphered the message, you will send it to PO Box 850 London, and add 'Garden' at the bottom of the information. You must do nothing else with the knowledge that you gain, nothing!

Never seek out your father through idle curiosity or any sense of finding an attachment or loyalty. He risks his life for you daily, and will do so until he has achieved all that he has set himself. I have been his only contact outside of Russia since you were born. Now you will replace me, and play the same role. There is no one who knows that you are Paulo's son not even Aunt Loti. His and your own safety depends entirely on how successfully you keep our secret. Never can anyone else know. Your life is in danger only if your relationship to Paulo is unearthed, because then your father's opponents could use you as leverage against him; forcing him to reveal his contacts in the West, endangering them in the process, and putting a stop to all his good works at lowering the levels of danger that exist in the world today.

You must at all time be diligent and restrained in what you say and to whom you speak. Trust only yourself and your father. He has trusted in me, and will now trust in you.

Along with the code and the names of those hotels in Berlin, there is also a means of communicating with your father for all things other than your own selfish ones which, as I have mentioned, you must avoid. There is an address of a house in a town near Hamburg. You must knock at this house and ask for the name that is written down, and if no one is there, then you will return until someone answers.

You will be told that the person you want is not there at present, and they will request your name, to which you will reply 'I'm Lord Paterson.'

From a Lutheran Bible, which you will find in the library at number sixteen, you will take a copy from page 64 of the scene where Luther is communing John the Steadfast, and another of article 18 'Free Will,' on page one hundred and eleven. The first of these is only to be used in an emergency; it will require Paulo to meet with you. The second means that you have a message for him.

Whichever one you use, it must be left in the choir pews inside the Church of St Anselms in the same town on the next Sunday. If it is a message that you have for your father, then write the number of the hotel where you will leave it on 'Free Will.' If you have used the emergency method, then pray to God that you will both survive!

George had been fortunate in his short life, never having to choose between flight or fight; at the age of twenty-nine, fear was still an alien concept to him. He had experienced what he would describe as fear on few occasions, and the scariest moments were always when Harry had been around.

Maudlin had once escorted them to an indoor riding school at Ripon, in Yorkshire, and somehow he had managed to fall whilst attempting to coax the horse to turn to the right at a walking pace. He fell on the mixture of sawdust and hay, young enough not to have hurt any part of himself, other than his esteem in the watching Patersons' eyes. As he looked up from his dusty shame, all that filled his vision was his mount with his right foreleg raised with what looked like intentions to stamp on him, adding injury to the already-suffered humiliation. Luckily for both him and his horse, nothing untoward happened that day, but the memory still haunted the otherwise-unchallenged George. Another time was when Harry, then twelve, had insisted on piloting their canoe over the weirs on the River Nidd near Knaresbourgh, when the rudder wires broke and they almost capsized. George had never learnt to swim, and Harry hadn't asked!

After finishing Maudlin's script of instructions, he felt more fear in that moment then when he had lain helplessly in the sawdust, or had been hanging on to his helpless paddle. Those in comparison were just anxiety. He wondered if he had the courage to do all that was being asked, and evidently expected. He was both mesmerised and bewildered, not only by the directives, but also by the amount of money deposited in Switzerland for him. He was a millionaire!

The first time that the ability to keep confidential insights to himself was tested just a few days later at the funeral, when the young Harry asked of his future intentions. He passed that examination, and all that had followed.

The story of Grönwohld was just that... a story. It was an excuse Paulo would use for sojourns into the West, and the substantiation of his role as spymaster. It had been told before, a story in which Paulo was the narrator but neither Maudlin, nor any other Paterson was the audience. It was the legend that Paulo attached to his operative. It was how, he told his compatriots, that his 'Mother' agent made contact.

Maudlin's solicitor's letter to Paulo arrived the day after the one to George, at the Grönwohld house of Dietmar Kohl. He read it in the comfort of room 501 of the Hotel Hackesher on Behrenstrasse, part of the English sector of the still-divided city of Berlin. Number five on the secret list.

His reaction was different to his son's. His was one of sadness and deep regret, even the news of the hundred million Stirling being added to the Swiss bank account he held in Zug on the banks of the Zugersee, did not dull or take away the feeling. It had been in this same hotel that he and his father had last met over five years ago, when the topic of succession had again been delicately discussed. Maudlin, more by accident than design, had told the right story to the right people all along the line. He had enabled George to fill the role of go-between admirably, beyond the attention and intelligence of politicians of both sides and those who serve them, who are meant to know everything and everybody.

Given normal circumstances you would think that this would be a strength and an added advantage in the game that Paulo played; but the games that were being played were not taking part in any form of normality. In reality, George's anonymity was the opposite. Maudlin's fabricated reference to enemies of his son were not that far from the truth. He had made many envious of his popularity, and they had long memories, and held grudges for longer.

Chapter Twenty-Two

Jerusalem Artichokes

The exploding bomb in Beirut had taught Paulo many lessons: one of which was that not all things were held as cheaply as the lives of practicing zealots in the minds of those who performed the persuasion. Information held a higher premium to them in their pursuit of antisemitism. He developed his political contacts throughout the region, feeding them what they required. Their appetite was, however, unquenchable. They were always demanding more in the struggle against Israel and their truly special relations, the Americans. Paulo needed a new supplier, and it was to *trade* that he cast his eyes. He needed knowledge of Western commercial ways now, rather than their not-so-secret desires to overcome the might of the Russian armoury.

The last communication received at Box 850, presided over by the last King when he and the Prince met for their final time, five years previously, detailed the invasion of Afghanistan. It was a political decision, and one which Paulo had adamantly opposed in the declamation he made to the Kosygin reform group in which he held the most prominent beacon.

The era of stagnation of the Soviet economy was drawing to a close, after the group's proposals of decentralisation, away from heavy industry and into consumer goods was beginning to show results. The foreseeable drain that a war would cause on the resources that these improvements had led to, was not acceptable to Paulo. He would not allow himself to simply sit motionless and permit the wastage to occur. With the continuing narrowing of the Soviet barriers to commercialism, Paulo hoisted himself onto the advisory body that examined the credentials of each and every trade delegation that wished to expand into the Soviet Bloc. He manoeuvred his way on to the reception committee to greet the British trade delegation due to arrive in February of 1992.

He had trawled the lists of too many to count in the preceding years, never finding what he really needed, and not willing to compromise. The gambler in him was waiting for the *one* big hand. It showed its face in the September, when a list of new names appeared in Moscow Centre for appraisal. For days and nights he hung his hammock in their shadowy offices, cross-referencing files and every scrap of information he could find, in order to scratch away at the surface of the fertile shoot that he had at last found in his sieve, and would not budge.

Mr Jack Simmons was a short, overweight, moustached man, of questionable fashion sense. Once a Royal Air Force sergeant, then, on retirement, a convener in the Telecommunications Union and member of the Fabian Society, and now, since Thatcher's realignment of the share wealth of the UK, an entrepreneur who owned Surveillance Cameras Incorporated. Paulo singled him out for his special attention. Jack had been an old-style socialist, as he told Paulo on the penultimate night of his stay in Moscow. Having at last seen the light and truth of capitalism, he had abandoned the philosophy of his previous society, and his militant ways, for the one of outright private enterprise, and therefore the advancement of oneself in the creation of wealth for the betterment of those less fortunate.

"Since Thatcher, without all the red tape and needless regulations keeping you looking over your shoulder all the time, companies can grow unhindered. We are able to make more money than before, and to keep it. We can also choose which markets to chase, and where to diversify to make our profits. I've seen the error of my ways in following Socialism. What I've made for myself has helped to smooth the edges of life, if you know what I mean.

The portfolio that I presented to your equivalent to our Minister of Trade today contains details of all our security cameras, including our latest product: a lightweight unit with exceptional lens capabilities, high zoom, and wide-angled. It comes in all sizes, and there's nothing like it in the world. It can be automatically set on a random pattern, or operated manually as is conventional in most systems of today. It's won us many orders worldwide, even in the States, where it's fitted on all their satellites, and I'm hoping for more from here. As I make more money, so I can pay the workers more, or employ more, and still make profits. As the workforce grows, so does the whole economy, and so they buy more goods and pay more taxes.

Your countries ten-year plans, and all that nationalisation, simply doesn't work. You've got to give the workers what they want and that's money in their pockets and the choice of where to spend it." His sermon was not needed; he preached to the converted. It was time for Paulo to strike.

"What is it that you really want of my country, Jack? Because, whatever it is, I can supply it," Paulo temptingly offered. He had managed to entice Jack away from the main group of business men and government personnel to the exclusive Zurich bar, tucked discretely behind the Kremlin. It was normally the province of the well-heeled, *haut monde* of Soviet patronage, where the private rooms above were used for more intimate words and actions than these opulent but open surroundings could decently accommodate.

"That sounds like an attempt to bribe me, Yuri. I'm a simple man, and open to proposals. Money speaks volumes to me and my other half; I have mouths to fed at home and ambitions to fulfil. I want contracts, and as many as can be arranged. If you can do that…what would you want in return?" He was hooked, as Paulo had known he would be. He had chosen the two hostesses well, and not only for their ability to serve drinks.

"Nothing is beyond my reach. I wouldn't want much, Jack. Just gossip on some Fabian members past and present, and the up-and-coming ones as well. Members and devotees that might make a splash in the future... you know the sort. I'm reliably told that the girls can be very obliging and quite versatile, if I tell them to be. Oh, by the by, if you could see your way to ignore any disapproval that might be thrown up by the purchasers and installation of those cameras of yours, and turn a blind eye to some of the places I want them sold. I'd be very grateful. There are millions of places in the USSR, and beyond, where surveillance could be a top priority if I made it so."

Paulo had his source, and his explicit photographs as well, as his way into the upper levels of Socialist Britain to use as he saw fit; or more pertinently, where Paulo saw the most advantage. They would be useful contacts for his previous employers in the secret offices, and to help his adopted England in its fight to regain the greatness that Maudlin personified.

At first, he offered his new friendship to those who sat in the dingy boxes of the KGB.

"I've got a finger in the UK Labour party, the opposition I know, but not forever in a democracy. Any use to you?" he asked.

"We have that avenue well-covered, Comrade Sergeyovitch. We have enough resources there already. Most are idealists and theologians who simply wear their red tie or red socks, but crave a knighthood or peerage too much to be good agents for us. We had one once who was ace. One who almost collapsed that special relationship that exists between the USA and the UK. Refused to allow British troops to support the Americans in Vietnam on our say-so, and told everyone who listened that it was in retribution for the Yanks' lack of nerve over Suez. It was his information that your 'Mother' confirmed all those years back, but since then we have had only the 'Ban the Bomb' enthusiasts, and not much more. How good is yours? Not much better, by the sound of it."

Paulo was amazed. He stayed to chat with his comrades, thinking he would share a few beers, then maybe vodkas.

"They give away Knighthoods and peerages over there, then?" He asked, after a long conversation in which names of British sympathisers were freely disclosed to their one time co-worker.

"Yes, apparently so, if they do worthwhile works or bribe someone or have something over someone. You know all about those matters, Paulo, don't you?"

Oh yes I do, thank you, he thought.

He travelled on to the more sumptuous, spacious rooms of the members of the Politburo and served Jack Simmons on a platter to them instead, washed down by their wine.

"Well done, Korovin! Take your seat beside us where you belong. We will need friends on our journey towards openness and restructuring. Perhaps Mr Simmons' cameras can help watch the old guard for us, in case the going gets tough.' Said the balding man with the birthmark showing through his thinning hair.

With one eye on the prospect of a Knighthood and the other on the opportunities that a materialistically driven corrupt Soviet economy presented, Paulo's version encapsulated his existing schemes in the Middle East to help his adopted country and line his own pockets. He needed his 'Mother' to further one of his aims, and his own greed for the other.

The King is dead, long live the King!

George took over the mantle, alternating from collector to delivery boy, overcoming his original fear of flying by necessity. For the remainder of that year George made collections from the same premises, near Earl's Court Road, that Paulo had first used as an accommodating postal address; only this time, the messages were from the more than satisfied Jack Simmons.

He visited Berlin several times and redirected other copies to Box 850, adding, as instructed, 'Garden' to the SIS copies; thereby swelling Dicky Blythe-Smith's file and causing consternation within the Civil Service ranks, and the Military.

Chapter Twenty-Three

Propagation Through Grafting

"What did your father ever tell you personally about George, Harry? How did he explain his being part of the furniture, and the special rights granted him?"

Judith and I, with Hector leading the way, had turned left from her home. We were heading away from the packaged breakfasts of the Common, and on our way to my favourite delights to be found nearby in Lachmere Road as Mrs Squires had reliably informed me, when I had complained to her of the fashionable virtual kind found in chic cafe's on the other side. I had already excited my appetite on some of her leftovers, and Hector could almost now speak in his admiration of her cooking. Judith was the only one of our number still in search of palatable satisfaction, other than what was edible. I was due to meet Sir David Haig in Whitehall that afternoon, and wanted a full stomach before, what might be, my execution.

"Very little...you've got to remember that we seldom met. Elliot was here in London, and I hated the place. All that congestion not only the traffic but the people as well, herded together like the cattle back home before they are carted off to market. Except I prefer to be around animals most of the time...they don't complain as much as people. It's gotten worse, if anything. Now there are tables and chairs outside everywhere you can't move, and if you stop for a tea or coffee, or, perish the thought, a meal, the stink of the diesel comes free. They should pay you to sit outside some of those places! Anyhow, he moved down here on a permanent basis when I was eleven and he must have been about thirty-eight. I imagine that he was still very active in his extra marital pursuits then because he wasn't seen much in Harrogate that I can recall. Grandfather Phillip was around in those days, hung on for another twenty years or so, but he had given up the bank by then. He asked me once how I got on with George, and it was he who told me that George was to join Elliot in London."

"What did he say?" She asked, expectantly.

"Oh, I can't remember, Judith. I was going off to Eton and had other things on my mind. I know there was something about Maudlin stepping in to resolve a difficult situation, and him being a distant relative, but I never took much notice about it. He was a friend, and it was as simple as that to me. I didn't care where he came from. He did say that, on holidays, I would see George but other than that, his time was to be spent here with my father, and if there were no more brothers in the family then Edward would be the next in line for the banking role of the family. I do remember thinking that it would suit my youngest brother, as he always seemed to cry and scream when it came to sharing anything. Hated parting with things, hung on for dear life. Even a football…he'd run off with it, if he caught Maurice and I playing."

"So, you didn't have much to do with George after that?" She persisted.

"No, nor Elliot. What is all this about, Judith? You don't seriously suspect George in all this, do you? You've been nagging on about him since yesterday. He wouldn't kill a fly…I've seen him avoid treading on ants! He really isn't capable, you know."

We had stopped our walk and were looking directly at each other, as Hector needed his umpteenth lamppost and I was beginning to regret my decision of bringing my new doggy friend along.

"Never be surprised at being surprised, Harry," she said loftily, as if she had invented the quotation.

"You're being silly, Mrs Meadows. Now, if the two of you wouldn't mind, I'd like my all-day breakfast, before I meet with your boss and have to listen to his verdict on my corrupt family and the sentence he wants to pass down on me." I hoped that it was now the end of the conversation about George, but it wasn't to be.

"I'm sure it won't be that bad, Harry; only a few years in the Tower, I assume. Seriously though, how about after Haig we take a ministry car to Radlett, and you and I speak to Auntie Loti? Are you up for it?" she goaded me, and I wasn't in the mood to give her the last word.

"Sorry, can't make it. Must return home I've duties to see to. They've had to close the gates at the estate. There were too many virgins queueing, waiting for my return."

Wishing that my imminent departure and the queue were true, I rudely read the sport pages of the Daily Mail as I fed myself and Hector, with the brooding Judith tutting at every mouthful of cholesterol-bursting hash browns that crossed my, otherwise closed, lips.

We returned the sluggish and sated Hector home, then tasted and smelled the delights of the London Underground system on our way to King Charles Street and the Foreign Office.

"Shall we drop the respected titles and adopt the '*tuo* mode, Harry? Is that all right with you?"

"*Certomente, perché no,*" I replied, showing I, too, knew a little Italian. I accepted his hand as he crossed his suite and met us at the double doors of what would have passed for a reception room at many a palace. The walls were draped in portraits of Empire building individuals. Clive of India, Wolfe, Cook, Rhodes, and others I recognised from somewhere in my dim past. Hung there against unfamiliar backgrounds, along with memorabilia and trophies, gathered from around the world when Britain ruled it, covering every piece of furniture that filled this cluttered place and leaving no room for much else. I was, however, shocked to find a portrait of his infamous relative; Field Marshal Douglas Haig.

David Haig was in his late fifties and used glasses to read, putting these in his top jacket pocket as he proffered his greeting. Shorter than myself by about three or four inches, balding, and not carrying my excess bulk, he wore a brown suit, which I found disconcerting.

Daniel Kemp

"Coffee, tea, or something a little stronger? Please take a chair, both of you. Good to see you again, Judith. Keeping Harry here busy, are you?" he asked, in a practised diplomatic way that needed no reply.

"Don't suppose you've got an Isle of Jura single malt floating around the building anywhere, have you?" I enquired, reckoning that I might as well be comfortable in my hour of need.

"Ah, forgot that! Had it delivered specially after Judith's memo. A large one I presume? And a coffee for you, Judith? Are you driving today, or tubing it?" he inquired, as he took his place behind the ostentatious desk that took up half of one wall, flanked either side by floor-to-ceiling windows with the same ill-fitting net curtains found in every ministerial office.

"Well, I was going to speak to you about that. We wanted to borrow a pool driver, and car. There is a lead I want to chase down in Hertfordshire." Judith was not slow in coming forward with her request.

"Hmm...let's see how far we get first, shall we?" He replied.

So, this was where she had picked up the habit. Imitation either being a form of flattery or a sense of insecurity, which I was sure Judith did not suffer from.

He buzzed for the refreshments, and moments later a seductively attractive vision of womanhood appeared, no more than twenty-five and oozing sex appeal. Judith kicked me.

"Watch out, Harry! You'll need a bib...you're dribbling!" She was right, I almost was.

"Come now, Judith. We men have to have distractions, otherwise life would be too unbearable. Don't you agree, Harry?" David had noticed my reaction, and Judith's jibe.

"Where's the paperwork? I'll sign up now!" I laughingly replied, rubbing away my shame from the point where her foot had connected whilst feigning pain and injury. "Ouch, that's some kick you've got there, my sweet."

With the goddess's departure, the room took on a more serious atmosphere as Judith, at David's request, began her report. She covered everything in fine detail, referring to her infamous book most often of

159

her own volition, but occasionally after David's intervention, asking how she had arrived at certain conclusions. It was an interactive conversation between just the two of them, leaving me feeling the same as the faces staring from the walls: inanimate and lifeless. My past was being dissected, without a chance for complaint. After an eternity of dismembering the Paterson family with facts and assumptions, none of which I could refute or argue against, Judith's speculation reached out further than those previously discussed.

"I would like to hypothesise a bit here, and take a risk. Let's imagine that Paulo and *Garden* are the same man, and Tanya was never a Russian agent, she was Paulo's make believe one, created by him to cover her defection. The first question my theory throws up is - where would Paulo send Tanya to run to, the day she skipped away? My answer is: straight to Maudlin's front door.

Whatever information he gave the Kremlin came from elsewhere. Whether or not this was damaging to us is unclear, but based on the evidence of what he supplied us, all thoroughly substantiated and proven, I would say of little value. Let's, for the sake of my theory, say he gained prominence first in the KGB, and then in his political life through other means, against targets other than our own. We know that he is a resourceful person, careful and precise. We can also presume, with some certainty, that he is rich and has had, over the years, little chance to spend that money on anything other than buying influence and power.

He could not have existed all these years through bribery alone, people and enemies he would have used and made on his way up, he would have to eliminate. If you remember, there was conjecture over the death of a head of the KGB a good many years back, just when Paulo was establishing himself. A heart attack, they reported. They're not going to tell the world anything else, are they? Particularly if I'm right and he was murdered, or assassinated.

If I *am* right, Harry, Maudlin was the best case controller there has ever been. Not only has Paulo escaped detection in his place of work, but his identity has been kept from everyone here and therefore has never been compromised. I don't want to vilify or malign our own Secret Service, but I don't believe Maudlin trusted them. Maybe he shared his sources that he ran in Ireland with them, and that was how the Republicans got wind...who knows. Maybe he was put off by those who were uncovered in the sixties as being tainted bright red. Something did it for him and this is where I'm going to shock you, H, so hang on for dear life.

I think Tanya was pregnant, and Paulo wanted his father to raise his child here in England as a punishment for what he saw as his mother's abandonment in Leningrad. There's no way that he wanted Tanya and a child to hold him back, and it wasn't for the obvious reasons. He didn't love Tanya when they married; she must have forced it on him, or forced *herself* on him. One day he, or she maybe not, don't think they were that progressive in those days, so I'll stick with *him* Paulo fancies a quick leg over and, by hook or by crook, Tanya falls. Now...if either of you two can tell me that, if you were in love with someone who carried your child, you could then leave her in a country when she was unable to speak the language and knew nobody, then never visit or contact them for fifty-four or five years, I would call you a liar. Not even someone who's as wrapped up in himself as you, Harry, would be that callous for so long. Nobody could, therefore he couldn't have loved her in the first place. And if there was no child, then why did Maudlin become involved?" She sat back, drank her coffee, and waited for the response.

I was the first. "You think it was a boy she had, and that boy grew up to be George, don't you?"

David came in a distant last, only just qualifying, avoiding elimination by a whisker.

"Sorry, you almost lost me there. Do you mean George, the valet-cum-secretary living at Eton Square?"

"Yes, to both of you and there's more. I believe Tanya, is still alive and living in that place I want to visit, about an hour's drive from here in one of your shiny limos, David."

"He's not a murderer," I blurted out.

"Did I say that? If I did, I can't recall it? Again, I've left you standing. You've have only just put the key in the ignition, and I'm racing down the home straight. I was implying H, and I'm sure David was following, that Paulo's weakness was George. He was discoverable, if someone looked hard enough. Think about it. Who could Paulo trust to pass on his information after Maudlin died? He could hardly write directly, could he? Even with Glasnost, after eighty-five, there wasn't that amount of openness. There was still censorship. I think one of the security agencies might have spotted Box 850 on an envelope!"

"What sort of stuff has been passed, then?" I asked, naively.

"Sorry, Harry, we can't go there, I'm afraid. But I *can* tell you that, not so long ago, some government Ministers were implicated. No stronger than that, but we did take precautions. Recently some questionable scientists applied for visas and, following advice from *Garden*, they were refused." David had joined us

"Not linked to the petrochemical industry, were they?" I asked, less naively, and was right. "That's one hell of a supposition to make based on the strength that he calls me by my first name, Judith. That would make him my…what, exactly? My step-uncle? Don't you think he would have said something down the years…claimed a part of the family silver, surely?" I continued.

"Step-uncle, yes, I think that sounds right. Probably best to consult a genealogist to be certain." It was David who ventured a guess and, having now wrenched the conversation away from us two warring factions in front of him, carried on in his assessment.

"You have to understand that what Elliot, with Phillip and Maudlin before him, were doing at Queen Anne's Gate was not conventional everyday banking. It's common knowledge that Coutts are the Queen's bankers, but that's for the civil list money, vulnerable to hackers and other like-minded nosy people. Your ancestors have handled their personal finances, along with the majority of the other Royal houses of Europe, since its conception. The British Government have also had money invested there for reasons they wished kept from the scrutiny of public auditors. You may have wondered why I handle the file and not 'C' directly; that is because the SIS have interests in the bank's dealings, and there may have been a conflict of interests there.

This Department was given the responsibility many moons ago, long before my time. It was in 1981 or '82 that we, here, became increasingly concerned. The information about previous and possible future Ministers being sympathetic to the Soviets was particularly unsettling, especially when it came to foreign policy decisions. There was a great deal of damage to repair from a past administration. The allegations about possible future serving Ministers had to be addressed. We couldn't ban them from holding office... after all, we are a democracy, despite what others may think." There was an almost undistinguishable pause, and although I was not looking directly at him, I sensed a glance in Judith's direction.

"We had to take precautions both ways, in case this was Moscow mudding the waters, so to speak. Judith was brought in for that purpose and the *Garden* file, the uppermost secret file we have, opened for glimpses from her eyes only... without causing ripples, you understand. There are very few definitive facts in all of this, and what there is could be discovered by anyone with access to that file or information about your family and its connection to the bank. That's no disrespect to Judith here. She came with the highest recommendations and clearance. She's very good at her job, but others could do the same research and connect Maudlin to a son born in Spain and evacuated to Russia. However, it's questionable if they would be as competent as Judith finding them in Leningrad! You must explain to me fully one day how you did that, perhaps when we have closed this matter." He turned to Judith and there was a slight bow of the head in recognition of her expertise.

"I think you should indeed follow up on your enquires in Radlett, and by all means take a car. I'll ring down now, and arrange it."

"There is one last thing I would like to say." The irrepressible Judith took her chance to grab the last word. "I'd like to answer Harry's question about the family silver, David, if that's all right?" He nodded his approval to her intervention.

"Suppose George doesn't know that Maudlin was his granddaddy, Harry? Maudlin wouldn't have said, how could he without upsetting the whole apple cart? Auntie Loti couldn't tell him, at least while he was still around, and it would appear that she hasn't said anything since. Maybe that's what Maudlin meant when he told you to bury a secret deep. He'd sworn Loti to secrecy, frightened her somehow... let's go and find out, eh?"

Chapter Twenty-Four

Lime Trees

The natural beauty of the lime trees that lined the avenue where the wife of Maudlin's illegitimate son once lived, was not reflected by the houses shadowed by their majestic spreading branches. We had taken the diversion simply to satisfy my curiosity, but it was not gratification that I found hidden there; only more unanswered frustrations. The sterile concrete forecourts that at one time, presumably, were complemented by those trees, now provided barren space on which row after row of vehicles were displayed. It was not a scene that I had imagined or had hoped for.

On very few occasions I had felt sorrow in my life. At Maudlin's funeral was one time, when it was for others rather than myself, and at Phillip's, when again, the full measure of that emotion escaped me. Nevertheless it was there. Perhaps, felt more by those mourners who wore it gravely on their faces as I listened to their grief. I had the misfortune of attending three more funerals before the one that had hit me the hardest and showed me what real wretchedness felt like... that of my mother's. I had arranged everything for that day, not wanting, or inviting, my father's participation. As I sat there, next to Judith, in the Ministry car, filled with morbid grey thoughts that matched the skies, I realised that I had wrongly blamed him for her passing. Although I accepted death as an end to mortal life I did not accept it as her ultimate end.

Today, in raking over the past, I had travelled part of the route that his and my brother's body would take on their return home to the place of their burial. The desolation of what must have been a better area when Maudlin choose this part of Hertfordshire as home to his grandson, had struck me with the misery that I had managed to avoid through, perhaps, my entire life. I despaired for Tanya and early George if it had always been so, but reason dictated otherwise. There hadn't been the same number of cars in those days that necessitated such grey, concrete provisions, and people took pride in where they lived. Rows of coloured plastic bins were never needed, and councils tended verges and swept pavements not like today, in this part of the changed world.

When Alice died, I had managed to keep my feelings hidden through the days of preparations leading up to her entombment, as there had been so much to organise and occupy my mind. Her family was vast and widespread. There were eight brothers and sisters with fourteen grandchildren scattered around the globe, all of which I had not only to contact, but first find out where they all were. I enlisted the help of my own sisters and brothers in this endeavour, but they, like me, had never been acquainted with each and every one of mother's family. I searched address books in hope of enlightenment, but against no name was there a note of relationship. I delved into everything I could think of, and again came up short. She had often spoken, with pride, of the numbers in her family, but never committed them to paper. Frustrated, I wondered why.

I tried to remember who it was that suggested her widowed sister Evelyn as the saviour in my quest, as it was to her that I turned and finally the grief inside me was released. I have no answer as to why, in her presence, I bawled my eyes out like a child, but I wished I did. It would have answered many questions that I had hidden away, somewhere out of reach. I had spent many hours with her late husband, and respected him highly. Perhaps that was the reason. Maybe it was because she had been the one I remembered beside my mother's bed the most, or maybe it was just her manner in submitting to the inevitable that was collapsing her world and about to collapse mine.

"You've shouldered the responsibility for too long, Harry. You should have let Elliot help although I agree with you, he would have been useless in this matter. A mind always distracted by something or other. Why haven't you let him do some of the arrangements?" she argued gently as I made excuses, never revealing the reasons for the blame that I had showered on him.

This disappointing place from which now, belatedly, Tanya had escaped, had caused me to visit that part of me that closed doors on the irretrievable past. I began to feel the loss of those that I should have been more understanding of and closer to.

"Let's get going, shall we?" I addressed my accuser and instigator of that egotistic label, who sat beside me. Judith had been right and I wrong, in asking for this diversion.

The depression had not fully left me on our arrival at Leighton House Lodge, advertised as a Luxury Residential Retreat masquerading, in all its grandeur, as the last place for those with less time to live with self-respect than the rest of us. I had expected very little from this Tuesday's afternoon drive north of London. I had not, however, anticipated the neglect I had seen at number 108, the address that Judith had discovered as being owned by Loti Martins. It was the last semi-detached house in the road and possibly the most dilapidated, although its overgrown and uncared-for front garden covered most of its ignominy. The property had been empty for over two years, with the 'For Sale' sign seeming to have taken root, sprouting red flowers that resembled the camellia bush some distance beyond, under a laburnum tree whose branches brushed against the windows.

During the journey I had quizzed Judith on how she had obtained the address of the house. Now I wished that I could believe she had made a mistake, but knew that desire would not be granted.

"It was easy, Harry. I've an old school friend who's the head buyer for Fortnum's. I've always been one to keep in touch with old school chums... never know when they might come in handy. Turns out

George is in the habit of sending presents of one kind or another, when he can't find the time to take them himself. I got all the information from her."

The drive through the gates of the Retreat resembled, on a smaller scale, the wide expanse of manicured grass at Harrogate Hall, but the happiness I felt at home was impossible to be replicated or imagined here, in order to dispel the torment that troubled me. What was there to find here of benefit, if George was to be implicated in the murders, or if Loti was married to my step-something Paulo? How could that knowledge compare to where Maudlin had left them? Was there an advantage in knowing that? Not to me, I doubted.

* * *

She was seventy-four, the matron told us, and I am ashamed to say that momentarily I wished that she had added 'senile and suffering from dementia' but she did not. The opposite, apparently, was true. "She's in good health and spirits and used to visitors… she is a very popular person, and a pleasure to have here." A part of me was relieved to hear that she had fared well, despite all of what Judith suspected and what I had witnessed. The rest of me, however, held on tightly to the apprehension that weighed me down.

"Follow me… I'll take you to her. She will be surprised that she has such important visitors as yourselves. I'm not sure that we have ever had a Lord here before and, of course, I've told no one, as you re-quested." It was Judith who replied *Thank you.*

As we trailed behind her, all my trepidation seemed to hit me at once. There was nowhere to hide from the truth. Was Maudlin a user of people for his own good, a sham who had fooled me, somebody not worthy of Judith's praise and my own admiration? Or, was he that knight in glistening armour I so wished he was? Was George capable of deception for forty years and, if so, could he really have killed my father and brother? Was I the next one, because of the way Maudlin had treated him and Loti? Was it as simple as that?

"Hello Loti, these people have come to see you. Lord Harry Paterson and his wife, Lady Judith. They would like to speak to you in private, if that's all right. Would you be so kind, ladies?"

The matron of the home stood motionless, her right arm extended towards the door we had just come from, ushering away the other residents seated in the conservatory, all dressed in white with their lawn bowls in carriers at their feet. I was wondering if they had finished their game or had not even started, due to the rain that had been on and off throughout our drive. The overhead clouds threatened more when the lightning strike of my married status was thunderously announced. A part of me enjoyed it, the part that enjoyed subterfuge and deception... what else did you expect me to say?

A tall, thin, dark-haired woman, with a black headband holding back her untidy tousled hair, rose somewhat awkwardly from near the centre of the gathered group. She looked sheepishly towards me and quietly said. "I'm pleased to meet you, Lord and Lady Paterson. I'm Loti Martins. It's not about my son George, is it? He's all right, isn't he?" she gently asked, with a heavy frown. A perfectly innocent thing to ask if you were unaware of the facts behind this visit. However, Judith had been right. It was no longer a theory and that gave the reason for us being here a whole new perspective.

The source from whom all knowledge sprung had no sympathetic disposition that day, and was not in the mood for idle chitchat. In the short time that it took for the forlorn, disappointed and inquisitive bowlers to leave, Judith had selected her tactics; a full-on frontal assault, covered on one flank by the fantasy of peerage, and the other by fear of repatriation. Her only saving grace was that she had waited until we were alone.

"Your son is fine... he is not the primary reason for our visit. You are Tanya Malonovna Kuznetsoka. Your marriage to Paulo Sergeyovitch Korovin, and also, your subsequent defection from the Soviet Union into the arms of Lord Maudlin Paterson in 1956, are the reasons for our being here. Would you like to explain what transpired to make that happen! When you have finished, we would appreciate if you filled in the details of what you and George have been up to in all those years. The future of both of you remaining in this country depends on it!" The barriers were breached and we were through the first defences. I wondered what both of them held in reserve.

She would, I guessed, have been an attractive girl and, indeed, woman as she had matured. Now the lines around her forehead and mouth rejected those looks, but could not deny what once, must have been. She stood upright and proud, every inch shouting determination and resilience. Maybe Judith had been wrong in her assumption that it had been Paulo's impulse alone that had led to George's conception. The women who stood before us was more than capable to decide on her own life's direction. She was smiling. A grin, that not only lightened those heavy lines on her face and made her brown eyes twinkle, but made me smile in return, as if we had both discovered something pleasant and satisfying to share.

"It would seem that you are right. There is much we must speak of, but the idea of sending me back to Russia is not one of them. Perhaps the first should be an explanation of who exactly you are, as I know that Lord Paterson here is not married. I have followed the family history for many years, sir, and know you are still single. If I was younger I would propose, and not take no for an answer! Your full title now, I believe, should be Earl of Harrogate, the same as Maudlin was when I arrived. Another veritable catch for a lucky woman. I have always imagined you were like your great-grandfather Maudlin in that way.

He had a harem of women around him, always a different one on his arm when I saw him, and I'm betting you're just the same? I would guess you are here because of your father and your brother's deaths. I am not laughing because of that… of course I'm not. It's because it has taken you so long to find me. Maudlin did well for his son Paulo, and for me. Now, it's George who deserves the accolade for all that he has done. Perhaps that is what we should speak of, eh, whoever you are?"

My smile had not been misplaced in any sense, particularly as she had found out Judith's lie. However, it was not just the two of us that were sharing the joke. As I glanced towards the interrogator she, too, was giggling, and was not averse to admitting her mistake.

"I apologise for misleading you...I shouldn't have done that. My name is Judith Meadows, and I work for the Foreign Office. I thought it might worry you if I had declared that when I rang. It was simpler to allow the woman who I spoke to on the telephone to assume that I was Lady Paterson, but that was wrong of me. As for deportation...that has never been a consideration. I expected that it would have been harder to get you to admit to being the person you have been forced to portray for so long. I expect your husband and son are very proud of you. You are right. We are here to find out if you can assist us in Harry's loss through memories of Maudlin and his friends, in order to protect Harry here from becoming the third Paterson to be murdered, even though it has not been reported in the newspapers or on television. Shall we start all over, and this time try to be friends?" Judith, holding an olive branch, was a surprise to me.

Tanya grimaced as she lowered herself back in her chair. Whether it was the news of murders or what I thought I detected as a stiff back, or both, I was not sure, but did not have to wait long to find out. "Are you all right?" Finally, I had an opportunity and the courage to speak.

"Yes, thank you. I suffer from rheumatism. I have cortisone injections for it but nothing helps, especially in the damp air of today. Most of us here do. That's why you found us inside, and not outside on the green." She straightened the cushions on her chair to support her back, easing herself slowly into the comfort they provided. I found the resilience I required.

"Would you prefer that we address you as Loti, or Tanya? It's all the same to us. We want you to feel comfortable in all this, and I'll be grateful for your help. There are many things missing in what we're trying to put together over Elliot and Edward's death...my only hope is you." It was a genuine statement, not meant to counterbalance Judith's abrasive opening, but it did no harm to endear myself to her.

"You are not dissimilar to Lord Maudlin. He was a polite and caring gentleman as well, gracious, I used to say. He was never demeaning in his attitude to either of us. I owe him everything, as does George. It broke my heart when he died, but I always understood why George had to go, and I never questioned it.

I would prefer Loti; it is the name I'm known as here. Tanya was in a different time, an unhappy time, one I'm not sorry to have left behind. Would you like me to start in Leningrad, or my escape when the ambassador's wife let me out of her sight in Harrods, in 1956? To be brutally honest to both of you, it will come as a relief. I've never been able to open my mouth about it for over fifty years. You don't know how hard that's been for a chatty person like me…you really don't." There was a pause in the conversation, neither Judith or I knowing who should start, and where to begin. However, Loti had not quite finished; she had a request.

"Now that you have found me, I presume that I am no longer the threat in Paulo's life that George goes on about so much. Could you, Lord Harry, consider allowing me to come with George to the funeral? I know that he would appreciate that, and I've never been able to say thank you for all Lord Maudlin did for us. It will be good to reveal the truth to my son who still believes me to be his aunt."

"Please, call me Harry," I said as I nervously looked at Judith, wondering if we had overstepped the mark and jumped too many hurdles before they needed to be jumped.

She was an affable, engaging woman, obviously sociable and apparently full of life. All this reconfirmed my confidence in Maudlin and restored my hopes in the closure of all that enveloped me. My one concern remained with George, whose name I saw Judith confine to that ominous red and black book of hers, underlining it heavily. As to what I would do with Tanya at the funeral, I left that at the back of my mind, to revisit another day.

Chapter Twenty-Five

Forget-Me-Nots

"The shared apartment block at 2397 Baskov, in District 19 of the City of Leningrad, had been progressively plagued by ever increasing numbers of rats for the three exceptionally harsh winters leading up to 1956. The sewers had frozen in places, and the stench of effluent and the screech of rodents filled the Arctic blasts of icy air that whirled endlessly around, never moving for months.

Paulo had money, and at first had bought special rat catching dogs, which soon ran away after seeing how many rats there were and the size of them. Then, when his Spanish mother's condition worsened, he made friends with chemists and some less qualified and legitimate bribing them for extra medicine or the like, and getting from them the poison that I used to pretend that I was going blind. That's how we fooled the *polits*...our name for the Cheka...those who checked everything, including his reason for bringing me with him to England."

Slowly, the corners and the side-pieces of Judith's jigsaw puzzle were being put in place by Loti, as we sat and listened whilst the hours ticked by. We were invited and accepted the invitation to stay for dinner. Apparently, we were told, it would please the others greatly to dine with a Lord, which Loti rectified quickly.

"He's an Earl as well you know, tell them that. Their tongues won't stop wagging long enough for them to eat!" She winked at me, revelling in knowing more than Matron, conspicuously happy as she took my arm and led me to the dining room and her collection of wide-eyed friends. At the end of an agreeable meal, the two of us followed Loti to her spacious rooms, where I could not stop myself from passing comments on some of the refinements.

"Wow, that's more a cinema screen than a television, very hi-tech, I must say. Bet those speakers blast out a noise. Don't you keep everyone awake with all that? Must have cost a bob or two!"

"It was bought by my George, and so was the smaller one in my bedroom. They're both high-definition, but I expect you've got that as well. Brilliant for watching certain films on Sky. Keeps me on the ball, does George. He just updated my computer. Nothing wrong with the old one, I told him, but he wants me to keep abreast of all the modern things going on. He says it keeps my mind active, and keeps me young at heart." There was a broken accent to her speech which, although her excellent English disguised it, could still be heard.

"I'm being a bit intrusive, I know, but does George pay for all this? Or did Maudlin provide for you?" I asked, with a degree of shame.

"Lord Maudlin provided for me throughout my life, as I told you. He left me a house and a tidy sum of money, but I had employment, you know, and it was he, my employer, that left George and I well off. The legacy is managed by a firm of advocates. You'd have to ask George the name…he deals with it all. I'll tell you something funny about this place though. They only invoice us all here every three months in advance - they don't want to have to refund large amounts to relatives, if we don't last longer than that. They only speak of next month's excursions, never next year's," she said, laughing as she did so.

"Not a cheap place to live, I suppose, but they do seem to look after you well." Judith ineptly put in her pennyworth.

"No, it's not," she replied defiantly, then added less severely, "I think it's just short of four thousand a month…but you're right, we are well cared for. George tells me he is at Eton Square. Will you move in there now, sir, become a banker?" She was able briefly, to ignore Judith, but was ambushed again only moments later.

The extent of her knowledge of Maudlin and the Paterson's was vast, as was her memory, aided by the shoe box she carried into her sitting room from the bedroom. In it were documentations of all manner of things. The original marriage certificate in Cyrillic, George's birth papers carrying an Irish Carmelite seal, a contract of employment drawn up and signed by a Feydor Grogonsky, and, to Judith's wonderment, the letter that Paulo had addressed to Maudlin as an introduction.

"Thank you for holding on to so much. It will help enormously," Judith delightedly exclaimed, carefully scrutinising it all.

"I'm nobody's fool, not even Paulo's. I trusted no one. I got everything in writing and kept everything I could, it was my way of getting guarantees. Paulo had a way with words, and he could tell you things that you'd never believe from anyone else. I'd seen him do it at local meetings of Bolsheviks, or at parties with superiors in that KGB of his.

He would praise them all, pledging his obedience to the red flag, telling them what they wanted to hear. The next minute he would be telling me a different tale of how they were fools, and how one day he would rule them and repay the Paterson's for their good works and kindness. He would do wonderful things for England, he said; he would make *nana* and England proud. What was I to think? Would you have believed him...that his *nana*, his dad, was an English Lord? I went along with it all because I wanted out of that repressive place, that country where you were told what to do, what to think, what to wear. Paulo would never have considered me as an equal in Russia, so I twisted his arm a little. I wanted a little protection, and a tie to him if his arm hurt in the future and he wanted rid of me and a child. A form of insurance, you could say." There was a single-mindedness that was apparent to us both. Judith's indecision about who had made the first move in the relationship had been answered.

I'm not sure which of the two of them was the more excited Tanya in her joyous recollections, or Judith in her reverence to all that she heard, but I can say for sure that some things became clearer to me. It was well past midnight when all of us became confused again.

"Loti, do you recognise this?" Judith asked, showing her the coded paper I had given Judith.

"Yes, it was the second letter Paulo instructed me to give Lord Maudlin. I imagined it was a secret code when he showed me. Was it?" Tanya asked.

"I was hoping you could have told me, and if it was, explained how you used it to contact Paulo?"

"You think this old lady was a spy, don't you? That's why you're here Foreign Office lady, isn't it? You can't be serious!" laughing loudly she replied.

The drive back south to Clapham Common was both swift and full of conjecture, not least the subject of overtime for our driver who, despite our assurances that we would both gladly sign his docket, refused to stop referring to it.

"They're cutting back everywhere, haven't you noticed? They will want written affidavits from the three of us just to keep my job, let alone the extra time. I made it three this afternoon, when we left. I'll be lucky if I'm home in Hammersmith by three, and I'm starving. Can't eat at this time of morning, no good for me...or the wife, if you get my meaning. Flatulence you see hers, not mine! Oh well," he muttered, when neither of us joined his laughter.

"I best leave a timed message on the FO drivers line when, and if, I ever get home. You'll have to add another half an hour on my time sheet when you sign me off. I'll try me best to be in me front door by then. Bet you'll be in for a ragging from the boss for keeping me out for so long. Anyway, hope it was worthwhile. I don't like seeing our own in trouble over nothing, do you?" he added solicitously, before recalling other occasions when he, or unfortunately for us, other drivers had been out for after-hours' expenses.

There were many in his repertoire, and neither of us felt cruel enough to beg him to stop relating. "Once, you know I had an SAS escort, back and front all the way from Portsmouth to Durham. Three and half hours we did it in. Flat out hundred miles an hour, police outriders on all the lights!"

"Exciting," I said, and regretted it as soon as I had done so.

"Bloody worn out I was, I can tell you!"

I felt sorry for whoever the passenger was, but I never voiced my opinion on this story or any of the others, unlike Judith. Oblivious to my own experience and indifferent to Steve's discomfort, she added, "Next time I'll drive. Then I won't have two fools to put up with. Do shut up, man, I'm trying to think!"

Steve decided that discretion was, indeed, the better side of valour, and kept his own counsel for the remainder of our journey. As for me, the few words that Tanya had spoken when we were alone, about George's valiant role in deserving a Knighthood, kept rolling around in my mind. Judith had sought permission to use the bathroom, and Tanya had quietly confided in me.

"With you not living in London, my Lord, you will not know George well. He has become a secretive man over the years, not even telling his own mother much. He spends a lot of time abroad, mainly Germany, I know that much. I have a photograph of him at the wall in Berlin when they pulled it down." She withdrew the cardboard-mounted snapshot from her box and placed it in my hands, as if it were a prized trophy. "Look at it carefully, sir. What do you see?" she asked, and I had nothing to quell her inquisitiveness.

"Exactly. There *is* nothing to see. No crowds, no television cameras nothing. An empty background, apart from concrete slabs. He took it himself, and I believe it was on the other side, from East Berlin… otherwise, why so empty? I saw the pictures on the television there wasn't an inch of space anywhere. Why not take it where everyone was celebrating? He gave me this, as well; it's a German Bible. He uses my printer when he visits, runs off copies from the pages. Why would he do that if he wasn't working with his father? I'll tell you why, Lord Harry. He's a spy for Lord Maudlin's England and working with Paulo…that's why. I have never forgotten the look on Paulo's face when he said what he did about Lord Maudlin and making England great again. He meant every word…it was a pledge, not an idle wish. You want to know his last words to me, the night before that trip to

Harrods? I'll tell you: *Never forget me, Tanya, because one day I'll be more famous than Lenin and Winston Churchill put together. Watch out for me, from England.*"

Chapter Twenty-Six

Dead-Heading

One of the first English words that Paulo learnt from the old man at the postal office in Leningrad was 'Garden.' At his tender age, everybody was old. Even his own mother was ancient, and as far as his father was concerned, the fact that he was nearing his fiftieth birthday was beyond his youthful comprehension. A colourful *garden*, however, was not. Yuri, a name he was to use himself later in his life, had been a gardener's apprentice on an estate in England before the Great War had started in Europe and he had begun Paulo's education by showing him pictures of how the huge kitchen garden looked, behind the walls that sheltered it and kept it warm.

The young, aspiring, Paulo found a parallel between life and gardening, and he became more aware of the words that Yuri used to describe the art in which he had wanted to prosper, before the world erupted. The sun and the rain were important, of course, but so too was nourishment and care. Knowledge of where best to grow a particular plant and how to prune it, to keep its shape, or to maximise its production.

"Have you ever seen a plot of land that's been left to its own and God's devices, Paulo? All overgrown, with the plants strangling each other?" he asked, then answered without delay, "Of course you have. They're all around you. That's what happens when nature has its own way, without us to supervise and manage it. The world would be in a sorry state without gardeners, that's for sure. Do you know what

God's answer to pruning is? It's war and desolation; that's what it is. A messy way of doing things," he sagely proclaimed. He had forgotten to add an important aspect of prolonging a flowering plant's life before it turned to seed; that of deadheading, allowing the production of more flowers to flourish.

To the ageing and sceptical, more pragmatic, Paulo, life was equivalent to war. The strong must survive at the expense of the weak. He had adopted and followed this philosophy, except for on one occasion; when he failed to spot a shoot left to grow from the base of his rose bush, one that threatened to suck the life out of its host, the merciful Paulo himself. This parasite had no Latin family name that it could be referred to in order to find a cure. Instead, it was homegrown, a Russian variant, a species hitherto unknown, called Dimitriy by his friends, his full patronymic name being Dima Nikolaevitch Lebedov.

Dimitriy was a brute of a man but not physically, in that department, he was not noteworthy at all. He was five foot six and skinny, with thinning white hair vanishing quickly, and thick black-rimmed spectacles that made him feel important. He was not a tyrant with a fear factor; instead, he frightened others by his mental dexterity. He was the type of man that never forgot a thing, especially about an opponent, and he saw competition everywhere. Any idiosyncrasy or fascination, perhaps a fetish or compulsion, a habit or a quirk… whatever it was, he never forgot it. Those who did not care for him, and these were many, told a story that said that his mother never knew she was pregnant until she gave birth in the town Library of Nyvina, whilst reading one of her favourite books.

She had a choice of two, both read a dozen times or more *Private Property* or *The Holy Family* two of Karl Marx's works, who she worshiped and preached passionately about. Dimitriy's father, unfortunately for his son, was of the same inclination. Consequently, Marxism took preference in their house over everything, including sex, and the unexpected baby boy when it came to mother's milk. In truth the story was told in a crude, more obscene way, with no respect to either of the parents, which sounds unkind and cruel, but not if you knew

Dimitriy. That was how he would be, if he found your weakness and had a dislike of you: cruel. He abhorred the version of communism that the young Korovin represented and that had been followed, by many in important positions so unashamedly. The trouble was that he had few friends he could turn to with his protest, and even less when he did. His first approach was to the city council committee on which he served as deputy secretary. He presented his damning indictment in a way that he just *knew* they would approve of,… and *knew* too that they would punish the pretender severely.

"This Korovin, a KGB officer, deals openly with black market racketeers, forcing them to sell him contraband goods through his position. He then entices senior officers to accept these goods as gifts, in order to ingratiate himself into their company. He is anti-communist, an opportunist, and a capitalist amongst our committed community. It is my strong recommendation that he be expelled from the party, and banished to a gulag in Siberia."

The six members of the committee were not privy to the less humanitarian reason for Dimitriy's protests. That they were not solely public-spirited, but more based on revenge and jealousy… a dangerous combination for a man who never forgave or forgot.

The Lebedovs had been relocated to Leningrad when Dimitriy was twenty-two, six years into his proposed elevation of becoming the youngest advising Political Officer to the Politburo in Moscow. He was two years senior to Paulo, whose path he often crossed. There were political meetings and discussions that the two both attended. Dimitriy, new to the city, watched everything and everybody with a view to doing exactly what he saw Paulo doing; cultivating favours within his clique of sycophantic friends. He wanted in, but Paulo refused.

"Comrade, you seem to be well-acquainted with all members of our local congress. I am new to Leningrad and it would help me, not only to settle in, but also to make friends here if you helped me. I have seen you at many meetings that I have attended…allow me to introduce myself. I have ambitions in the political field."

"I heard you speak at the last conclave, Comrade Lebedov. Your type of Marxism, with your own brand of emphasis on the class struggle, is anathema to me. Too many times that has been bred in the houses of envy. Throughout history it has meant the replacement of one dictator by another, and still the poor are the oppressed. Lenin taught us more than that. He taught us to be self-reliant and supportive of one another, not adhering to an unjust philosophy of the idealism of consumption and production. We are practising communists not theorising about life, but living it. We have no room for you," Paulo responded.

Rejection planted anger into a Marxist heart, and after hearing the deliberations of the council on considering his recommendations for Paulo's future, the anger turn to hatred and, in turn, the pledge of retribution.

"We find your objections puerile and fatuous, Comrade Lebedov. Comrade Sergeyovitch Korovin is well known to all of us here, and many within this great city. He is beyond reproach in the execution of his civil duties. We have considered why you have brought this to our attention and concluded that it is for your own selfish ends. Which is something a political official should not contemplate. Our recommendations are to be sent to Moscow, where you will report immediately. We believe that time to evaluate your position, and to meditate on your situation within the party, would be beneficial to all concerned."

By 1974, the increasingly disgraced Dimitriy was further away from the damning tribunal than Moscow, much further, than even they had imagined when they had passed their verdict upon him. He had become the principal political official in the town of Jakutsk, in Siberia, near what Russians call 'The Pole of Cold.' Here, deep in the permafrost, where jackhammers are needed to break the ground, local Yakuts say that if you shout to a friend who's standing a little distance away in winter, your words will be frozen by the wind and your friend will have to wait until the slight thaw of spring to hear what you said. Here, he burst his lungs screaming his protests, but he got nothing for his efforts, as the Yakuts would have told him, had he asked. The nightly prayers he had pleaded to his God to assuage that hunger and quench his thirst for revenge seemed to have been answered, when he came across a convicted drug dealer delivered from Moscow a year before his own exile.

Dimitriy soon tired of the reports he read of the many poets and writers, academics and philosophers who had been abandoned and forgotten here since Stalinist days. There was no profit in such reading only boredom and frustration. His lethargy, however, was lifted after one assimilation class he took where he was approached at its conclusion.

"Comrade Nikolaevitch Lebedev, I am a good communist and do not deserve to be here. I was forced to do some work for the KGB that I am ashamed of." Dimitriy had heard many cries of innocence from the condemned but this one, with the mention of work for the KGB, was not the usual repetitiveness.

"I was a student chemist in the University of Leningrad when I was first contacted by an officer who wanted more of a special medicine for his dying mother. He threatened me into supplying this with fabricated evidence, telling me that he would put that evidence to the local congress to have me barred from my studies. I graduated, and went into agricultural chemistry for the state industry in Moscow, where this same officer found me. This time he wanted an odourless, colourless substance that could be mixed with cocaine, a substance that would kill. He did not tell me who it was intended for, nor did he ask me to supply the cocaine. I extracted the potassium chloride from ordinary fertiliser and gave it to him. The next thing I knew was that I was being suspected of killing the head man of the KGB, and it was the same officer who was accusing me! His name, Comrade...I'm sorry, have I not said? No? It was Sereyovitch Korovin."

Sixteen years passed for Dimitriy in his squalid isolation, watching many of the radicals who had been committed to his care for re-education into the communist regime, pass on from this life. One such inmate was the only one whose death he regretted, and that was not for the life that had gone. It was for the life that was going; his own, never having had the opportunity to present the evidence that died that day in front of the abomination of a man far away in Moscow. Korovin was finally out of reach of Dimitriy's damning, accusing, letters.

In them, he told of the conversations that he had with Paulo's man from Moscow, whilst eating the foul and rancid meat, drinking from the contaminated still, and smoking anything that would burn between his blue, thinning lips. The intense, unendurable cold was the thing that eventually had dulled his protestations, but it had taken many years of tolerating frozen and bent fingers before his pen stopped, and he accepted that nobody was interested. He died the same year that Paulo was expanding his life, an embittered morose man. However, he left his mark, albeit a small one. Paulo might well have put himself forward as the first to recognise the validity in the accepted truth that, 'oak trees grow from tiny acorns'.

Most of us are indifferent to the ways of others in this life. To those not included in this generalisation, some are mildly curious, while others are positively nosy. Curtain-twitchers, gossips, the sort that prefer maligning the ones that live differently to themselves but there is another variety, employed in one secret agency or another, throughout the world. Within the KGB ranks languished the majority of the greatest inquisitive minds the world has ever seen. However, they were arrogantly neglected by their pompous principals, who were more interested in conformity than confrontation. For Paulo, this was fortunate, otherwise he may have had the full weight of the Sixth Directorate on his back instead of the minor department, manned by an Army Colonel and two subordinates. The destination where most of Dimitriy's acorns had found a home.

"Keep it simple," Colonel Vladimir Sokolov told them. "You only have to look at what he has done for us to know there is no truth in it. One liar to another, no doubt. This Lebedov has form in that direction. Nevertheless, it will do no harm to look gently. Be careful! It will be your careers on the line, not mine. He has powerful friends, this Korovin."

Chapter Twenty-Seven

Wistful Ducks on Ponds

"You know that I believe everything Tanya told us, and I believe she knew no more, don't you?" Judith announced. We sat with our own thoughts as we returned to her house, which I had now designated the derisory Kennel. As to who was the principal resident housed within, Hector, or myself I'm not sure! It had crossed my mind to keep what Tanya had told me to myself, secretively, again trying to discover the killer's identity on my own. However, it was an impractical idea when I first set out on that road, and nothing had altered to make it easier. Circumstances, if anything, were stacking up against me.

"Tanya thinks that George is working with his father and spying for us. I think she's right; he's certainly in contact. He's got the Lutheran Bible and takes copies of the plates, the one Peter sent me to make contact with. That means George must be with 'C' on this, and running Paulo together."

"She's a sneaky one, the old girl, isn't she? Wanted you all alone for that one, eh? Anything else you feel you should confess, Harry? Like written confessions to the murders, or something similar?"

"No, ha ha, but there was a photograph taken by the Berlin Wall. Tanya thought it was taken on the wrong side, but there was no evidence," I declared.

"Nor is there anything to back up your belief that Peter and George are together on this. Remember what Paulo said to you when you told him of Trimble's involvement? He said it was old-school, that method of leaving things in churches, and no doubt sounded surprised?"

"A little, I guess, but I could be wrong," I answered.

"I don't think you're wrong, H. Nor do I think that Peter knows about George. George is winging it, Harry, flying solo; and, if I'm right, he hasn't got a parachute, hoping that if he needs one, he can use his dad's. I'm staying up for a while, Harry. I'd invite you to share a dram or two, but I won't. I need to speak to Haig privately, so if you don't mind toddling off to bed, I'll see you later."

I couldn't resist. "Shall I wait in your bed, or in the single one you've given me? Mine would be more intimate, don't you think? You could fall asleep on top of me!"

"I wish you'd be more serious, Harry, and less flippant. It's for your sake that I'm doing this."

"You are aware that it's five in the morning, Judith? I doubt he'll be best pleased, or take your call. But if he does, don't tell him that you're lonely…it will ruin my reputation!"

"Bye bye, Harry. Sweet dreams."

I had been in and out of the bathroom, when I heard her speak into the telephone.

"It's Judith Meadows for Sir David. Mark it *Highly Sensitive* at the top," she demanded authoritatively

I wasn't that tired but hadn't bothered to shave, preferring to simply lay and think about all that had happened since the Sunday of my father's death. That wasn't the only thing that filled my head and kept me from sleep. The other was the trill of the blackbirds in their morning chorus, soon to be joined by the single ring of the downstairs phone.

"Get up, Harry, and make yourself presentable. He'll be here in thirty minutes."

As permanent First Secretary to the Foreign Office, Sir David Haig warranted an apartment in town for the occasions that required him to remain in London, such as war or the immediate threat of it, and perhaps the assassination of the Monarch. Political scandal that could overthrow the elected Government would not be on his list, nor normally the murder of an Earl and his youngest son but, to his annoyance, these were not normal days. He was far too important for trivialities to upset his family life in Oakley Green, just outside Windsor, with his wife and two dogs and his favourite Michelin-starred restaurants in nearby Bray.

Life in London was not as bad as it used to be in the old fashioned, sparsely appointed flats in Dolphin Square let out to his predecessors along with scruffy under-employed spooks on compassionate leave or plotting to overthrow regimes still worth overthrowing. Nowadays he had the converted once hospital in Marsham Street to reside in. At five in the morning, a twenty minute drive from the Kennel of Clapham.

I could smell coffee being prepared, and in the kitchen, from where all the commotion was coming from, a loaf of bread was being sliced, ready for toasting and the spreading of marmalade from the jar that stood benignly beside it. Grey coloured cups and saucers, that I had not seen before, were being dusted, and knives in white lace napkins rested on three plates, arranged around a cut-glass butter dish, a nicety I had not been privy to before.

"Very artistic, Judith. Part of your apology for dashing my invitation to sexual bliss, is it?" I yawned, and therefore lost the impact I hoped my sarcastic remark might convey.

"I will seriously have to consider adding 'delusional' to my assessment, H," she scornfully retorted, before adding, caustically, "No more impudence... now is not the right time. Do go somewhere else, you're in my way here. And if you have to smoke in the lounge, open a window."

Duly reprimanded, I sulked away, muttering loudly enough for Judith to hear, "I hope he brings that Goddess to brighten the place up." I made my own tea in the mug I had previously been allocated on my arrival at the Kennel, as David sipped his strong smelling coffee and Judith buttered his toast. He set about explaining why his presence had been necessary both at Marsham Street and here on this sunny spring morning, now mysteriously devoid of songbirds, except the one being fawned upon.

"Judith feels that you should be brought up to date and given information that I was unable to declare yesterday in my office." He had come alone and I can't say that he had my full attention, as I expected another deluge of senseless facts with no distractions over which to fantasise.

"She says it will help you to focus and concentrate more fully." There goes that psychoanalytical mind of hers on its travels, again, I thought.

"Twelve days ago, the Friday before your father was killed, I received a message marked *Garden*. It did not go through the normal channels of SIS first. In it, were the names of two specific high-ranking officials of the European Parliament's Trade Committee, listed as being operatives in the pay of the Russian Mafia. It contained photographic evidence of money changing hands for, what we confidently believe, was information into the research that you were involved with; petrochemicals. The men were the same Willis and Howell who met your late father at Harrogate, when Peter Trimble introduced them to him, and the intervention into the company you're now employed with was first discussed. They were both arrested immediately, and Judith and I feel that was the reason your father and brother were killed; not as revenge, but as a way of finding out how *Garden* passed on his messages to us, or to me in this particular case. The idea must be to uncover *Garden* and stop further information coming our way...perhaps implicating someone closer to home."

"Could it be a set-up, the money, and Willis and Howell?" I asked, fully attentive.

"Unfortunately, no! In 2007, my office received direct warnings about leakages from fields in which this country excels: your industry, in scientific development, and in pharmaceuticals. A couple of years ago, strange occurrences happened to both Willis and Howell. Willis's car was broken into and his briefcase, which he had inadvertently left on display, was stolen. Then, Howell was arrested in Dresden for being drunk whilst driving. He had benevolently given his driver the night off, and he too had department material with him. Both of them explained the situations admirably and, after due consideration, were allowed to continue in their jobs. The consideration that we gave to the situation was driven by Peter. He thought rightly, in my assessment, that by allowing them to continue, the damage could be limited by the observance of their contacts. Interrogation would then reveal what had been divulged."

I interrupted the nonsense I was listening to. "So you had them and let them go, and because of that you're telling me that my father and brother lost their lives. Is that it?" I angrily accused not Haig, but Judith, looking directly at her for the answers.

"It's not as simple as that, Harry. It never is," she answered apologetically, as I detected a deep sense of regret in her voice.

"Well, tell me how complicated it got, then!" I directed my accusations at Haig, as images of trench warfare came into my mind. With eyes wide open he climbed the bloodstained wall, and over the parapet he charged all in the cause of freedom from tyranny or, in this instance, if not the great sacrifice made by so many in the Great War, protection of our resources.

"Look, Harry…these things have to be judged on merit. We never had enough on either of them to make a case. All *Garden* had was suspicion at first, until two weeks ago when he was certain. You've got to realise that we sponsored their original idea in involving ourselves in that company. We were willing to go the extra mile with them because we trusted them, and we didn't want to believe anything different. Peter did say, on record, that he had personal concerns over the acquisition, but not over their particular involvement. We all made mistakes, Harry. We all do."

"No one could see it happening, Harry. Not even Elliot, when he found those ledgers." Judith and I were on our own once more, ambling aimlessly across the Common with Hector running free ahead. The regret I had detected whilst Haig had been present resurfaced, but this time, with an added explanation.

"If we had the gift of foresight, maybe we would be more circumspect in certain relationships we make or conclusions we come to. I'm about to spill my heart to you, Harry…so don't mock me, or make any contentious remarks, please." We had stopped at a hollowed seat-shaped trunk of a fallen tree, a place she chose to disseminate her life to me, trying to make her own sense of it all. The sun was on our backs, but that was not the only source of warmth for me. Being the special guest to her hidden revelations warmed me more.

"I met Tony at university, about twelve years ago, now. He was younger than me by six months, and I called him 'Toy' for short. We were both in groups that seemed to gel together regularly. To be honest, I fancied his mate more than him, but he was never interested. Got off with someone else I forget her name…well, that's not true, but it's to cover my shame, just in case you couldn't control yourself. He was like you, in someways. He was not quite so flippant, but untroubled and unconcerned, certainly. Another similarity was his branch of discipline chemistry. The two of you would have got on well, and would have had lots to discuss, Maybe you two would have built your own atom bomb in that laboratory of yours. That's what he was really interested in, you see, bombs, and how they were made. He joined the Territorials whilst still at uni and was away every fourth weekend on courses, or what he called 'his banging weekends'. He would tell me of the sophisticated American equipment he would use; remote-controlled machines they could send into situations instead of men, and how the British Army were to get them. And, of course, the body armour they were promised, but never got. It was all done to calm my fears, my anxieties for his life, although he seemed to have none. He was a good-looking man with exuberance and energy, exciting to be around, with an enticing personality and intelligence. I fell in love, Harry. I couldn't do anything else.

He signed up for the regular Army, passed all their boards, and was commissioned a Captain. Within nine months this was in November 2001, he was with the Special Services in Afghanistan. He wrote, or called me, which was worse because every time the phone rang I thought it could be his father or mother and the news would be bad. I should have walked away, Harry. No sane person looks death in the face every day, as he did. My father told me once how he measured bravery. He said there were two kinds. One was irrational, spontaneous, *heat of the battle* stuff. 'You're pinned down by machine-gun fire when someone charges the pillbox, in open ground, and blows it to high heaven.' The other sort was more calculated, fully conscious of the risks to yourself. 'You've had time to weigh up the situation and death is the odds-on favourite, but still you go in, putting the lives of others before your own.'

They had said that they were short on trained men and equipment, and so it was to be a quick turnaround. They had ten days leave maximum and they counted from the day you set off! All heart, that Blair, and the rest of them, with their free wheeling holidays up each others' bums. I think it was round about this time that he declared he found God, the sanctimonious prick. Next thing he was the Middle East expert…the only thing he was expert on was pissing on other people. I'm sorry…I got into one, didn't I?

I married Tony on that leave; I put all that my brain told me away. I'd even told myself that I would be a widow, a brave dead soldier's wife, but nothing and nobody could stop me from doing that. He was posthumously promoted to Major, and the citation read something along the lines of *'in honour of his thoughtless bravery.'* Tony was among many good men that died. Had they have known the truth, and not what Blair and his cronies peddled, do you think they would have gone, Harry? I wish my Tony hadn't. He was too good to die, and leave me."

Chapter Twenty-Eight

Harvesting

The meeting in Moscow had unnerved Paulo, a sensation he rarely felt. He had lived on the edge all his life in one way or another, but this was different, and much closer to home. The kneeling figure of John the Steadfast was a last-resort card to play, and nothing in his son's life had indicated its need. The description given to Paulo of the depositor of that print in St Anslems did not match the ones he had been given of George since he had first seen his son in Maudlin's photographs, but it came close to another. George had used Grönwohld on several occasions, forwarding on Jack's insights into the English commercial and political life, when his father had notified him as to which hotel to leave his messages.

Paulo's friends, both in Russia and the Middle East, avidly embraced Jack's company's products in ever-increasing numbers. Mr Simmons grew rich investing his money in further projects, as did Paulo with the commissions he made. George had last used the drop-off point eight months earlier, and had been described by Dietmar as no different to the other times. A man in his late forties or early fifties, about five foot ten inches, with black hair, hazel eyes, an average build and a goatee beard nothing like the description of this caller, but very much like the same person Paulo had heard of years ago. The other difference to the man, on this occasion, was that he had wanted to be seen. George had not.

Since Maudlin's death, Paulo's motives for assisting the English Secret Services had changed slightly. Money had ceased to be one of his incentives, since George had been given a position in the Paterson home in 1970, and, he had accepted as the truth that Maudlin could not go on indefinitely siphoning off money from wherever it was that his father was finding it. He had no knowledge of a private bank, nor did he make a connection to George's name. Had he done so, who knows the outcome?

Another incentive had gone completely: Maudlin. Paulo had great regard for the *Old Man*, considering himself a 'chip off the old block,' as he father had once declared him to be. He believed it, and took pride in his words. Now, however, his reasons for continuing were twofold; one being pride in his success and undoubted ability, the other the safety and welfare of his son. He was caught in a situation that he had made, that much was true, however, at its onset, not even he could have seen its full implications.

How could he unite himself and his son? He certainly could not bring George to Russia, not without exposure. George would not be able to withstand the onslaught of interrogation that would come his way. As far as he knew, George may well have discovered that the Aunt Loti that Maudlin had invented was his mother; and then his agent *Mother* would be discredited, along with himself. Defection was never a course that would cross the mind of a man so self-absorbed and conceited in pride. That, to him, would mean admitting failure, and no amount of money stashed away could make up for failure. No, there was more to do in his motherland than risking everything for his own survival. There was more work to do in defeating communism. As a consequence of this forthcoming defeat, Paulo could make whatever he had in Switzerland ten times over. He decided that he would use that bank account to make his wishes come true.

By the late eighties and into the nineties, 'Glasnost' and 'Perestroika' were the words in vogue, and Paulo followed his friend with the port-stain birthmark closely behind the banner that he carried. The trader in Paulo had no wish to be too close to either side in what he could see as the oncoming confrontation. He knew it was coming, because he was going to arrange it. He met with a worried General, always preferring single numbers to consort with, when he was considering the craft of conspiracy.

"Comrade General, the Berlin Wall has come down, but the barriers are going up. The economy has become stagnated, and all we hear from the Union of the Soviet States is *give us freedom, give us self-determination*. It will happen, and soon, Comrade. Can you imagine what will become of the military, the cutbacks, because we won't be able to afford to maintain what we have now? Can you imagine the unrest throughout the Union, when all the technicalities are being considered and the rebels want more than we can possibly give? Could it ever be right that this nation of ours, with the most mineral and energy deposits in the world, gives them up to help create democracies on our borders? We have, Comrade, a quarter of the world's fresh water in our Mother Russia. Should we give murdering greedy thugs access to this, in this federation of ours? We know the Americans and their allies in the West...we know them well. Do we want adversaries on our borders? Have you not heard the war drums in Chechnya, the rumblings in Poland to join NATO? I would urge you greatly to consider your support for all this radicalisation. I cannot support you openly, but...well, given the right circumstances...I could support you financially, if the two of us could think of a way that does not compromise me."

A few weeks later, when Paulo had laced the Generals', and several other General's previously unknown or unused private bank accounts, he approached his banner-carrying friend and sympathetic fellow Politburo members with the story of an impending military coup. Again, Paulo was the hero; irreproachable, proving his innocence through beating off accusations by a plotting General who had no evidence of Paulo's involvement. The money, hidden so well by the conspirators that only someone as bright as Paulo could *find*, was traced to a dead criminal figure with known connections to a newly discovered circle of such miscreants, with a structure that distinctly resembled the American Mafia.

The banner of privatisation, along with trade and market liberalisation, was soon taken up by another recipient of Paulo's generosity.

His largesse not only went directly into this man's pocket, but also helped persuade the fortunate plebiscite to cast their votes in his direction in the first ever election held behind the, now fully open, Iron Curtain. The first tentative steps towards complete capitalism were heavy footed ones, taken by the new standard bearer often more consumed by alcohol and other drugs, than forward thoughts along economical lines. Vast sums of cash were taken from a declining Russian economy by those with connections with government officials to further individual ambitions. Stepping ever forward in their wake was a never-hesitant Paulo, reaping the harvest that he had sown. Who else was better placed? Not only firmly cemented in government, but also having friends within the newly discovered Mafioso circle who had more attachments and interests elsewhere, some of which Paulo could facilitate?

* * *

"What are you doing, Harry Paterson... what is it you want?" Paulo asked himself.

* * *

When the mighty Soviet Army left war-torn Afghanistan, it did not relinquish all of its interests there. It left behind many communist sympathisers and others who were forced to follow the creed. One such unfortunate, Mullah Wardak, was of the latter variety. His mother, father, brothers and sisters had been taken from their home by the withdrawing forces and were promised safe return, one by one, in exchange for information Mullah would supply to the departed Russian authorities. He had seven brothers and four sisters, and six of his siblings had been released by the time Harry Paterson saw his first tour of duty in that country in 2002.

It was winter in Afghanistan when Harry had arrived from the rain-sodden barracks at Aldershot, his right knee already swollen and stiff. The cold of Kandahar did not help to alleviate the discomfort that caused his pronounced limp. For the first few days in the Mess, his fellow officers would bow sarcastically on his entrance and announce his appearance with a cacophony of simulated triumphant salute. He tried to protest against the deafening sounds of mouthed trumpets and beating cutlery.

"I'm only an Honourable! Not Lord Paterson, until my father dies," he proclaimed.

Mullah was employed in the kitchens, clearing away the garbage or washing dishes, far from any sensitive duties. However, he managed to hear the greetings, and put a face to the name. His report and description landed on the by then *Colonel General* Vladimir Sokolov's desk, along with his second report, three months later, on the same man. Only this time, Mullah said, the limp had disappeared.

Vladimir, as head of the newly structured FSB, or Federal Security Service, was not that interested in would-be English Lords. It was worth noting, but little else. Certainly not worth the release of any Wardaks, he arrogantly stated to his friend Paulo Korovin.

* * *

"You've put on weight, Harry. If it hadn't been raining, I would never had known." Paulo blessed arthritis and the rain soaked hamlet of Grönwohld.

"Has George given you my secrets, or has he found out about your great-grandfather being his grandfather? Is that why you want to meet me? You must be a very clever man, Harry, to have come this far in discovering me. Did you leave the army and grow fat on a master spy's salary…do the others know of me, too? I shall have to research you thoroughly, find out more, before I agree to your request." Unnerved Paulo told himself.

Chapter Twenty-Nine

Bending Branches

Colonel General Vladimir Sokolov's renowned belief in self-preservation had saved him from Paulo's driven purge, which amongst other things had brought the toppling of the last Head of the now-defunct KGB, who had been implicated in the failed attempt to change the constitution of the government. His promotion and subsequent escalation from his cheerless, bleak office were due entirely to that basic instinct honed over countless years of sitting back and watching his subordinates do the hard graft, whilst taking the glory bestowed on him.

He also excelled at spotting an opportunity whenever he saw one, and head of the fledgling FSB was one he could not resist. The advancing capitalist approach to the outside world, teamed with the escalating corruption within Russia, could result in an untouchable organisation more powerful than anything before if handled in the right way. With the right men behind him he could be as powerful as any one sitting on the highest throne in the Kremlin, which could, in time, even be him! Another contender for that seat was beside him now: the sole presider over the transfer of the enormous scattered and divided Soviet assets in the former federation, back into the hands of Russia alone. A favourable time for both of them, but only one would be the President, and Vladimir had it fixed in his indistinct sights.

Paulo genuinely liked the man who sat beside him. He admired his introspectiveness and how that had helped to survive the conflicts and competitiveness that had surrounded him throughout his career. That was why he had suggested him.

'*Some plants have to be supported, Paulo, otherwise the wind rocks them and the roots are disturbed. Then the growth will be stunted, or their fleshy stems break and the flowers are lost. Others bend in that wind, accepting the squalls, whilst gracefully arching their backs, dancing like ballerinas on a stage. Not fighting against nature by rigid resistance, but growing stronger against each blow. Every plant of substance will need support at the beginning; leave it there until it has the strength to stand on its own. Even Nureyev fell, occasionally.*

Yuri would have made a good teacher of garden husbandry or, if he had wanted, the understanding of the human psyche had he trans-posed his insights into that field, instead of sharing them only with Paulo.

Quiet introspection can be extremely valuable. It allows the exam-ination of your own strengths and weaknesses, as Vladimir would gladly testify to, having practised the process for many a long year. However, as he was the subject of his own analysis, whilst dreaming of the forthcoming days of power and influence, it would take some-one else to show him that his strength could also be his weakness. As someone, somewhere, once said: *A man who looks too intently into the fog should be careful not to trip on the stone directly in front of his feet.*

His strength lay in his pliability. His willingness to go where oth-ers lead, never seeking the mantle of a celebrity, preferring relative obscurity to one of fame. His life had been spent in obsequious infe-riority to those above. But now there was no one to placate, no one to make those decisions that he could concur with. He would have to make them himself. That was his weakness, never having had to make those hard choices; the one that Paulo had identified.

* * *

"We can find no evidence to incriminate Comrade Korovin sir. He has travelled many times to various hotels in Berlin, both before the Wall came down and since. He has reported these occasions as contacts to the source that he has reported to us, an Englishman, who we ourselves have checked and attempted to use. He met his daughter there after she was taken on by CNN. All have been checked against corresponding files, and all are genuine sources that Korovin has registered. The one thing of contention that we found was his meeting with General Gromov who was subsequently found guilty of organising the coup in 1991 but, as we explained to Colonel General Vladimir Sokolov at the inauguration of the FSB, he answered that at the hearing, explaining it was his attempt at stopping it before it occurred. There is a curious fact that has been troubling me for some time, however, and I would appreciate your opinion and instructions."

Alexi went on to tell his new boss Valentin Antopolov of his delving into what he described as the myth... or called, by others, the legend of Paulo Sergeyovitch Korovin.

It had taken almost twenty years before a decision was reached on what Sokolov initiated with his then two subordinates, all based on what Alexi Vasilyev said that day about one man's foolishness, and another man's sense.

* * *

On a distinctly hot and humid June day, Jack Simmons gave a speech to a gathering of equally ambitiously minded captains of industry at the Institute of Directors in London's Pall Mall. The summer that year had started with a bang after a conspicuously uninteresting spring, the south-east of England had been bathed in clear skies and temperatures in the high eighties for the last ten days or so. Jack's never ending summers had been seamless, with his particular branch of industry never experiencing the variances of climate or change. Telecommunications had been added to his company's name, as he told his audience how his innovative business brain had developed new strategies and products to complement his established all-seeing cameras. He closed his address with a short summary.

"In my line, as in all of yours, it's vital to stay one step ahead of the competitors. With us, we originated a directional hearing device to attach to a camera, one that can be operated on its own if more covertness is required. In the beginning we were able to offer our clients minute coverage of all ground activities covered by their satellites. Now, not only do we supply many countries with pinpoint accurate surveying using GPS technology, but the ability to intercept both terrestrial and cellular conversations. It gives us that all-important edge in foreign markets, in which it gives me great pleasure to say we dominate. British innovations are exported worldwide, gentlemen, closing that never to be forgotten trade deficit."

He chose not to add, at that moment, his connection to a powerful influential figure, holding his hand and lighting the path for him. He did that later.

"Hi Jack, I'm Geoffrey Rowell. I run Refining Derivatives Ltd, a petrochemical company based in Surrey. I was very interested in your presentation. I'm trying to accelerate my company into those foreign markets you mentioned and I wondered if, over a drink, you might give me a few tips. I'm at the Sofitel Hotel, it's just across the road. Can I buy you one?"

Jack had no pressing engagements, no clock regulated his life, and he was sorry to say there was no wife at home to worry about where he was. The divorce had been made absolute about four years after meeting Yuri on that trade delegation to Moscow. They had lived apart for two years and Dotty, his pet name for Daphne, had sued on those grounds. But that was not the reason. At first, Dotty admired Jack's enterprise and dynamism, the zest for life he had, in driving his organisation forward into those new markets abroad with more exotic names than Basildon where they lived. The move to Hadley Wood and the six-bedroomed detached house showed the world in particular, the clique in which she moved, who valued the friendship of those who could afford the price of everything just how much his tireless efforts were worth.

Then, the problems began. His time spent away, alone, in pursuit of the lifestyle that they had both craved started to irk, then worry and distress Dotty. She listened to the suitably impressed friends pass their assessment and judgement on his wandering life, by praising her trust and indulgence. "He's a man, out there on his own. I wouldn't trust my husband!They're all the same, my dear. Only a place for one thing in their mind...and it's not always football!"

Doubts set in, so much so that on his return she started to check the pockets of his clothing and laundry. The clues were there, but she never found them, assuming the dampness of his underwear to be simply a sign of the hygiene he employed in those faraway places. The suspicions grew when the same pattern appeared at home, always damp, as if pre-washed before ending up in the linen bin.

"He's having an affair," she thought. "Someone he's impressed with all our money."

That was not the case, either, but she was close to the truth. She came even closer one morning when she went through the pockets of a suit jacket he had worn the previous day. She found a short letter, but it had long consequences:

The London Clinic
1 Devonshire Place
London
W1 2DY 3TD
Dear Sir,
I have the results of the tests and they prove, conclusively, my first diagnosis of gonorrhoea. Please contact my office at your earliest convenience, to arrange an appointment so we can discuss the treatment.
Signed: R. D. Lawrence
Sexual Health Clinic Consultant

The first call she made was not to Jack. That came later in the day, after the locksmith's visit and the telephone conversations she had with their son and daughter, both away at college. Jack faced a scathing and withering attack, face to face, at his Edgware Factory, under a barrage of clothes slung at him from a vitriolic, suitcase-emptying, Dotty. Jack never again lived with Dotty, or had the same relationship with his children that he had before that disease was announced to them.

His problem had started many years ago, the ugly stains staying hidden until too late. He never could recall the name of the bar in Moscow where he guessed the cause, or causes, of that problem had originated. He could not remember their names either and, helplessly, the night spent in their company seemed to pass quicker as every year past by. He paid a substantial price for his indulgence, but now, nine years on, he had recovered all his costs of divorce, all of his dignity, and all of his health, after following his consultant's advice. This harrowing experience had left its mark, leading him to become well-versed in the art of guidance on many subjects, including patience, the divergence of assets and his most prolific subject...the advocating of 'saying no' to unprotected sex, a campaign he rigorously spoke out on.

"Sure Geoff, love to. I'm at the same hotel," he replied.

"I was on the board at BP, when the chance to front a government backed takeover of a company owned petrochemical plant in Antwerp was put to me," Geoff announced to the waiting Jack in the bar. "I could realise the potential that I knew was there, and with government money behind me, everything looked rosy. They'd even recruited the eldest son of an Earl to open doors that might otherwise been closed to us. It didn't work out that way, though.

I wanted to push the company forward into the twenty-first century not just producing by-products of the oil industry. I even had my sights on being the first to discover an alternative to unsustainable resources, and we're not that far away, despite the uncooperative attitude of my overlords. All they want to do the government, that is, is to find out what our competitors are up to with no thought to where we should push on with our efforts. I think, for example, that the Russians have deliberately cut back the supply of oil to push the price up, thereby making the cost of crushing the rock strata that holds billions of barrels of reserves more cost effective. I want to develop our position in two different directions. One where we benefit from the excavation of this new oil in Russia, and two, establishing ourselves in countries where there is no oil. And then developing our technology further for when there is no oil left anywhere. I need contacts, Jack, to convince the officials on my back that I'm right and that our markets are out there. The world needs us, Jack."

"I know just the man, Geoff. He's a Russian named Yuri, a finger in every pie going. I'll get word to him…set you up a meeting. By the way, you ever been tempted at home or while away on business to pay for sex? If so, I've got a story to tell you. Sit back and enjoy your brandy…I'll educate you."

George collected Jack's communique and read of Geoff's conundrum, then found himself in a pickle as well. He had never instigated a meeting for his father before, ordinarily handling messages containing mention of politicians or individuals working against the best interests of GB Ltd, for Paulo to do with as he wished. This was different. A stranger would be meeting his father, something he would dearly love to do and had dreamed about. He remembered Maudlin's cautionary written words of not being inquisitive nor acting for personal reasons, but those warnings he had read before he became a qualified spy. Now, he was one that others wrote books about, a furtive figure hiding in shadows doing the legwork for the important spies hiding out of sight. He had mastered this role, and avoided detection by sticking to the rules. Could he bend them ever so slightly to make his dreams come true without the use of John the Steadfast?

Chapter Thirty

Autumn Colours

"I'm sorry about that, Harry. I don't know what came over me...I'm not normally that open about that chapter in my life. I think it was seeing you trying to make sense of what David said; how there were doubts, but nothing was done. If it had been, I mean, if Willis and Howell had been arrested sooner then all this would have happened before now. You can see that, can't you?"

"Yeah, of course I can. It just seemed so futile, having intelligence and not using it. I wish I had cottoned-on sooner, or that you had. I keep thinking that if I had told Trimble all I knew on that Wednesday, or better still on the Sunday when Special Branch told me, then maybe Teddy would still be around. It's like you said...we all make mistakes."

"Yours wasn't a mistake, Harry. If you had known everything, which was impossible, you wouldn't have changed a thing. The person who did this had already worked it out for themselves. I reckon that all the information that I put together about Paulo and Tanya was already known by him. What I *am* confident about is that he does not know that George is Paulo's son, but he has obviously made the connection between Paulo and your family and the bank. I'm doing my best, Harry but it's not easy. Whoever it is, it's deep, H...well covered. I think he's frightened that Paulo will expose him. He's trying to find how he contacts us here, plus he wants to discredit Paulo back home and have him arrested. I don't think it wise to trust anyone but ourselves in all of this. Treat everyone as suspicious, then we won't make any mistakes…either of us."

She stopped for a moment, simply staring ahead, her face cupped in her hands, elbows on both knees. I was torn between believing that she was remembering Tony, or looking for answers to fill in the centre of that jigsaw puzzle that surrounded me. I didn't have long to wait to find out.

"That's what I do well, nowadays, since Tony died…you know, Harry?"

"What's that?" I asked.

"I've reverted back to my childhood, not trusting anyone. I believed Tony you see, all he said about staying alive. I forgot to question things when I was with him, and he was the only person I had ever known to make me daydream about life. When I was young my grandfather took me to Blenheim Palace, to show me what being English was all about… *how we fought for our heritage,* he said. The two of us were taken on a private guided tour from one room to another full of trophies, gratefully given, the guide said, to the Duke of Marlborough by the villagers or townsfolk he liberated during his campaigns. I was nine and didn't believe a word of it, so I spoke my mind.

"He stole them, you mean?" I said, out loud, to the guide. As I was so young, she never deemed it necessary to answer my accusation, but my Grandfather simply smiled at me. For a while I forgot that scepticism, but after Tony died; it came back with a vengeance."

"What did you do after Tony's death?" I asked, not as an unwarranted question, but one I hoped carried the sincerity I felt.

"I screamed, I shouted, threw things at the television, drove a car into a brick wall while I was thinking of topping myself. The department offered me counselling, my GP offered tablets. Tony's family gave me a place to grieve and deal with it. You'll find your own place, Harry, but for now we've got work to do. Don't get like me and blame everybody. Let's concentrate on what we know and find whoever it is that killed your father and brother, before I get into one again and you go all sentimental on me."

"I'm not the sentimental type, Judith. Haven't you noticed?" I said.

The characteristic 'Hmm' was followed by her proposal to return to find George. "He's the key to all this, Harry. I just hope he knows how to open the door."

We left the Common with Judith humming a tune I did not recognise, one that had no name to others, one that only she found significance in. I felt a closeness to her that allowed me to use that name she had suggested a lifetime ago and had resisted until now. I was falling.

"Let me drive us to find him, Judy. Let's see how that German car of yours deals with London traffic. There's always plenty of room to park in Eton Square, as all the residents use the underground car park. Can't leave the Rolls and Bentleys on show, can they? Who would believe we were in a global financial meltdown if they did?"

"Am I converting you, H?" she asked, smiling at me.

* * *

Paulo had found George once. It was not at Eton Square, though, and he wasn't meant to. His discovery was a lucky accident; the only trouble was that nobody benefited by that discovery.

George left the *Free Will* on the hymn book shelf and, about a month later, planted himself on the same plane as Geoffrey Rowell. He had done his homework on Mr Rowell after retrieving Paulo's invitation, checking to see that he was indeed who he said he was. However, he could only be marked five out of ten for his effort, as he had never set eyes on his man until at the booking-in desk at Heathrow.

They travelled in separate cabs to the Westin Grand Hotel, number five on the updated list of Berlin Hotels. George was the first to arrive, and found himself an empty table by the window, ordering a beer from one of the attentive waiters walking the floor of the foyer. Being a conscientious, shy man, he was embarrassed by the assiduous attention his near-empty glass caused the busboys, so he ordered another and wondered why Geoffrey was taking so long. An hour passed in agitation, frugally sipping his now-warm beer, his stare fixed firmly away from the interior into the night, beyond the ever present industrious floor-walkers imagining all manner of things that could have happen. An accident, a mugging? Perhaps a breakdown of the bus he must be using, or the cab? Then, it came to him. He must have been accosted by a tout from the unregulated taxis at the terminal and taken one of those…poor man! No doubt driven by an illegal from Poland, one of the thousands from that country taking their economic revenge on the citizens of Berlin, using Geoffrey's money to help the rebuilding of Warsaw by taking the scenic route. *That has to be the reason,* George thought, as he smiled at his own reflection in the window.

Paulo was standing on the pavement outside the Westin Grand as the evening commuters spilled from their offices and hurried along Friedrichstrasse on the way to somewhere, but his view of his son with the goatee beard was not obscured in any way.

At last, Geoffrey arrived. He was cutting it fine to make the appointed time of the meeting, which was dinner at seven-thirty. George had already checked that he had a room reserved, and imagined him rushing there to shower and change, so as to present himself and his case for benevolence to his father in a presentable fashion. *He must hurry,* he thought. *He only has an hour to go.*

Going, was on George's mind, also. He had come for a glimpse, no more than that. He had no reservation in the hotel, only a table for one in the restaurant at the same time, hoping to make sight of the enigma that was his father before the last flight home.

Both men ate alone that night, on separate tables no more than twenty feet apart, and both had regrets and unanswerable questions. George could never ask his; it would tell Paulo that he had disobeyed his instructions. Geoffrey had asked his, but not of Paulo, the man he had hoped to have met but who had never showed. He had asked, instead, a colleague who was an expert in certain matters, their conversation causing the delay that George had fretted over. They had a common need, a business matter…something Geoffrey could not soil his hands on.

* * *

"The non-appearance of Korovin, made me look again Comrade Colonel General Antopolov, I was very suspicious. Was it simply a coincidence? I reviewed all reports concerning the British as far back as 1956. In almost every case, whatever we discovered, they were informed of by an agent known to them as *Garden;* sometimes before or sometimes after. In one particular case, the Stonehouse affair, an English MP working for the Czech StB, was uncovered by the British. It was Korovin, then, with the KGB, who advised the Czechs to tell him to run. Given the right circumstances it was the correct advice, but these were not the right circumstances. The British, I have been very reliably told, never knew of him until his faked suicide in Florida...perhaps another coincidence. What sticks out, however, is the lack of investigation by the late Colonel General Vladimir Sokolov into the circumstances. What is more confusing is that it was Sokolov who suggested Australia as Stonehouse's retreat where he eventually was found.

Korovin's subsequent role in the return of Soviet assets within the Federation brought him in close contact with many ex-political leaders and Mafia associates if you remember, and it was they who were thought to be behind Sokolov's death. As you are aware sir, Comrade Korovin has grown extremely wealthy through those associations, and Sokolov's widow and family are enjoying their life in the affluent south of France to its fullest." Alexi Vasilyev finished his report, but not his investigation.

* * *

"That reminds me, Harry...I think I must have left my riding boots in the boot of my car, and they'll need cleaning. Come on, Hector! Time for home."

Hector was harnessed, sadly not to a leather-studded collar and thick plaited leather lead that his namesake might have needed for control, but to an elasticated variety, his freedom controlled by a plastic grip. As we neared the car he became increasingly agitated, sniffing the air instead of the grass, wagging his tail, and barking as if challenging Achilles to battle.

"What's the matter with him?" I asked.

"I'm not sure," she replied, reeling him in. "He's never acted like this before."

"Perhaps he's seen a fox and it's the beagle in him that wants to chase it?"

We stood beside her car as Hector performed his impersonation of a 'Whirling Dervish,' jumping in the air and chasing his tail, emitting a muffled bark as he did so.

"He's seen plenty of the furry kind on the common, Harry, believe me. This is somewhat more serious…he was Tony's dog, trained to sniff out bombs. Fancy opening the door to find out if I'm right? Brought your passport with you, H? I think it's time we left, don't you?"

"Where are we going, Judy?"

"Let's try Hamburg to start with, and see where it leads."

Sir David Haig was still in his London apartment when he received Judith's call, preferring to recover there, from his early morning rise than in the clinical surrounds of Whitehall, Goddess excluded. She was not from his private life…he was not that type. He was a straight up-and-down honest guy, not cheating on his family or his country, as Judith explained to the worried, questioning, Earl of Harrogate.

"Yes, we can trust him, Harry. If he had planted the bomb, then there would have been no need to have asked me yesterday if I had driven into town or caught the tube, would there? Plus, he might have looked a mite surprised when we arrived, huh?"

"You're assuming that he never left it here this morning on his way home. Maybe you didn't put enough sugar in his coffee, Judy!"

My mobile phone was in hyperdrive in the back of a turbo charged London cab. I had already made and received more calls than I would normally make in a week before we were over Albert Bridge, on the way to Heathrow, by way of a surprised George.

"Good morning, Lord Paterson…it's Detective Chief Superintendent Fletcher here. We can release your father and brother's bodies. They're being held at Southwark mortuary. I will text you the address, if you would like to notify the collections to your undertakers."

I had called Joseph to complete the arrangements with the funeral directors, telling both sisters, and Maurice, who was now at Harrogate; but I told none of these of my destination, nor the fact that I was lucky to be alive.

"Not really the time to go swanning off somewhere with your latest, is it, Harry? No matter how important you say it is! What am I expected to do?" Maurice had asked.

"Do what you do best, Maurice, and moan. Failing that, ask Joseph what needs to be done and help him out. I'm trying to find whoever it was that murdered Elliot and Edward for God's sake. Show a little bit of understanding!" I curtly replied, and promptly closed my phone. I had left instructions at Eton Square for George to contact me, and when he did I followed Judy's biddings.

"It's all a bit sudden, Harry. Where are we going, and what will I need?" George asked. Judy had decided that the explanation would be better heard from me.

"It will come as a shock to him, Harry…I'm not sure how he is going to react. Don't go into too much detail at this point. I think we can leave out the Maudlin tie-up, and Auntie Loti. Let's stick to Paulo…that will be enough for now." The best-laid plans having been formulated and decided upon, we set about our mission

Chapter Thirty-One

Snapdragons

"I haven't got copies of what I leave in the church for him to contact me, you know. How are we to do that, then?" George asked, as I finished the first part of the story of why we were going to Hamburg to meet his father. I had covered the murders and the attempt on both Judy and my own life, adding her thoughts to the reason behind these things. Sir David Haig had called Judy and told of how the mercury switch to the bomb would have activated the sophisticated device on the first corner we would have taken.

"It may have been crude in its objective, but not in its design. It was expertly balanced, so that no amount of leaning against the car would trigger it, nor simply getting in. However, I'm told that as the car would have gone over one of the many humps in the road surrounding you, or around a sharp corner, the mercury would have completed the circuit and well, they would be scraping the bits up," was the succinct way in which he put it!

"We are all targets, it would seem, George… and maybe your father Paulo Sergeyovitch Korovin knows why," was the last thing I had said to George, before he mentioned the means of contact. I could not pass up on this opportunity to bring up Loti, but Judy got there first.

"We know you haven't, George. The bible is with auntie Loti, except that isn't her real name. She is Tanya Malonovna Kuznetsoka. Your real mother."

It wasn't the plan to get this far ahead but, as with so many plans, improvisation is a fundamental and necessary tactic. During the next hour and a half remaining of the time before the flight to Hamburg, Judy went back to 1956 and told of the legend that involved Paulo and Tanya, but omitted one important detail, which was spotted and leapt upon by George. And it was not the discovery of both parents.

"How did Maudlin fit into all of this? Why did my mother arrive at Eton Square?" he asked, simplistically.

"That's your domain, Harry. I'll let you answer that one," Judy declared adamantly, looking away from the two of us. She stared into the distance, as if wanting to detach herself from the answer.

"You're his grandson," I answered. He wasn't as surprised as I thought he would have been.

"I did wonder, you know. The story in the letter that I received after his death was all a bit fanciful and heroic. There was not enough there to justify the money he bequeathed me; nor, looking back on things, the effort and attention he bestowed on me throughout his life. I sensed I was special to him, but I didn't know why. Loti being my mother makes more sense. She kept her secret well, didn't she?"

"To protect you, George. That's why you're still alive," Judy announced.

"You have a step-sister named Katherine. Did you know?" I stupidly asked.

"No, how do you?"

I related the story of Vancouver, and told him how I had felt in Grönwohld and of the ensuing conversation in Moscow. That's when George dropped it; the same story as Alexi's but from a different perspective.

"You're lucky to have met him. I tried, once. I shouldn't have, mind you, but it didn't matter…he never showed up."

It was Judy's turn as she rejoined our conversation and started her questions, black and red notebook to the fore, pen waving in tune to that metronome, marking the time for the notes of his replies. The flight was short, as was the journey to the hotel, but the dialogue between the two went on into the night, neither of them noticing my return with a torn page showing the kneeling figure of one steadfast man whilst another anointed him. I decided that, having defaced a Bible and my sins being done for the day, I would punish myself in the bar resorting to red wine in the absence of anything from the Isle of Jura. I never even asked…it wasn't that classy a hotel.

There were three full days left to unravel this mystery before the funeral on Sunday, not sufficient time to wait for replies and set up meetings in Berlin from numbered lists. This was too urgent for such niceties, regardless of bombs or whatever else had to be settled. There was a way that had not been discussed. Perhaps it was guilt that had caused me not to; but I wondered why Judy had not broached the subject of Katherine.

* * *

Paulo had done great work for the Soviet Union in the Middle East, and for himself. The loss of Anacova had not stopped him building relationships with militant groups and ruling families throughout the area. Katherine had been eight when she lost her mother to Hamas, being then raised by an array of nannies under the watchful eye of her father. He had previously firmly eschewed away from meaningful partnerships. They had brought him no satisfaction. What had, though, was what he saw as his duty to his daughter.

He loved her, but his love was impassive, unemotional. He was detached yet systematic, everything placed within a structured plan, as though one would when designing a house for someone else to live in, not a home for yourself. No subtleties, no spontaneity mirroring Paulo himself, for whom everything was predetermined. The foundations had to be laid, and she was to be cocooned in luxury and shielded from danger, never to know anything of his many double lives.

The walls were made from images of him leading the way towards political reforms, restoring Russia to the pinnacle of world power by adopting Western ideas, but ones sheathed in communist principles.

The roof was his money and his influence. These would protect and guide her, countering the corners of life where ordinary folk can become snarled, entangled with backward views of despair instead of forward ones towards glory. Paulo's vision contained that glory; one where reliance on wits alone within a closed society unwilling to look forward, such as the one that had strangled his own notional ambitions, would not exist for her. His wealth would see to that.

Her vision never extended to her father's role in identifying terrorists whom the Soviets could use in their subversion against America and their ally Israel, nor the arms deals he arranged for the less stable regions and organisations. Paulo was instrumental in the decision taken by many of the OPEC members to cut back on oil supplies to the West in the 1980s. It was in order, he said, to cripple their industries; but, in reality, it made the extraction of Soviet oil from the Caspian basin and Siberia more cost-effective. She may well have approved, had she known.

He invested his time and his money early in such ventures, enhancing the education of his daughter by the employment of specialist governesses in both academic and cultural fields. She attended the Russian Academy of Science in Moscow from the age of eleven and, by the time of Paulo's elevation to the Presidium of the Federation of Russia, the International University of Russia. She majored in economics and social studies in the place of learning that Paulo had helped establish when 'Glasnost' was the byword for radicalism and outward-looking.

Katyerena Illich Sarenova, she was given her mother's name, married Richard Dwight Friedal, an American working with Cable News Network, in 2004. The wedding took place in Brussels, where Richard was based as the news channel's NATO and European Union representative. Paulo was delighted, as it had been his suggestion that Katherine spread her wings from Russia. The headquarters of the European Community was a place where she could hear the wise speak of profit and capitalism and perhaps, he thought, pass some of that insight his way. He did not know of her change of name, nor the real reason for the marriage.

She had been inducted and trained in the ways of the FSB whilst at the Academy of Science, the cradle for its operatives. Her father had no knowledge of this, or of the fact that Katherine was in love with another. From her husband and his many acquaintances, the FSB in Moscow discovered multifarious facets of the working of North Atlantic Treaty Organisation it had never known before. Her identity was clouded by history. Her papers said that she was Estonian, born in the city of Tallinn, and that both parents were descendants from Russian migrants drafted into that country to bolster its industrialisation and militarisation after the Second World War. They replaced the millions that had been deported or murdered by Stalin, then Hitler, then Stalin again, firstly during the Soviet conquering, then the German occupation, and finally the retaking by the communists. The antecedents of such people were impossible to validate, as it was the old KGB who had destroyed them, and the new FSB who hadn't replaced them. In the same year as her marriage, Estonia entered the European Community; giving Katherine free unrestricted access to all of Europe as well as America, thanks to her matrimonial citizenship.

* * *

Alexi Vasilyev had tended his student well. He had always been a good listener, trying to hear the footsteps before the knock on the door came. He heard what the late Vladimir Sokolov was saying when only a Colonel in a dingy office, to him and the other incumbent, who had quickly organised a transfer, leaving Alexi with no one to blame if the knocks were in the middle of the night. He had hidden away his doubts of Paulo in a windowless vault with no filing cases; just his memory.

He stepped quietly through the offices of the ranks above, carrying Political Officer Dimitriy Lebedov's letters of protestation as an introduction. He found no substance, as he reported, but wondered at Paulo's meteoric rise and the lack of evidence as to a Strategic Studies Group in President Reagan's time. Alexi had been born in Warsaw six years into the Soviet occupation of Poland, and had witnessed the carnage that followed Stalin's death, as positions of power were fought over by previous family friends. He knew what naivety was and the punishment it carried. He clung patiently to Sokolov's flowing cloak of anonymity and indecision, until one day he found himself in the stratosphere of the FSB, along with Korovin, amongst Vladimir's visitors. That's when he knew that Lebedov's suspicions were valid.

His decision to seduce Katherine was not a hardship. She was an extremely attractive girl and, although twenty-seven years his junior, not beyond reach of his shrewdness and well exercised prowess. He began his task at the Academy, giving lectures on counter intelligence and its importance in every walk of life. He singled out Katherine for his special tuition. They extended this 'one-to-one' and began their special relationship when she was sixteen. Paulo was seldom at home in Moscow throughout the early nineties, away fostering his own affinities with foreign governments or less reputable individuals who wielded power. His connection with oligarchs and the Mafia were growing stronger by the minute, and he noticed nothing closer to home.

* * *

Richard Dwight Friedal did not appear to be an easy target for Katyerena. Outwardly he was a consummate man, proficient in his vocation and assured around women. He had never married, presumably preferring the single life of transient affairs to one of nuptial vows. This judgement, however, was wrong. At thirty-four years of age he longed to be settled into a partnership with someone to fill the void in his life that his housemaid could not adequately accomplish. Past liaisons had been with already married women who were unwilling to leave one domestic role for another, or single women, who had no wish to become his replacement housekeeper. Washing, ironing and cooking did not rate as highly with them as it did with Richard. Katyerena's joyous agreement in fulfilling this role changed everything and made his dreams come true; in the most important parts of his home, that is. Richard had at last found his surrogate mother, and was happy.

Paulo's daughter never intended to share this confused happiness of Richard's idyllic life. She had what she and Alexi wanted. She left a note, stating the days she spent washing his well-used, smelly golf socks as a reason for her leaving, and disappeared, carrying her American citizenship, occupying her talents elsewhere. Katherine met Donald Howell in Silvio's wine bar in Downtown New York in August 2009, and the name of Paterson was mentioned again.

"Oh yes, it was Paterson money from the private bank they ran for us that set up Refining Derivatives four years ago. Have you heard the name before, then?" Howell asked: A name she could never forget. She put the love of Alexi before the familiarity of a father, telling her handler of a meeting in Vancouver and of a flamboyant lover who went by the same surname.

"My father met him in Moscow, and said he would be useful to him at some stage. He kept calling him Lord Harry. I slept with him, Alexi…it was before I loved you. Will you forgive me?"

Alexi was instructed to continue in his rumination on Paulo Sergeyovitch Korovin; only this time, he was authorised to go further.

Chapter Thirty-Two
Weedkiller

Dietmar Kohl had spent the best part of forty-seven years, in one capacity or another, in the Lutheran Church, before his sudden death at the age of sixty-seven in 1987. He had lived for the first twenty-five years of that life in the unified German City of Leipzig, then for five further years in the same place. Only this time, Leipzig was under Soviet control in the Eastern partitioned sector of Germany, from where he and his wife and eight children were deported into the allied controlled democratic West, and it was not only for his religious beliefs that this action was taken. By the time he fathered his final child he had five boys and three daughters, none of whom knew of the dark secret he and his wife had borne, carrying it throughout their lives, until it was swallowed up by the consecrated ground in which they found their eternal rest. Well, almost.

Dietmar had been conscripted into the Wehrmacht three years before the start of World War Two, and by its end he could be implicated in the death of 6 million Jews, along with millions of others disapproved of by the German Army leaders. He was the Gestapo Oberfeldwebel who directly passed on Heinrich Himmler's orders of extermination to the death squads who carried out Himmler's orders of genocide. Like many Germans at the end of the conflict, he would profess his innocence to this crime by proclaiming that he was simply doing his duty by following instructions. However, his case was more complicated. It was not repulsion that was instrumental in his deportation for the governing Soviets, as repulsion was an everyday sentiment of those who held different views than their own.

The Stasi, the East German secret police, and the KGB were as equally hateful of Jews and misfits as were the Gestapo, dispatching millions more to their death. His crime was more repugnant than even that. He was manipulatable and easily led, believing the propaganda that Hitler preached above that of his church; he had betrayed his own, believing it his duty.

Out of uniform, and carrying no insignia of office or rank, Dietmar and Steffi, his wife, had covertly organised small congregations of churchgoers, extending their open arms to all creeds of religious believers. She had secretly photographed them, then together they had reported them to the Gestapo, who had administered the appropriate punishment for being a follower of Christ and not a full time member of the Nazi party.

'Give unto Caesar what belongs to Caesar,' was their combined justification to this sin. Obligations are written in the Bible as well as by Senior Gestapo officers, they told themselves, conveniently forgetting the rest of the quotation.

* * *

Anotoly Petronikov had told Paulo of Dietmar's existence at the onset of the plan to plant an agent codenamed 'Mother' in the West.

"We have just the man for you, Paulo. He has performed tasks for us before. He is not far from Hamburg. An easy place to contact, and close enough to Berlin for him to place the messages."

"What happens when he dies, comrade? Do we look for another way?" the young naval attaché and assistant translator had asked.

"Do not worry, comrade Korovin. His secrets do not die with him... they are a never-ending damnation on his family. We have seen to it!" Petronikov told his underling.

The method of collection of those *Mother* inspired messages was also discussed and decided upon that day in the yellow stone building in Lubyanka Square.

"Do you know what they call this place, Paulo? It's called the tallest building in Moscow. Do you know why? Because they say you can see Siberia from its basement, that's why!" Anotoly slapped his new friend's back, sharing his joke heartily.

"Since 1948 and the airlifts into Berlin, passage between East and West has become harder and will get worse. Beria built on what Stalin wanted; a divided Germany and Khrushchev will be no different. Berlin will see changes, Paulo. You will need a good reason to visit West Berlin... they will be watching everything you do."

Paulo met Dietmar Kohl in the Soviet-administered City of Schwerin, by the side of the lake, three months before he travelled to London. Here he established the rules of communications in the same way as he and Maudlin had discussed. Dietmar suggested the Bible, and the encryptions therein. He would do anything, he said, to avoid the shame of what he had done being made known to the outside world. Paulo made it clear what would happen to his family if he or any of his descendants ever broke the promise made that day.

The once impoverished Paulo stood on the battlements of Schwerin Castle, and gazed astonishingly at the vista he beheld, lavishly reflected from the waters below. He had never seen such beauty and he found it impossible to convey in words, as he declared its magnificence to Maudlin. His father wrote back, using the code for number 29 the next prime number in the sequence, on the way to 101 and the return to 7.

You will have the breath taken from you when you see the Zugersee from the town of Zug. On a summer's day there is no more beautiful sight that I have ever seen.

* * *

When Harry Paterson left *John the Steadfast* in the church, it required Dietmar to deviate drastically from the normal routine of message collection. *Free Will* could take its time; being steadfast needed urgency. Fortunately, mobile texting had evolved, taking over from the written word. The message Paulo received on the spare cellular phone that had never been used before contained an innocuous question: *What is the difference between Public and Private International Law?*

Paulo found a bar away from the Hilton in Brasilia and called Dietmar. After deliberating on the answers he received from the voice at the other end of the telephone, he made his decision. On his arrival back in Moscow he contacted Katherine, and arranged the meeting that night in Vancouver.

The message he received this time was exactly the same. *What is the difference between Public and International Law?*

It was Judith who knocked on the door at number 17, and enquired of the middle-aged man who answered it as to the whereabouts of Dietmar Kohl.

"Hello, we're looking for Dietmar Kohl. These are both Lord Patersons, and it is rather urgent that we meet. Could we give you this directly, or must we place it in the church and waste valuable time?"

"Er ist nicht hier," the man said, as he closed the door firmly in Judith's face.

"Now, that was stupid. We should have played the game as I said," George indignantly stated. "Maybe we've screwed up altogether," he added, as his opinion.

We sat on the same bench that I had occupied that second Sunday amongst the gathering there that day. This Wednesday evening, the church was different in two ways. It was empty, and we did not have long to wait for a reply to Judith's demands.

He spoke in English. "I am Dietmar's grandson; he and my grandmother are buried in the cemetery behind this church. I have two messages from Goganof one for you, and one for me. First my father, then I, have carried on this procedure of being a go-between, whilst serving the brethren here as preacher. Before I read you your message, please answer a question regarding my own, and please tell me that it is now all over. Mine reads: *In my mind there is no longer any difference between the two.* It is the first time any of us have had anything in print from him. He has contacted me once before, and never contacted the others of my family."

"When was that?" I asked.

"After you came here and left the same picture. I sent the same text as I have just done, but I had forgotten what was expected of me. It was twenty years ago that I was instructed what to do if that depiction was ever left in our church, and I had forgotten the procedure. I panicked a bit, but eventually I found Dietmar's old prayer book in which everything was written down, and sent this."

He showed me the text, and I showed Judith.

"What did he do the first time you sent that message, when Harry here came along, causing all your anxiety?" Judith enquired.

"Huh! I thought I was in the middle of some Hollywood spy film. My father and I never knew what we were doing, but both of us were told never to ask. Luther, my father, told me that Dietmar had said that it was old lovers communicating about the past, but neither of us believed that. He did say, though, that an English Lord was involved, and it was all very secretive. It was something to do with the war, and imperative that we kept it all going until we were told it had finished. I thought it might have been, that last time, but he said he needed me for a little longer."

"What did he say exactly?" Judy asked, impatiently.

"Sorry," Dietmar's grandson was not focusing on what was being said. His thoughts were elsewhere. "It's just that I'm hoping whatever hold this man had over us has gone. I had sent the text as soon as you had left, and hadn't long returned from evening prayers when the phone rang once, then stopped. It rang again, the same one ring and then for a third time. I had seen this sequence mentioned in Dietmar's book when I had searched it before. If it *was* him, the next time the phone should ring five times before stopping and it did. When it rang again, I answered. A man's voice asked, simply, "how is the weather there?" I replied that it was fine, 'sunny,' I said. "Then go to the call box beside the water wheel, I will call you there in precisely four minutes."

He told me his name, and that corresponded to what Dietmar had written. He then asked about you. Each time, you see, that a message was left, I, or my father before me, had to describe the person who had called in the letter that we sent to numbered listed hotels in Berlin. This time I said that you were different, and he asked me to describe you, which I did. He said he would send me a message to leave in the church the following Sunday, and told me to be at the same call box before the midday service. There was thunder and lightning with a deluge of rain, if you remember, and I told him so when he rang because he mentioned the noise it was making. He asked if I had received the photograph of a young woman with a message on it. When I replied that I had, he asked me if you were the same man as before. I said yes, but this time you had a limp. He laughed, and said, 'I thought so,' then told me to leave the photograph for you to find. It was then that he told me 'It won't be long now that I require your services. Soon, it should be over'...which gave me hope."

"I think, then, that you can take it that it *is* over," I emphatically declared.

"What message did he send us, then?" This time it was George who asked, with an increased degree of impatience. Which was not assuaged by any reply.

"Please ask Goganof to text me if it is over. Just those two words will do: *it's over*." He directed his plea to me, then, passing his phone to Judith, added "You may wish to write the details down."

He never volunteered his name and we never asked. Perhaps we all felt an empathy towards him, which was reflected in his closing statement as we left.

"If it is all finished, then I shall leave this place. There is something not right here in Grömwohld."

Chapter Thirty-Three

Glow-Worms and Fireflies

Paulo, like George before him, was not completely scrupulous in his homework. If he had been he would never have instructed Katherine to meet Harry in her capacity as a CNN reporter. He could have offered age as his defence, instead of his disregard of nepotism and apathy towards his daughter's career, whereas George, on the other hand, had only ineptitude as an excuse. If Paulo had been thirty years younger than the age that he was, he would have made the same mistake. He could never have imagined that the deepest cut, into his ageing veins, would have come from his own flesh and blood, sheathed in another's hand.

Alexi easily found Maudlin Paterson's name in old KGB files, as was Andrea Cortez. The bank was already known to him. Harry Paterson proved the link that he'd suspected. Now he needed proof that the fable of Paulo was a myth, and in Katherine he had the catalyst to bring about the reaction he required.

* * *

We all met Paulo in the Hotel Baur Au Lac in Zurich, Switzerland on Thursday, late in the afternoon. He was alone, and looked considerably older than the three years that had past since our last meeting. He rose from his seat, and greeted us.

"I am Paulo Sergeyovitch Korovin. I was sorry to hear of your father and then your brother Lord Harry…I expect that is why you have come to talk with me. Also, let me apologise for misleading you when we last met, although I doubt the deception worked." He bowed slightly, but offered no hand in my direction. He did, however, to his son; but the gesture was difficult to understand or interpret.

"I am pleased to make your acquaintance, George. However, I fear it is too late for us to have a meaningful, close connection. You must know by now that your aunt Loti is…or was…?" The lines in his forehead deepened as he quizzically gazed at George, requiring an answer to his bemusement.

"She is still alive, and yes, I'm aware that she is my mother, but it would have been nice to have known before this week," George replied, abruptly, to Paulo's implied question. I worried about George and his seamless acceptance of his past.

"Well, there were reasons." Paulo left a pause hanging in the atmosphere, mingling with the smell of coffee. "I'm sure it must have been this young lady who has discovered them, no disrespect to you, Harry, but I think your time with the SIS has been spent in other directions. Would you be so kind as to introduce us, George?" He didn't have a chance, as Judy was biting at the bit to get into the conversation.

"I'm Judith Meadows. I work directly for Sir David Haig, the permanent Secretary for Foreign Affairs, and I am currently the one exclusively in charge of a SIS file named 'Garden.' I think you are the subject of that file, and someone on your side is trying to expose you, and intending to kill George and Harry here as an afterthought. What do you think, *Paulo*?" She contemptuously emphasised his name.

He took a deep breath, and again the ageing dull grey of his eyes could be seen clearly, overshadowed by the etched burrows above them.

"It would seem that my efforts in assisting my father's country has not impressed you. You did realise that we were related, Harry? Ah…of course you did. Your work again, Judith? I may call you Judith, I hope? I wouldn't like to incur more scorn from you."

We were seated in a corner of 'Le Hall,' an opulent cherry coloured panelled bar, full of portraits of studious men drinking and sniffing wine, or smoking cigars and pipes. Paulo sat with his back to the wall, stretched out in the middle of a three-seater settee, while we occupied the three chairs the other side of a low, highly polished table. On the table rested our glasses, two plates of hors d'oeuvres and a tabletop grill, with small wedge-shaped pans to melt the Raclette cheese displayed on a huge plate, surrounded by sausages and shredded hams. With my glass of Jura lovingly cradled in one hand, I had already visualised eating the delicacies and finishing on some chocolates I had seen on our arrival. Dieting was not prevalent in my mind at that moment in time. My step-uncle read my mind.

"Don't be so chivalrous, Harry nor you, George. I think Judith here has other, more pressing, things on her mind than local specialities. See, I've already made a start…I couldn't wait, I'm afraid. Where were we, Judith? Ah yes. You believe I'm in danger of being exposed as a traitor to Russia, don't you? And why would you think that a seventy-eight year old would attract that amount of attention? Surely whatever I've betrayed is well known by now…who could benefit from my exposure?"

"I don't know, but you have obviously ruffled someone's feathers, haven't you?"

"I like that word, *ruffled*. Such an English word…I can't think of a Russian equivalent for it." I watched him shake his head from side to side, as I alone wantonly melted more cheese, conscious of Judy's distraction and George's obstinate attitude.

"It is time that I enlighten you. My adversary's name is Alexi Vasilyev and, although not Russian by birth, he shares the same qualities of persistence in pursuit of what they see as right. It's because of our harsh winters. One becomes single-minded in survival, indomitable. That steadfast figure of John sums them up. They need a Luther to stir them, but once awake they don't sleep with bad memories."

"You know this man wants me dead, don't you?" George offered as a way of reconciliation with his father and to gain significance in the two-way conversation, but it backfired.

"One thing that has always intrigued me, is how people blame others for their own shortcomings. Are you accusing me of being inconsiderate towards you, George? You, the same person who has had everything found since birth? Did I not arrange enough money for you in Lord Maudlin's will, or have you not checked the balance in that account recently? Please don't answer me with any sickly claptrap. You were asked not to do one thing, and that was too much for you. That trip you made to Berlin could have cost me my life…did you think of that when you ignored Maudlin's instructions, or was it sheer selfishness on your part? I put you in a place of safety, George, with a cover that not even Vasilyev has been able to break. He has discovered a connection to my father, and knows about a bank but not of you, George. He's still looking. I have been indiscreet, Judith. I may well have made mistakes in the past, but the mistake I made regarding Howell and Willis was my biggest. I presume they were arrested after my message to your man, Haig?"

"They were, yes, days before Elliot and Edward's death," I answered, my attention now on George and what on earth he had done to warrant his father's censure let alone Haig, who I heard Judy tell of our plan when he had called about the bomb. I was worried, and wished I had a gun in my hand instead of sausage.

"I had knowledge of them before, but nothing concrete until a couple of weeks or so ago." He sat forward in the settee, staring blankly at the table.

* * *

"Katyerena, your father has become a very insular man. He has detached himself from Moscow politics, existing in Switzerland, doing nothing for his beloved Russia. I want you to visit him there, and tell of your handling two English agents; he is bound to be delighted by your exploits. He was, you know, one of our finest intelligence officers in the Cold War. He achieved many great feats, including seeing off that belligerent Ronald Reagan a warmonger, that man, you know. Almost blew us all up, but your father stopped him. You didn't know? I must tell you all about it before you go visiting."

She would not have been a willing participant in Alexi's scheme of dethronement had she been aware of that deviant side of her lover's nature. But she suspected nothing underhand in his proposal. It was a tragic assumption. On her arrival, Paulo's mood brightened considerably. He had been thoughtful since meeting Harry in Moscow, preferring his hermit status away from the limelight. She was young, with all the exuberance of youth. *Let's go here, Papa, let's eat there, let's sail your boat around the lake! Praise me, Papa, because I'm following in your majestic footprints! I'm a spy runner, just like you with 'Mother.'*

The promise he'd sworn in Beirut had not been broken by himself but by an arrogant Polish upstart. He was too laboured in his ways now for journeys to Berlin, and had not been there for over a year. He decided on the course of action he took when he first heard of British industrial spies giving up information regarding bio-fuels from an associate within the circle of oligarchs who frequented his favourite eatery, the Seerestuarant, before spending the night at the card tables in the casino up the stairs. Switzerland had become a favoured tax haven for many such millionaires and they came no bigger than Paulo, to whom they all owed greatly.

* * *

"If this Alexi knew so much, why do you suppose has he waited so long?" Judy asked.

"Perhaps for the conclusive proof that he now has...who knows?"

"Then why the need to find George? Why not just come here and confront you, scurry you off to Moscow and hang you out to dry?" she continued.

"I have been expecting that since I read of Elliot's death. If he were Russian, I'd say he was after the Order of Lenin and on his way to becoming the next President. He has me... so why, indeed? Unless he wants something else... and there is a second game that he plays. The clues are there for you to find, Judith. Look closely, and maybe, like me, you will find them."

He sat back, smiling victoriously, then added, "I have been in this business for over sixty years and am still alive to tell the tale. I had Maudlin to guide me at the beginning, and he taught me well. *Keep things close,* he would say. *Do everything yourself; never involve more, or speak to more, than is necessary.* Call it luck, call it what you will, but I survived all those years following that simple advice. Alexi has not got a Maudlin in his life to advise him but he has someone else, maybe of an equal standing. He never killed your father and brother, Harry. He persuaded someone else to have the deed done, and I use the word *persuade* intentionally."

"How could you persuade someone to kill?" I asked.

"Oh... hundreds of ways. Loss of pride, loss of face. As they say, to-day: *how could you allow that to happen without retribution?* Or, *is it not time you took your revenge for what he did to you?* Conceivably, in this case, my name was incorporated with the very worst thing that the Russian secret society can envisage; a traitor who lived amongst them. We are proud people, peddling our wares of lies and misinformation. If we took no pride in ourselves or in our work, then our errors would be like fireflies in the night, easily preyed on. We don't like mistakes that haunt us, and we would like to eliminate those memories before our fellow merchants remind us of them. People such as I don't mur-der anyone. We arrange death with about as much regard as a normal soul would select from this menu.

You seem to be the only one eating, Harry. I was told once by a Georgian General that the best snipers he had ever seen had huge ap-petites... particularly after a killing spree. That would make you very good in the role; and you, George, very poor. Did you see action in Afghanistan, Harry? No, don't look surprised. You were spotted your first day there. That's how I knew it was you in Grömwohld. Your limp gave you away. There is more, much more I can tell all of you but I am tired, even if you are not. I have arranged three rooms for you, and the keys are with the concierge. I will continue this elucidation to-morrow after breakfast. Let's say, eleven-thirty. I take life at a leisurely pace, nowadays, I'm pleased to say. If you don't mind, I would ask you to indulge an old man and excuse me from your company. However, George, if you have the stamina, and the interest, I invite you to accom-pany me to my room. I think it best that I fill in the details of my life that affected you. It may help to placate your anger, if not your dislike of me." George left with Paulo without a grin or a frown, leaving me wondering what was going through his mind.

"What was that all about with George in Berlin? Sounded a bit up-tight about that, didn't he? What do you make of him, Judy?" I asked.

"I'm reserving my opinion at the moment. He certainly appears to know about you, though," she replied, looking distinctly pensive and lost in thought.

"And Haig seemed to be implying that he's behind all this. Was it really necessary for you to tell him we were coming here? I think I should check out your room for explosives, and perhaps park myself in there for the night...what do you think?"

"I don't think he was implying that at all, and if you applied yourself, rather than occupy whatever it is between your ears on foolishness, you may have worked that out. I won't comment on your offer, Harry. It's like the rest of you: superfluous." The wistfulness I thought I had detected had been replaced by anger.

"I knew you would come round to liking me...I'm only surprised it took so long. Shall I order something from the kitchen for you? A bag of bones, perhaps? You can gnaw on them while your superior cerebral content churns over. Bet that sounds really appetising, huh?" I retaliated, in the only way I knew.

"Be careful the cheese doesn't give you nightmares, Harry. You might see yourself in them. Drink some more of your single malt, and let the real world pass you by." She disappeared after offering her advice, giving 'work to do' as an excuse. I hoped it was simply that, and not a return to her isolation before our candid conversation of the Common.

My world was empty of real people and meaningful emotions. The simple summary that Judith had awarded me was correct. Alone, on Paulo's vacated soft settee, watching groups and couples laughing or in earnest conversation, I felt as wanted and welcome as the hot roast pork sandwich that I had ordered would have been at a bar mitzvah. I was lonely. I had always been at the centre of things, from school days to squire, the one everybody chose to know. Now, examining those relationships, not one of those souls who had rubbed shoulders with me could I truly call a friend. My family name had been the fly in the web that had attracted all this attention, yet I felt outside of what was happening. Even the threat of my own death was abstract and speculative. If an attempt was to happen, then I would feel connected; as it hadn't, I had nothing to equate it with. I was detached from it all, impervious to everything except my own superfluous life. "Superfluous," I said aloud, then quietly to myself. "You're right, Judy. I am."

Chapter Thirty-Four

Help With Parasites

"You're a fool, Harry. Most importantly, a fool to yourself. Move up a bit...I want to sit next to you." She had been gone for about an hour, but to me it felt like a lifetime that I had been on my own. "I was pretty hard on you...I'm sorry. I had forgotten what grief can do to a person, and I was being completely thoughtless in not considering how you felt. Please forgive me for my selfishness."

"There was a lot of truth in what you said, Judy. It made me think about things and reflect on my sorry excuse for a life. I seemed to have screwed up somewhere, particularly in relationships, where maybe I've put myself before others."

"You haven't screwed up on anything. The trouble with you is that you have never known anyone that you wanted to share that life with. You've got some high principles, Harry, tough for others to live up to, but you're not wrong in having those ideals. It's just that you haven't met the right one who believes in the same."

"Perhaps I should have met you before we both became so cynical?" Perhaps it was the flight and the drinks that had made be become sentimental, or perhaps it was something else entirely.

"You're not cynical, Harry. You're just fed up that you can't get your own way all the time, and when you do get your own way you want someone to tell you that you're right. You're just a little insecure like the rest of us. Like me, you need to be reassured sometimes." The uncertainty had left her, and her confidence had returned.

Suddenly, a spotlight hit me. Someone had fired a flare gun and the gloominess that had overshadowed me was lifted. There was a distinct sly grin on Judy's face, and it was widening as she rubbed her hands together, with relish.

"You're the most big headed person I know. You've found something out, haven't you, Judy? And you've come back to gloat. That's it…and there was I thinking you cared for me? You had me going there, almost fooled me completely. Go on, then. What have you heard at Paulo's keyhole?"

"No, not there, Harry, from Sir David! Both Willis and Howell have confessed to dealing with the Russian Mafia. They gave away more than that though, playing for a pardon, I expect. They said a Katyerena was the link. Alexi Vasilyev has fingered Katherine for us. Why has he done that? I hope you're on the same page, Harry. Snap out of the melancholy, and start following what I'm saying. The first rule of name change is *what*?" She was sitting opposite now, having moved hurriedly away when I had regained my sanity fearing, I hoped, that I might have strangled her.

"Change them all," I obediently answered, the same question that she had put before.

"Correct, he never changed hers far enough. Take a coveted gold star, and put it on your chart. Alexi's done it on purpose. What's he telling us, H?"

"I've no idea. Have you thought that maybe it isn't her, or that he doesn't follow the same rules as you, or perhaps he just slipped up and made a mistake, like Paulo, with those two names? We're not all perfect like you, my dear. That would make for a dull unedifying world, where people like me could not exist."

"Oh, stop feeling sorry for yourself! Of course he did it on purpose. I reckon he had Katherine tell her father about Willis and Howell so that he would turn them in. He was on to him, but needed cast-iron certainty. He had all his money on it. He's done it, you dumb head, because he's on *our* side. Leaving Katherine's head on the block is his signature on the surrender letter...*I'm yours.* Read the signs!"

"Wouldn't you know if he's SIS? Wouldn't Peter have told you? Or, if he didn't know, how about Haig? I'm still unconvinced that he isn't involved."

"Of course he's not involved...I've told you that. Change your life, and stop being wrong all the time. Alexi is one of our cousins, Harry divided from us, thank God, by a huge sea of water. He speaks the same language some of the time with different spelling and a different dialect, often unintelligible, especially where humour is concerned. If I'm right, and I just *know* that I am, he's been hanging out in Paulo's Russia for a very long time. What's worrying me is why drop his trousers now? Can you figure it out?"

"I know I would like to ask Korovin why he changed from the SIS to Sir David. That is, if Paulo made the choice, or if it was forced upon him," I had fully recovered from the conceptual mentality that had overcome me, but still suspicious about Haig.

Chapter Thirty-Five

Beneath the Topsoil

Theoretical concepts made up the main part of Rudi Mercer's life that was devoted to the cause of American security, conducted from various bunkers around the world; but his all-time favourite was in Regent's Park London, beneath Winfield House, sold to the American nation by Barbara Hutton for one dollar at the end of the Second World War. As heir to the Woolworth Winfield empire, she could afford such charity. When in 1955 the Ambassador to the Court of St James took up residence he, and those that followed, praised her bigheartedness. They strolled around the private garden before being ushered, on yet another practise drill, into the nuclear war protection level, five hundred foot below those manicured grounds.

Rudi, on the other hand, could ill-afford philanthropy in his daily dealings with the secret world through which he travelled. Magnanimity of spirit was a phrase never heard there, as generosity and understanding of failure could not exist side by side with international deceit and duplicity. Rudi was an asset runner, not an operative living the lie, but the orchestra conductor who signalled the time for the soloist's performance.

Over the decades that past, since Rudi first appended his signature to the CIA, his twinkling light had held the gaze of his masters as they scanned the skies searching for new stars to pin their hopes on in the fight against the communist enemy. Rudi's personal star was coded

Vagabond, and Rudi became the sun and water bearer. He brought forth a steady growth of information on which that glint, spotted in dark space, grew into a huge planet. A planet around which dignitaries as powerful as Presidents orbited, lured like moths to his atomising radiance.

Mother had been *Vagabond's* first significant disclosure, and Rudi had feasted on it in Regent's Park like the lions caged in the zoo next door gorging on the food thrown to them by their keepers. *Mother* had been traded around the ears of the whole floor of the Sixth Directorate in Moscow, reaching as far as Alexi Vasilyev who was diligently obeying his Colonel's orders. Except Vladimir's directives were not the only concerns for Alexi; he had Rudi Mercer's desires to consider. Alexi was the star of the show with top billing as *Vagabond*, and it was his investigations that uncovered more about Paulo than any Chief of the SIS or Permanent Secretary of the British Foreign Office ever knew, or was written in the *Garden* file. Unfortunately, there was more to come that Rudi kept to himself, not even telling his priest or his granddaughter. However, he did share it with the third member of his holy trinity: the President of the United States of America.

Margret and Mikhail were doing bundles of business with Ronnie, setting the price they could all live with for the Intermediate Nuclear Force Treaty which was up for auction. The year was 1986 and Mikhail, with Paulo at his side, was speaking words of détente and the reduction of Nuclear Arsenals, of more cooperation with the West and a free and just world for all the oppressed that live in it. At least those that lived next to oil; and Mikhail had it leaking out everywhere. The meeting took place in Iceland where, to the surprise of almost everyone, Ronnie struck a deal with Mikhail. ICBM's were to be cut back: *no need for so many, we're friends now,* they said. Then the world went topsy-turvy again when a bomb blew up the 'La Belle' discotheque in Berlin, detonated by the Red Brigade and killing hundreds of nightclub users.

Vagabond had the intercepted communications from the Libyan Embassy in East Berlin, and it did not take long before Margret stepped in with offers of RAF bases for her best mate's use. When France and Spain refused air passage, the Sovereignty of the Straits of Gibraltar were given for the bomb-laden jets to fly through, on their way for revenge on Gaddafi's head. Ronnie would not allow his support for the perpetrators to go unpunished this time.

Alexi had intercepted more for Rudi. "Mr President, I have disturbing news. Evidence from *Vagabond* shows conclusively that London is not secure. Our Cruise Missile sites are known to the Soviets. We have arrested a Navy Commander who's a faggot, sir. He gave away firing sequences and targets. We're unsure if codes were disclosed, but we're changing them anyway." Rudi relayed the news to the leader of the free world.

And so it began, way back in 1986, that the 'special relationship' that is predominately referred to over *here* was severed by those over *there*. Margret was left in the dark as an American flashlight was shone on the green and pleasant land where England will always be found, in the quest to find the hidden nasty who had sold the missiles not included in the treaty to Mikhail's nemesis: his military.

In the USSR, the still-smarting hawk Generals, suffering from Able Archer, were ripe for Paulo's suggestions and innuendos, and he applied them well. "You see? What did I tell you? Is now the right time to split up our Federation? I think not...how about you?" He added fuel to their fire of disenchantment, supplying the bullets that they would fire in his already decided plan that their power had to be addressed, as would Mikhail's position.

Alexi's grading throughout the concluding years of the Cold War never allowed him to eat from the same table as those who feasted on London news, and when the need for conventional political espionage was replaced by one more concentrated on industry, his opportunities of discovery of the leakage were not readily enhanced. He had all the qualities needed to be a sleeper, including the most important, exceeding those of belief and aptitude: he had endurance and stoicism in abundance enough to wait for the chance he and Rudi knew would come their way.

Enter one Geoffrey Rowell with capitalism, couple that with the shrinking of the Russian Federation and an ever increasing eager craving for monetary reward, and the cake was baked for Alexi's inclusion as he keenly listened to Antopolov on the day he told of the missing Paulo at a hotel in Berlin, and he was made aware of why that meeting had been arranged.

"We have a man deep inside the British secret intelligence," Antopolov told him. "Who, for some years, had spoken of a *ghost* within our organisation, someone none of us could see. He was telling London all about our assets and turning our friends against us. He discovered the possibility that Korovin had connections to an English Lord who was extraordinarily rich, owning his own bank. There was speculation among the less cautious of the Politburo that Korovin could have been that ghost. The evidence pointed elsewhere until my predecessor, your once boss, cast his vote alongside those doubters. His motives behind that vote were questioned. He had ambitions of acceding the throne vacated by our last First Secretary and was miffed when Yeltsin was elected. That, along with Korovin's increased power, nullified his protestations, and the others had been similarly tarnished by envy.

I also could have been counted amongst the envious in those days, but not now. The FSB is more powerful than the old KGB. We answer to no one, and we have no fear of Korovin or his kind. It is us that control the oligarchs, the Mafia and the Government. We are omnipotent, doing whatever we please, and it pleases me now to look further into Comrade Sergeyovitch Korovin and the money he has hidden away. I was the one who read all of Dimitriy Lebedov's original letters and passed them on to Colonel Vladimir Sokolov, as he was, then. It was I that handed them on him and you. I didn't want to touch them back then…Korovin was too powerful for me to reproach. But the tables have turned. Now it is my turn, and I am too powerful for him.

A chemical company has been set up by our friend's influence in London. It has recruited amongst it number, relatives of an English Lord that may have supported Korovin, and his American agent named *Mother*. It might help to flush out Korovin…make him let down his guard. It was our man who arranged that meeting you referred to in Berlin, and it aroused my suspicions as well when Korovin did not show. Work on it, Alexi, and work stealthily. He has the ears of many influential figures, and not even I will be able to save a Pole from them. If you nail him, I will take the glory; but I promise that you will drink from the same nectar as I and taste the ambrosia on which I will feed."

Alexi with Rudi had their incentive. They could kill two birds at the same time and elevate Valentin Antopolov, with *Vagabond* following behind. Nobody was to be told not even Peter Trimble, when he became 'C' in 2007.

Paulo changed his alliance from the SIS to the Foreign Office in the same year, but not, however, for the same reasons as Rudi's mistrust of the SIS. Paulo's reasons were purely based on what Maudlin had told him of Peter's inane attempt at incrimination of himself in his financial dealings with Andrea.

"Dicky Blythe-Smith sent a bloody fool here! Name of Trimble…didn't know his arse from his face. They're employing anyone today…next they'll taking them from redbrick universities, or straight out of school. The Empire is in ruins, Paulo, only you can restore it!"

Another quality a sleeper must have is luck, but Paulo was fast running out of his quota.

Rudi Mercer voiced his misgivings in the Oval Office to a taciturn President, where the reliance on luck would not normally be entertained.

"He's either a fool or a very brave man," Rudi offered by way of explanation. "That message he made up could well have backfired. It was clever, though, I'll give him that. Only President Reagan knew exactly how far he was prepared to go, and if it had been to Armageddon, then there wouldn't have been much of him around to apologise. I wonder if the British knew how much damage he did to us in his days in the KGB. Three complete cells he destroyed, fifteen men and women up against a wall and shot. We should be treating them like our enemy if they knew about that. For the Brits he would sell his soul, but for us, a boot in the face. To me, he's fair game. We owe him, and the Brits, nothing."

"I wish everything was as simple as you would like it to be, Director Mercer, but it's not. I'm going to need the British vote on the Security Council at the UN if we are to liberate Kuwait. What I have in mind can't be jeopardised by whatever you've got going with the British. It will have to wait," said President Bush.

"I would like my reservations in this to be noted, Mr President. The last time we worked with the UN was in Bosnia. At that time we believed it was the French who were muddying the waters...but now, I'm not so sure. I think it is a mistake to work with the British too closely in intelligence. My department's advice would be to act with caution in your discussions and disclosures with them."

"I note what you say, Rudi. However, it is a shame that we can't use what you yourself describe as this man's undoubted expertise in the region. He's probably been entertained in every one of Saddam's homes, and could point them out for our missiles."

"Not only Saddam, Mr President. If he is who I suspect, then he has the background on every intelligence operative in the whole area. We could kick ass from Libya to Syria, and back again. We could turn them inside out!"

"That is a thing to think about, yes indeed...but it will have to wait, Rudi, for another day. Who was it that used that quotation, once...it's slipped my mind?"

"We'll have to do it the hard way then, or perhaps make a direct request to the KGB? Who knows? They might just come across."

In total, Rudi had served under five Presidents, just missing J. F. Kennedy, but he would not continue past Bush. He was forced to take delayed retirement over a matter he had very little control of, but it was not to do with *Vagabond* or *Garden*. The manner of his retirement was a regret to Rudi; but not as much as not being there when the sleeper in London was unearthed by the compromising of Paulo, nor not being able to use the valuable information that Alexi supplied about Shias and Sunnis and the others of the Islamic faith in that huge region.

Chapter Thirty-Six

Heavenly Scent

Judy and I, were still in the bar talking until almost three that Friday morning, swapping stories of misspent youth and adult adventures we had never shared. I spoke of shooting parties, rugby pitches, girls, and jumping out of airplanes. She spoke of birthday parties, family, friends, and falling in love with Tony; and I fell in love with her. *Why*, would be a question I could never answer. It just happened that way.

* * *

It was with George that I travelled in the elevator later that morning, listening to the list of praises he lavished on his father. He, too, had been up half the night reminiscing.

"He is a truly great man, Harry, as was Maudlin. Two lion hearts battling the world. He brought forward peace by many a long year. I reckon a Knighthood wouldn't go amiss... do you think you could have a word somewhere to that effect, after you listen to him, of course?" George wore a solemn expression as extolled his father's virtues.

"You're missing the plot, George. Whatever Paulo has done, it looks as though he has been well and truly caught. The Russians won't want him back to embarrass themselves. They'll want him dead, then write a glowing obituary about him. A Knighthood would only make that more certain."

"Yes, you're right. I hadn't thought of that," he replied, ruefully. Then, as the doors opened, he added, "Couldn't he come and live with us at Eton Square? Then maybe Loti could come too. They would love Mrs Squires' cooking, and I could look after them both. What do you think, Harry? Does it sound a good idea?"

The idea of his reunited family had possibilities; however the security issues would, it seemed, prevent this being practical. My mind was lingering on Eton Square, and the problem I had there, when Judy appeared from the front desk. Her attention was on a letter still unopened in her hand and she was agitated, not looking where she was going. Fortunately, it was into George that she collided.

"He's gone, Harry! Paulo left this as by way of explanation." Abruptly, and without an apology, she forced the thick envelope into my hand. It was addressed formally to Lord Harry Paterson, Earl of Harrogate.

"It was under the door to my room this morning, Harry. I checked at the concierge desk, and they said our friend had settled his bill early this morning and left with his chauffeur. What the fuck's he playing at?" She was more than agitated, as the look on her face and her language betrayed; she was almost white with anger.

It has been my pleasure to meet you all especially you, Harry. I could see the same devil-may-care attitude that I believed to be in your great grandfather. Alas, I will never be around to ask you if this belief of mine was true. I trust that by now your companion, Mrs Meadows, has worked out exactly who Alexi Vasilyev is, and who he represents. Please forgive me for my intrusiveness in regards to Judith, but I had to be sure she was who she said she was. It's my carefulness. The same caution that has kept me alive all these years. Alexi is American CIA, but you can never use that information; it would not only cost him his life but many others as well. You are not built that way, Harry, and I suspect neither are George and Judith.

You see, Katyerena was my daughter's name before we all became Westernised, and the name Katherine would suit her better in her career in the CNN organisation. It would save unnecessary questions, you understand. When she told me that was her cover name when she met Howell, I knew that Alexi was sending me a message. So I met him and made a deal, the last one I shall ever make in the life that I have previously led. I intend to retire, Harry, and live out my remaining days in a less complicated manner.

I became suspicious at our first encounter when I asked who authorised Grömwohld as the contact point. Up to that time only George and old hands at Moscow Centre knew of the means that I supposedly used to keep in contact with Tanya, or 'Mother' as the natives had come to know her as. I knew then that there was, what dear old Maudlin would call 'a bad apple' in the new FSB with contacts in London. That is when I began my preparations to disappear, so I have had ample time to make them with the same degree of carefulness I have already mentioned. You will not find me, Harry, so don't waste your time, or allow the lovely Judith, and whatever department she works for, to waste theirs. At this point of my final communication with you, there is a part of me that wishes I could say sorry for what I have promised in my side of the bargain I have made with Alexi. The truth is that I cannot; I am many things, but not a hypocrite. I have never experienced what others describe as a family, even when I had Maudlin in my life, or Katherine now. There is something missing in me to understand what that words means to others. I have heard it referred to as love and devotion, or duty and support. My response has always centred around me. I came first in every thought I have ever had, and it is still the same. When George and I were alone, I attempted to explain what it is that has moulded me into becoming the inconsiderate person that I am, but it was impossible to convey my life in mere words… and in any case, I'm not sure that I really wanted to. I felt it more as responsibility than an effort to find the connection or attachment that I'm certain George was looking for. The accountability that I feel is not confined to the past where I had little control, but more to the present and the immediate future, that I do indeed control.

You see, it was I who exploited the circumstances that dictated the need for your visit. My meeting with Alexi was before Katherine told me of Willis and Howell. Her telling me was done to confirm his suspicions to Moscow, and then for them to believe in what now happens. I am to die, Harry, or at least seemingly so.

The easiest lesson I ever learnt is that money will buy you anything, I have bought Alexi, and I have bought my death. A few hours from now my car will explode outside my home and three burnt-out bodies will be found, two human and one of a dog, they will be unrecognisable. Viktor, my driver, will be one. (there are good reasons for this that I cannot go into) The other human, I'm grateful to say, has been arranged to take my place in this tragedy. Alexi cannot go back on his word, as I will expose him if he does, and I cannot go back on mine. I have given him George, and that was why you were enticed here. The killer you search for will settle on nothing less than everything, and he could not discover who was communicating with me after he discovered the link to Maudlin. He is Russian, you understand. Treachery of the Motherland is an unforgivable, unpardonable crime. They are embedded with patriotism, particularly if you were born in Stalingrad and had read your history.

Hitler hated the whole Russian population, and his propaganda machine portrayed the people as neolithic subhuman creatures with deformed skulls of huge proportions. His barrage and destruction of that city held more of a symbolic significance to him than a military strategy. It was one dictator against a city named after another. He intended its obliteration as a sign that his will was the strongest. After complete destruction of the place he planned on bulldozing whatever was left, after the artillery and bombing had finished, and erecting, on Mamayev Kurgan the highest point, an allegorical monument designed by his architect Albert Speer. It would show Mother Russia suspended upside-down from a gallows, clutching her heart whilst a perpetual flame burnt below her head. That was how the German's hung their captives; upside-down, in rows upon rows, until they died from pain or hunger. When they were able, Russian snipers were ordered to shoot them dead, to put them out of their suffering and silence their cries.

In my own city of Leningrad the siege lasted almost three years, and until recently the plans that Hitler and Speer drew up for his victory over Russia were displayed in the Astoria Hotel. It shows palaces for Germans, with his subhuman depictions of Russians chained as slaves and housed within a separate moated and walled section of that city. It was their intention that whoever remained after the war would die inside those walls. There was to be no sanitation or fresh water supply to the area. It would save on bullets, and was a cheaper way towards annihilation of a race. When all were gone, it was proposed to use the area as a rubbish dump. If you are Russian, Harry, these things stay in your mind forever. You become protective and solicitous about the welfare of your homeland.

Alexi does not know the identity of your killer; if he did, I would tell you. But I know this much; he will attend the funeral of your father and brother. He needs to see George in the flesh. Tanya, or Loti, as she is known, is also at risk. I was required to give up that information as part of the arrangement I made... it settles the matter, you see.

If you feel what I don't, then you must discover the identity of this man before he takes that revenge. I do sincerely hope that the steps that I have taken in my attempt to expose this killer to you are successful. No doubt you will discuss what I have detailed here and shower me with your condemnations, but remember one thing. This man who has murdered your father and brother has been looking for me over a long period of time. It is only recently that he has discovered what he searched for. You have the advantage; for the first time he has shown himself. When you catch him all is finished, and I will be out of your life forever.

It was signed simply, *Paulo.*

I had opted for the emptiness of the terrace, and the crisp fresh air, to read alone the letter Paulo had addressed to me much to the undisguised annoyance and frustration of Judith and George. The feeling of love that I had declared to myself earlier this very morning had been overtaken by the words that I had finished reading, now neatly refolded, resting on top of the roughly torn beige envelope. Although, as I say, I had finished reading it, I had not finished with it. In the seconds it took for my companions to descend on me, I stared at the blue water of the lake, trying to find something in my memory that would rationalise his sentiments towards his son. But I could not. No other written or spoken words came to me. I was ashamed of myself for thinking that I could have helped this man. George was the first to speak, as Judith, unopposed, grasped the letter. "Well, what did he say?" He asked.

I did not reply; not because I wanted to ignore his question, but because I could not find the right words to hide the betrayal and condemnation from the man he wanted knighted. Nothing I could find felt adequate for him, his son. Experts could argue forever over which form of narcissism Paulo suffered, but I was not one of their number. All I knew was that I wished Maudlin had never gone to Spain to record the names of those who had joined the International Brigade.

My personal expert, Judy, added her analysis as an opening to the debate. "He is a manipulative bastard of the first degree, and no mistake! Clever, though...I'll give him that. It's simple really, then. All we do is look out for someone with 'killer' written across his forehead on Sunday, and we've cracked it. Shouldn't be so difficult to do for you, Harry, with your shrewd judgement of character!" A waiter appeared with two coffees and one tea at that precise moment, stopping me from shouting my reply, but not stopping George's persistence. Judy had reached into her bag for her cell phone.

"Someone tell me what's going on, please?" he asked.

"Here, read it yourself, George. Don't take her interpretation as gospel...sometimes our Mrs Meadows gets confused by facts. Who are you calling or is *warning* a better word to use?"

Chapter Thirty-Seven

Horseflies

It was late Friday evening when we arrived at Harrogate. Joseph and Mrs Franks, had been assiduous in the painstaking detail they had taken over my late instructions regarding our arrival and needs. In all, twelve more rooms had been made ready, and dinner for fourteen prepared. Tanya, with her escorting team drawn from the Static Protection arm of Special Branch, had already arrived, but she had chosen to wait for us before eating, excusing herself from their company by saying, "It will give the soldiers here more time to get organised without having an old fuddy-duddy like me around in their way."

"The gun room is awash with weapons, sir. Might I ask why?" Joseph attentively asked, after reporting Tanya's words.

"Oh, it's nothing really. They're for all the dignitaries on Sunday…you know all the protocol and procedure that has to be seen to be done before they can tick the box. There will be more from the Yorkshire Constabulary here for the funeral, so you'd better warn the kitchen. We don't have to, I know, but better to stay on the right side of the law. It won't hurt to give them a few rounds of sandwiches," I replied, trying to divert Joseph's enquires.

"Your brother Maurice has compiled a list of those who have accepted. There are 387 names down for Sunday, and there are a further 22 names on a Home Office memorandum that arrived yesterday. I have left the details in your office, your Lordship." I had succeeded, and I nodded my recognition to his information while studying farm reports on the computer in the estate office, attempting to distract my mind.

"I think between the two of us, with help from Lady Elizabeth and Lady Rose, we have covered everyone. There will be one notable absentee Miss Stella Anderson, away in New York, giving one of her virtuoso performances. Maurice argued against her inclusion, but Rose and Elizabeth said that it would be callous not to do so, at least now any embarrassment has been removed. Had you not have left a note regarding her, I would never have known," Joseph said, but I wondered if he had never heard her name mentioned. I had not yet become accustomed to this formal address of Lord, and for a second imagined Elliot to be in the room with us. I hesitated in my reply.

"No reason for her to come, Joseph. But I thought it might have been father's wish that she attended."

On the Tuesday, following my father's murder, Joseph was there when I heard how Elliot wanted his private property and money divided. To avoid the taxes that follow us in death, the estate and the family homes had been amalgamated into a Limited Company, and the bank a separate entity, all unaccountable to mortal parasites. Mortality, however, is inevitable to everybody. The only advantage some have over others is their ability to influence the two certainties. Primarily, if they are lucky enough, by having the best medical practitioners at their side when death is nigh; and secondly, if prudence and foresight are part of their make-up, with the best financial advisors alongside to mitigate matters before the event. Elliot never expected death so soon in his life, but did heed advice and make provisions long before that day. One beneficiary was Joseph.

In the early seventies, when Phillip my grandfather tired of Maudlin's interference in London and spent most of his time in Yorkshire, Harrogate Hall was extensively refurbished, with particular regard to the housing of the staff. Before this time, their individual rooms contained simple washing facilities and a bed, and bathrooms were a shared utility, three for each gender. All this changed partly because we did not need as many staff, and partly due to Phillip having little else to occupy his mind. It wasn't that we didn't care, but it had more to do with the fact that we were slow to recognise progress. Rooms were combined, incorporating integral bathrooms, and an outside area was designated for staff use only. These were not the only changes he instigated. Four houses were built on the edge of the estate intended for the retirement of retainers of long employment. Elliot and his advisers saw tax benefits if these homes were written into employment contracts as a bonus after thirty years of service, rather than an old-fashion monetary tradition that was given as a 'custom and favour' gift. They were to be leased at a nominal rent for the life of the occupier, tying the buildings to the estate and the Limited Company. Along with this, the Company would pay the occupants a lifelong salary and expenses for a car, not a gratuitous amount of money conferred as a bestowal, as before. These arrangements created tax deductibles and were not counted, as would have been the case, towards personal wealth, attracting death duties.

When told that he would benefit for these arrangements, I had expected Joseph to show more satisfaction that his future had been safeguarded than he did. Not being an outwardly gregarious man, I thought little of it at the time; but now, when anyone could be that killer, I wondered about his reaction. Since leaving the hotel, I had looked at everyone with suspicion. My paranoia was not helped by Judy's phone call to Haig, which I had vehemently opposed, but as before, I had been ignored. She was not the only one to disregard me. George, too, paid no attention to my counsel of not attending the funeral. He couldn't have been more enthusiastic about being there. The only trouble was that he would not leave my side, insisting on walking in front of me.

"You or I might be able to spot anything unusual if I'm in front, Harry. Keep your eyes peeled."

He had refused to shave away his goatee beard, and offered no token gesture as a way of disguise. "Judith is right. It's the only way to make him show himself, me being there. There's no point in trying to hide. I'll be looking over my shoulder for the rest of my life if he's not caught, and I don't want that. I'd rather face up to it now and get it over with," he stubbornly announced.

With Tanya being here at the Hall, I reckoned on being able to leave George safely in her company; thereby ensuring that he did not appear on Saturday, when the bodies of my father and brother were to be laid out in the chapel with the book of remembrance opened for all those that wished to pay their respects. At least, I thought, that would be two worries off my shoulders until Sunday. Judy had tried to reassure me that all was taken care of, even attempting to persuade me that the actions taken by Paulo were in our best interests, but I saw demonic killers everywhere.

"Harry, it's someone high up in London, not the butler. How's he able to send and receive messages from Russia? Whoever it is will be here for the funeral. What I want you to do is go through those names, and highlight the ones you don't know. Paulo's done us a favour, Harry. He has drawn him out. All we've got to do is narrow it down and catch the bastard. The protection is just for us... there'll be more here for the real event."

"The trouble is, I won't know most of those names. The majority will have come from his London club, or other associations down there. Maurice would have gone through his personal book and found the names. Nobody here would have met them."

"George might have done. Get him and Tanya working on it. It will give them both something to think about and keep them together, make them easier for the boys in blue to look after."

"I thought you said nothing will happen until Sunday?"

"It won't, Harry. Believe me, may not even then." She replied more in hope than belief, I thought.

That was what was missing: trust. Judith had lost mine when she had called Sir David Haig. I mistrusted him and I had no confidence in the police being able to capture the murderer. As I have already said, the police and I had an indifferent history, and I had little faith in their competence.

It was some three or four years ago when I first had need of their services. I had read about the atrocities in the national newspapers, and began phoning around. There had been a spate of attacks on horses overnight in the immediate surrounding area and beyond, with some of the devastated owners known to me. Four had been killed outright, and eight others mutilated by knives and axes. Luckily, our stables had been unaffected, but I wanted insurance that they would remain so. It was early summer, with little to do around adjoining farms, and I was fortunate in being able to hire some labourers and pickers for extra night-time work in guarding our stables. Some of my friends were not so prosperous, having to rely on good luck and police patrolling for their protection; both let them down. The carnage continued into a second week, with maiming and crippling being the main objectives for whoever was doing this.

The death of these poor animals was a secondary consideration to the abject mutilation, leaving the owners with no choice but to execute the animals, in order to stop the terrible suffering they endured from such evil attacks. The stories I was told were horrific. None was more so than the one relating to a child who found her pet, which had been left out in the paddock, recovering from sedation but not and never to recover from the contemptible damage inflicted by a chainsaw. The animal was left to lie in agony, waiting for a humane end.

I approached the Chief Constable with the aim of asking for more help, more patrols, a more obvious presence as a way of deterrence and for the prevention of these heinous crimes. I quoted the opening sentence of his own Police Instruction Book: 'The primary purpose of a police constable is the prevention of crime.' I will admit that, at that stage of our conversation I was far from calm and conciliatory. I had listened to his category of higher priorities and his repeated statements of understaffing due to underfunding, not enough petty cash for such unfortunate things - his phrase and choice of words, not mine. I had, as they say, lost my cool.

"What do you, and all the others idiots like you do on a weekend, then? Watch the news on the television and say, *ah, what a shame, what is this world coming to?* Perhaps you are more comfortable discussing the number of parking tickets issued, and how many more local shops have had to close as a consequence of that process? Why don't you and your cronies do some policing for a change, and earn your keep, protecting people instead of interfering with them?"

He wasn't too pleased with my suggestion, nor with the actions I proposed to take when he would not budge from his stated position.

"In that case, if you won't help us, we'll help ourselves and on your head be it if someone gets killed!"

That appendix of mine, about someone being killed, didn't help my case when I was arrested for attempted murder. I had fired two rounds in the air and then at a pickup truck Jack Jeffries and I found on his land as it made off, dumping a chainsaw from its open tail gate. I, naively, reported the incident that Saturday at three in the morning after trying to chase the truck, but by the time we had reach our own vehicle it was long gone, perhaps luckily. I gave the police its registration number then returned home, thinking no more about it, until Joseph woke me at ten.

I was charged, and held in custody, until I appeared in a Magistrates court for bail proceedings on the Monday morning. When the charge was put to me I pleaded not guilty, and my solicitor argued that there was no case to answer. I had fired my service pistol, for which I held a licence, on private property, with the owner's permission. The alleged intended victim could not be found, the number on the truck was false, and my service records showed that, had I wanted to kill someone that night, my ability with a gun would have meant that whoever it was would be dead. Paulo was right in his assumption that I would have made an expert marksman, I had done the course.

It was a convincing argument professionally put and keenly listened to by the Magistrate, who, after declaring his knowledge of me and my background, and the circumstances surrounding the event with the effects that it had brought to the community, dismissed the case, censoring the Police in bringing such a matter to his court.

"It is my opinion that the defendant has every right to raise a civil procedure for wrongful arrest and imprisonment against the police authorities who have dealt with this abominably. Surely a degree understanding should have prevailed in this case before the use of the law with all its wide ramifications, and the time of this court, were required? In such a matter, the attempted murder of another, a senior officer would have to authorise this action. I will have the name and rank of that officer delivered to the clerk's office by midday. If you have nothing else to waste my time on?"

He glanced at the prosecutor's bench, where the representative from the Crown Prosecution Service simply shook his head. "Then I dismiss this case. You are free to go." He addressed this remark to me. Eyes fixed firmly on the uniformed senior police officer seated beside the advocate.

I never did sue, nor did I send any flowers when Chief Constable Rainer was posted to the Northumberland Constabulary a few months after my court appearance. I had no reason to disrespect ordinary police officers going about their duty. I knew several personally and shared a drink with at the Spyglass and Kettle when, eventually, the two I fired at were caught for another offence, and admitted their guilt. However, I never forgot what was said many times whilst I was at Sandhurst: that the men under command are judged by the quality and competence of their officers, who are expected to exercise good sense at all times. In my view Rainer acted in an imbecile way, showing poor judgement and even less common sense.

* * *

The smell of grease mixed with boot polish and waxed jackets that invaded my nostrils as I greeted the Chief Inspector in charge of the armed blue-clad men of assorted sizes sitting around my gun room with their Hecklers, magazines still attached did nothing to alter my conviction.

"Quite a collection you've got here, sir," he remarked, attempting to engage me in conversation as he gazed at the gun cabinets.

"Yes," obliquely I replied, shaking his offered hand but declining to continue or offer an opinion on the competence of his group. Nor did I remark on their overzealous conditioning of their weapons. I simply walked away reminded of a different life when all was more clear and defined.

"Never put grease on the outside of a Glock. It's made of a superior plastic, and it will slip from your sweaty palm the first time in action. The metal parts need a tender wipe, no more. Imagine you're stroking your lover's nipples for the first time... be gentle, gentlemen. Treat her as a lady would like to be treated, and if there are any amongst you who don't know how to treat a lady, it might be better that you transfer to the Navy; they have a lot of ladies there!" The staff sergeant would say, at weapons training.

Chapter Thirty-Eight

Water Features

Life changed suddenly for Igor Stanislovich Abishley, and it started as a river boat trip that the tourists who take it now marvel at. One of the reason Igor did not appreciate it in the same way was because the year was 1953, one year after the canal opened, and the land had yet to recover from the ravages of the siege. Another reason was more pertinent to the situation. Igor was only three years and eight months old and didn't appreciate much, other than the meagre food his mother fed him and the clothes that she found to clothe him in. Then, however, purely through the fault of lack of age, he never realised that the sacrifice Yelena made helped to keep him safe from the pneumonia epidemic that Stalingrad suffered that year.

The elder Abishleys had experienced a rare war, and a common war. They had both survived, which was rare, and had lost loved ones, which was all too common. Their home, near the port, was one of the first to be hit by aerial bombing on the 23rd of August 1942, killing their two sons outright and burying Yelena beneath tons of rubble somewhere between the ground floor and the remains of the four-teen storey building. When her screams for help were heard, after four ceaseless days and nights of bombing and shelling, her left arm had to be severed at the shoulder before the gangrene, caused by the nails protruding from a shattered floorboard, travelled further into her body. She was reprieved from the sentence of death that she faced, but not the limitations in what little life was left open to her.

The men in grey dusty overalls fed her half the rations of other workers, arguing that she only worked half as much as the others. Clothing, medicine, and water were also halved, as the men in the not-so-dusty grey overalls argued that she couldn't survive long because of her injuries, and more would be a waste.

Stanislav, a river boat pilot by trade, helped his wife when he could. He scavenged and hoarded, like the rest of the conscripts, fighting each other over the scarce morsels that could be found. Dead Germans were, at first, a rare opportunity with pockets full of rations, but that lasted only a year or so, as the German sixth army was slowly starved into surrender by their Herr Hitler. The parachutes that missed his army were another blessing to Yelena. She had friends who did not wear the authoritarian grey coats to cover their bones, but did have knives and scissors as arms and tools from Stalin's communist regime.

Yelena and Stanislav outlived the war and brought a new life into the sorry downtrodden world in which they lived in the March of 1950. They were happy with each other, proud of the new born Igor, and content in the dreams they had for his future. Such is the way of Russians. They are proud, defiant, friendly dreamers, with a splattering of poets who fuel those dreams. But there were no poets watching when Yelena gave up her struggle for survival and fell beneath the hammer of that epidemic she had fought against to save Igor. Now it was Stanislav's role to deliver the salvation they had dreamt of. After saying goodbye to his wife, Stanislav piloted his river boat through the Volga-Don Canal, carrying his son concealed below the timber he ferried to the Sea of Azov and then on to Sevastopol.

Stanislav knew Ibo Pasha well, and they had met many times at the site of one of the battles fought in the Crimea War. Their countries were friends now, not enemies as in the 1850s. Pasha was Turkish, hailing from Istanbul, and had access to the Western world where dreams came true, or so Stanislav had been told. Without exchanging a word Stanislav handed a canvas seaman's bag to the silent Pasha containing his son Igor. That trade, unseen by the Chekists in their wooden huts, was not for money but for a promise made by one man of honour to another. It was not the only thing exchanged that night between those two. Stanislav gave his friend a carefully sealed envelope, bearing his son's name on the front then broke the silence. "Whoever takes Igor, make sure that they disclose the contents of this to him when he is ready, Pasha. You must promise me this, on your children's lives."

Pasha never liked his shortened Christian name, finding it some-what effeminate when mouthed by other men; he had a hang up about names. He had wanted for ages to fully embrace Islam, and change both names into something that he considered more dynamic and meaningful, like Abdullah or Mohammed; but the hectic life he led left little time already, let alone any spare to indulge himself in trivialities. He admired the English habit of addressing one another by their surnames. He found that convention respectful and dignified and adopted that mode for himself, as, in his own opinion, he had both of those English attributes.

Some, like Stanislav, and there were many likeminded, thought Pasha the most honest man on earth. Others within the many legations found in Istanbul viewed him suspiciously, but all were well aware of his worth to them. He spoke Turkish, Greek and English exceptionally well, with enough knowledge of French, German and Albanian to understand and communicate.

Pasha passed Stanislav a note, because Stanislav earned money from the KGB. That's how Yelena beat the odds and stayed alive as long as she did and that's why the Chekists turned a blind eye but discovered two other children hidden on the river boat *'Alanta'*, and that's why Igor ended up where he did. As well as the qualities previously ascribed to the Russian race, adaptability should be added; the adjustment to differing conditions had been inbred in that nation's people from the beginning of time.

* * *

The infant Igor Abishley was placed in the loving care of the Consul, the head of the British Consulate in Istanbul. This man was a career diplomat destined, he believed, to become an Ambassador not continually travelling from one consulate to another dealing with bureaucratic issues of Brits abroad, or Turks wanting to live or trade with Britain. He wanted to leave this transient life and settle permanently in one part of the world to enjoy what that world had to offer him. He was forty years of age, aesthetically missable, and socially definitely to be avoided at any cost. He had forfeited some of that dream when he lost his wife and son to heart failure, following a severe illness of diphtheria. It had been at a time when he was happy as the Cultural Attaché at the British Embassy in Tehran. Here in Istanbul, after months of compassionate leave, he was morose, having little more than the graphic details of that loss with which to engage most of whom he met and conversed with.

"One's throat becomes enflamed, and the neck swells out of all proportion... it's commonly known as the 'bull neck disease.' It stops sufficient air getting to the vital organs, particularly the heart, as in the case of Mildred and Robert, our son. The local Iranians are apparently hosts for the toxin as they've become immune over the years. They are working on a vaccine all over the world. One day, I suppose, it will be eradicated, but at the moment it's very contagious for us Westerners. They suffered dreadfully, you know, my wife and son. I have never got over their loss, and I don't think I ever will. I love them, you see, as if they're still with me," he stated, not really knowing whether it was the audience he was trying to persuade, or himself. At that point our man would normally excuse himself from the gathering, finding a private place in which to grieve for the past; leaving the new recipient of awareness on the 'bull neck' syndrome wondering whether to follow and console, or run somewhere else in case the morbid conversationist returned.

They say it takes up to five years to recover from a close bereavement, and that, almost to the exact month, was how long it took for the widower of Mildred to come out of his shell and venture into the unknown. His marriage, and most probably the pregnancy, had been ordained by others. His father had wanted him gone *as soon as possible*, he would often voice aloud, and although Mildred's father was more reticent, he felt the same reluctance of unending shelter and benevolence about her. The two had known each other since childhood, got on well enough for the parents' satisfaction, so *why not?* A father of one or a mother of another asked. Neither one of the inhibited couple could think of a reason not to comply; so, in St Margaret's Westminster, their knot was tied.

"When are you going to give us a grandchild?" a doting parent on one side or the other enquired pontifically? *Why not?* they thought, and so they did.

Mr English, the Consul, that's how Pasha referred to him, made his first and last attempt at seduction within earshot of the ever listening wannabe Muslim who would have preferred to have been deaf or, at least, not conscious of the balls-up his friend made.

"Would you consider having sex with me and bearing my children?" Mr English asked a rather respectable, beautiful young Turkish girl, at a trade gathering held in the British Embassy. Then, as the girl who he had never spoken to before lost all colour in her face and seemed on the brink of fainting, Pasha thought of striking out at Mr English who hastily added, "for money, of course. I don't expect you to love me...heavens, no!" The shocked indigenous lady hit Mr English so hard that he spun uncontrollably into the Lady Ambassador, knocking her glass of champagne to the ground. All were distraught. The girl left hurriedly with her father, mouthing a torrid diatribe in the direction of the prostrate wounded figure, and Lady Ambassador called anxiously for another glass, asking, "What did that girl say?"

Pasha knew that his friend, Mr. English, would never find happiness again if left to his own endeavours. He would be, more likely, murdered by an irate husband! So, he and Mr English came up with a plan, whereupon it was decided that Pasha would supply his willing youngest sister, aged twenty-one, to become the new Mrs English. A child would be procured and pronounced to be Pasha's nephew, the result of a previous fictional relationship of said sister, who now loved Mr English as far as the second star on the right and back again. The sentiment was shared ditto, with a capital D.

* * *

Ibo Pasha became, some twenty something years after this event, a fully fledged Muslim. He finally took the name of his liking: Abd-ul-Rahim, meaning Servant of the Merciful. His downfall was, ironically, connected to this choice.

Although he held no aversion to change in his religious calling, he did in his way of work. He joined the jihad and the Mujahideen as his main employers at the Russians' instigation, before they invaded Afghanistan. The idea was, that he would serve by doing what he did best: telling secrets. However, within his new ultra-suspicious brotherhood, it didn't work, he came up short, as he always had seemed to do. He was found out before he really began, and was shot, never living long enough to see Igor scale the heights he was destined for.

Mrs English survived the boredom of her marriage by seeking and finding her solace from her husband's timidity elsewhere than their separate rooms and beds, satiating it often with a wide variety of lovers.

* * *

In 1970, at the world-weary age of twenty-four, Rudi Mercer came across the beautifully displayed Mrs English in Washington, DC, and quickly became the Adonis to her hungry Aphrodite. He was a willing and excited participant, never having had an older and more exciting lover before. He would possibly say there was no one like her ever again, if he was gallant enough, which must be doubted.

"No wonder your old man looks worn out, Ceran. I envy him having had you all to himself. He's been a very selfish and inconsiderate bastard," Rudi once said, exhausted, discourteously drawing on one of Mr English's scented Turkish cigarettes and not realising how true his words were. Ceran never enlightened him; she couldn't, because she was unaware of just who Mr English truly was. It had been him who had told of the American Thor missiles stationed in Turkey that were used, five years previously, in the secret bargaining that ended the Cuban crises. It was something that better placed people than Rudi never found out about, and they were not here lying next to the surrogate mother of Igor, the forthcoming arch enemy of Paulo and inciter of slayers of Patersons. Had they have been, the future would not have altered.

"Ciao, honey," Rudi said to Ceran on her departure from his apartment, back to 3100 Massachusetts Avenue and her home within that compound of the British Ambassador. Life been kind to Mr English, fulfilling his dream of an Ambassadorship. "Che sarà sarà" Rudi added, as the door closed behind her.

Chapter Thirty-Nine

Crazy Paving

Igor was sixteen when he was given the sealed envelope that his father had handed to Ibo Pasha, by which time he was skilled in both the spoken and written word of his native Russian language. Stanislav began it with a poem:

Not for every plashing wavelet, watches keen the helmsman eye.
He awaits the last huge roller, when the ninth wave surges high.
But until that last strong roller, swells with deep decisive roar,
We must meet the strife and effort, of the waves that go before.
Even though we scarce perceive them, sinking vanquished to their grave,
Wait, O brethren, wait with courage, for the ninth all-conquering wave.

He handed the metaphorical verse to the Ambassador, and asked for an explanation. To the man seated before him, Igor was known affectionately as Iggy, but never beyond these two was that name mentioned, and Mr English is no longer referred to as such; he is now dead.

"Well, Iggy... let me see." He pouted his lips and tightened his jaw, the usual mannerism he adopted when his full attention was needed. Next came the reading spectacles, meticulously adjusted onto the bridge of his nose, and finally the deep, noisy intake and exhaling of breath that would follow his acceptance of whatever written material was passed to him. Mr. English adjusted his not considerable weight into the reclining red leather chair, lit one of his sweet perfumed cigarettes and began to give his interpretation.

"It's symbolic, especially to a seafaring man and river boat captain such as your father. The rhyme suggests to me the ups and downs of life; the very rhythms, in fact. There we are, smoothly going about our daily whatever-it-is we do with the occasional bump to overcome of course, but nothing too serious until something unseen or unexpected comes along to knock us out of kilter, as it were. What he's saying, in effect, is to be wary at all times, just as a ship's captain has to be, expecting the unexpected. Not in complacency and triumph, however, in knowing what's coming; but in a circumspect way, heedful of what that rhythmical wave might bring." As a diplomat, Mr. English was accustomed to being verbose.

At sixteen, Mr English decided to reveal all to Iggy; his real parents, their history, and his own. It wasn't so much decided by age, but more by the defection of a Major in the Sixth Directorship of the KGB. Mr Ambassador did not feel directly threatened by this, but he knew that this army officer threatened a very delicately balanced arrangement that had been struck between himself and a sympathetic Russian friend.

"It was the politics of the time that lead me to believe in Lenin's dream; I obviously still do, I should add. My father was in the Foreign Office and knew that war was coming, speaking often about the criminality of it all. He and some associates had been approached by several high-ranking Germans alerting Britain of Hitler's ambitions and asking the British government for their support. The aristocracy, for their own avaricious ends, wanted no part in another war, and so they did their upmost to retain the status quo. Intellectuals advocated peace at all cost, conveniently forgetting the atrocities the Nazis committed in Spain and that they were still perpetrating against their own people, so the leaders did what they are good at: nothing. They sat on their hands, hoping it would all go away. When it didn't, opinion became polarised and, in certain people's minds, mine included, the only side that promised to put an end to Fascism was Communism. The Western world had nothing to offer the populous, except greed and war.

I, and many like me, despised the totalitarian and despotic views of Hitler garnering support by appealing to popular bigotry, whilst the supposedly enlightened world did nothing other than consider profit and loss accounts. Lenin had offered a revolutionary ideology of self-worth and equality, one where everyone benefited from each other's labours. There was no other choice for us. I stayed alone in the support I gave the Russians. Other sympathisers went about things in their own way, and our paths rarely crossed. If they did, I was far removed from the outcome. You would do well to ensure the same, Iggy, as a similar role beckons you."

Iggy was used to playing roles. From the approximate ages of three to six he had spent many hours with the flamboyant Ceran, his mother. He was, to her, a little doll to be dressed and displayed as such, fawned over by her and the glittering circle of friends she moved in. Comparisons between their children were made. "Oh, mine was able to configure a Rubik's cube correctly by three," or "mine could understand Einstein's theory of relativity three weeks after birth!" He was in a competition, one in which Ceran was the official and he had no alternative but to enter.

In Istanbul she dressed him in blue and white sailor outfits or shirts with imitation decorative ties attached, as the other British mothers did to their own offspring. In whatever country he found himself in, he had to adhere to the local costume. The *jilbab* in Beirut and Damascus, where the traditional Arab conformity in dress was observed. The latter was where Dad was the *Chargé d'Affaires* for a brief time, before moving to Athens as British Ambassador, where frilly blouses and skirts were Ceran's orders of dress. No matter what the code, she would add a feminine touch, such as a pretty bow to his long curly black hair, or a beaded amethyst bracelet. In Greece, topaz earrings were hung from his juvenile lobes to match the colour of those frilly skirts that were mandatory to wear.

All this done with one thing in mind: to get Ceran noticed and spoken of. From six years onwards, when Ceran was more occupied, Igor was consigned to his father who used him in the opposite fashion…one in which his father could be inconspicuous. Kicking or hitting a ball in a park with your son does not bring the attention that doing the same with another man, without children around, may. Fishing in Lake Assad in Syria whilst holidaying alone with your son, and bumping into strangers and exchanging conversation, would not cause undue anxiety to anyone watching or happening to pass by. Even in Washington, the same was true. The Potomac and Great Falls Park was an ideal place to wander around whilst chatting aimlessly with one's son, eating ice-cream and hot dogs and avoiding as many as you could, but obviously not all, around the kiosks. Then of course there was the inevitable stops to purchase sweets and other essentials at the petrol stations on the drive home, when encounters *just could not be avoided.* Opportunities arose more often to accumulate information, and to pass on your own revelations, when you had a child in tow than when you did not. Dad, the Ambassador, was one of the very best in being inconspicuous. Another thing he was good at was clearing up uncertainty and loose ends.

* * *

Have you ever looked at a child whilst they are questioning you with their eyes? Weighing you up mentally, as if they can see beyond the facade that you portray in front of them, particularly one where you look happy at being used as a punchbag when suffering from a migraine? There comes that time when you must tell them off. Not for your own gratification, for shouting doesn't help that headache, but in the pure wish that you could save them from your own mistakes.

Have you seen their eyes when that happens? Is that mistrust, or just confusion, that you see there? We can all see the signs of growth physically and can alter things in that regard by adding more of this, or less than that, but how do you change the intellect and percipience?

By saying sorry when the reprimand was justified, or tempering the occasion by explanation or a cuddle? But whichever way you believe to be the best for that child, he or she change. They either accept the situation that their mother or father have become different and have developed an angry side. Or they think: *Mum and Dad are inconsistent. One minute they are my friends, playing with me, but the next, after that thing they call the 'television' is laying in bits all over my floor…they are shouting just because I was strong enough to pull it over! There was I thinking I would be praised for my initiative.*

The mind is formulated by such occurrences, affected by the parent's personality. The odds are that, if you are kind and considerate, so will the person growing in that tiny body grow up to be. The reverse is also true, if you are a user or a manipulator….well, that's how Igor grew after Ceran's control and his father's exploitation, and it was with that as his background that he listened to dad's problem relating to KGB Majors.

* * *

"So you see, dear boy, that Stanislav was a pragmatic person, taking advantage of the situations that presented themselves to him and Yelena. You have a special opportunity to repay your father's courage."

"What must I do, dad?"

"Learn from me, Iggy…that is all. I have an example for you of that ninth wave your father mentioned, and how, if we are not circumspect, our boat can be overturned. Perhaps you can recall fishing off the rocks in the Mediterranean when we were in Beirut? We did it quite often do you remember? Of course you can it was great fun, wasn't it? I used to leave you occasionally and speak to a man there. A tall chap, stocky build, with a mane of blond hair. He helped you land a fish once, had a deep laugh, and made a great song and dance about it all, almost falling into the sea! That man and I, along with several others, sympathised with the left wing of persuasion before the War. We all wanted a strong Russia to be able to defeat Germany, and we thought that Britain and her allies were not doing enough in that regard. We thought that the emphasis was too loaded in the American direction, at the expense of the Russian people.

It was obvious to us that after the invasion of Poland the treaty of peace between Germany and Russia would not stand for long. The Russian armed forces were no match for Hitler, but the treaty bought time to reorganise and rearm with modern weapons. The allies would not help with information on even the basic items like bomb sights or tank technology. But we were working behind the cover of diplomacy. Through one source or another, those things and more, were delivered to our friends, eventually enabling them to wage the war that was inevitable...And win it!

Before the war finished, it was by efforts made by like thinking sympathisers that allowed Stalin to sit alongside Roosevelt and Churchill while they divided up Europe, predominately in American favour. Had he not been there, the Eastern Bloc would never have happened, and capitalism, backed by American armed forces, might would have ruled Europe. In our eyes, we needed the Russians to have the bomb. It negated the Americans, and their wish of world domination. The British and the French got theirs later. You have already learnt, I understand, about British and French colonialism, and the tyranny that brought upon people in India , the Caribbean, the whole of Africa, Cambodia and Vietnam? The conflicts that ensued in those places when freedom was denied? You only have to look at Korea and the indiscriminate killing to understand how much human life means to an American General or their President.

The only concern was one of balance, you understand. The Americans had rid the world of the Nazis but, in doing so, had peddled their own dogma wherever they could. They insured their prosperity by fostering loans on stricken countries. Even the British had to pay for its efforts to hold off Hitler when it stood alone. They despised communism and its furtherance of the common man for the common good. They believed in the power of money, but only in their own pockets. This is still true today as you can see from their interference in

Iran, and now the fighting in Vietnam in which they always wanted to fight, after funding French resistance to a free country's wish. We have not been wrong in our ideals. Russia grows stronger as communism is embraced by more nations willing to fight against American capitalism. Materialism is everything here. You are judged by where you live, what you wear, and the car you drive. Communism is more of a levelled plane, one where it is important to help one another. Do you see that often in the West?" Mr. English sat back to consider his words not looking at Iggy for a reply and nor did Iggy feel the necessity to offer one. As far as Igor was concern he was in the presence of greatness and luxuriating in every syllable.

"The man we met in Lebanon was a believer, and he was an enigma to the British. He had served Queen and country well, yet was suspected by America of being one of those hated commies, so he was sent away from here, back to England, and on to retirement for his brave service. He is one of us and, when discovered will be rowed down the Thames and through Traitor's Gate, spending the remains of his life in the Tower, or shot, according to English law.

The defecting KGB Major knows all about that man's past, but that is all he knows in that direction. However, the man in question knows much more, and could, if pressed hard enough, point his finger in other directions. Being in the diplomatic corps has made things easier for me to pass on the knowledge that has helped your father and your true Motherland to get where it is now, and in so doing I have been privileged to more information than most. There is an arrangement in force that my position cannot be compromised by any ninth wave or man-made disaster. Your position will be equally protected…but neither can be so if our friend in Lebanon is exposed." Iggy could wait no more, Mr. English needed help it seemed.

"We are a long way from Lebanon, dad. Have we got to go there and kill this man?" the worried Igor enquired.

"Goodness no Iggy. People like us do not kill, and in this case it is far from necessary. Eventually he will be found out for what he was by the testimony of this Major. Remember, Iggy…you cannot stop the ninth wave. You can only expect it, and ride it out. He will not be found out for what he did, nor whom he knew. They will not catch him for that ride down the Thames because of me. In a last resort, we have others to do the unpleasant side to our work. We specialise in knowing those people and in knowing how to arrange the disappearance of embarrassments without bringing suspicion upon ourselves. I shall tell you how this will be done, old chap. You never know... one day, it might come in handy,"

Igor's education up to this point had been exclusively handled by Mr English, with hand-picked tutors in whatever country they stayed in for a while. But all the tutors had one common denominator: dedication to their well disguised communist leanings. This subterfuge was never discovered,. And on return to England a few years later, when Igor was sent to Cambridge, he presented himself as the staunch patriotic Brit that dad had portrayed, and had envisaged Igor following.

With his background and pedigree, it was not long before he was recruited into the British Secret Service. He never parted with the words contained in that letter written by his Russian father, nor the lessons of deceit and misrepresentation of the truth his dad had taught him so very well. His impression of a desolated and rejected Russia never left him, so when he found out about an English spy working against the land that Stanislav and Yelena gave their lives for, he felt sullied and defiled, as though he had suffered personal violation and betrayal.

* * *

At the end of Stanislav's letter, there was a long appended paragraph, written perhaps as an afterthought. It had no real bearing as to the previous content that told Igor of the lives his parents had lived and how they had met, but it had significant resonance to remain in his life forever. It read:

That day in August 1942 when both your brothers were killed and your mother was so badly injured, I was with my unit on the hills to the south of the city overlooking the Volga and the Western suburbs. Although not the highest point in Stalingrad, we could see virtually the whole city. I was a field gunner in the Fourth Brigade of artillery, and we had been stationed here for some time, expecting the Germans. They had already overrun the Ukraine, with several thousands of refugees arriving in our city by the day. They were a mixed bunch of different nationalities, all fleeing from the Nazis, and had been scattered around families for shelter and whatever food could be provided. Our block, where we all lived, was in front of me and to my right. I could see it clearly, and on one occasion, when the officer lent me his binoculars, could make out our own part of it on the fifth floor. It was one of several of the same height and had spotters for the guns situated on the roofs. These, too, I saw through the binoculars. When night came, there was no light shining from the city but for the searchlights that lit the sky as the sound of planes filled the darkness with the droning of heavy engines. As the guns on the far outskirts of the city opened up, there was a blaze of light on top of our block and other buildings around Stalingrad. Bonfires had been lit, marking them out for the German bombers. We had been betrayed. Amongst those refugees had been Romanians spying for the Germans and pinpointing important targets for them.

When our forces were strong enough, and the German Army was surrounded by our troops, it was the flanks held by Romanian soldiers that we drove through. We took a bloody revenge on them that day, slaughtering many without mercy in ways only battle hardened soldiers could think of. I took my own revenge for your wounded mother and my dead children in a manner I will not describe to you, but I was not alone in this brutality. The betrayal their fellow countrymen had wrought upon us had gnawed deeply into our souls, driving any thoughts of compassion far away. Never forget where you came from, my son, and never forget the evil that man can do to man.

Chapter Forty

Resting Time

What remained of Friday quickly passed. I read the list on which were more names unknown to me than the reverse, and of those that I did recognise, none jumped from the pages screaming *Murderer!* I seemed inundated by detail. Everything appeared to have been covered for both days by my brother, but still I fussed and had to check. I hadn't seen Maurice for several years, and had no desire to rush and reunite. There was no hostility between the two of us, it was simply that we had drifted apart through the ages and now had little in common in which to engage. I was not in the mood for idle niceties, nor was I looking forward to the conversation with my recently extended family at dinner.

Joseph carried my excuses, blaming tiredness and weight of responsibility as reasons for my absence, but really I was being selfish. I wanted to be alone and to rationalise my thoughts towards the future and those around me, including Tanya and George. If there was only one thing that I had learned from all of this, it was that I did not want the uncertainty to continue. I wanted a quieter, more settled life. I filled a glass from the office decanter and, with a packet of cigarettes in hand, went to find a degree of solitude in the courtyard beyond my office doors, watching the pairs of armed police patrol around this old house of mine. I felt a heavy load of responsibility.

The persistent drizzle turned quickly to rain, with a distinct smell of salt pervading the air. The strong pelting raindrops bouncing on the cobblestones seemed to me to resemble small people, like broken matchsticks, hurrying away, where to or where from, I wasn't sure, but I pictured myself running from here.

George was my main concern. I could only marvel at how he was still standing after all the revelations of the past week, combined with the knowledge that he was next on the list. If it had been me…well, I'm not sure what I would have done. Then Tanya, thrown into the mix at the time of life when lawn green bowls was the highlight of the week. I was mulling over the thought of turning Eton Square over to them, and how everyone else there would react when my third and immediate problem appeared. I had wanted to put her to the back of my mind; she was, if I'm honest, why I had not joined them all at dinner.

"Would you like some company, Harry?"

"The stone seat might be a mite uncomfortable for your skinny bum, but yes, why not?" I just could not help myself, using the derision that came so quickly and easily to my tongue as a shield against what I was trying to hide.

"Ha ha. Look, Harry, I've not come to fight you. I've come to…well…to say sorry, really. I've been hard on you these past few days and for that I'm sorry. You've been the admirable Paterson in all of this, and I salute you. I can't imagine what's being going on inside that mind of yours, losing two close family members and then discovering three you never knew about hidden away by the man you so revered, and now facing up to it all. George is a friend of yours and the thought of him being used as a coconut at a fairground can't be easy, despite the precautions. We'll catch him, Harry. Paulo seemed confident of that."

"*Seemed*, Judy. Got nothing more positive than that to reassure us? I know that no one's coming here on Sunday with guns blazing in George's direction. I'm not silly. In some way, I wish they would…at least then it would be over and done with, and this lot might get a clear shot and get in first. No, I doubt it will play out that way. Whoever it is wants a sighter; they want to taste the kill before the revenge is fully satisfied."

"Then what's bothering your size twelve feet, H? They're twitching... it's a habit I've noticed you've got when you're not comfortable with what you're about to say." She said, nodding towards my dangling right foot.

"Perhaps I'm just going through the male menopause, or got a gnat bite with all this rain around."

"Don't shut me out, Harry. Over the days we have spent together, I've come to like you around. You've grown on me. At first, I meant to be demanding, but somehow I just carried on being a bit of a cow, when I didn't have to be. You got under my skin, I think, but in an affectionate way. Otherwise, I would never have told you of Tony. You're a friend now, Harry, and friends tell each other what's on their mind."

I had never felt as close to a women as this in all my life amongst them, and I had no idea how to express my feelings. What would happen if I suddenly announced "I love you, Judy," would she hit me, or just laugh? I had never finished the book on women, only getting as far as how to make their acquaintance and what to do to satisfy mine, and on occasions their lust. The end, from what I had seen of it, looked boring, finishing in separation or divorce. My right foot was now firmly against the stone floor, but this stability did not improve my situation, or my confused thoughts. I decided that perhaps I was wrong in the interpretation of my emotions, and time for a re-examination was needed. I took the cowardly approach, and said nothing of them.

"No, it's nothing... it's just me. I'm a bit weary, that's all. I guess I've been trying to think of too many things at the same time. I'm having one more drink, then turning in. Would you like to join me, and then I'll go through what will happen tomorrow?"

* * *

Saturday arrived, with the doom that hung over me reflected in the dark rain-laden clouds blowing in from the moors.

"It never seems quite fitting, a funeral or a wake in the sun, my Lord," Joseph offered solemnly on greeting me in the breakfast room. The two caskets were due to arrive from the funeral directors at 3 pm and placed, opened, in the family chapel for the visitation starting at 4. Flowers were already being collected at the Gatehouse to the Hall.

"There has been an unexpected amount delivered so far, my Lord. It may be wiser to place only the immediate family floral tributes inside the chapel, and perhaps line the path with the others? I have had the remembrance book placed at the lichgate. There it can be signed before, rather than after respects, easing the passage around the coffins. Shall I see to the flowers, Sir?" It was a woman's soft step that I heard after Joseph's departure, but not those of my dilemma. Tanya was as early as I this morning. She greeted me with a bearlike hug, as though we had known each other all our lives.

"Hello, Harry. You know, the more I see of you, the more I see of Maudlin. He was a brick of a man, a tower of strength in a crisis, just as you are now." I didn't feel much like a *tower of strength*; more like a whimpering idiot with thoughts of stupid love floating around my mind, clouding every feeling I had this morning. Without Joseph, I didn't know where I would be.

"George acts so strong, Harry, but he's as worried as hell about today and the internment tomorrow. He wants to be a pallbearer, as he has said, but thinks that will be when it happens, you know…gets killed. He feels exposed out there. He admires you and looks up to you. Do you think you could persuade him to step down? I'm sure if you could think of a reason he would, but it must come from you, he won't listen to me."

She too was a small eater, reminding me of Judy as she sat with her single slice of plain toast and black coffee. I shook my head, involuntarily trying to remove all thoughts of stick insects.

"Are you all right, Harry?" Tanya asked, with genuine concern.

"Yes, I'm fine. I'm sorry. I'll have a word, but I don't know if it will do any good. He was firmly set on doing it when he asked, he said it was not only his duty, but his privilege and honour. I'll do my best Tanya."

I replied, but held no belief in the success of my efforts nor in being able to rid myself of my distraction. It was Tanya's turn for confession.

"He feels alone, abandoned and, I suppose, betrayed. He's feeling a bit raw round the edges, and I can certainly understand that. The cosy world he lived in has been turned upside down by people he trusted. Take Maudlin, for example. Okay, he looked after George financially, but being his grandfather and never saying? How would you react to that? How would any of us? Then there's his father. He saw him for what... an hour or two in Switzerland? Then he disappears, leaving him facing a killer, out for some sort of Russian revenge with no real explanation other than that Paulo saved the world. So he's a superman, but won't stay around to save his son!

Strike that one up to experience, eh? Now, we come to me, his mother, who swore an oath to the man who abandoned him and for fifty-four years leads him to believe she's his aunt. Very maternal, wouldn't you say? Understandable to you and your lady friend because you know the facts, but George doesn't... not all of them. How could he in two hours, with Paulo and then me trying to justify what I can't? Lastly, there's you. You've been complacent at best, and at worst you've been downright disgraceful towards him. He grew up looking out for you, playing at being your elder brother when he was your uncle. I'm no genealogist, but maybe he should be Lord Paterson and not you. Have you thought about that, Harry? As of yet it hasn't crossed George's mind, but it will do. It's bound to." Thinking her coffee may be ready to taste, she stopped her analysis. Giving me time to reflect.

* * *

Wrapped up in my own self-interest, I had been neglectful about George with all that had happened in his indirect life, and how the revelations must have affected him. I had given him little or none of my time to help him adjust to the changed situation he was in. The last thing I could remember was asking Judy what she thought Paulo meant by saying that George had somehow let his father down in

Berlin, and since then inconsequential things had driven him out of my thoughts. There had been opportunities, if I had wanted to take them on the plane, for example, to ask about that and how he was dealing with matters but I hadn't taken them, and now I felt guilty, deserving of Tanya's rebuke. There was not long before I had other things to consider. Tanya had finished her coffee and was back on track, speaking of her son.

"Has he shown you the letter Paulo left him yet, Harry, or have you hidden yourself far enough away from him, so that he hasn't been able to find you? Last night he was too worried about *your* lack of sleep to wake *you*. Do you know that he wouldn't wake you when he found it, even though I told him he should? That's my George for you... considerate to a fault. He was always that way with me when he thought that I was just his aunt. Where's *your* consideration Harry, to the family name, or that *auntie* woman, eh?" The seventy-four years of her far-from-normal life had not dulled her perception or awareness, something I was sure she always had, after seeing that box of hers.

Leaving a simplistic "I'm sorry," hanging in the air, I left immediately, determined to find George and his letter, but it was Judith who I first encountered coming from his room.

"If I were you I'd leave him, Harry. He's very confused. He will work it out, I'm sure of it. He's trying to think back to something, trying to remember a face from years ago. If you have to, just poke your ugly one around the door and say hello, then leave him, H. I have to tell you about his letter." *Superfluous* came back to haunt me, and with a nervous knock, I did what I was told. "I'll sort it all out, George, believe me. I'm going to talk to Judith now about that letter. When you're ready, come and find me. I could use the help of a friend... bit thin on the ground, aren't they?" Without waiting for a reply I closed the door on him, but not the gaping hole in my heart.

* * *

"He took his jacket off when he went to Paulo's room for their get together on Thursday night. Last night he was hanging it up and checking through his pockets, when he found it: his father's final attempt for a reprieve in his son's opinion of him. Paulo has told George that when he went to Berlin for a chance meeting with his father, the man that had come to see Paulo is the man behind the murders, and now he's trying to remember what he looked like. The name he gave George was Geoffrey Rowell, and he said he was head of the company you work for, H. Know him?" Judy asked, eyes bulging in expectation whilst jumping from foot to foot. That stopped on my reply.

"Never heard of him, I'm afraid. I didn't get invited much into the elevated realms of the top flight premier management of the company…I simply sat at my microscope and ran errands for SIS in my spare time. Nobody told me anything." Her excitement had not completely disappeared.

"You should read it. Skip past the first bit it's Paulo-speak for — *I'm an asshole please forgive me for being one.* It's the second part that you'll find interesting." Those skinny arms and hands of hers, once my bête noire, were gesticulating in all directions, holding fast to that letter that I so dearly wanted to share.

I never had that chance, Judy summarised it for me. "Alexi told Paulo everything he had memorised from Willis and Howell; how they had been instrumental in the pursuance of government policy towards the chemical industry, and how easy it was to convince them into the takeover. They had used private funding to conceal HM involvement from audit companies answerable to parliament. The real purpose was to pass on, to interested parties in Russia, current work and direction in bio-fuels, and spin-off enterprises being developed in what was fast becoming the leading company in those fields in the world. Maybe that was your doing, eh, Harry? No don't answer that one, I'll take a stab at it later. Anyway, Willis and Howell's interest was purely monetary, however, Alexi believes that your company is only a cover for a wider operation run by this man in London, set up to avert attention away from his major operations. Bio technology in the pharmaceutical industry is the main interest, but the man has a finger in many pies, including telecommunications and armaments manufacture.

Paulo was in charge of the repatriation of all the state owned Russian assets when the Federation of Soviet States broke up. He imagined that this would be directed at military equipment and the like, and he came across the same project codename many times. In the portfolio that he was given, were several laboratories that had to be retrieved, along with scientists and technicians and an enormous amount of stock, this, too, carried the same coding of *Pasha*. Paulo offers no explanation to any of this. He suggests that these portable laboratories were simply operating for profit in supplying the markets that Russia dominates in several African countries, along with its own neighbours and the emerging markets of Brazil and India. However, he added a sinister overrider. He made tentative investigations into the stock held at these sites and came up with mostly conventional medicines and vaccines along with mainstream research, some of which he could trace to the same name. But, when he tried to look deeper, he was blocked out of their system. Even he could not access the data. The only thing he can testify to is that there had been regular shipments of material classified as 'Pharmaceutical Compounds' to very volatile Middle Eastern countries: Iran, Iraq, Syria, and Lebanon. He put this with his knowledge of those regions, and came up with biological weapons as being another explanation. He leaves it hanging like the sword of Damocles suspended over our heads, Harry." Judy left me to find George, a computer and a safe line to Sir David Haig passing me the beige envelope stamped Hotel Baur Au Lac, bearing the Swiss flag.

I found no rest that day, unlike the eternal rest found by my father and youngest brother, laid in their opened caskets in the chapel. A part of me envied them the peace that had been thrust upon them, but whatever small piece of sanity was left to me, wished them well in a safe part of heaven; far away from the hell I now dispatched my memories of Maudlin to.

Chapter Forty-One

Mystical Garden Light

The intense two-year affair that was mutually enjoyed by Rudi Mercer and Ceran English ended when Mr English was recalled to London to be awarded the KCMG and retirement from his distinguished time spent in diplomatic service to his country. At the age of sixty it was considered that he had done enough good deeds for the Crown, and could now be released to spend his time and influence elsewhere. He joined a leading pharmaceutical company as a market advisor, lent his name to less well-known charities, and saw out the remainder of his days coercing former associates, and their friends, into opening doors that would normally be closed to his multinationally financed corporation. He gave lectures and after luncheon speeches, shunning the after-dinner circuit to spend time with his son whenever the term ended; or, when time allowed, at the rooms he took in Cambridge, sharing his evenings with Iggy, discussing their mutual future. The lack of clarity of Igor's background curtailed a career in the diplomatic corps, to which the doors were only open to those of at least ten generations of upstanding British descendants, but the antecedents of his benefactor opened many others for him, including the one hiding the British Intelligence safe.

At university, Igor had been studying mathematics and history in the period he had spent there before Mr English and Ceran arrived from America. He had fared well, but had not excelled in his studies.

His talents lay in being like Ceran: noticeable. He had produced and starred in many productions for the Footlights Company of comedy shows, touring at Christmas time with the King's College Choir. The tendency that Ceran had for dressing him up had stayed with him, and now, with the addition of makeup and the limelight, he had found a place for one side of his diverse private life. He did not hide his sexual orientation nor did he display it wantonly, but it was there for those who possessed the same traits to notice. Mr English could not be counted amongst that number.

For the holder of the Knight's Cross of St Michael and St George, sex seemed a troublesome thing to be avoided and left unspoken of. He had seen many lives ruined by it, marriages and prospects ended by indiscretions *committed in the cause of what?* he had wondered. Ten minutes spent uncomfortably in the back of a car or worse, a series of sweaty nights like the ones he had endured with Ceran when they had first married? He had dismissed the idea of satisfying her passions when not even two nights had passed of their honeymoon period, retreating to a separate bed and setting the pattern for the rest of their life together. He did not blame her for his inadequacies or offer lies in his defence. On the contrary, he spoke the truth to her disconsolate questioning eyes. As a diplomat, he was well versed in words of deception and vagueness, or variances of truths. The outright truth was a commodity rarely used between practitioners in verbose and reportage speech, but Mr English was a principled man, and knew when honesty was the best policy.

"My dear, I don't want you to be offended...but, you see, I'm not a very sexually driven man. I never have been. Mildred was not like you in that department. She was more timid than I was, if that was possible. It was the first time for both of us and, well, it was awkward, so to speak. If it hadn't been for our parent's wishes, I doubt we would have done it. They expected a grandchild to carry on the name, and we were lucky that the child was a boy. If it hadn't been, then heaven knows what might have happened. How can I put it? Mildred was not keen to try often and it would not be a lie, as far as I am concerned, to say that what I hadn't enjoyed, I didn't find the need to repeat. I hope you understand!"

She didn't, but wouldn't waste precious time surrounded by desirable, willing men in trying to; her sensuality needed satisfying. When Ceran started her liaisons they were not looked upon, by her husband, as acts of unfaithfulness. They were considered by him as a natural form of progression for her to indulge herself in. For those who wanted to put him straight on what he already knew; he would simply shrug his shoulders and lower his eyes, as his way of acceptance. To Mr English, it was an advantage. Her behaviour distracted onlookers away from the fight that he was engaged in; the one he could, and did, eventually win. No one would ever suspect that a man who could not keep his wife satisfied, would have the balls to screw his own country!

Igor's penchant for male company was not unsettling for Mr English either, nor the nodding heads at Moscow Centre. What was once described as 'the English disease' by the French had never been frowned on by the Russian puppeteers. It had always been a way into the upper spheres of decadent society, and not just in Britain but the world over, including the self-righteous French. To Igor's youthful good looks were added confidence and charm, and his desire to be noticed was not long in being fulfilled. He joined the young Fabian group of socialist thinkers, joining debates on the gradual reform of society towards democratic socialism rather than a revolutionary approach. He was an erudite orator, and soon published in the New Statesman.

In 1972, Britain was in darkness for four days a week, because of fuel shortages caused predominantly by the left-wing socialist-led coal miners being on strike. Prime Minister Edward Heath would not govern for long; the few would defeat the majority in a weak democracy governed by greed and self-preservation. The irony of the situation was not lost on Igor when he was approached by the British civil service, one not known to favour votes of reform to its own constitution. He was invited to enter the battle on the side of the Right. It was Dicky Blythe-Smith who made the offer.

"These are turbulent times in which we live. We risk elected governments being controlled by outside influences and not being able to represent the electorate, but more inclined to render assistance to vested parties. The British Secret Service must see to it that privileges of citizenship of this country are enjoyed by all. Your adopted father's name is held in high regard in the country of his birth, and I'm sure you would welcome the chance to build on the reputation of that name. I am offering you such a chance. We want you to continue to build on your affiliation within the Labour Party. Become a card-carrying member, and, in time, ingratiate yourself into its inner sanctum. Give them stories of depravity abroad, hedonism you've witnessed at the Consul's table, at the Ambassadors Ball. You have a vivid imagination, so use it with tales of self-indulgence, drunkenness, frolicking under the sheets and behind the shed…that sort of thing. Throw in a few underhanded deals, like turning a blind eye to certain transactions for acceptance of a Roll's Royce bid, or one from BP. Better still, use the British Leyland name. They're dying on their feet, and the next in line for another handout from the public coffers. Pull this off, and there is a great future here in England for you. My office door will be open, and that of my club. We'll make you truly English…one of the chosen race. If not, well, don't want to go down that road, do we?"

* * *

"Ironic, indeed, the use of implied threats to induce me into the very organisation I want to enter, the head of the serpent knowing nothing of the trail already laid! How easy it is to work amongst snakes," Igor related to Mr English the following mist-shrouded morning, drawing on Turkish cigarettes and gazing, emotionless, at the London skyline from the boardroom of Smith Kline Beecham, the domain of he who wore the Knight's Cross of Saint Michael and Saint George. "We have done well, Igor. My intuitiveness into the British nature, and your…" Mr English paused for a while, pondering on the right expression to use in describing the next in line as Russia's ears and eyes on America's ally… "*exuberance*, have seen us through. You are in, my boy; make it count!"

That is exactly what Igor did. For the next thirty-nine years, he doubled as a double. A complicated thing to do for the ordinary man, but with genes from Stanislav and Yelena and the interference and guidance from Mr and Mrs English, Igor was far from ordinary. At first he began spying on the Red English for the Red, White and Blue English, and then spying on all colours of them for the Russians, who laughed all the way to their bank. The only trouble for this association of reptilian minds was that eventually, when Paulo owned the bank, the deposits made by Igor were never securely underwritten by anyone. Paulo pocketed most of them, never passing on a return on the investments in the depositor's direction. Instead, he returned the capital from whence it had come, insuring Igor's wrath.

With the qualifications he gained at Cambridge and the patronage of a KCMG father, a significant place was found in Price Waterhouse for Igor's material talents, whilst his spiritual ones prospered inside the Labour Party. He walked in exalted air, perfumed by success and dressed in the refineries of wealth and prominence. Paraded to all and sundry as 'the son of our distinguished last Ambassador to the United States' when accompanying his elders at development conferences for business purposes or for political ones. There, he tagged along behind the very leaders of the Socialist party as a volunteer aid in his spare time. For years he enhanced Dicky's knowledge of the left wing of British politics, while at the same time alerting Moscow of pickings to be found among the disillusioned far left-thinking periphery. These, Moscow instructed, were to be encouraged and developed by hands other than Igor's in replacing the ones that Dicky had told Igor to concentrate on; the ones already suspected as Russian sympathisers, and now confirmed by Moscow. These were the same names that Paulo was informed about when he found Jack Simmons. They were spent, used up. Igor could confirm Dicky's suspicions and make himself indispensable in the cause against the *subversives*. He dutifully obeyed his instructions, putting an end to several established and potential political careers in the process. As his reward, he was presented with the Official Secrets Act document, and asked if he would be good enough to add his signature. "Become one of us, dear boy. Make daddy proud." They never gave him the combination to the safe that day. Even fools don't always make mistakes. However, no amount of education can turn a stubborn fool into a wise man, and they awarded it later.

Mr English was indeed proud and satisfied that their plans had been completed, and he danced around that second star on the right, that Ceran had so liked, with excitement. Stanislav never came to hear of his son's elevation. Had he done, I'm sure he would have laughed whilst tending Yelena's grave, whispering "All will be avenged, my love, Russia is to be great again."

Chapter Forty-Two

Shadows Along the Path

"There must be something you remember about him, George. What about the colour of his hair?"

"I've told Judith, Harry. There is nothing. At the check-in he wore a hat, and I was never that close in the hotel. I never saw his face only the name I heard when I was beside him at Heathrow. I never looked across in case it spooked him. He was taller than me…that's all I have. It was a long time ago, and I never thought it would end up like this. If I had, I would have taken a photograph or maybe a gun would have been better, and then we wouldn't be where we are now! Look, it's no good how long you go on…I just can't remember." He was agitated, as we all were, but George was more so. His frustration was born from all that Tanya had said, and I hadn't had a chance to address any of it. He had spent almost the entire day exclusively in Judith's company whilst she had 'walked him through' the episode ending with his abortive attempt to find his father in Berlin. We had met for the first time on our way to the chapel for the memorial service held after all the other mourners had left, when the two households combined for their own private show of grief.

The rain had persisted all day and as we walked towards the chapel, under the canopy of the overhanging ash trees, the polyethylene protecting the gifts of flowers crackled, as though several cars were being driven across gravel. On our return, the rain had finally stopped. Now the droplets from the overhead leaves made the sound of a single pebble being kicked along a cobbled path, as if Elliot and Edward were now saying their final good-byes to us on our walk home.

I had locked the doors on the coffins and the three of us followed the poignant procession of the umbrellas, paired off in twos and threes, back to the welcoming warm glow of the Hall. The severity of the situation was not lost on any of us, but it was George who commented on our escort.

"Are they any good with those guns, Harry, or are they just for show do you think?" His previous bravado was abandoned. The reality of the heavily armed police and their purpose eating away at his confidence as Sunday drew ever nearer.

"Nobody will blame you if don't want to carry Elliot's casket tomorrow," I responded. "We can keep you out of sight you know. It's not as though you have to do it or be at the graveside to be seen to pay your respects. Everyone knows how you feel, George, how you loved Elliot and what you did for him when he was alive,"

"I don't know. I don't know anything at the moment...I'm a little scared, if I'm honest. The truth is I would rather be anywhere than here right now. Lying on a beach enjoying the fortune I knew nothing of sounds pretty good to me! But I can't, Harry, can I? No, it's got to be done. One way or another, I have to be here. Oh, I don't know. Let me sleep on it and make a decision in the morning. Maybe I'll find some Dutch courage by then."

"Okay, George. But remember, everything is fine by me. You do what sits well with you, old chap," I added, still trying to reassure him.

Judy had been quiet throughout the sojourn to and from the chapel but now, as we reached the warmth of the Hall, she spoke to George. "We will have to go through it again, now that Harry is here. He may think of something I've not mentioned or asked. Another mind on the job George, perhaps a different perspective, eh? Then, if we come up with nothing, so be it. We face it tomorrow, and catch the bastard."

"All right. Now that you're here, Harry, it would seem a shame that you have missed out on all our fun." For the first time in days I saw his self-assurance return with the flicker of a smile.

"That would be an ideal place to start, George. Tell Harry about the fun and games you had at the check-in desk that day." We were in the library, the site of my own interrogation but without the machines which had gone. I was sure, however, that Judy would have some means of recording our conversation.

"It was a joke, really. There I was, with just the name on Jack Simmons' message to Paulo. I had no way of knowing what he looked like, so I had to find out somehow. Well, as I said, it was comical in the extreme. I made out that I was nervous about flying, which wasn't far from the truth, There were about five or six girls on duty behind the check-in desk and it wasn't a busy flight by all accounts, so it was easy for me to walk up and down, pretending to decide whether or not to board the flight. I kept talking to myself, saying — *Shall I get on it, or not get on it? I'm sorry, can't make up my mind yet, give me time!* I had to do it for about half an hour, you know. Made myself look an idiot, but they were ever so polite and understanding, especially as I told them that I was like this every time before I boarded an aeroplane, made them laugh that did. Each time someone checked-in, I hovered around them like some eccentric old fool until I heard their name, then off I'd go again, apologising to all. That's how I discovered Mr Rowell and knew it was him when he eventually arrived at the Hotel."

"That was clever! I wouldn't have thought of that, George... showed some high quality initiative there. Did you get a glimpse, anything we can build on?" I asked, knowing that Judy would have covered it, but I was trying to help.

"Look, I used to play a brain-teasing game on one of Mrs Squire's nephew's electronic Nintendo, one where it shows you words for about a minute or so and then you have to write down as many as you can recall. I was useless at it. Got about three out of forty. I'm just no good at that sort of thing and, as I've said, I didn't know that this day would arise, did I?" George was not made to remember facts about people in airports or hotels. It's an art that can be taught, but George had never had the need for the lessons.

"How were they, Rowell and Paulo, to recognise one another?" I asked. "Oh, that was simple. Rowell would lay his briefcase flat on the table, handle pointing away from himself. He put that in his message."

Judy went back over everything she and George had covered in my absence; what he was wearing, what he ordered to drink at the Hotel and on the flight, whether he was right or left-handed…even the size of his shoes. There was nothing constructive that I could add.

"There was one thing, he smoked." George suddenly announced. "The waiter lit a cigarette for him when he sat at the corner table in the restaurant. Yes, I'm right. He sat facing the door on my left side, with his back to the wall."

"Did you see what brand?" Judy asked, excited by this new lead, but it lead nowhere.

"No chance, he was too far away. But there was something though. I remember the waiter picking up the packet and looking at it as though it was special, and I saw him blush. I thought it was the light at first, but it wasn't…it was a definite blush."

"For someone who says that they can't remember anything that's quite a lot, George. Thank you, I'm sure we'll find some sense in that," I replied, not knowing what that meant.

"We can assume that this man Rowell met someone on the way to rendezvous with Paulo, and that's why it took so long but what I can't understand is if that *was* Alexi Vasilyev, then why didn't he give Paulo a description?" Her question was addressed to me as I was the only one in Judy's company, but I had no answer to it, nor to others that my cowardice would not allow me to ask.

"Maybe it wasn't Vasilyev that he met, or maybe he was in disguise," I added my pennyworth, just in case she was about to leave and find more intelligent answers on the telephone or in her computer.

"Hmm…could be." Those long fingers were drumming against her knee, tucked under herself in that usual repose of hers. With her un-painted nails and absence of make-up, she seemed vulnerable and naked, without the pretence of infallibility coupled with supreme confidence that she usually gave to the voyeurs of the outside world. Was I being allowed further within her inner refuge, or was I an avuncular figure around whom complacency could be casually worn? I felt clumsy and uncomfortable as I tried not to stare at her, silhouetted against the iridescent flames from the fire that again coloured her hair a twinkling orange, and shimmered from her skin. She looked as if she belonged here; it was *I* who didn't.

"Do you think that you will keep in touch once all this is over, Judith?" I asked, boyishly… hoping for the stupid romantic answer of *I'm never going to leave you Harry, I'll stay with you forever and a day!*

"What did you say, Harry? Sorry…I was miles away. I wonder if it was the killer he met, and not Alexi? That would explain why he doesn't know what our man looks like, don't you think, seems to me to be the only answer? Go on…what was it you were saying?"

I was in a no-such-place without any room for a lovesick Harry Paterson. I offered up Edward's friend, the one who had found him, and some of his other friends, as my excuse to leave. I said that I was expected to meet with them at their hotel in Harrogate before the next day's funeral. It was a lie, but it was all I had in the locker left to use. I retreated to my office and watched the fading sun paint the sky red between the remains of the disappearing clouds. I brooded on what I could not change, and what was impossible to have. My frivolous past had caught up with me, and now was the time to pay.

For the three years between the end of Able Archer and the death of Mr English, nothing about Igor was frivolous. He diligently went about his Moscow-driven assignment of tracking Tanya, but to no avail. He could neither support nor disclaim the fact that *Mother* was in America. He was back on familiar ground, being posted as an attaché to the British Embassy in Washington after GCHQ picked up radio traffic from Moscow to the squadrons they readied for retaliation, had Reagan not stopped his psychological games. Fleming was then 'C', and Margaret Thatcher had promised her soul mate, Ronnie, all the assistance she could. Fleming, however, had never been briefed, and wanted to know "what the f—k was going on!" As he succinctly put it. "No one told me that we were about to start the thing for real! I was told it was an exercise no more. It came too bloody close for my liking!"

So Igor went and had a meeting with American middle ranking officers of the intelligence community, swapping stories of tactics used, radar station locations, response times, and who the hell knew who this *Mother* was?

Igor played his ace. "I do," he said.

With lecherous ears, Rudi Mercer listened carefully to all Igor told him about Tanya. "How do you know all this?" Rudi asked.

"We know because, in 1956, Paulo Sergeyovitch Korovin left her in England to spy for the Russians. She somehow came here and is now on your Strategic Studies Group, thank God. That cowboy Ronnie of yours almost tipped the balance. He had them going for a while, you know. According to our reports, they were really spooked," Igor told the all attentive Rudi.

Rudi had never wanted to liaise with the Brits, but he liked London, and a few crumbs in their direction occasionally kept their plumage plumped up. It allowed them to believe the fabrication that they were the most important among the equally unimportant rest of the outside world. He didn't take kindly to this effeminate Turk insulting his President, either. Turks were, in his opinion, *only good for one thing*, but he never elaborated on what that was!

"We don't have any *Mother* over here, because we don't have that kind of a Strategic Studies Group. How's your mum these days? I knew her *very well back in the day.* Send my regards when you get back," he said. He wanted to add *Faggot!* but restrained himself.

So Igor knew what Alexi thought he knew, that *Mother* didn't exist. But Alexi didn't know Igor's identity, and neither did Igor know his. Fortunately for Paulo, the strong willed Valentin Antopolov was still walking the corridors of Moscow Centre, the money minded Vladimir Sololov was sitting in the top chair.

At this early time in his life, Rudi had no granddaughter to share his stories with. The President could not be bothered with such menials and as far as a priest was concerned well he just didn't know any well enough, so Rudi told Alexi, instead of one of his yet-to-be trilogies.

"They've got another one of those homo queers in that SIS. Genetic Vice International I think I'll call it from now on! Never trust them...they don't know a bat from a ball."

By the time of his retirement in 2007, it cannot be known if Rudi used his misspelt anagram again, but his dislike of Igor was well-founded, and returned with some interest.

The night before Mr English's funeral, Igor met with a man that Mr English had previously recommended as the best in the business at clearing up unwanted loose ends. The settlement of an insult to Mr. English was on his mind. The topic they discussed was not Paulo, but Ceran. She was an embarrassment that no longer needed to be tolerated.

* * *

The sky was black, the moon shrouded by the quickly scurrying clouds, as Scarlett's immortal words of — *tomorrow is another day,* were confined to the dark screen of the television, and I wished "goodnight" to Rhett and the others in *Gone with the Wind.* My tomorrow was now my today, it was after midnight but my thoughts of Judy would not go away and allow me to sleep curled up on the office divan beside the window. I imagined Judy as Scarlett and myself as Rhett, wondering why there had never been a sequel. A part two, perhaps *Blown back by the Wind,* where they got back together and life ended happily. Or maybe Rhett, like me, found the circumstances of their relationship too difficult to continue with and never pressed it further. As I lay there, with only the occasional passing sentry to interrupt my thoughts, I recalled part of the conversation I had with Paulo that I had forgotten all about. The second time we met at the concert in Moscow. He was talking about himself and Katherine, but it could well have been me or any number of Patersons. It had started completely innocently, with me complimenting his choice of seating.

"I sustained an injury to my knee many years back, and the cold and the rain affect it badly. I do appreciate the ability to be able to stretch it out. Usually I find I'm in an uncomfortable seat, where it's not possible."

"Ah the misfortunes of life, we all suffer them in one form or another. I have had a few, but not, in all honesty, many. I doubt there is much time left for me to experience more than I have had. My deepest regret is of one of a higher plane… more transcendent a pain than one so physical. Love seems never to have smiled upon my family, Harry. My mother lost my father early, and then when she found happiness in the arms of another man it was short-lived. Death took her before she had finished with it. The same applies to me. I lost someone close… she was taken from me by men not like us. There was no love in their hearts, only hatred of something they did not understand, knowing only that it was different, and that they were frightened by it. Katherine is not frightened by love, but it still escapes her. The married title, and her change of surname were for convenience, in order to get something that marriage would provide. In her case, the deception was quickly over. She could return to normality and the pretence was put aside; for another day, perhaps.

Convention, protocol, propriety… call it what you want, but people like me embrace it. It means conformity; we blend in. We don't get noticed the way that those who display their difference to that state do. Being married and having children is the norm, and it opens doors usually closed to the single man unless, that is, he knows the right people, or has secrets about them to use as a leverage. Excuse me, Harry. I've drifted away from what I was speaking about. You're perfectly normal in your sexual orientation, I know that much, but why no band on your finger? Nobody good enough yet?"

I wondered where that knowledge had come from, trying not hard to glimpse at Katherine.

"No one silly enough, more like," I had replied.

"They won't have to be silly, Harry. They will need to be as clever as you are. If you get the chance, think about what I have said...things might get clearer for you, if the need arises."

I sat bolt upright, reaching for the phone as soon as I did, and punctuated the darkness of the room with the light from the computer screen. The answers I received from both, however, were painful.

Chapter Forty-Three

The End of The Path

"Wake up…I need you!" It was my turn to disturb Judith's sleep. How is it that the brain works overtime when the body labours through loss of sleep?

The cortege was due at eleven, but I doubted that by that time I would feel as wide awake as I now did. I was shaking with excitement and trying my damnedest to hold it all together. The penny had dropped, well to be precise, more like a halfpenny and now all I needed was to prove my deduction and get the other half.

"Go away, Harry, I'm sleeping. I certainly don't need you."

"I've worked it out. I need David Haig's number it's urgent Judy. I've got him by the balls. Do you want to sit in on the call and share the glory, or to lay here all alone?"

"Lay here…no, all right, I'm all yours. Figuratively, not literally. Don't let your imagination stretch too far H, you might get carried away. Why have you got David by the balls incidentally? Would you like to elaborate?"

"It's not Haig, but I need him to do something for me, I mean us."

After some banter of "I told you so," and "don't involve me in your fantasies," she dressed, and from my office phone, dialled his London number. "He said he would be in London until after the funeral. Put the phone on speaker, and you do all the talking I want to keep my job, thank you. This had better be good, Harry." Judy pulled up a chair and sat opposite me, as if distancing herself from the conversation.

"David...Harry Paterson. Sorry it's so early, but this won't wait. I think I've found who's behind the murders. Judy's here, listening in." I saw her scowl at me, but then she smiled, as I added, "She knows nothing of this call so I need you both to listen and hear me out."

"Judy? Oh, I see...you mean Judith Meadows, on more friendlier terms then? Sorry, I was still half-asleep. You do know the time, Harry? You're not in a different time zone up there, are you?" he asked. I ignored the intonation carried on his voice with Judy's name, and the chance of declaring independence for Yorkshire, and dived straight in.

"That club that my brother was supposed to have gone to last Saturday night, was it quite an exclusive club?"

"I don't know the exact details but I believe it was, yes," he replied

"Then it would have had a membership list. Did the police check it?"

"Harry, they are very good at their job. I don't hold their hand through everything, but if you asked me to hazard a guess then I would say yes, most definitely," the sound of a kettle boiling did not overshadow the condescension in his reply. I glanced at Judy to see if she too had caught it, and she turned her green eyes towards the ceiling with a finger in each ear, waggling the rest, imitating a bird in winged flight.

"Then get them to check it again, only this time look for Geoffrey Rowell. It's a name that has been used before, and could well have been used again. Get a description. Then if I'm right, you're both in for a tremendous shock." Judy had her black and red book with her, opened and ready for the off, but she did not pen anything into it. I thought I knew why.

"It will have to wait until Monday, now, Harry. I would doubt that there is anyone there at this time of day with a list of members. Tell me who you suspect, and I'll have him detained until we can follow this up." Sir David replied.

"No, that won't do. Get Special Branch to knock down doors. You are going to need hard evidence for this. I've downloaded a photograph and I'm sending it to you now." I pressed the *send* button. "Take a good look then you will understand the severity and urgency of the situation." Judy tried to get a peek but it had gone and I'd cleared the screen.

"While you're waiting, let me ask a question or two David. Who was the permanent secretary to the Ministry of Defence in 2007, the one who makes suggestions to Prime Ministers for appointments?"

"Something makes me think that you know the answer to this already, Harry. Will it confirm your suspicions, or have they passed that page and moved on?" he asked.

"Both barrels are loaded, but the safety is still on. Have you got the photograph?" To the muted sound of his "*Yes*" I added, "Then take a deep breath." I looked at Judy. "Do you want to kiss me now for ruining your prospects, or save it for later when we're both in the Tower?" I asked, as I turned the screen towards her.

"You can't be serious, H! You've lost whatever marbles you had!" she replied, leaving her mouth wide open, as I contemplated the lack of a refusal as an open invitation. The phone connection had gone silent, but not Judy. "Are you going to explain the logic that led you to this fanciful conclusion, or is Prince Phillip the next on your list? They've had some bad barley harvested and distilled in the Isle of Jura, and you've drunk it!"

"Yes, you could be right, Judith, but, then again," it was David. "The answer to your question, Harry, was Sir Gordon Spencer. He was a very close friend of the outgoing PM of that day, and the one-time holder of my job. He was called to give evidence to both the Hutton inquiry and the one into the Iraq war. He was retired by Gordon Brown in the first year of the new administration because of his ill-health. His sickness began to show virulently, as he was in a constant sweat, and could not swallow or keep any food down. The evidence he gave in the Iraq case was taken at his home, because by that time he was too weak to travel. He had a cancer of the immune system, lymphomas. A symptom of HIV, from which he died four weeks ago. Your man in the picture was at the funeral along with many other distinguished notables, including myself. But one thing I, and a few others, did not have in common with the majority there that day, was that we were not from the gay fraternity. Your man, however, could have been, or could still be, I suppose. To my humiliation, I must confess that I have had little dealings directly with him including on that day, and it did not appear to be of great significance that we were receiving the *Garden* information at the FO. But then, and please remember that it was only four weeks ago, having seen the way he conducted himself, I wondered if there was a connection.

The war in Libya and the death of your father in suspicious circumstances took pre-eminence over approaching the PM over that slight concern. However, being sexually motivated towards one's own sex does not confirm him as being your murderer. How can you relate this orientation to the murders of Elliot and your brother, Harry?" Judy was saying nothing, sitting motionless, impassively staring at the image that stared back.

"Through George, and through a lot more digging into his past than has been done. He has an association with a killer somewhere in his past, and it has to be found between now and sometime soon, do you agree?""I will do my best Harry. How did you know about Spencer?"

"I knew about Edward. He had mentioned the name a few times in the past. Seem to remember a case that Mrs Tony Blair had brought to the Court of Human rights for poofs to be included everywhere, including on the education curriculum or something similar. Sung his praises, did Edward. He banged on about the liberalisation of sexual awareness whenever he had the chance. Was she and the other half there at the funeral, or was he still into his 'holier than thou' stage and soaking up the American oil dollar, hiding his face with disclaimers of all responsibilities from any indiscretions?"

"I'll call you back if I find anything, Harry." Sir David's phone line went dead, and I was left alone with Judy, her attention still glued on what was before her.

"I can understand the connection with the name of Spencer and the funeral H, but I fail to see how that leads you to him as your killer.

It's preposterous! I've never met a nicer man. For pity sake Harry, his father was awarded the KCMG for services rendered to this country. He spent about fifty years in the diplomatic corps and must have done wonders for us. Do you suppose that his son was disenchanted with what daddy was awarded? Maybe he thought he should have been made King and that's what turned him? Perhaps Moscow visited him and said the same... *a mere medal for all those secrets of ours you gave away, old chap? Come to us and we will appoint you as our next Czar!* That might have done it for him, don't you think? I think you're barking mad, Harry."

"Did you know that he is Turkish by birth?" She had moved from her uncomfortable position and was spread out on the divan, the blanket that I had minutes ago over me, draped around her body and tucked in at the chin. Cold but cosy; neither words that would rush into my mind to describe her. "I didn't, but so what? Does that make him a spy?" Her eyes were closed, but she was not about to fall asleep.

"Why do you think that it was covered up by his father, the Ambassador? By the time he took on the role of Ambassador in Washington his son was a British subject, and all reference to his birth in Istanbul had been removed. Incidentally, although I expect you have an answer to this, why was his original birth certificate not filed until 1953, when he is said to have been born three years before?"

"Could be completely innocent. Perhaps his parents forgot, thanks to the pressure of work on Sir Raymond. An oversight so what?"

"He's adopted, Judy. He's said to be the outcome of a previous 'you know what' of Ceran, his mother. No name under the 'Father' column, and a secret made of it at the time... why should it have been. Surely another notch on Sir Raymond's belt of humanitarianism, goodwill to the underprivileged furthering the gospel of British altruism but was it? Sometime in the sixties... I'm not sure of the exact dates, but perhaps you might know as you were what, twenty something then?" I said with a sarcastic grin on my face "the Soviets found out about American-built intermediate range ballistic missiles stationed in Turkey, pointed down their throats. So they thought *what the hell, let's put some of ours on that insignificant island of Cuba, and see how the Yankees feel about that!* Sir Raymond moved from Turkey to Syria in 1961 just before it all got rather warm in Cuba. And where was Philby when it was finally decided that he was a Soviet agent, Judy?"

"Not far away, Harry." She had opened her eyes and propped herself up on an arm of the divan, looking directly at me. "How do you know all this, H?" My attention was concentrated on her lips mouthing the words, taking no notice of the sounds that came from them.

"The same way I found out about Spencer being in charge in 2007. I had heard his name as I have said, but didn't know that he was the number one chief mandarin at the MOD. It all came together when I remembered some words of Paulo's. I have friends in the war office. I've just woken a few up and then suddenly, all the bits fitted. You started it rolling, Judy, in the library when we were speaking about that grouse shooting weekend and I mentioned Howell being in 2nd Para. You asked if he had said anything about the UN and it whetted my appetite, so I began to ask around after that."

"Come on, then! I'm all fired up don't stop now, you heathen. Where are you going with all this?" The blanket was off, and sadly I admit, I unashamedly fantasied what lay beyond my reach.

"I'm making tea. Do you want a coffee?" I needed to move, the tension inside of me was becoming too intolerable. "Come with me, Judy. I need you to hold my hand, I'm shaking."

"Sure, I might need the caffeine." She did as I had asked, not, I've got to say, to my surprise. Her soft hand felt good in mine, but other things kept me from announcing my proposed devotion, not simply the thought of rejection. "If we bump into any full red-blooded plods, they'll probably use you as a spoon," I joked, attempting to lift the tension that I thought we both could feel. "Ha bloody ha. Be careful they don't confuse you as a traitor," her gentle voice proclaimed.

There was a distant sound of voices as we used the back staircase to the kitchen, the one with the no carpet and painted bannisters instead of thick pile and shiny polished ones elsewhere. Judy, wrapped only in her dressing gown, complained about my 'meanness' in having the heating turned down and about being disturbed, and not being told earlier about my enquiries and anything else she could bring to mind.

The kitchen door was closed on the people and voices behind. She was still moaning as I opened it, only to be surprised by the number there. I had expected one or two with the rest patrolling around, but there were over a dozen, and more coming down the main stairs. The reinforcements for the day ahead had arrived. I recognised one, with his Yorkshire Constabulary insignia. "I'm sorry, your Lordship, I didn't think anyone was up. If I had known I would have asked your permission. We're just assembling, ready for the day ahead. Were we making too much noise?" It was Superintendent Ryan, who I had met in my duties as a lay magistrate. All heads had turned in our direction, and neither of us could confuse the leers that were levelled at us.

"That's all right, Alan carry on. Had I known, I would have laid on more refreshments. We're only here for a tea and a coffee, so we won't get in your way." I was I confess, a little embarrassed.

Judy was busying herself at the sink filling a kettle, with the cups already prepared. I joined her, parting from the attentive company. "Are you quite comfortable here or shall I make them, and bring them back to the office?" An innocent and, I assumed, gallant enquiry as to my companion's welfare and feelings, but I was wrong.

"You really are a sexist pig, aren't you? Would you feel uncomfortable if our roles were reversed, and you were surrounded by beautiful women all staring at you, lusting after your body? Of course I'm comfortable, you twit!"

"Well, I wouldn't go that far. I can understand the use of the phrase *lusting after me* if the roles were reversed. In your case, it might well be that they're thinking about what you live on apart from air, or wondering what a handsome fellow like me is doing with such a scrawny girl. They do look confused, wouldn't you say?" We sat at the end of the long white scrubbed table with our mugs, and Judy's eyes seemed to be everywhere other than on me.

"Go on, Harry. You were about to fill me in on the UN. Don't ask again if I'm comfortable here…it's warmer."

"I can see that. Are you sure that you're able to concentrate?"

"Even better. Now go on, and show off."

"I took part in Operation Resolute in 1995 as part of the implementation force, or IFOR, at the end of the Bosnian War, following the Dayton Agreement. My role was in gathering military intelligence on two individuals a Bosnian named Dario Kordic, and a Serb named Milomir Stakic, both of whom have been tried and sentenced to forty-year prison sentences. I've kept in touch with my commanding officer from those days, and have met him several times. He will be here later today for the funeral. He's at the MOD now, collating information for the NATO forces operating over Libya. Anyway, when I was recruited into the SIS we met in London, and I stayed at his house for a few days. On the Friday he and his wife had a dinner party, and among the guests was a guy that worked in the same sort of field as myself for Pfizer, the American drug company. Sandy, that's Sandy Barrington my ex-chief, and I were chatting about our days in IFOR, when this guy joined in the conversation. It moved on to chemicals used in warfare, and he asked if we had come across any usage in Bosnia, particularly in hostage taking. Part of the evidence against Kordic concerned a concentration camp at a village called Ormarska, where it was found that experiments were conducted using an analgesic pain suppressant drug.

It was a war within a war: Bosnian Croats against Bosnian Serbs against Serbia and Croatia with Bosnia Herzegovina as a side line. No one knew who was fighting who, most of the time. In the concentration camp, it was simpler. It was run by Serbs holding non-Serbs, and some of them were selected for these experiments. They were given ever-increasing dosages of an opioid-based drug, and then subjected to ever-increasing levels of pain. The drug used was Fentanyl, a hundred times more powerful than morphine, for which there is a worldwide shortage. Did you know that six countries in the world use and hold almost eighty percent of the supply of morphine? No matter just thought I'd throw in, show how intelligent I am.

Pharmaceutical companies are searching for a substitute, and some of what they have come up with are killers as well as pain-suppressants. The guy was an American...Doug someone. He had a great deal of knowledge of this Fentanyl and its derivatives. According to him, it had been used by Mossad to kill a Hamas leader in 1997, and by the Russians in 2002 when Chechens held hostages in a theatre in Moscow. Another use is in recreational drugs. It's called China White on the streets when mixed with heroin and gives a greater sense of euphoria and feelings of untouchability, it commands a great premium, so he told us. It was a German company, taken over by Smith Kline Beecham, that discovered Fentanyl, and none of the conversation that night at Sandy's house had any bearing on me, or Elliot and Edward's death until I contacted Sandy again this week and mentioned your question about the UN in Bosnia.

As far as I knew the UN were not involved, but almost every major country in or out of the UN were, including Russia. I knew there was a UN arms embargo, and again they got involved when it came to Kosovo recognition after the NATO bombing of Belgrade in 2000. Sandy knew more. There was a UN delegation visit to Ormarska at the end of the war, to a chemical stabilisation unit, led by a British scientist. Apparently they wanted to examine Fentanyl with the idea of using it for military purposes as a lollipop for pain killers. You can suck on it if you're wounded and still kill people, what will they think of next? I looked it up, and recently a derivative has been accepted as a cancer treatment. The licence for Fentanyl, along with every derivative, is held by Smith Kline Beecham and its manufacture should be governed by that company and controlled in distribution, but do you know that it's already available in Brazil and India? And, of course, Russia, where I suspect there are a lot of lollipops just in case. Did you know that Sir Raymond was on the board at Smith Kline Beecham and his son is a major shareholder and, I believe, a Russian spy?"

"That's a great deal of research you and Sandy have done. If what you're alleging is true, it will be catastrophic for the government. It could bring it falling at our feet," she declared quietly.

"Not necessarily. Most of this happened before the last election but then again, you knew about the delegation to Ormarska and what it

was for, didn't you, when you asked that question about the UN?"
I asked.

"No, not really. It was a shot in the dark, actually. I joined up in
2002 after it had all finished over there, but there was a dossier doing
the rounds about leakages from America and from Russia which we
weren't being directly spoken about. GCHQ had traffic emanating out
of the UN in New York and out from Moscow which they couldn't
analyse. All we knew was that both America and Russia had been
compromised. As we weren't being told about the stories coming out
of Moscow, we couldn't tell our erstwhile cousins anything about the
intercepts, and they wouldn't have liked the idea of us listening in
on their private conversations. Antony Willis was at both the Foreign
Office and the Home Office, and I just threw it up in the air seeing if it
landed on solid ground, that's all. Now there's a part of me that wished
I hadn't." Her gaze was now directly on me.

"Do you know who was the scientist leading that delegation, Judy,
or would you like me to share his name just in case it wasn't on that
dossier?"

"If it's relevant, then yes, Harry, please enlighten me."

"David Kelly."

"What, that wasn't on there!" she exclaimed in utter surprise.

"No, it was mysteriously removed, so I'm not surprised you never
saw it. When was that delegation sent, Judy?"

"I think it was in 1997, not long after the election, when we all
embraced Islington socialism as the second coming." She was still in
shock and put both elbows on the table, leaning closer towards me, her
mouth slightly open and I wanted so much to kiss her. But I didn't!

"Let's go forward a few years, and here I might need some guidance.
Wasn't there a British Ambassador who gave evidence at that Hutton
Enquiry, said he met Kelly in Geneva and asked him what would happen if Iraq were to be invaded? Do you remember what he said in
reply?"

"He said that *he, Kelly, would probably be found dead in the woods*,
Harry."

"That's right. And the ambassador thought he meant that the Iraqis would kill him, didn't he?"

"Yes, that's what he said."

"Do you remember the ambassador's name, Judy?"

"David someone, I believe."

"Almost spot on. David Richmond he served with Sir Raymond when they were at different British consulates in Athens."

"Is that important?" she asked, but I declined to answer that question, I didn't want speculation to interfere with what I knew to be factual. "They said that Kelly was in contact with what they called *dissidents* inside defence intelligence, and that his remark about the Labour Government *over-sexing* the WMD report was made to further their aims in calling for a rethink. Is that right?"

"In essence, yes."

"You remember all this so clearly because of why, Judy?"

"Because of Tony, of course. My one, not the lying cretinous one. It was the first chance for anyone to get at some of the truth that they had been covering up. Why there were no weapons of mass destruction pointed at UK bases in Cyprus, for example." We were both running on pure adrenaline at this stage. I asked another question as soon as she had stopped speaking.

"Now for the biggest cover-up answer of all time. The *sexing up* was in line with available intelligence to the Joint Intelligence Committee who may have been *subconsciously influenced* by HM Government…is that what was said?"

"Most definitely yes. I can almost see the squirt who wrote that sitting next to the cretin." Wide green eyes answering with hate written inside them.

"Just for old time's sake, Judy when did the cretin step down in 2007?"

"In June, late June, Harry, if I recall correctly. He stayed around long enough to do what you're suggesting, and then did a runner. I hate to say it, but you could be right and not about to hit your thumb instead of the nail!" The smile that emanated after that remark was not, unfortunately, her usual radiant one.

"I'm sorry to disturb you, your Lordship, but there is a Sir David Haig on the telephone for you," Joseph announced, on his arrival in the kitchen. As to how he had known that I was there I never did find out.

Chapter Forty-Four

The Compost Pile

"He's in custody, Harry. It's over…all of it."

"I only wish it was, David. There's the small matter of a killer still at large, plus I think Judith here is about to add to your many troubles." There were six hours to go before the two black state carriages pulled by two teams of four matching black horses arrived for the caskets, and what remained of the immediate Paterson family led the way to St Michael's and All Angels to attend the obsequies.

"Has he said anything?" I asked, praying that he had, but knowing that it wouldn't be that simple. "I was only told ten minutes ago, but don't worry, he will," David replied, confidently. Although one part of me shared that confidence, another part, the rational side, wondered if all would be revealed.

"You should be looking happier than you are, H. You were right, and you have stopped him. The interrogation will get it out of him Harry, I know the methods." Somewhere those words from Judy found a resting place but it wasn't in my heart. We were back in my office and Judy was touching my hand, but not even that, nor her approval, could lighten the depression I felt.

"Why should he tell us, Judy? What's another murder to him? He's implicated in Edward's death, but by what? He was a member of the same club and used a name that had been used for a proposed meeting with a British spy. That's all we've got. Okay, his belt is undone, but the trousers are still hanging around his waist. If my suppositions are correct, then it goes deeper than just this one man. Maybe your cretin isn't involved directly with him, but you can trace their paths crossing on many occasions. It will take months, Judy, possibly years to unravel. Joint Intelligence, SIS, Defence, the FO everyone will want a piece of him. I doubt that the murders will be mentioned at all, and if they are, they will only be a side show to the wider picture. If members of the previous government were compromised or, at best, naïve in their appointments, the repercussions will be immense. With the cost of whitewash on the High Street set to rise through the roof. Tell me something...did nobody think it strange that a single man had been given one of the highest chairs in which to park his bum? Or, was it just taken as gospel that things were as they were being told?"

"A few down the pecking order made comment, but we all assumed that God knew what he was doing. With hindsight, now that the dead Sir Gordon Spencer has been exposed and his shared preferences with the man he appointed let out of the closet, it should never have happened. But then, nobody knew."

"You can't be sure of that. Maybe the cretin knew. Maybe he was party to the appointment. After all said and done, he would be the one who would sign off on it. Another thing I found out was what our man did when he signed on the dotted line way back when. He was sent burrowing into Harold Wilson's Labour Party becoming an aid, and probably a confidant, to the Home Secretary of the day. A man once described by Wilson as more a socialite than a socialist because of his lavish lifestyle. That same man was in charge, you know, when George Blake made that miraculous escape from Wormwood Scrubs, and he even kept his job in the Cabinet after it. Other notable achievements he went on to make in parliament were the decriminalisation of homosexuality, being made head of the European Union, getting a peerage, and cancelling a military aircraft so far advanced in avoiding radar that it had the Americans dribbling in envy and the grateful Russians rubbing and clapping their hands together, not bad for the son of a miner from the Valleys. Oh, one more thing...he became an advisor for the chosen one you referred to… the cretin himself. Now if our man pointed him in the wrong direction at the beginning, particularly in getting Blake back to Russia, then who knows how far cretin's mind was influenced? Maybe as far as direct contact with Moscow centre. That, fortunately, is not my concern, but George and Tanya are. I need help, Judy, and I need it fast." I willingly gave up the speaker's platform and welcomed her involvement.

"I've had a thought, H. Want to hear it?"

"Can't resist. Does it involve churches and rings?" I cracked, trying desperately to lift the gloom that I felt. It was instinctive.

"I'll take a pass on that one, Harry. Let's get back to the point. When he used the name Geoffrey Rowell to meet Paulo in Berlin, it was to mark him as the target for the man he uses as his assassin. He maybe many things but as you say he's not your killer. It would have been too awkward to take photographs. Paulo would have noticed. But an onlooker, another person inside or outside the hotel could have taken one. I don't think even he would have registered that. With Edward, it was the same idea. Join the same club, socialise, then point him out for the future kill. Paulo said as much. George would be at the funeral for our man to identify and then either describe him or, point him out and say within earshot, *There he is go about your work when I'm not around.* Seem reasonable to you, H?"

"I'm right behind you, Judith. Got the ring in my inside pocket." Still trying to keep my shattered dreams alive, I replied. "Then why don't you contact Sir David again and ask if Edward signed a guest in at that club anytime before he was murdered?"

"Good idea, but there's no need. With that photograph I sent over to Haig I attached an email asking the same question, Judith. I've got the answer right here. Want to take a stab at it or do you already know what it says" Not shattered any longer, now destroyed.

"Not on the same page, Harry, sorry. Care to elaborate?"

"Do you remember I told you about some photographs taken at Maudlin's funeral that I had discovered? It was when you told me about your great-grandfather knowing him, and how your grandfather had attended his funeral. Well, I had another couple of photos emailed to me earlier this morning from Sandy. One was of Sir Raymond, one of those I didn't recognise at Maudlin's entombment. But there was another of Sir Raymond, taken a good few years before his death, with his adopted son, and guess who's holding the other hand? Can you see her? An eleven year old girl with red flaming hair, looking remarkably like a younger version of you? Am I right Judith? I asked with a huge lump in my throat. "You should consider your answer carefully." I added, swallowing hard.

It broke my heart what I believed to be true, but then again the old proverb of — *There's no fool like an old fool* must have been made up for a reason…And I was it. There was a sigh from her to begin with, and then a confession that ached every part of my body.

"Hmm…you really are a clever man, Harry. I wondered if I might have been in one of those snaps that you found. Is that when you first started to suspect me?" There was no pride in her question and no pity left in my heart to answer her. She had stood by now and had her back to me, staring out of the French doors to where we had sat only a few hours previously. There was no conceit in her voice; only sadness. I gave in to my own sense of shame.

"You know what, Judith? I tried not to. I even thought that I had fallen in love with you…almost told you so, and had my head bitten off. Could say I'm pleased I didn't, but deep inside I can't be sure about that. If it wasn't for the photograph and Sandy, who knows? You might still be waiting for a chance at George even though Paulo's been unearthed." There was no reaction from her and I'm not sure what I would have done had there been.

"Looking back, there were little things that puzzled me. Like why was a case officer running a file on the Patersons and why such vehement distress when Paulo vanished? Both could have been explained, but when the photo of Sir Raymond came through…I knew, then. And I knew where you had gone last Saturday night."

"I wasn't going to kill George, Harry!" She still had her back to me as if saying *I'm defenceless, spare me!*

"Oh, that's nice of you, I'll tell him, shall I, or do you want the honours? How many in total, Judith? Done it before, tried it, liked the thrill? Get a huge buzz out of Edward, did you?" The anger inside of me was building, but I think it was directed at me as much as her. I had been such a fool.

"I'll tell you something, H, now that it's too late. If you *had* proposed I would have turned you down…not because I don't love you, but because I do. I wasn't going ahead with his plan; I was looking for a way out. I made up my mind before tonight. Before you found out. It was only a matter of time anyway, and I knew that I couldn't cover his back for long. I even told him that. You won't believe this, but that's why I suggested that you get back to Sir David and ask if anyone had been signed in as his guest to that club. I wanted to be caught in the end. Don't ever worry about that bomb, Harry. I knew what I was doing when I assembled it. I learned more from Tony than just how to worry without showing it." Another sigh but still no face to accuse.

"Why Edward, Judy? You had me by then…surely you both knew that I would lead you to who was supplying Paulo?"

"He wouldn't take the chance, H. You had no direct connection to the bank. He knew it all started there."

"Did you know about the connection between the FO back in 2003? About David Kelly, and the man you refer to as cretin?"

"No, I most certainly did not." Why wouldn't she turn? With a heavy heart, I asked my final question.

"Tell me about Peter Trimble. How did he make you into the monster that I fell in love with?"

Chapter Forty-Five

The Lifeless Winter Garden

"In the beginning, when I was young, he was simply a family friend, that's all. One who told amazing stories and recited poetry. Most of all I liked him because he let me paint his finger and toenails, and put make-up on him without being asleep. I had done it once on my grandfather when he had dozed off one Sunday afternoon, and although he laughed about it, it wasn't as much fun as doing it to Peter. He enjoyed it. I was ten in that photo, not the eleven you guessed at, and he was thirty-five. He still had his fingers and toes painted, you know, when that photograph of him was taken. Peter was a laugh, a joy to be around for a ten-year-old." We were seated now as far apart as it was possible to be in my office and I had shown her the damming evidence of association.

"His father died a year after Maudlin, and his mother a few months after that. He admired his father but was always a bit secretive about Ceran, his mother. Much later he confessed to me that he had arranged her death, and he told me why. I was in his confidence, you see, and he had me spellbound. You're right about the adoption, of course, and I could tell you why the papers couldn't be backdated. It was simple, really. There had been a census done in 1952, and the following year was the first opportunity for Sir Raymond Trimble to register the birth. Peter did worry about that, but didn't think that it was so important that it would catch him out. He's Russian by birth, Harry, born in Stalingrad. He carries his heritage like a sickness that can never be cured; that's why he wanted Paulo, then George. It took so long because he never knew that Tanya was pregnant in 1956, I never put it all together until I'd killed Elliot." Still she would not look directly at me, preferring the window where still she sought peace.

"Peter dropped the Willis and Howell thing on that Russian, Alexi Vasilyev, gave them up to flush Paulo out. They had worked it together. Vasilyev's boss was an old adversary of Paulo's, apparently, and half-suspected him of being an English agent, but Paulo was too powerful and too clever. Peter admired him… he told me so. It was Trimble who recruited me, straight after Tony died in Afghanistan in 2001. I didn't need much selling. I hated the British way of things, with the double standards for those in power, and the lies that flowed every time they opened their mouths. I wanted to get my own back, and to get revenge for Tony. Peter gave me that chance. I don't know if there is any substance in what you hinted about the other Tony; the cretin, I'm not sure that you do either, but I do hope that someone takes up the challenge." Her voice had dulled and weakened as her fingers trembled holding on to one cigarette after another. I had nothing to say that would take away any of our sorrows.

"It was Peter who put me up to Hendon for the driving bit, then through a SAS course for self-defence… only it was never about self-defence It was for taking lives, not saving them. I learned about disguise and how to pose as a man, as you so rightly suspected. I have the figure, don't I. I even danced with Edward the night Peter signed me in as his guest, and Edward never noticed. My name, the one I used that Tuesday, the night before I met you, was Rufus Abbot. I thought I wouldn't forget that. That name will be in the book at the club. Elliot was easier, of course. I followed him out of Queen Anne's Gate, just to make sure, but we knew where he lived whereas with Edward, we didn't. Peter wanted Paulo's source as well as Paulo himself, and then, when I gave him Tanya he said he could die a happy man. I'm dead as well; aren't I?"

She stopped and at last turned from the window. "I'm so sorry, Harry." Then she burst into tears.

* * *

The weather had been kind and fitting for the funeral, apparently suiting the majority of those who attended who, like Joseph, preferred a dark and sombre day for burials. Now, after dinner, the heavens opened again as if washing away the memory of the day; as Sir David Haig had tried to do, when I asked him what would happen now. He made no mention of Peter Trimble when I had given him Judith, and the only response to my question was, "It really is better not to ask, Harry. Somethings are best left alone."

He relieved the Paterson family of their obligation regarding the Bank of St George, conjuring a diplomatic answer to the problem from his hatless head. "Obviously there's no reflection implied on yourself, Harry. God knows where we would all be without your astuteness. But Annie's is no more. It's been taken on board by the National Audit, and it's all in their hands now. I expect that's a relief for you. You are *numero uno* in our books, Harry. You have only to ask, and it will be given."

I settled all family affairs at dinner that evening explaining as fully as I could, why George and Tanya were there and why Judith was not. I ended the wild stories Maudlin had perpetuated regarding George and the Northcliffe family, then resolved my worries over everyone at Eton Square. I gave the house to George and Tanya to live in together as they might have been able to do, if only Maudlin had been more prudent in matters of love. One other thing I privately decided to do and that was not to investigate George and our genealogical relationship. He was my friend and I was his. I wasn't going to confuse that by labels.

As for myself... well, I concluded that not always do you gain something when you win, and by that I don't mean just the collection of medals and trophies. I had lost something in winning and saving two lives; but the victory tasted sour, as if I had cheated by playing outside of the rules. I had allowed a part of me, my heart, to control whatever brain I had, which was something I had never been guilty of before. Judith was wrong about me being clever. I was anything but. If I had taken more care in my investigation and not been sidetracked by affection, then maybe I could have saved Edward, and if I had been more forthcoming with the police when Elliot had first suspected something amiss at the bank, then possibly my father would still be here for me to dislike.

Despite the protestations from George and Tanya and petitions from the others, I found sleep readily that night, with only self-pity as company. I had nobody to paint my nails or tease me before sleep and dreams overtook my sense of right and wrong and, although it shamed me, I missed her. If the God we had all prayed to earlier had read my thoughts, then I was indeed a condemned man because I wanted her back and beside me. Paulo's cynical, but accurate, description of the lack of love was right for this Paterson. If only I had taken notice of his words before!

I dreamt heavily that night overdosed on regrets. In my dream I was beside a lake, pointing out the oversized fish to Judith, when a telephone rang. I ran around in circles until I found it, nailed to a tree. As I picked up the receiver both Maudlin and Paulo appeared standing in front of me, but neither spoke. On Maudlin's shoulder was a dead dove, and Paulo was indicating the ground at my feet, where lay an empty nest. The next thing I knew I was emptying the lake with a plastic bowl. The water had turned red and the fish were all dead and I didn't know why. I looked for Judith everywhere... behind trees, under bushes, even in the water. Diving in three times and swimming with a fin attached to my feet to find her. Eventually, I did. She was kneeling on a stony shore, staring blankly at a wall in front of herself. She never spoke, despite my shouting. It was my screams that woke me.

I have never had that dream explained to me, never having a Mrs Meadows to analyse it and never sharing it with anyone else. But it must have meant something, as I have had it several times since. I wish it would go away and just leave the part where we are together beside the lake. I have never seen her or Peter Trimble again, and unlike Maudlin, I have still to find love.

THE LITTLE DOVE
By Ivan Dmitriev, 1760-1837

The little dove, with heart of sadness,
In silent pain sighs night and day;
What now can wake that heart to gladness?
His mate beloved, so far away.

He coos no more with soft caresses,
No more his millet sought by him,
The dove, his lonesome state distresses,
With tears his swimming eye balls dim.

From twig to twig, now skips the lover,
Filling the grove with accents kind,
On all sides roams the harmless rover,
Hoping his little friend to find.

Ah vain that hope his grief is tasting,
Fate seems to scorn his faithful love,
And imperceptibly is wasting
Wasting away that little dove.

At length upon the grass he throws him,
Hid in his wing and beak and wept
There ceased his sorrows to pursue him
The little dove forever slept.

THE END

Dear reader,

We hope you enjoyed reading *The Desolate Garden*. Please take a moment to leave a review, even if it's a short one. Your opinion is important to us.

Discover more books by Daniel Kemp at

https://www.nextchapter.pub/authors/daniel-kemp-mystery-thriller-author

Want to know when one of our books is free or discounted for Kindle? Join the newsletter at http://eepurl.com/bqqB3H

Best regards,

Daniel Kemp and the Next Chapter Team

The story continues in:

Percy Crow by Daniel Kemp

To read first chapter for free, head to:
https://www.nextchapter.pub/books-percy-crow

About the Author

Danny Kemp, ex-London police officer, mini-cab business owner, pub tenant and licensed London taxi driver, never planned to be a writer, but after his first novel —The Desolate Garden — was under a paid option to become a $30 million film for five years until distribution became an insurmountable problem for the production company what else could he do?

Nowadays he is a prolific storyteller, and although it's true to say that he mainly concentrates on what he knows most about; murders laced by the intrigue involving spies, his diverse experience of life shows in the short stories he compiles both for adults and children.

He is the recipient of rave reviews from a prestigious Manhattan publication, been described as —the new Graham Green — by a managerial employee of Waterstones Books, for whom he did a country-wide tour of signing events, and he has appeared on 'live' nationwide television.

http://www-thedesolategarden-com.co.uk/

Printed in Great Britain
by Amazon